HURLEY LOWE MANAGEMENT
3a IMPERIAL STUDIOS
IMPERIAL ROAD
LONDON SW6 2AG
0171 384 3322
FAX: 0171 384 3344

The Anniversary

For David
and for our children
Tanya, Michael, Katrina, Nikki and Richard
with love

THE ANNIVERSARY

Ann Swinfen

C

Century · London

Published by Century Books in 1996

1 3 5 7 9 10 8 6 4 2

First published in the United Kingdom in 1966 by

Century,
Random House UK Limited
20 Vauxhall Bridge Road, London, SW1V 2SA

Random House Australia (Pty) Limited
20 Alfred Street, Milsons Point, Sydney,
New South Wales 2061, Australia

Random House New Zealand Limited
18 Poland Road, Glenfield
Auckland 10, New Zealand
Random House South Africa (Pty) Limited
PO Box 337, Bergvlei, South Africa

Random House UK Limited Reg. No. 954009

A CIP catalogue record for this book is available from the British
Library

Papers used by Random House UK Limited are natural, recyclable
products made from wood grown in sustainable forests. The
manufacturing processes conform, to the environmental regulations
of the country of origin.

ISBN 0 7126 7687 2

Printed and bound in Great Britain by
Mackays of Chatham plc, Chatham, Kent

Acknowledgements

My thanks go to Murray Pollinger, my agent, for his warmth, loyalty and encouragement (and for some excellent lunches), and to Kate Parkin and her team at Century, whose kindness and enthusiasm have been stunning. Above all, my thanks go to Mary Loring, my editor. Mary is the kind of reader every writer dreams of finding; working with her has been a joy.

With love also to my family, who viewed my abandonment of lucrative employment with a mixture of amusement and tolerance, and were even heard to say, on occasion, 'Go for it!'

Natasha's Family

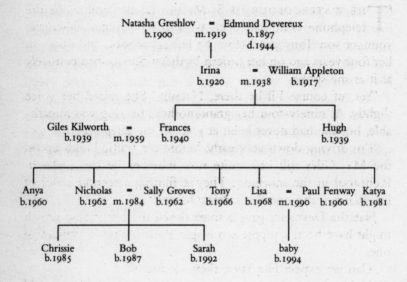

Natasha Greshlov = Edmund Devereux
b.1900   m.1919   b.1897
d.1944

Irina = William Appleton
b.1920   m.1938   b.1917

Giles Kilworth = Frances   Hugh
b.1939   m.1959   b.1940   b.1939

Anya   Nicholas = Sally Groves   Tony   Lisa = Paul Fenway   Katya
b.1960   b.1962   m.1984 b.1962   b.1966 b.1968 m.1990 b.1960 b.1981

Chrissie   Bob   Sarah   baby
b.1985   b.1987   b.1992   b.1994

Chapter 1

THE WATERCOLOUR OF St Martins on the wall above the telephone table had been painted by Frances Kilworth's younger son Tony just before he left art school, and given to her four years ago on her fiftieth birthday. She looked pensively at it as she spoke.

'Yes, of course I'll be there, Natasha.' She raised her voice slightly. At ninety-four her grandmother's hearing was remarkable, but she had never been at ease on the telephone.

'I'm driving down very early, before the traffic builds up on the M4. Giles still isn't quite sure whether he can make it. Rehearsal in the morning. They're filming a second series of his sitcom – the one that's doing so well.'

Natasha Devereux gave a snort down the telephone, which might have been a suppressed laugh. Probably not a favourable one.

'Can we expect him later, then, doushenka?'

'He's going to try to come down after lunch. That would mean he could manage most of the day.' Frances recognised a familiar note in her voice, at once apologetic and pleading. It often surfaced when she spoke of her husband to Natasha. She despised herself for it.

'Drive carefully,' said Natasha automatically before ringing off, as if Frances were still a teenager, dashing about the Herefordshire lanes in her beloved soft-top MG. Frances sighed. Gone. Long gone. Vanished with that younger self, who now seemed as remote as a stranger.

Frances stood for a moment with her hand still on the telephone. The watercolour constantly filled her afresh with delight. Tony had managed to catch the endearing atmosphere of the place – the jumble of styles, from the mediaeval tower and the half-timbered sixteenth-century main house to the elegant Georgian frontage and orangery (now dilapidated), added when the family had aspired to gentility in the mid-eighteenth century. By showing it from an unusual angle he had been able to reveal its haphazard chronology. The horseshoe formed by the house and stableyard was flung round like the rough embrace of the military cloak St Martin himself had wrapped around the shivering beggar. In the right foreground (slightly shifted by artistic licence, she thought) was the great copper beech, planted in 1790 and recorded in the estate book of the period. Its partner, mirroring it across the lawn, had begun to rot in the sixties and had come down in a storm seven years ago. The surviving tree was the first they had learned to climb, she and her brother Hugh, soon after their mother had brought them to St Martins to escape the blitz.

★ ★ ★

Hugh will never find me here, thinks Frances, crouching under the rhododendrons. She holds her breath. He is ranging about the lawn, poking at shrubs with a stick, peering down the well that Mummy is always so fussed about. Then he seems to lose interest. He throws down his stick and starts to climb the copper beech. He jumps and catches hold of one of the lower branches, then walks his feet up the trunk and claws at the branch until he gets his tummy over it. Soon she can see nothing of him but the shaking of the branches. Furious, she crawls out from under the rhododendrons and runs across the lawn.

'You're supposed to be finding me!' she wails.

He drops neatly from the tree beside her, and grabs her arm. 'Got you!'

'It's not fair!'

She hits him.

Soon they are rolling over and over amongst the dead leaves under the tree, punching each other until they are tired.

Later, when they are lying on their backs, gazing up through the branches at the patchwork of purple leaves and blue sky, she complains again.

'You are a beast. It wasn't fair.'

He rolls over on to his stomach and grins to himself.

* * *

The morning of Saturday, 11 June, 1994, dawned milky white as Frances joined the M4 at Junction 10. The road stretched westwards ahead of her, almost empty. In three hours' time the tarmac would be hot with the friction of the hundreds of tyres rolling over it, the trees in the adjacent fields shaking with the thunder of lorries pounding to and from London.

Now she could see a kestrel hovering lazily overhead – not three miles from Reading. She reached up and wound back the sunroof, then pressed the buttons to open both front windows fully. Her sensible Cavalier hatchback could never rival the excitement of her old MG, but she still drove in a wild tangle of air when she was alone. Giles objected peevishly when he travelled with her, closing windows, hunching down with his coat collar turned up when she refused to turn on the heating, ostentatiously coughing into his handkerchief with unspoken reproach: My voice has to be cherished, I need to be cosseted, my looks and my voice are my fortune.

She shook herself in irritation. No need to think about Giles just yet. She would reach St Martins in time for breakfast. Probably before the children had even woken up. Yesterday afternoon Tony had collected Katya after school, on his way from London, and driven her down to Herefordshire; Lisa and Paul had planned to drive over from Worcester during the evening. It was only a month till the baby was due, but Lisa had insisted that she could not possibly miss the party.

'Not come to St Martins' fiftieth anniversary, Mum? I wouldn't miss it for the world. Anyway, Natasha would never forgive me.'

Frances had made protesting noises down the phone.

'If anything disastrous should happen,' Lisa said stoutly, 'Paul can always run me into the hospital in Hereford. It only takes twenty minutes. But I'm fine, really. Never felt better.'

This was not strictly true, but for Lisa Fenway the birth of her first child and Natasha's party for the fiftieth anniversary of the St Martins community had become somehow entangled in her mind. She had an odd, superstitious belief – which she would have admitted to no one, not even Paul – that if she did not go to the party something dreadful would happen to the baby. Which was idiotic of her, as she knew very well.

★ ★ ★

Frances switched on the car radio, tuning in to Classic FM. It offended her by playing only fragments, never completing a piece, but it provided an agreeable and undemanding background to the drive. She had always preferred driving alone, but since her marriage it was a pleasure she had rarely been able to enjoy. For years there had been the demands of others, creating tensions, making the metal and glass box into a prison. First Giles. In those days (before he had lost his licence) insisting on driving, though he was not nearly as good a driver as she was. Then Anya, fretting in her carrycot, the back seat around her wedged with carrier bags full of nappies and baby powder and made-up bottles of formula. Then Nicholas and Tony and Lisa. All of them quarrelling, wanting to stop, demanding to be sick or to go to the loo, and being pacified with chocolate by Giles, who laughed at Frances's rules about no sweets between meals.

Then, much later, when Anya and Nicholas were almost grown-up and Tony and Lisa were bored and aggressive teenagers, it started all over again with Katya.

I'm too old for this, Frances had thought, assembling a new set of baby paraphernalia, alien in design and purpose from the objects that had cluttered her early motherhood.

Tony and Lisa had complained and bickered about the space in the car being encroached upon by the new baby. Who – then – had been angelic. Quiet and good, with a smile to melt hearts. But her brother and sister had been unmoved.

'Honestly,' she had overheard Lisa saying to Tony. 'At *their* age. I think it's disgusting.'

Tony had snickered. 'Just Dad trying to prove he's still virile. Or Mum trying to stop him straying.'

★ ★ ★

Giles cried, that time, in the autumn of 1980. Tears, of course, came easily to him. They were one of his professional skills. No more to be trusted than his charm, once so enchanting.

'I swear to you, Frances,' he said brokenly, burying his face in her breast. 'You are the only woman I love. That little bint who's been in the Noel Coward with me – honestly, I was just giving the kid a bit of fun, showing her the sights, introducing her to some useful people.'

He heaved himself up, glowering. Frances noticed that he was beginning to thicken about the waist.

'How dare she ring you up like that! Who does she think she is?' he demanded crossly.

Ah yes, this is the real Giles. His sense of dignity is offended. Little Ms Bootsie Fabersham (what a ridiculous name) is finished. She has not played the game by his rules. She has invaded his bolt-hole, his private place, my home.

Her eye was caught briefly by a cool still life painted by Natasha and hanging on the bedroom wall. It was a study in yellows and greens, with a shaft of sunlight falling diagonally across a table.

He kissed her hair, stroked her.

Why don't I have the strength to throw him out of my bed, out of my life? Frances asked herself resentfully, knowing that she would not, feeling herself melt. Pitying him, with his injured pride.

She had not taken the pill for months. Until now there had been no need. She was not really worried. After all, she told herself, I am forty. Nothing can possibly happen after just once. But it did. And the result was Katya. A beautiful baby. Perfect in every way.

And three months before her birth, Giles was photographed with his latest girlfriend, attending the première of a film in which he had played a minor role.

5

★ ★ ★

In the bedroom she liked best at St Martins — a queer, lopsided space up under the mediaeval roof beams — Katya Kilworth stirred and pushed back the duvet, but did not wake. Her clothes were scattered all over the floor, a heap of black — skirts and sleeveless tunics and baggy jeans and boy's football boots. In bed she wore a grandad woollen vest with buttoned neck and long sleeves. It sported a wartime utility label in the back, which was currently considered by Katya's peers to be cool. She had bought it in the local Oxfam shop for 50p. After she had worn it for an hour or so, it developed a curious smell — reminiscent of wet dog. It was scratchy and too hot, but she had bought it to annoy her mother and so felt obliged to wear it.

Irritably she half woke, threw the duvet off the bed entirely, then stripped off the woollen vest and flung it across the room. The pale light of early morning fell on her from the uncurtained window, and she looked at herself in disgust, loathing her body. She threw herself on to her face, clutching a pillow in her arms and remembering, as she drifted back into sleep, her balding teddy bear. She kept it hidden at St Martins, to avoid the shame of Mum turning it up in Reading. Tomorrow she would rescue Ted and bring him back to her bed. No one disturbed your privacy at St Martins. Which was odd, really.

★ ★ ★

Two floors below, Natasha Devereux lay awake on her high, severe, four-poster bed. She slept very little these days. Not profound sleep. On the other hand, she dozed frequently. During the day, sitting in her favourite high-backed chair in the window bay of the drawing room, she would be dozing and yet at the same time aware, in some part of her mind, that she was still present in the room. So that Irina or Mabel, coming in to urge unwanted cups of tea on her, would start to tiptoe out again — only to be confronted with her disconcertingly sharp eyes. Sometimes they manoeuvred William into the chair opposite, where he would sit, quiet and biddable as a well trained dog. My son-in-law, since his stroke, looks older than

6

I do myself, thought Natasha a little complacently. Even though he is seventeen years younger.

The white voile bed curtains stirred and billowed in the breeze from the windows. She had caught from her English husband the habit of leaving the windows open at night, except in the most severe weather.

'Leave the windows *open*, Edmund dousha moya?' she had exclaimed, scandalised, the first time they had slept together, that joyful night in Paris, the spring after the Great War. 'The night air is poisonsome, everyone knows this.'

'Poisonous, my darling, not poisonsome,' he said, laughing, touching her lips with the tip of his finger. 'And that is foolish nonsense taught you by your Nianyushka. I have slept with the windows open all my life, and look at me!'

And she had looked at him. He still wore uniform. It was not so splendid as the Russian uniforms of her childhood, but the sober, well tailored lines defined the shape of him, filling her with longing. He started to undress, exposing the scar on his chest that he had earned at Passchendaele, still pink and vulnerable. She began to kiss it.

Now, lying in the bed at St Martins, she was filled with wonder that she could have survived this last half-century without him, after a second war, nearing its end, had taken from her the man the first war had brought to her. It seemed inconceivable – such a gulf of time. By tenuous links her thoughts slid to Anya, her troubled eldest great-granddaughter. At thirty-four, thinking her life was over. Anya was only just beginning.

She keeps too much to herself, thought Natasha. What is going on in that tight, well controlled brain of hers? Too much she thinks of things, of ideas, of theories. All beautifully categorised and indexed and filed. She never speaks of the feelings. Irina, now, my so-disappointing daughter, she speaks of feelings all the time, her own feelings. Always they are hurt or offended in some way. But Anya – no, she is like Edmund, very British. Does she even speak of feelings with this man of hers, whom she is so reluctant to bring to my party?

In the tiny bed-sit in North Oxford, which was all she could possibly afford – no, more than she could afford – Anya Kilworth lay very straight on her back under a single plain white sheet. She was not asleep. Probably she had not slept all night. She loved this room, especially when the trees were in leaf. Without lifting her head from the pillow she could look out through the uncurtained window at a rolling seascape of tree-tops, just now heaving gently in the light summer wind. The spiky candelabra of horse chestnuts, pink and white, caressed the looser, wilder, yellow cascades tumbling from the laburnums.

The back garden of this house – divided for many years amongst a shifting population of students, graduates and university hangers-on – was in a state of rampant neglect. The laburnums had seeded themselves, and were scattered about in every size from finger length to a height of twenty feet or more. If you ventured into the garden you had to fight your way through an undergrowth of cleavers and bindweed and ground elder, clawing at you to waist height. There were tunnels where the secret cats of North Oxford patrolled on their nightly business and at the far end, beneath the crumbling garden wall of brick, lay the remains of an asparagus bed, from which Anya had been able to pick a few shoots last week when Spiro came to dinner.

It had been meant as a reconciliation. They would have a pleasant, relaxed meal and talk about neutral subjects. Make a fresh start. But somehow it had gone wrong. They started to quarrel, and then they were shouting at each other. To her horror, Anya heard herself telling him to leave. It seemed to be some other person speaking – a shrewish woman with a harsh, self-righteous voice. She did not want him to go, and had been cold with shock ever since.

She had seen him once, two days ago, in the Bodleian. They had nodded at each other and walked on without speaking. He was supposed to be coming with her to St Martins today. A month ago at least, they had arranged to meet at the station, in time for the Hereford train. Should she ring him to remind him? No, it would be too humiliating. What if he did not turn up at the station? Should she wait? He had the infuriating Greek habit of indifference towards time. If you missed a train, so what? Another one would come, today, tomorrow.

I wish I could talk all this through with someone, thought Anya. Though I know I'm not the kind of person who talks about such things. I wish I were the sort of daughter who can talk to her mother, the way Lisa talks to Mum. Though Mum is hardly the best person to give advice. Granny Irina is useless. Once, I might have gone to Natasha, but she is getting so old now, and frail. I can't burden her. And although I have lots of acquaintances − colleagues, people I go to pubs with − I don't really have any close friends. Mum would at least understand the dilemma I'm confronted with.

Anya smiled a little bitterly, flung herself crossly on her side and looked at the clock. God, it was still only six.

★ ★ ★

Frances Kilworth stopped once only on her journey. Not because she needed petrol, but because she liked to get out and stretch and view the countryside away from the tunnel-like motorway with its monotonous scenery. She had turned off the M4 at Junction 15, to take a shortcut cross-country, instead of following it the long way round to the M5. Giles always wanted to keep to the motorways. It confirmed his perception of himself as busy and sought-after, dashing about the country on the blue lines radiating out from London. It was the source of one of the many irritations between them that Frances much preferred the adventure of unknown country roads. Little hidden villages, valleys concealed from the major highways by enfolding hills, were to her an enrichment of the experience of travelling. She had never been able to make him see that her cross-country routes often shortened the journey as well as making it less tiring.

'You're always getting stuck behind some damn tractor thing,' he would complain, impervious to the fact that tractors usually turned off the road within a quarter of a mile or so, while tailbacks on the motorways moved far slower and stretched out for interminable miles. He almost appeared to enjoy them,

9

drumming on the dashboard with his fingers, exchanging exaggerated, comical faces of woe with fellow sufferers in the cars around them.

In the same way he seemed tied to the crowds and traffic of London by an umbilical cord of emotional needs. The furthest he had been prepared to move, when they had felt they could buy a house thirty years ago, was to Reading. This was not Frances's idea of the country, but she had still been in love with him then and the house would do for a few years, till they could afford something better. But that had been, as it turned out, one of their most prosperous periods. Giles had secured his first West End part, in a lightweight play that for some inexplicable reason ran and ran, so that, together with the tiny bits of money she had been carefully putting aside for five years, they were able to pay in full the £4,000 the house had cost. (No right-minded building society would have given an actor a mortgage.) Frances managed to find some work translating correspondence for a local firm exporting to Italy, which she did while Anya was at her morning play group and Nicky took a nap. The work was badly paid, but the money covered their modest daily spending needs, with a little scrimping and saving.

'A hundred and ninety thousand pounds!' she had repeated to the keen new man in the insurance office last week.

'Oh yes, Mrs Kilworth,' he assured her. 'It must be worth at least that, even with the present difficulties in the housing market. Five years ago it was probably worth well over 200 K. You really must not under-insure. If you had a fire . . . '

She found it difficult to attend to him. When they had bought it, the house had overlooked fields at the back, giving at least an illusion of the country. But in the early eighties new housing developments had begun to encroach on them, nearer and nearer. Now the view from the main bedroom and the kitchen below it — a view once moving in a cycle through the colours of the agricultural year, and framed by willows along a stream — had been replaced by the severe backs of identical houses, row upon row, whose windows were too small and whose roofs were too shallow. The stream had been culverted, and the willows cut down – one agonising afternoon – by an indifferent man with a chain-saw.

This leap in monetary value was ludicrous, almost obscene. Because the house was much nastier now than when they had bought it. And the streets were no longer safe. When Anya and Nicky were small, she had never worried about them playing with their friends up and down the road, or on the small area of grass around which the houses were grouped. Now, whenever Katya was just a little late from school she would begin to worry.

After Junction 15 she bypassed Swindon and headed for Cirencester on the A419. She thought at first that she had missed the lay-by where she wanted to stop, but spotted it at last and pulled in. It was disconcerting not to find it where she had expected it to be.

I know this road so well, I could drive it with my eyes shut, she thought. But I suppose it must be three months since I was last down at St Martins. What can I have been doing with myself all that time?

She got out, stretching slowly and luxuriously, like a cat. Then she locked the car. And not long ago I would not have done that, she thought. She pushed through the dusty, sickly-looking bushes that edged the lay-by and climbed the slight rise beyond. North and west of her the soft lines of the Cotswolds rose, looking larger than they really were in the horizontal light of early morning which dramatised their contours.

* * *

'I'm going to find some real mountains to climb,' Hugh said.

They were eating a clotted cream tea in one of the golden Cotswold villages, sitting outside a cottage in the unexpected sunshine of July, 1958. Their bicycles were propped against the low garden wall, the over-full saddle bags bulging into the hollyhocks and foxgloves.

She was only half listening to him. It was, although they did not know it then, their last cycling holiday together. Since their early teens they had taken cycle trips every Easter and summer, even after Frances's acquisition of the MG. Last night they had stayed at the youth hostel in Gloucester. They planned to make their way through the Cotswold lanes at a leisurely pace, then go on to Stratford and buy standing room tickets for whatever play was showing. The tickets cost only half a crown, and sometimes the usherettes would show you to an unoccupied seat at the first interval. Once, they had found themselves in the front row of the dress circle.

'There's a field trip going out to Kashmir. I'm going to try to stay on afterwards and do some real climbing after the others come back.'

'Won't it be frightfully expensive?'

'I'm going to use my prize money, and Natasha said she would help. Mother, of course, is dead against it. Dad just humphs.'

'Mmm.' Thinking about Stratford had filled her mind even more intensely with Giles, and she felt her stomach churn. It was just possible they might run into him in Stratford. He had some sort of job at the theatre for the vacation – selling programmes or something. Would they see him? Would he notice her? She was so insignificant compared with his usual glamorous girlfriends. Dark, studious, shy, she was acutely embarrassed whenever she had to mix with his set, who all seemed larger, more vivid than anyone she had ever known. They called each other 'darling', were wantonly careless about lectures and tutorials, flouted the rules about staying out of college late, left Oxford without permission.

One day in the seventh week of last term, Giles had taken her with a crowd of his friends to London to see a show. She persuaded another girl to tell lies to their tutor, saying she was ill and would have to miss her mediaeval history tutorial. The entire evening was ruined for her by her guilt and terror.

'Look at my little bluestocking,' Giles said, parading her before his friends and covertly caressing her, so that she blushed an ugly red.

They had dinner afterwards at Rules, and celebrities of the stage were pointed out to her. Giles's OUDS cronies themselves could not quite conceal their awe. Then they went on, somewhat drunk, to a Soho night-club, which was horrible. Frances thought the floor show ugly and degrading, and a swarthy, middle-aged man pawed at her in the dark corridor near the Ladies.

They began the drive back to Oxford at dawn, tired and quarrelsome. Giles seemed morose and withdrawn, so that Frances sat, biting back tears, looking out of the window, past Beaconsfield, past High Wycombe, into Oxford through Wheatley. She asked to be dropped near the Martyrs' Memorial, and wandered about disconsolately until well after the college gates were opened. The last week of term had been spent trying to avoid the Dean, in the fear that somehow she would reveal her guilt in her face.

★ ★ ★

At the end of that summer Hugh made his Kashmir journey, arriving back late for the start of term at Cambridge. But, as always, he was forgiven. He had managed to lose himself in the mountains. Had fallen in with a remote local tribe, and lived at their village for a month. By Christmas he had sold an account of his adventure, with photographs, to one of the major Sunday papers.

The following summer Hugh graduated, staying in England only long enough to attend Frances's wedding to Giles in the chapel at St Martins. Then he had left for a two-year expedition up the Amazon.

★ ★ ★

Giles Kilworth did not sleep as well these days as he used to. In the past he had stayed up till the early hours, keyed up after a performance or drinking with chums when he was resting from work. The moment he laid his head on the pillow — unless, of course, he was otherwise occupied — he had always been able to fall asleep immediately, not waking until a civilised hour of ten or eleven, in time for a leisurely shower and a half-breakfast, half-lunch with the papers.

Lately — and he could not quite trace the beginning of the change — he had found it increasingly difficult to fall asleep. And then he would wake in the dark reaches of the night, or

13

in the early morning. Partly, it was due to the twinges of pain he sometimes felt in his hips and knees. Stupid, really. Nothing to worry about. But just enough discomfort to keep him awake. Partly, too, he was keyed up about the filming of the new series of *Vet in Hot Water*. The first series was just finishing its run on ITV, and was a smash hit. He'd never had so much fan mail in his life. Odd, when you thought about it. He'd always seen himself as a serious actor, and he'd done his Hamlet in rep in Birmingham and his Romeo (rather late, when he was nearly forty) in Huddersfield. He'd had supporting roles at Stratford and the National, but somehow had not made it to the top at either. He was looking forward to his Lear some day, but not yet, for heaven's sake!

The trouble was, there were so few good parts for Shakespearean actors in their fifties. Though Larry Olivier had got away with it. There was Malvolio, of course. And Shylock, though Giles wasn't the right build for that – you ought to be gaunt and hungry-looking, and he *had* put on rather a lot of weight recently. As his agent kept pointing out to him, quite unnecessarily.

Caesar? Mark Antony? Not that anybody seemed to want to do the Roman plays at the moment. Derek J. was a lucky bastard getting Claudius for that great long Robert Graves thing on telly back in the seventies. A toga is quite flattering if you are, well, a bit on the heavy side.

There were other possibilities, of course. He'd like to try his hand at Ibsen's *Master Builder*, but Brian was doing a run with that. Up in the north, though. He shuddered at the thought of a Scottish tour. Those freezing digs.

Really, it was much better to stay in London. That way, people didn't forget about you. What a stupid idea that had been of Frances's, years ago when he was just getting known in the right circles – some idea that they should live in the country. He could commute to London when he had a show, she said. Perhaps have a little flat there for sleeping over. The point was, you had to be *seen* about the place, all the time. He couldn't make her understand that.

He had never supposed he'd be so good at comedy, though

he had done his share of the usual frothy things in the early days. And there had been the Noel Coward about fourteen years ago, when that stupid little cow had tried to make him leave Frances and marry her, for God's sake! He'd paid for the abortion and sent her packing. Nasty little piece of work. She'd only been trying to use him. You saw her all the time on the telly these days, in some soap, playing a brassy barmaid. That was about her level, he thought with satisfaction. She looks older than Frances now, though she must be nearly twenty years younger. Not much older than Anya. Saw her the other day at a party. That was a lucky escape, that time.

One more rehearsal tomorrow, then we'll get the last episode in the can next week. He turned restlessly on his side, grunting as a pain stabbed briefly in his back. He wasn't *absolutely* happy about the new series. There was a different screenwriter, who just didn't have Max's zest. And then Judy, that clever little kid with a face like a monkey, who'd played the part of his assistant, had already been sewed up tight in a stage contract she couldn't wriggle out of, so they'd had to drop her character from the second series. Didn't think it would matter, he thought grimly, but somehow the whole thing seemed to be falling flat without her, even though hers was only supposed to be a minor part. She has absolutely no sex appeal, not for me anyway, but she's a real pro, bright as the proverbial button.

The worrying thing was that there wasn't anything definite fixed up to follow this second series. Of course, with the reviews and the ratings, something was bound to turn up soon. Still, he hadn't been happy when Frances had said that she was thinking of giving up her part-time lectureship at the poly.

'Now that you're doing so well, Giles,' she said, 'and with only Katya left at home, I thought I might stop. It takes so much time and energy, all the preparation and marking and examining, when I'm only paid on an hourly basis for the hours I'm in college lecturing. No pension. No paid holidays. No sick pay.'

'Not for me either, darling.'

'But you knew that when you went on the stage. My full-time colleagues at the poly have everything very nicely provided. It's just the mugs like me – married women working part-time – who are exploited.'

'Now don't go all *feminist*,' he said, in the beguiling comic tone he used so effectively in the series.

She looked at him coolly.

'There are other things I would like to do. I think that it's just about my turn. At last.'

That was unfair of her. They'd agreed right from the start that she would take all the part-time jobs she could until he made his name. Of course she had to give up that notion of going to Italy to do a PhD – on apprentices in Renaissance art studios, or whatever it was. Boring trash. What with Anya arriving while they were still undergraduates. It wasn't *his* fault. She said she wanted to put his career first.

The trouble with women of Frances's age was that they were both too young and too old. They were too young to be like their mothers' generation, accepting their place in the scheme of things, staying at home and supporting their husbands. And they were too old to have the freedoms of younger women. But now some of them were trying to grab those freedoms in middle age. It was laughable.

Uncomfortably, he thought of Natasha, who disproved his theory. Now Irina, Frances's mother, was the old-fashioned wifely type, irritating though she was. But her grandmother! By all accounts, Natasha was quite a girl in her day, back in post-World War I Paris. Part of a real bohemian living-in-a-garret set, from the tales told by those odd characters who used to wander in and out of St Martins. All dead now, probably.

* * *

'Natasha Ivanovna, she comes from great family of Russia, you understand, my friend.' The man, a morose White Russian in threadbare clothes, has warmed to Giles over the vodka bottle, in the little back sitting room at St Martins. 'She saw terrible things in Revolution, terrible, when she was just girl. All her family slaughtered by those pigs of Bolsheviks. Not clean with gun, oh no. They make long time fun with swords taken from wall of Petrograd mansion. This she watches. Her mother,

her sisters, her little brother. Her father is already dead, you understand. They climb over his dead body to get into house.'

He pours himself another glass, staring red-eyed into the fire.

'When they finish with others of family, they turn to her, Natasha Ivanovna. All this time they hold her and she struggles. She thinks, I will throw myself on sword and it will be finished.'

'But she didn't.'

'No, my friend. Natasha Ivanovna is very beautiful. They do not use sword. They rape her. All of them. I spit on them.' He spits into the fire.

'But how did she escape?'

'One of this rabble – he was once servant of Greshlovs. He is ashamed. While pigs of Bolsheviks are stealing bottles from cellar, he manages to make escape her.'

For a long time he is silent, turning the glass of clear liquid round and round in his hand, staring into the past.

'When she is in Paris, she becomes part of bohemian set – artists and musicians, living on Left Bank. She is now painter. She comes also to quarter of émigrés, where myself I am living. She is become very wild, you understand, my friend. For some it was like this, for others – nothing but grieving. Once, there is party at Russian club, and someone begins to play balalaika, very sad songs, mourning our lost Mother Russia. No, says Natasha Ivanovna, play fast dances, play for me!

'And she dances on table amongst glasses and food, wearing nothing but her petticoat. *Nothing*, my friend! This you must believe.'

It is certainly true, what he says. His eyes gleam at the memory and his lips are wet.

★ ★ ★

Glumly, unable to sleep in the brighter light now slipping beneath the thick curtains, Giles thought of Frances. Certainly she had never shown any sign of dancing on the table in nothing but her petticoat, like Natasha. But some women did turn *odd*, didn't they, at her sort of age?

The latest red-head, stirring and moaning a little in the bed beside him, broke his train of thought. He had completely forgotten about her. Disconcerted, he eyed her pink freckled shoulder with distaste. High time to end that particular liaison. He would slip quietly out of her bed now and go to his club for a shower and breakfast before tootling along to the rehearsal room in Ealing. He would send the aspiring starlet a graceful letter of farewell, with some roses and a bottle of bubbly. Something fond and fatherly, making her see that it was only a diversion, helping her to find her feet in London.

He started to ease himself out of the bed, groping for his slippers. A large, firm hand grasped him about the upper arm in a grip it would have been difficult to break without rudeness.

'Darling?' said the red-head.

With a groan, Giles sank back on to the pillows.

★ ★ ★

Irina Appleton, daughter of Natasha and mother of Frances, was not quite awake, but she was going over her lists in her mind:

Send Katya to village to collect extra cheese
Check enough glasses
Get Mrs D to wash glasses
Get Mr D to put out tables
Tell Olga to lay tables in garden
Mabel to make salads
Mabel to bake quiches
Mabel to see about tea urn
Get cakes from Sally
Nicholas to put up signs on drive about parking
Mabel to phone wine merchant about one case short
Sally to set up old dairy as crèche
Tony Nicholas & Paul to put up marquee

She stopped trying to pretend she was still asleep. In the other bed William's breathing was deep and regular. Fretfully, she felt he had fallen ill just to spite her. Not retiring from his solicitor's practice until he was over seventy, when he knew how difficult it was to deal with St Martins and Mother, despite

Mabel's splendid help. He could have been some use to her during these last ten years. Then he had a stroke and became just one more worry for her. Thank goodness he didn't seem to mind Mabel nursing him.

And I do think Frances might have come down yesterday to give me a hand.

The voice inside Irina's head was so indignant she could almost hear it in the room.

She could surely have cancelled that bit of teaching she does, they wouldn't have minded. It's not as if it is a *real* job. People are so inconsiderate. And Katya looked dreadful when she arrived last night. Why ever does Frances allow her to wear those appalling clothes? I would never have allowed *her* to dress like that.

Briefly, she recalled those disgusting short skirts of the sixties. But Frances was married by then. She *would* marry Giles, and much good it has done her. Though I will say his new show has been a real laugh. Quite made me forget my sciatica for half an hour.

That marquee. It looks awfully complicated. I hope the boys can manage it. There could easily be rain. Not that it is a marquee really. Just something the Scouts use at their summer camp, but it was kind of Mr Peters to lend it to us. Mother has no idea, really. How did she suppose we could afford a real marquee? This isn't pre-Revolutionary Russia, I ask you.

Dreading the day ahead of her, Irina climbed slowly out of bed.

★ ★ ★

Frances had left Ross-on-Wye behind her. It was fully morning now, and the Black Mountains stood out clearly on her left as she headed north through Herefordshire. The cloud cover was thinning out. It might be a sunny day after all. Oh, I hope so, thought Frances, for Natasha's sake.

Only five more miles to St Martins. She was nearly home.

Chapter 2

IRINA APPLETON SAT at the kitchen table, cradling the mug of tea Mabel had made for her. She much preferred tea out of a proper cup and saucer, but thought it wiser not to object, this morning.

'I've been up since six,' said Mabel happily, hurrying across the kitchen with her clipboard and ticking off some items on the master plan she had pinned to the community's kitchen notice board. 'So much to do, so much to do. I don't know how we're going to be ready in time.'

Her cropped grey hair flickered from almost black to almost white as she moved in and out of the weak sunshine shafting through the window.

'Have you had any breakfast?' Irina asked. 'It's going to be a long day. You'd better have something.'

'No time for breakfast,' said Mabel. 'Now, Irina dear, if you could just shift a *wee* bit, along to the end of the table, it will give me more room . . .'

'Yes, of course.' Irina picked up her mug and moved to the chair at the far end of the table, noticing absently as she sat down that its rush seat had reached the point of no return. Hadn't she heard something about a new man in the village who could do that kind of thing? She leaned on her hand. Really, she did think she was beginning to get one of her heads.

'Sorry!' said Mabel, leaning across her to lift baking tins out of a cupboard. 'I'll just set these out for Sally and Olga. They thought they'd work together in here. They've divided up all the cooking between them. Of course I would just *love* to have the time to make some of my famous quiches, but I'm so busy seeing to everything . . .'

The clatter of the tins was dreadful. I'm probably coming down with one of my migraines, thought Irina. Mabel is a good friend, and a really excellent person, but I do wish she wouldn't chatter so much.

I wish I could get Irina out of here, thought Mabel. She will be under my feet all morning, getting in the way. It's not as if I could delegate anything to her, she would just get in a muddle, or leave it half done. You would think that a daughter of Natasha's would have inherited *some* of her mother's talents.

Rubbing her temples, now definitely throbbing, Irina watched Mabel set out the tins and stoke the Edwardian cast-iron range with coke.

The back door was pushed open with a muddy Wellington boot. Gregor staggered in, carrying a large cardboard box filled with vegetables. Irina could see the fronded tops of carrots and three or four big lettuces.

'Morning,' said Gregor. 'Where do you want these, Mabel?'

'In the scullery, please. Oh, Gregor, your *boots*!'

'Sorry. I stamped off what I could, but it's been drizzling in the night. Ground's dampish. But it looks as though the clouds are blowing away now. I'll sweep up the mud in a minute.'

He disappeared into the scullery.

★ ★ ★

We have been asked if we will take in some refugees for the duration. A Polish family – mother, father and little boy. Mother, of course, says yes at once, although the house is still almost derelict.

'They will be the first new members to join the St Martins community. This is good. They must come to us at once.'

It is May, 1944, and Irina has been at St Martins for a week, working like a skivvy and wondering whether it is really worth it. She had to get Hugh and Frances away from the bombing in London, but could not bear to send them off into the unknown like the other evacuees. You couldn't know what sort of a family they might end up with, perhaps really dreadful people, with disgusting table manners and an earth closet in the garden. You heard such tales. And already Hugh, who is five, has started running off to play with any child he meets in the street. So unsuitable. Frances is an easier child, but she follows her brother around no matter where he goes and thinks everything he does is wonderful.

Now Mother and Father have inherited this ramshackle place from some old childless uncle of Father's that I've never even heard of. When Mother offered us a home for the duration I had no idea there would be nothing but primitive plumbing and no electricity. And pigeons nesting in the upstairs rooms. And rats and cockroaches everywhere.

Irina shudders. Her hands are raw with scrubbing down the kitchen and scullery.

What is worse, Mother didn't say a word in her letter about this 'community' they have set up. They have always had these odd, foreign, artistic friends, but at least in London they used to go home at night. Most of the time. I hated it when I was a child. I know the other girls at school laughed at us, and at the way Mother dressed – like an actress. But now eight or ten of these awful people seem to have been invited to live here too. In fact, I think she invited them before she invited us. They have set up some sort of a trust, and it looks as though they will be here permanently. Well, I can put up with it until the war is over and William comes home, then you won't see me for dust.

Mabel Owens is scrubbing potatoes at that dreadful sink.

On the whole, it was a good idea to bring her. Luckily she'd just finished her teacher training when the house where she boarded was bombed. It seemed providential – just the week before we came down to Herefordshire. She's a hard worker, I'll say that for her, and she is good with the children. She can make herself useful around the place for the summer, until she gets a teaching post and somewhere of her own to live. And help keep an eye on the children. This place is a nightmare, with that open well, and broken glass everywhere from old greenhouses and cold frames.

That must be the billeting officer at the back door, bringing the refugee family. I'm glad to see he understands the proper place for them. What peculiar people! As thin as scarecrows and dressed like them too. The coat the man is wearing was quite good cloth at one time, but it's full of holes now. Probably his master gave it to him when he was throwing it away. The woman looks consumptive. Oh Lord, I hope she isn't carrying TB. What large, dark eyes that boy has. He doesn't look – well – normal, somehow. Perhaps he is a bit . . . How tiresome of Mother. She knows I brought Hugh and Frances here to protect them from just that kind of thing.

The man claims to be a count or some such. What nonsense. He needn't think we will be taken in by that. I wonder whether he knows that Mother is really a Russian princess, and thinks he can impress her? Mother, of course, is speaking Polish to them, so I can't understand a word they are saying.

★ ★ ★

Gregor looks about cautiously. The house reminds him a little of home, but it is not very clean and the garden is horrible, choked with weeds and overgrown bushes where anything might be hiding. He remembers home very clearly, although he was so small when the Germans came and they had to run away into the woods. There is a woman with a round shiny face at the sink. That is probably the cook. And the woman with the cross face sitting by the table – he cannot imagine who she can be. She does not seem to be doing any work, but why is she sitting in the kitchen? Perhaps she is a lady's maid. And neither of the women curtsy to Mama and Papa as the servants used to do at home. But he does not know if this is done in England. He has been here two months now, living in a camp, but this is the first time he has been inside an English house.

The strange language washes over his head. The man who has brought them talks a lot, and says something about Papa. Count Baranowski, he says. Countess. Gregor. Now there is another lady coming in, with fair hair piled up on her head. She is laughing and holding out her arms. This is certainly the lady, the Russian lady. Gregor pokes the stone-flagged floor with his boot, which is too tight. He doesn't like the Russians any more than the Germans, but Mama says they are our friends now.

He looks at the lady suspiciously from under his thick black eyebrows, eyebrows which he can see if he frowns hard. He can see them now. She is kissing Mama and Papa. She is speaking Polish!

'Oh my dears,' she says warmly, 'I am so glad to welcome you to St Martins. We are still in a muddle here, but you are home now. This is your home, as much as it is mine.'

Mama is crying, but she is smiling too.

Then the lady kneels down by Gregor, and puts her arms around him. She doesn't say anything, but she hugs him tight. She smells nice, like the ladies who used to come to dinner parties and balls at home. Gregor is crying into the lady's dress, making it all wet. He is ashamed of himself.

* * *

'I think it might turn out fine after all,' said Gregor, prising off his boots and putting them outside on the step. He spoke with the soft broad vowels of the Herefordshire–Wales border country.

He fetched a dustpan and brush from a cupboard under the sink and began sweeping up the clods of earth from the floor. His big, bony hands were ingrained around the fingernails and in the creases of the knuckles with fine white stone dust, and he handled the brush as delicately as his chisels.

'I thought I might get Nicholas to help me wheel my Venus Rampant out on to the lawn for the party. We could hang a tray of refreshments round her neck, like those girls in the cinema. Make her work for her keep, see.'

'Really, Gregor!' said Irina crossly. The least he could do was to take his sculpture seriously. That Venus had been commissioned by a Texan with more money than sense, in her opinion. It might look all right in its ultimate home, some hi-tech mansion, she supposed, all marble and art treasures and security guards, but it simply would not do in the middle of St Martins' lawn. Certainly not with children about.

Gregor looked up at her sideways under his eyebrows from where he was kneeling in front of the scullery door.

'We could drape a shawl around her juicier bits, if that's what's bothering you, Irina.'

The quirk of his grin was hidden by the corner of the table as he watched the red slowly creeping up her neck. He loved taking the mickey out of Irina. She always rose to it, then struggled conscientiously to keep her temper like a lady. He had no intention of moving the Venus. It would need a fork-lift truck.

'Now, Gregor,' said Mabel briskly, 'stop talking daft and get yourself out from under my feet. Unless you want some breakfast.'

Gregor had minimal cooking facilities in the rooms he had made his own, over the old stable he used as a studio, but he often forgot to buy food or cook meals. When hungry, he would go and pull a few carrots or broad beans from the communal vegetable garden and walk up and down outside eating them raw. Although Mabel treated him with firmness, she could never quite forget the ravenous waif he had once been. About half the time he sat down in the main kitchen with whoever happened to be eating there.

'I wouldn't say no.' Gregor shook the dirt outside the back door and put the dustpan and brush away. 'But you get on with whatever it is you're doing. I'll make myself a good rib-sticking fry-up.' He opened the fridge and began pulling out eggs and bacon. 'What about you, Irina? Bit of fried bread? Bacon?'

Irina pulled a woebegone face. 'No thank you. I think I'm getting one of my migraines. I couldn't face a thing.'

Mabel, seizing her chance, said consolingly, 'Oh, you poor dear! Why don't you just go back to bed for a bit? You know you'll never shake it off unless you lie down in the dark for an hour or two. I'll come and see how you are when it's time to get William up.'

'I think perhaps I just might,' said Irina, allowing her voice to tremble a little, bravely. She put her mug on the draining board and left the kitchen with the air of a martyr going to certain punishment.

'Was that my fault?' asked Gregor, contrite, throwing food lavishly into the frying-pan. The bacon sizzled, and its tempting aroma filled the kitchen.

'Oh no, she really can't cope with today. She'll be glad of an excuse to lie low for a while. Well, perhaps I will just have a bit of bacon. Fried bread? I shouldn't really — they say now that it's so bad for you — but perhaps just half a piece. And an egg. Yes, that would be lovely.'

★ ★ ★

Katya dressed with care. The trick was to arrange the layers so that all of them could be seen. This meant that you had to start with the longer garments and work your way upwards and outwards. She pulled jeans on first, then discarded them in a corner and tried leggings instead. That was better. She could wear her long black skirt over them, and it would add another layer.

On top she wore a greyish sleeveless man's T-shirt that hung down to her knees, about a foot shorter than her skirt. Then a black, collarless, long-sleeved man's shirt, half buttoned. Then a shorter shirt, open. Then a long sleeveless waistcoat. Then a funny sort of short coat with big baggy pockets, another of her Oxfam buys, which the woman had said was a poacher's jacket. She pushed her feet into her football boots. They were heavy and uncomfortable, but they made a terrific noise when she banged up and down the shoddy staircase in Reading. Here at St Martins the stone spiral of the tower did not resound to them at all, while the wide oak treads of the main staircase leading up to her room gave only a faint tolerant thud.

I wonder if Tony will let me go with him to meet his girlfriend at the station. What will this one be like? He sounded quite serious about her when we were driving down yesterday. If I don't like her, I'll have to think of some way to get rid of her. Thank goodness Nick's Sally is OK. Pretty cool. And I suppose Paul is all right, though he's a bit of a bore. I wonder if Anya will bring her Greek fella or not? Maybe he's about to join the ranks of her ex's. She didn't sound as though she wanted to bring him, but Natasha was pretty firm on the phone last night.

Katya kicked aside some clothes and a canvas bag so that she could open the door, and ran down the stairs towards the smell of frying bacon.

* * *

Frances pulled the car round off the main drive and into the stableyard, parking near the coach-house door that served as the main entrance to the part of St Martins where her elder son Nicholas and his wife Sally lived with their three children. Curtains still drawn. If Sally (as she suspected) had been saddled with most of the cooking, they ought to be getting up soon. At a tiny window high in the gable a curtain twitched and Chrissie's sleepy face peered out.

'Hi, Granny.'

'Hi yourself. Aren't you lazy people up yet?'

'I am,' Chrissie pointed out, rather hurt. 'Are you going to have breakfast in the big kitchen? Can I come too?'

'If you're quick.'

The face disappeared, and by the time Frances had unloaded her suitcase and some cardboard cartons from the boot, Chrissie was letting herself out of the door, none too quietly.

'Ssh!' said Frances.

'Well, they ought to be up. It's the party today.'

'I know. Do you think you could help me carry these boxes? Heavens, darling, you're still in your pyjamas!'

'It doesn't matter. It's not *raining* or anything.'

Chrissie seized the largest box and began to carry it across to the back door. 'What's inside?'

'Food for the party. Cakes, and biscuits, and two of those salmon pastry roll-ups you like, and some other things. Careful, darling. Keep it the right way up.'

As Chrissie was struggling to open the door without dropping the box, it was opened from within and Gregor scooped Chrissie, carton and all, inside. He smiled at Frances over her head.

'Hello there. You must have started before dawn!'

* * *

Natasha says we have to be kind to this funny boy who has come to St Martins. But I don't like him. He's bigger than Hugh and me, but he can't say anything except nonsense words, like a silly nursery rhyme. I think he's stupid. He just stands around at the edge of the garden, watching us. This is where Hugh and I live. We don't want him. I hope he goes away soon.

* * *

Chrissie edged past Gregor carefully, with the box hugged to her chest. As Frances paused on the doorstep, he could see the low early sun catching the curve of her hair against her cheek and bringing out the polish like dark mahogany, which was hidden as soon as she stepped into the dim kitchen.

* * *

It is the summer of 1957. There is a dance in the village hall, and we are all going – Frances and Hugh and I, and that Latvian girl Olga who came last month. Since Frances and Hugh are brother and sister, I suppose you could say that he is going with Olga and I am going with Frances. But it probably won't work out like that. Hugh and Frances will dance with each other, because I dance like a bear, and I shall be stuck with Olga, who is boring and plain and four years older than I am.

Gregor feels some sympathy for Olga. She has lived most of her life in a camp for displaced persons in the British sector of Germany, and only recently, through some negotiations that he is not clear about, has her family been able to leave and come to settle in England. She has very poor English, but he suspects that even if she were fluent she would have little to say. The only thing she seems to have done since her family came to St Martins is to poke about in the garden with Birgit and Peter. No doubt they could do with some help.

At least their positions in the car tonight are to his liking. Frances is driving the second-hand sports car Natasha gave her for winning a scholarship to Oxford, and Gregor is sitting in

28

the front beside her. Occasionally her shoulder or her thigh brushes him, and he feels the blood come and go in his face. Hugh is trying to make conversation to Olga, squashed together with her in the back, but he is having a hard time of it, poor fellow. Very polite. Very Cambridge. At Gregor's art college they wouldn't bother. Take it or leave it, that was the philosophy. If someone didn't want to mix, you left them to get on with it.

The night is soft and warm. Someone has strung fairy lights around the prefab hall – an army depot during the war, left behind when the military moved away. A semi-professional band has been hired from Hereford for the night, and the strains of the latest hits from *My Fair Lady* float out of the windows. The prefab looks incongruous by day, an eyesore amongst the ancient half-timbered houses of Clunwardine Priors, but tonight it is softened and transformed by the lights and the music.

To his surprise, Frances seems to want to dance with him. He holds her uncertainly. Her waist is tiny, her skirts full. The bodice of her dress is so tight that it both excites and embarrasses him. But all the girls are dressed like this tonight. When they sit down on the hard wooden chairs around the edge of the dance floor, the hoops and the tiered petticoats of paper nylon that they are wearing tip up, showing layers of lace and glimpses of leg.

It is late now. The hall is very hot, and couples have spilled out into the market square, dancing round the trees and on to the castle green. Gregor is still dancing with Frances, and they are waltzing under the beech trees, stumbling a little and laughing as they avoid the cow pats and thistles. They have both drunk a good deal of the fruit cup and Gregor has begun to realise that it is stronger than he suspected. Frances is not used to drinking, and clutches him a little to keep her balance. The music stops and they pause in the shadows.

God, I love you, Frances.

* * *

That was a long time ago. We are middle-aged now, Frances

and I, thought Gregor. And Frances is a grandmother. But there is still something about her. Like Natasha, you notice her. In a room filled with people there is a different quality about her. He turned away, so that she would not see the expression in his eyes.

Chrissie was pulling packets of cereal out of a cupboard. 'Oh, Mabel,' she cried pathetically, 'aren't there any Coco Pops?'

'A new box at the back of the cupboard. But you ought to finish the opened packets first.'

'I hate all of those. Anyway, it's Natasha's *party* today,' Chrissie argued with cunning.

'Oh well, go ahead then.'

'Eggs and bacon, Frances?' asked Gregor quietly, teasing.

She laughed at him and poured herself coffee. And helped herself from a packet of muesli spurned by Chrissie. The kitchen door crashed open and Katya burst in.

'You haven't eaten all the bacon have you, Gregor, you pig?'

'Darling!' protested Frances.

'Hi, Mum. I didn't think you'd really make it by this time.'

'What time did you leave, Frances?' asked Mabel, guiltily getting up from the table and putting her dishes in the sink. She became busy with her lists.

'Five o'clock.'

Katya groaned and clutched her head. 'I'm glad I came yesterday with Tony. Shove up, Gregor.'

'It was a lovely drive. Dawn was just breaking as I left and there was hardly another car to be seen. I stopped just before Cirencester to look at the view and stretch my legs.'

Gregor caught her eye and looked away.

'Now, Mabel,' said Frances firmly, 'what's the timetable and what are my jobs?'

★　★　★

Lisa and Paul Fenway had been lying awake, each keeping still hoping not to disturb the other. They heard Frances's car arriving and Katya running downstairs, and the back door opening and closing. The thick walls and floors of the house usually insulated the different groups from each other's noise, but Lisa had been feeling the mild heat and left all the windows flung open last night after they arrived from Worcester.

She sighed and turned over with difficulty.

'Lisa?' Paul whispered, 'Are you awake?'

'Mmm. Have been for hours.'

'Are you all right?'

'I'm *fine*,' she reassured him, a little testily. He asked her too often. 'I'll just be glad when it's all over.' She cradled her swollen stomach with a protective arm. 'If I ever go through this again, I'm going to make sure it's a winter baby. No one warned me what it would be like, lugging all this extra weight about in the summer.'

'Less than a month to go,' he said comfortingly, running his hand down her bare arm. He was awkward with her in these late stages of pregnancy, averting his eyes from her shape. He wanted the baby, but he had not realised how much he would mind what it would do to Lisa. Already the unborn child seemed to come like a threat between them.

Lisa stared out at the curtains stirring in the breeze. She felt strange. There was no pain, not exactly that. But some change had taken place in her body during the night. The position of the baby was different. Under her hand she felt the baby kick twice, hard.

★   ★   ★

By half-past eight most of members of the St Martins community were up. Tony was leaning against the dresser, drinking black coffee, and Olga and Eric Collier had joined the others at the breakfast table, both of them quiet amid the chatter. Eric – who did silk screen printing in one of the studios – said he needed about an hour to finish a piece of work that was promised for Monday morning, but then he would come and help.

'Did you finish the drape for the mossy bank in the play?' said Chrissie.

'Yes,' said Eric. 'It's in my studio.'

'Me and Samira are going to fasten wild flowers to it, so it looks real. She's going to get here right after the service, so we can pick flowers from the meadow.'

'You can come and get it now,' said Eric, pushing back his chair.

'Not until she puts some clothes on.' Sally had come in the back door carrying Sarah. Bob followed her, glowering at Chrissie.

'Why did Chrissie get to have breakfast in the big kitchen?' he complained.

'Because I was already up, and I helped Granny with her boxes,' said Chrissie smugly.

Sally set Sarah on her feet and straightened up, tossing back her single thick plait over her shoulder. 'There are lots of things you can help with, Bob. *Outside.*'

Like a wheeled toy rolling down a slope, Sarah toddled precipitately across the floor until she collided with Tony's legs, and sat down abruptly on the flagstones.

'Outside for you too, shrimp,' said Tony, picking her up and tossing her in the air. Sarah squealed with delight.

'Not wise,' said Sally, tying on an apron. 'She's just had breakfast.'

'Spoilsport.' Tony tucked Sarah under one arm, where she hung happily, with her arms and legs swimming like a fat starfish. 'Come on, Bob. You can help us with the tables and chairs. Your mum is going to be cooking us something super for later on. You coming, Gregor?'

Sally and Olga chased everyone but Mabel out of the big kitchen and began to prepare the rest of the food for the party with the easy co-operation of long practice. Sally was the one with real flair, but Olga was a good sous-chef. The cooking she did for herself and Eric was dull but wholesome. Sally brought all her talents as a fabric designer to her cooking. Cakes became floral studies. Salads were transformed into tapestries of shape and texture. The older woman peeled and chopped, separated eggs, weighed and measured. And washed up.

From time to time Katya would pop in to give them a hand, or to carry trayfuls of food into the dining room, where everything was being stored behind closed doors, to keep it safe from cats, dogs and Sally's younger children. The kitchen was rich with the smells of chocolate and hot bread, chicken and onions. To her surprise, Katya found she enjoyed helping. In Reading she would only help Frances if asked repeatedly, and then banged about sulkily in the small kitchen where they had to sidle past each other sideways. The big old kitchen at St Martins, with its range always hot, its large table and collection of unmatched chairs, had always been the general gathering place. The drawing room had been intended as the community's common room, but gradually had come to be used only for the monthly committee meetings. It was Natasha's domain, though anyone who wanted a quiet corner to read or think would gravitate towards it. The kitchen was the social centre. It was here that things happened, day-to-day decisions were taken, quarrels flared and were made up.

In setting up a community for musicians and artists and refugees Natasha and Edmund had been mindful of the fact that volatile tempers would lead to arguments. There was only one rule of behaviour at St Martins. You must make up any quarrel before bedtime. It was not always – or even often – done with a good grace, but over the fifty years the rule had proved its worth.

'I wish I could live at St Martins,' Katya burst out.

'Do you, Katya? Pass me that cup with the gelatine in it, will you?' said Sally.

'I hate the house at Reading. I hate school too. I'd much rather go to school in Hereford.'

'But your parents want you with them.'

Katya kicked glumly at the table leg, then stopped as she saw that it was making Sally's garnishing difficult. 'I don't see why they should care. I hardly ever see Dad. And Mum . . . '

'What?'

'I don't know. She just seems – she's just so boring these days.'

She seems unhappy, thought Katya. But that sounds so gross. It can't be Dad's girlfriends. Even I know he's always had those, though they think I'm blind. I hate it in Reading. I wish they'd let me come here.

33

Mabel bustled in. 'How's it going then, girls? It all looks lovely. Katya, could you take these parking signs to Nicholas and tell him to get them put up? A few people are coming for coffee before the service at half-past eleven.'

* * *

Birgit and Peter Kaufmann, who had looked after the garden since joining the community just after the war, had grown too old for the heavy work, although Birgit still weeded and pruned with her special long-handled tools and Peter supervised from his wheelchair. Mr Dawlish now came up from Clunwardine Priors three times a week, in return for a nominal wage paid out of the trust's funds and a large patch of ground for an allotment. Mrs Dawlish, who preferred flowers in her small garden, approved of this arrangement and occasionally helped out herself at St Martins.

Frances, Paul, Gregor and Tony were helping Mr Dawlish put up small tables around the lawn, while Nick's children wove in and out around them. Bob was struggling to keep up with Chrissie, carrying out chairs from the barn, but he tripped over the legs every few steps. Watching them, Peter recalled how, at one time, the members of the community all seemed to be growing old together, until Nick and Sally had moved in when he joined William's law firm in Hereford. Now Chrissie and Bob brought their friends up from the village to run free over the garden and woods, and Sarah's toddlers' group met once a week at St Martins.

The sounds of children playing in the garden have brought back some life to the old place, thought Peter. He watched in frustration as the others carried out the tables and winced as the legs dug into his beloved turf. The smell of the sun on the newly cut grass was sweet, like a hayfield, and he wanted to be down on his knees, digging in the crumbling earth, making things grow. I'm nothing but a parasite now, he fretted, but I suppose I should be thankful I kept going as long as I did, after what they did to us in Auschwitz. And I can still play the piano a little, though not with the *brio* of the old days.

Frances grinned at him as she came past with two chairs.

'You'll just have to shut your eyes to the damage all this is going to do to the grass, Peter. At least it's only June. In a month you won't see a trace.'

'Hmph,' said Peter, disbelieving. But he appreciated the way she behaved towards him. So many people had started to treat him gingerly, as if he were senile, now that he had to use a wheelchair. It made the hot rage of his youth rise up in his throat, to be swallowed down with difficulty.

'Do you want to pick Anya up from the station, Mum, or shall I?' asked Tony. He was sporting a pair of French sunglasses and looked very like Giles at the same age.

'I'll fetch her, darling. I promised I would. And you would just have to turn around almost immediately to go for Alice. Paul, can you and Peter keep an eye on the children?'

'I'll go, if you like,' said Gregor. 'If you trust me with your car. I wouldn't ask Anya to sit in my filthy van amongst the stone chippings.'

'No, I'd quite like to go, Gregor.' She shaded her eyes against the sun, looking up at him. Then she added impulsively, 'Why don't you come with me?'

* * *

Gregor has been sitting in the hollow under the rhododendrons for hours now. The cows in the field opposite have been taken in for milking, but he has not noticed them. They let him see Mama for one last time in the hospital, and then Mabel led him away. It was better for Mama now, she said. She was in such pain with the tuberculosis, coughing blood. She didn't even know him when he saw her two days ago.

Ever since Papa was shot down in his aeroplane over France, flying with the Polish free air force, this is what he has been afraid of. He has nobody now. Will Natasha let him stay at St Martins? Perhaps they will send him away to an orphanage.

There is a rustling of the leathery leaves behind him, and Frances crawls through. She doesn't say anything. She puts her arms around him, the way Natasha did the day he arrived at St Martins. Except that Frances's little arms don't reach very far around him, and she smells of Pears soap instead of scent. He does not cry, now. Boys of twelve do not cry. But he is glad to have her there, sitting beside him.

* * *

Gregor swung shut the heavy barn door. All of the chairs had been moved out to the garden. The guests had been warned that they might like to bring a rug with them, for there were not enough chairs go round and – with all the events Natasha had planned – the party would go on until ten in the evening.

'What are you working on now, Gregor?' asked Frances, pushing the hair back from her face with the back of her arm. It was getting warmer all the time.

'Still the Venus Rampant. Do you want to see it?'

'Please.'

'You won't like it.'

'Why should you be so sure?'

He smiled to himself, turning away. 'Oh, I'm sure, all right. Not your sort of thing at all.'

Frances felt a little spurt of anger. How dare he! I suppose he thinks I am not artistically sophisticated enough.

He led her into his studio, flinging back the door so that the sun flooded in. The Venus Rampant stood bathed in light, motes of fine dust dancing round her like insects. Frances swallowed. He was right. She did not like it.

'It's a bit brutalist,' she said, walking slowly round it, to see if it improved. It did not. She looked across at him, where he was silhouetted in the doorway, a black figure against the sunlight. His face was unreadable.

'Is that what you really think of women?' Her voice faltered.

He turned away, fiddling with the tools meticulously hung up above his bench. 'Perhaps not all women. Venus is, after all, the goddess of love.'

'So that is what you are trying to show? The voracity of sexual love?'

He shot her a quick, startled glance, but did not answer.

'Come on,' she said. She sounded tired. 'We'd better hurry if we're going to be in time for Anya's train.' She glanced at her watch. 'She's due in just before ten.'

He followed her out of the studio. He did not show her – would not show her – the figure he was modelling, which stood at the far end of the studio, covered with damp sacking.

'I'll just go and take Natasha her breakfast, then we'll be off,' said Frances.

* * *

Natasha was up, sitting beside the window in her dressing gown of scarlet silk. She had heard Frances arrive, and watched the tables being arranged round the lawn. Poor Peter! she thought. He is hating this, but once the party starts it will be better. He loves a party. It reminds him of those wonderful days in the thirties, when he was the darling of every society hostess, and all the girls were in love with this glamorous Hungarian-German Jew. Irina was in love with him too, though she never suspected I knew. The first love of her life. A rising star at twenty-one, he was – with the beautiful face and the music in him like an angel. I begged them not to go back to Berlin in 1937. Begged them. So did Edmund. But he *would* not listen. He was arrogant in those days. It was part of his charm – that and his wildness.

She sighed. In a way, it was for the Peters of this world that St Martins had been intended, a place of sanctuary and healing. And he had been able to rebuild his career after the war. But his music was never the same again. Before, the rage and the joy had blended into a single, wonderful whole. Afterwards, there was only the rage, and bitterness. Then, eventually, contentment, peace. At least she had been able to give him that.

There was a tap on the door, and Frances came in with her breakfast tray.

'Good morning, darling,' said Frances, kissing her grandmother. Natasha's cheek was smooth and cool, like the silk of her dressing gown against Frances's arm.

Natasha eyed her shrewdly. 'You are looking – what was it Edmund used to say? Fine-drawn. Are you tired? Have you been working too hard?'

'Not really, no more than usual.'

But she looks exhausted, thought Natasha, with those grey

37

shadows under her eyes. I do not like this. Always in the past she has been the resilient one, whatever life has thrown at her.

Just for a moment, Frances dropped on to the footstool beside Natasha's chair. I must leave soon, she warned herself, but it is good to slacken off for a minute. With Natasha I never need to put on an act.

Natasha poured the strong black coffee she liked for breakfast, and buttered a roll. Frances will tell me what is bothering her when she is ready. She has always resisted if you try to rush her, she thought.

'Some time today, if we get the chance, I wish to have a talk to you, Frances. About St Martins.'

Frances looked up in surprise. 'Yes, of course. We can probably find a corner of the afternoon, once everything is under way. After a certain point, parties of this size run themselves.'

'The excellent Mabel,' said Natasha, with a wicked grin, 'would not agree with you. But yes, doushenka, I think some time in the afternoon, before drinks on the terrace, perhaps. Then, we should have our talk.'

* * *

Anya Kilworth sat on the train, looking out at the familiar landscape. She had changed at Worcester, and the last part of the journey took less than an hour. She would be in Hereford before ten. She closed her eyes and leaned back against the prickly seat. Although this was supposed to be a non-smoking compartment, the upholstery reeked of stale cigarette smoke. It must be one of the many smoking carriages simply redesignated by British Rail, as fewer and fewer passengers wanted to smoke. She imagined the carriage as it had once been, with soldiers, and girls with bright crimson lipstick and hair rolled up in improbable shapes, all chain-smoking, permeating the very fabric with an odour it would never lose.

No, that was fanciful. Even on a British Rail rural line the carriage couldn't be that old, could it? What she was visualising was a scene from the forties, conjured up by all those old wartime films shown in endless repeats on television. She watched them compulsively. The world they showed was so alien that they provided a balm for the tension that had become part of her life. Despite the violence of the wartime background, they had a kind of innocence that was totally remote from her own experience. Last night she had dozed off while watching one, then was jerked awake by a raucous burst of canned laughter. It was the last episode of Dad's sitcom, *Vet in Hot Water*, that he was so proud of. She had opened her eyes to see him wallowing about on his back in the mire of a cowyard. You could bet that the mire was something hygienic provided by the effects boys. Dad would never set his expensively shod foot inside a real farm. The skinny little girl who was supposed to be his assistant tried to pull him to his feet, and then she went down too, rolling him over in the mud. More canned laughter. Now she was dunking him in the horse trough to wash off the muck. Anya watched the girl thoughtfully. She's enjoying that. Getting a kick out of making the arrogant old bastard look a fool. She switched off the television.

God, men! she thought, opening her eyes now and watching the passing line of trees beside a hidden stream. She had waited till the last possible moment to get on the train at Oxford station. When the guard blew his whistle at 7.28, she had known for sure that Spiro wasn't coming. Up to that very moment she had clung to the hope that he might, that he would forgive her for the unforgivable things she had said last week. Why couldn't she have held them back? Shown some dignity? Always, in the past, she had been able to keep her feelings under control, to take them out and examine them rationally to herself, then tidy them away out of sight.

But with Spiro it was different. Probably because he himself was so different. The men she had gone out with over the years, even contemplated marrying, had all been British. And not only British but scholars, like herself. Like her they contained their feelings, put barriers round them. Were cool, rational, detached.

Right from the start, Spiro had awakened something in her that she hadn't known was there. She could not be sure whether it was because he was Greek, and so spoke easily of his feelings, without the inhibitions and embarrassments of her own set. Or whether it was because, for the first time, she was really in love. His presence disturbed her physically; no other man had affected her like that. It was not particularly pleasurable. Her feelings were so intense that she almost felt nausea. This angered her. Was, indeed, largely the source of her anger with him. Her life, for the first time, was getting out of control.

They had met at the tutorial college where she taught two days a week. This, with a little teaching for her own old Oxford college – Mum's old Oxford college – was her sole means of support. Despite her First Class Honours, her D.Phil., and three papers published in leading economic history journals, she had been unable to secure a permanent university post. After gaining her doctorate she had spent a year in Newcastle, filling in for someone who was away on sabbatical. After that, nothing full-time. She had come back to Oxford because you could usually pick up bits of teaching, but she did not earn quite enough to live on.

Spiro had a degree from the University of Athens, where his father was a professor of philosophy, a doctorate from Lille, and was now spending a year in Oxford, perfecting his English. He was very different from her other students at the college, who were mostly female, under twenty-five, and northern European. They were in Oxford primarily to look for husbands. They were pleasant enough girls, but Anya had little in common with them.

She had begun to go out with Spiro after breaking up with an unsatisfactory boyfriend, and saw it as a casual relationship. But some spark of attraction had caught between them. They had spent a good deal of time during the last months travelling about the English countryside on trains and local buses, sampling little restaurants and visiting the more out-of-the-way corners of the Cotswolds and the Welsh border country. Spiro had fallen in love with Britain – surprising, Anya thought, for a Greek. While she had talked of her academic ambitions, he had talked of the countryside. He was supposed to be going back to his previous university post in Greece, but seemed less and less enthusiastic about it.

'I am beginning to feel stifled by universities,' he said as they were travelling back by bus after a warm spring day spent wandering about Northleach. 'Whenever I pick up an economics textbook, I cannot breathe. Can you understand this? I want something different.' He smiled at her ruefully. 'Until now, I think I have been following the path laid down by my father, as a dutiful son should do. But I want to stray off the path. I want something free and open, where I can be in control of my life.'

Anya, leaning her head back against the plush cushion, had smiled at him sleepily, barely listening.

Then, three weeks ago, he had exploded his bombshell. He had asked her to marry him. And he had said he wanted to open a Greek restaurant in a Welsh village. Anya had reacted with contempt. 'Just like any greasy little Soho Greek,' she had said. She could still hear the words as they had hung in the air between them.

There is no way, Anya thought grimly to herself, that I am going to allow my life to be ruined the way Mum's was ruined. I don't want to look back on my life from my fifties and know that *I* have been a failure. That the whole of my life has been spent as the compliant shadow of some man, bearing his children, keeping his house, tied to his second-rate career, denying all my own talents and – yes – what I have to *offer* to the world. Mum is a dire warning to us all, of what happens to gifted women who mess up their lives with the wrong men.

The train intercom over her head crackled and emitted heavy breathing.

'Hereford, ladies and gentlemen. We are now approaching Hereford. Will you please ensure that you take all luggage with you when you leave the train. We are approximately six minutes late. Hereford.'

Chapter 3

A T THE FAR end of the lawn, Nicholas, Tony and Paul were struggling to put up the Scouts' big faded green tent. Tempers were growing a little short. Bob was banging tent poles together, while Sarah sat at the edge of the grass pulling up daisies and tasting them, with a thoughtful look on her face.

'Well, I don't think everything is here,' said Paul, who was in a jumpy state. 'I don't see how there can possibly be enough poles there to build the frame for all of this.'

They stood around the mass of limp canvas, which had a distinctly discouraged look about it.

Tony was being very offhand about the whole thing. 'Scrap it,' he suggested laconically. 'It's not going to rain anyway.'

Nicholas was systematically trying out different combinations of poles. 'It would help if we had some instructions,' he muttered.

'Shall I go and phone Mr Peters?' suggested Paul, who wanted to get back to Lisa. He had left her sitting quietly in the small sitting room, but he didn't trust her not to go and start helping Sally in the kitchen. He was uneasy about her. The party was sure to tire her, and she looked fagged out already.

* * *

From a wicker chair on the terrace, Natasha watched them. She was too far away to hear their voices, but she read their movements with amusement. It was as clear as a mime. Nicholas was slow and thorough like his grandfather, William. It was what made him a good solicitor. He would probably solve the problem while the others argued. Paul had the schoolmaster's tendency to take verbal charge, ordering the others about while doing little that was constructive himself. Just now he was suggesting something that the other two ignored. Tony was lounging back against a tree, watching his brother struggle with the poles. He would hold aloof until Nicholas failed to fit the last part together, then point out the obvious and take the credit. Poor Nicholas had always regarded his younger brother with a mixture of admiration and irritation.

It hardly seemed to justify their efforts. This tent Mabel had borrowed from the Scoutmaster was a poor thing, not at all what she had had in mind when she suggested a marquee. She had mentioned it quite idly to Irina and Mabel, remembering parties on the lawn of the British embassy in Paris in the twenties.

'Don't you remember, doushenka?' she said to Irina. 'You were only small, but you were always so thrilled with the ices, for we never had them at home.'

Irina did remember. She had worn a white dress, with a bright yellow scarf of her mother's tied round the waist as a sash, and shiny black patent leather shoes. She had been very proud of those shoes, but a horrid boy had stamped on her toes when they were waiting to be given their ices. She had almost fled back to her parents, but greed had held her. And it had been worth it. She could still see the silver dish, and the heaped spheres – cream and pink and pale yellow. She remembered rolling the ice-cream on her tongue, stunningly cold, so that you only began to taste it as it melted.

Was that one party or many, telescoped together in her memory? She couldn't be sure.

'When I was a girl in Russia,' Natasha explained to Mabel, 'there were always pavilions in the gardens, to shelter from the sun or the rain. So we had no need of such a thing as a marquee. But in your terrible English weather of June, nothing is certain.'

★ ★ ★

It is Petya's eighth birthday, and Mama and Papa have arranged a party. It is a great secret. That is, Natasha and her sisters know about it, and all the servants. But Petya does not, or at least he is not supposed to. But he must have seen the tables that have been set out in the pavilion, and the Chinese lanterns suspended from the trees. Petya, however, is pretending to notice nothing.

Natasha does not mind that Petya should have so much fuss made of his birthday. She remembers her parents' joy when at last a boy was born after five girls. Like the poor Tsarina, Mama had almost given up hope. There was a wait of eight years after Natasha, the youngest girl, and it seemed that the Greshlovs were not to be blessed. Despite the gap between them, Natasha and Petya have always been close companions. When he was a baby, the eight-year-old Natasha guarded him fiercely, driving away any nursemaids she did not like. It was she who spent hours tenderly assisting his first toddling steps, who bandaged his knees when he fell, who taught him – first his nursery rhymes and later his letters. Mama might have been jealous, but for the love glowing from Natasha like a lamp, and her pride in each of Petya's achievements.

Now Natasha is a tall girl, almost grown up, and Petya has friends outside the family, boys of his own age, but it is always to Natasha he turns when he is in trouble.

The party starts at lunchtime. The Greshlovs and their friends are to take a simple summer luncheon in the garden. The table is laid with starched linen. Columns of footmen carry out the Sèvres *bleu du roi* porcelain, the Venetian goblets, covered dishes, bottles of wine in ice-filled buckets. Then suddenly crowds of little boys and girls rush from the house, where they have been waiting with their nurses. Each has a party hat of satin, feathers and sequins, and each carries a balloon, which they tie to the trees. The footmen lift up the smaller ones so that they can reach.

After the meal, the children play quiet, organised games, but some of the older boys become rowdy and run off down to the lake. One of them falls in and there is great drama and excitement while he is fished out by a gardener, dripping and chastened.

Then a group of players arrives and everyone gathers below the terrace to watch them. First they mime the story of Baba

Yaga. When the black witch suddenly whirls round and rushes down amongst the children, one little girl starts to scream and scream, and has to be carried indoors to recover. Natasha becomes uneasy watching the players. There is something sinister about them, with their leering masks, through which the inscrutable eyes glitter remotely. Petya is standing beside her, and she feels his hand slip into hers for reassurance.

The performers throw aside their masks and change their costumes, and suddenly they are wearing embroidered peasants' clothes and dancing to the balalaika. Everyone laughs and claps in relief.

By evening the children are tired and fractious, and are taken away to bed. But Papa has another surprise up his sleeve. There is to be an evening party as well, with an orchestra and dancing under the stars. Everywhere there are young men wanting to dance with Natasha Ivanovna, who has grown so beautiful. Young men in dazzling uniforms, young men in cut-away coats and shirts of a dazzling white, with diamond or opal studs. And Natasha dances and dances until she is drunk with the music and the spinning.

'Beloved,' whispers a second cousin, who is rising fast in the Tsar's court, 'your hand is as white and as soft as the neck of a swan. Your hair is spun gold. Marry me, Natasha my darling, white rose, heart of my heart.'

* * *

'Natasha?' whispered Katya cautiously.

Her great-grandmother appeared to be asleep. Katya was about to back away when the heavy eyelids — softly purple where the veins showed through the papery skin — fluttered and opened. For a moment Natasha looked at her in confusion, then she smiled, blinked and shook herself a little.

'I am sorry, lyubushka. I was dozing. I am afraid I quite often slip away like that. Come and sit with me for a while.'

Katya, who would have resented being called 'little dear' by anyone else (wasn't she nearly five foot seven now?), did as she was told.

'I mustn't stop long. They want me to cycle down to the

village for some things, then I'm going with Tony to the station to meet his girlfriend. We have to leave in three-quarters of an hour. Everybody's getting in a panic – they don't think we'll be ready in time for the service.' She waved a shopping list. 'I came to ask whether there was anything you'd like me to get for you.'

'No, I don't think so. Tell me how is your life.'

Katya cupped her chin in her hand and stared gloomily across the lawn, where the tent had just fallen down again. Two shapes could be seen thrashing wildly about inside. Tony watched with detached amusement from his position by the tree.

'Everything is *dire*, Natasha. I hate it in Reading. Dad is away more than ever with this telly thing he's in. Not that I mind, really. Mostly he's only at home when he's out of work, and then he mopes around the house and drives Mum and me wild. Even when he is home . . . ' A fragile loyalty held her back for a moment, then she went on with a rush. 'They don't exactly row. They've always done that, off and on. Now they just don't seem to have anything to say to each other. Or to me. And when it's just Mum and me, well, she seems kind of switched off, you know? As though she isn't hearing what you say. And she isn't. Because when you ask her afterwards, she doesn't remember a word. And school is *foul*.' Her voice shook a little. 'I've never liked that school, not from the day I started, but it just gets worse and worse.'

Natasha took her hand, but continued to look out over the lawn. 'Frances tells me that now you are always top of your class, the others have been making things difficult for you. This is true?'

Katya wriggled with embarrassment. She was conscious of the social unacceptability of academic success. 'Mum told you that? I didn't think she even noticed.'

'Oh yes, doushenka, she noticed.'

'I don't suppose,' Katya asked, her voice tense with longing, 'that I could come and live at St Martins?'

'Only if your mother says you may. Have you asked her?'

Katya shook her head numbly. A sense of responsibility, of guilt even, had held her back from saying anything to her

46

mother. As the last child remaining at home after Tony's departure for a shared studio flat in Notting Hill, she had come to
see herself as Frances's ally against an obscurely hostile world.
She longed to help, but was tongue-tied when confronted by
inexplicable adult emotions. Frances, who had been her rock
and her refuge, seemed nowadays to be frail with fatigue, her
eyes drooping with sadness. The whole house was filled with
it. Once or twice Katya had even come upon her crying, and
had fled in horror.

'I will speak to her,' said Natasha decisively, giving Katya's
hand a little squeeze. 'We will discuss it before the day is over.
Now you must go to the village.'

★ ★ ★

When Spiro reached Oxford station a minute or two before
half-past seven that morning, he was just in time to see the
Worcester and Hereford train pulling out. He saw Anya leaning
out of the open door, and then retreating as the guard slammed
it shut. From the far end of the platform he had shouted and
started to run, but she did not look round and the train pulled
away imperviously.

These British trains! When you were on time, they kept you
hanging about for hours on their cold, windy platforms. When
you were just a tiny minute late, of course that was the one
occasion they would manage to run on time. He stamped off
to the refreshment counter and bought a cup of disgusting
watery coffee. He would just have to catch the next train.
There was to be some sort of service of thanksgiving in the
chapel of St Martins at half-past eleven. The train Anya had
taken would get her to Hereford an hour and a half before
that. Surely he could catch one that would make him no more
than a few minutes late for the service?

After a few sips he pushed away the coffee. He could not
get used to this insipid English stuff. What he needed was a
strong, reviving cup of real Greek coffee, black and sticky as
pitch. It sent a surge of energy through you like an injection
of adrenalin. Thinking of Greek coffee made him think again of
his fight with Anya about the restaurant. He had managed that

badly. He had so fallen in love with his idea that he'd blurted it all out, like a fool. He should have come at it crabwise, round about. He should simply have asked her to marry him, and then later broken the idea of the restaurant. He had no discretion with his feelings.

He didn't want to lose Anya through his ineptitude. For several months now he had known how much he loved her, known that marriage to her was the most important goal in his life. Her cool competence soothed him and gave him a sense of security. And he knew that beneath it lurked all the passion he could desire, passion that had clearly surprised Anya herself. He must be diplomatic. And he certainly must not miss this celebration given by her great-grandmother. That would do him a lot of harm in Anya's eyes. Anyway, he was intrigued by the idea of St Martins.

Standing in front of the train timetable posted on the wall of the station, he stared in horror. The next train did not leave till ten, and would not get him to Hereford until after one o'clock. He would still have to cover the distance between Hereford and St Martins, about twelve miles out into the country. By taxi, he supposed. It would be two in the afternoon before he could be there. He began to feel guilty about the extra minutes he had spent polishing his shoes, brushing his clothes. What a fool I am! he groaned to himself.

There was nothing else for it, he would have to find some other way to get there. Rather than waste time going to enquire at the bus station, he decided to hitch a lift. In his pocket he carried a dog-eared miniature atlas of Britain, which he had used on his trips of exploration with Anya. He would take a city bus up to the northern ring road and see if he could get a lift from someone heading for Cheltenham or Gloucester.

Spiro was luckier than he deserved. Up on the city bypass, the first car that stopped was driven by a middle-aged couple travelling to Brecon.

'We'll drop you at the railway station in Hereford,' said the man helpfully. 'You'll be able to pick up a taxi easily. If the traffic isn't too bad we should be there by half-past ten.'

* * *

Frances took her preferred back road from Clunwardine Priors to Hereford. Everyone in the village always called it the 'back road', though she was not sure why. Both were B roads, winding around the ancient boundaries of fields, obeying the needs of an agricultural population which had made this landscape centuries ago. Both slowed briefly through villages before diving once more between the hedgerows. This road had always been her favourite because – as the car swooped around bends deep amongst blackthorn and cow-parsley – it offered sudden amphitheatres opening out towards Wales and its mountains. This combination of the pieced, careful, farming landscape and the jagged outline of the mountains seemed to her deeply satisfying, at a level beyond expression.

Gregor sat beside her, relaxed in the seat with his legs sprawled out and his hands loosely clasped in his lap. He was looking across her, also towards Wales. He had always had this capacity for stillness, from the time he had first come to St Martins, after experiences so terrible that she had known nothing of them in her childhood. It was only after her marriage that Natasha had told her the full story of Gregor's flight from Poland. His stillness came in part, perhaps, from that early childhood training, hidden in barns and cupboards, afraid even to breathe. She remembered him lurking on the edge of their play when she and Hugh had been young. Very quiet and still, not daring to intrude.

Yet she felt now that this stillness came also from personality. Gregor was self-contained. A man who did not need other people. He had never married, and was totally absorbed in his work for most of his waking hours. Compared with Giles, he was profoundly restful. Giles fidgeted constantly, looking about him to see what impression he was making on other people. She had not been conscious of this habit when they first knew each other, blinded by her own awe at being singled out by him, but she knew now that her compliance, her early near worship of him, had been nourishment essential to his own ego. Nowadays, even though she knew that his tendency to

49

put on a public performance in his private life arose from a deep uncertainty about his talent on stage, she was perpetually irritated by it. On the rare occasions when they had a meal in a restaurant, she found it humiliating – particularly of late, when people had at last begun to recognise him.

With Gregor it was no more necessary to make conversation than it was with Hugh, and for the first few miles they drove in silence. Past the redundant church converted into a house, past the tiny black-and-white cottage where the old man stood with his border collie outside the front door, winter and summer, leaning on a wooden railing. Frances, as usual, raised her hand to him as she passed, and he, with dignity, returned the greeting.

'Does he stand there for entertainment,' she mused aloud, 'or because his married daughter finds he is in her way and parks him out there? I've always wondered.'

Gregor turned a humorous glance towards her. 'You could stop and ask. Why his married daughter, anyway?'

'If he lived with his wife, she would make sure he sat by the fire in his slippers, at least in winter. He must be eighty-five.'

'You're a romantic. His wife is probably a shrew and a scold, and he is wishing he had never married. He stands out there, eternally hopeful, waiting for something to turn up. Given the chance, he would be away from there, he and his dog, up to Lunnon and away from domestic bliss.'

This was getting too close for Frances's entire comfort. She drove for a few minutes in silence, thinking about her own first escapes – as she had perceived them at the time – driving away from St Martins on these unchanging roads.

'Remember your MG?' said Gregor, reading her thoughts. 'How I envied you! Wished I had a generous granny.'

'It wasn't fair, was it? Not that she usually spoiled us. I think that was the only big present she ever gave me. She was so proud of my scholarship to Oxford. What she didn't realise was that the scholarship in itself was reward enough for me. I never expect to be rewarded for doing what I had set my own sights on.'

'Still.'

'Still, as you say. We had a lot of fun in that car, didn't we? You and I and Hugh.'

★ ★ ★

'You did *what*?'

'Sold the car.'

'Sold *my* car?'

'We need the money, darling,' Giles nuzzled her ear, but she pulled away, furious.

'It was *mine*. Natasha gave it to me. How shall I be able to get about with Anya and Nick? Fetching all the shopping, with both of them under two years old? You never lift a finger to help.'

'Other people manage. Plenty of buses in London, not like still living in country-bumpkin-land. I have to go up to Edinburgh for an audition. Got to find the fare somehow. This could be something really good – a pre-West-End run.'

'You could have borrowed the money from Peregrine. You have before.'

Peregrine was Giles's agent, and had indeed loaned money before. Giles did not want to tell Frances that he was now £200 in hock to Peregrine, a terrifying amount in 1962. Also, since that episode of the weekend in Brighton, Peregrine had been asking awkward questions about what the money was for. Giles had managed to do a deal with a fellow actor who had had his eye on Frances's MG for some time. He had given Giles £375. Cash.

'I got £200 for the car. Jolly good price. Look, here's £100 for you. I'll hang on to the rest for fares and hotel bills.'

There were tears in her eyes as she looked down at the handful of grubby money, £1 and £5 notes. She had hardly seen a £5 note before. Her beautiful car, as dear as an intimate friend, reduced to this. The anger she felt was so strong she was speechless.

Giles, taking her silence for acquiescence, was pleased with himself. He would give Peregrine £100 to keep him quiet, get a lift up to Edinburgh with the friend who was going up for the same auditions, and keep the remaining £175.

It was their first real quarrel. Shaken by the intensity of her feelings and her sense of loss, Frances side-stepped difficulties with Giles for a long time afterwards.

★   ★   ★

'Do you think Hugh will turn up for the celebration?' Gregor asked, leaning his elbow on the open window and turning towards her. 'I don't think Natasha will feel it is complete without him.'

'Well, it won't be, will it? I just don't know. I haven't heard anything since Christmas. He was in India then. Just a postcard of a temple with a couple of sentences scribbled on the back. Usual thing.'

'I liked his book about the Inuits in Alaska. I sat up all one night reading it, couldn't put it down. Do you suppose he'll ever decide he is too old for that sort of thing? Decide to settle down?'

'Hugh!' Frances threw back her head and laughed. It was the first time he had seen her laugh that day. 'Can you imagine him settling down? Not like you. You were a bit of a wanderer for a while, but I always knew you would come back to St Martins. It's the right place for you.'

'Unadventurous and boring, you mean?'

She gave him a steady look. 'Not that at all. The still centre of your world. You do your exploring through your hands. Through your stone and clay.'

★   ★   ★

They face each other across the pile of logs in the outhouse. Frances is wearing a cherry-red scarf wrapped high round her ears, and matching mittens. Her breath steams in the frosty air.

'You're so unadventurous and *boring*, Gregor. All you want to do is mess about here at St Martins, with your lumps of stone and your little clay models, like a child at nursery school.'

What she is saying is unpardonable, and her knowledge of this has made her cheeks colour up, but her anger has overcome her. It is the Christmas of 1958, her second year at university, and she has brought Giles home to St Martins for his first visit.

It has not gone quite as she planned, and she is ready to lash out at anyone.

'Unadventurous and boring, is it? I suppose your Oxford friend is oh so exciting, daahling!' he affects a posh accent, angering her further.

'If you want to succeed as an artist, you'll have to go to London. Get a studio. Get away from all the comfort and cosiness here, all the *old* people. We're moving to London as soon as we graduate.'

'We?'

'Giles and I. We're going to get married.'

There is a sharp silence between them. Then Gregor draws a long breath, and reaches across the logs for her. He pulls her angrily towards him, so that she stumbles and falls with her knees on the logs.

'Married, is it?' He kisses her violently. It is like a blow in the face. Furiously she fights free from him, and hits him across the cheek. Her mittened hand makes no impact. Then she runs back to the house, leaving him to collect the logs and follow her slowly – dragging his feet.

* * *

Natasha switched on the radio, to catch the 10 a.m. news and the weather forecast. After the overcast start to the day it was looking a little better as the morning went on, but she wanted reassurance. Yesterday evening she had asked Mr Dawlish whether it would stay fine for today. He had shaken his head and said, 'The clouds be too frivolous and clibberty.' He might have been right, but she hoped that it would be no more than one of the light showers he called 'gnats passing over'.

The news was just finishing, with an item about the concluding D-Day events. For days now the news had been dominated by the 'celebrations' or 'commemorations' of the fiftieth anniversary, depending on one's position in the controversy. Natasha had been unable to take sides on the issue – whether it should be a celebration of the beginning of the end of war, or a memorial to all those who had died. Her own private feelings about that month of June, fifty years ago, were in the same painful state of confusion – happiness and grief blended.

Edmund had ten days' leave at the end of that May, which he spent helping her move into St Martins and clearing out a corner to live in. They stowed all their furniture in the vast drawing room, arranging it in groups, saying to each other: 'This is the bedroom, and this is the dining room and this, with the fireplace, is the kitchen.' Edmund had propped up Natasha's canvases in one corner, announcing, 'This is the Long Gallery. Admission sixpence extra.' They had laughed a good deal, like excited children, planning how they would run the place as a communal home for creative artists of all kinds, and for refugees from war-torn Europe. Since the early thirties they had provided temporary shelter in their flat in Chelsea, but knew it could not be a permanent arrangement. Irina had arrived at St Martins the day after her father, with her children and some girl who had been bombed out. The children ran about shrieking with joy, but Irina was grim-faced, and her nostrils curled at the state of the house.

★ ★ ★

'I have been to the solicitor,' said Edmund, holding up a bundle of papers for her to see, and putting it in the central drawer of the big desk. 'I have made over ownership of the property to you, just in case, don't you know.'

She made a sound of protest, pushing his words aside in the air with her hand.

'It has to be thought of, my dear. The war isn't over yet, and the invasion will be bloody when it comes. I'm only doing what is practical.'

'I cannot bear to think of it.'

'I know. I know.' He stroked her hair. 'He has also drawn up the trust deeds for us. You will remain the outright owner of St Martins, able to live here, and your heirs, for ever. But the trust will pay you only a peppercorn rent. You will also receive the rent from the farm, so you will have a little to live on, but not much. You won't be rich. Are you sure you are happy with this?'

'You know this, dousha moya. Such a place has been my dream since – '

'Yes, don't think about it.'

'And I need very little money. I am a very good maker of soup from the peelings of vegetables,' she said proudly.

He laughed. 'The trust papers lay down that members of the community will pay rent to the trust according to their means, to be determined by the community committee. The trust will be responsible for maintenance of the property, and any improvements decided on. The regular bills, like rates, and electricity – if we ever get it – will be divided amongst the community in the same proportions as the rents.'

'It is all very excellent and very English.'

'Aren't you happy with it?' He looked at her anxiously.

She was sorry at once. It all sounded so dull and formal, when her heart was bursting with joy, but Edmund was right. One must be sensible. These things cannot be left, casually, to chance and goodwill, or they deteriorate into the ill-natured squabbles she remembered from her days in shared *appartements* in Paris in 1918 and 1919. Then, whenever there was a bill to be paid, some people would simply disappear. Those left behind would fight, with all the intensity of those who have spent their last few francs on wine and theatres instead of putting it aside for the rent. She remembered clearly the time she threw the frying pan full of hot onions at Jean-Claude. He had ducked, and they had all had to find some extra francs for a new pane of glass.

* * *

The trust came into effect on the 11 June, 1944. By then Edmund was gone, back to his regiment, and for the last few days they had all known why. The Allies had invaded Europe. The Germans were starting to be pushed back. D–Day. And Natasha demanded of the unloved and inscrutable Deity why Edmund should have so mistimed his birth that he should have to fight in two wars.

They had launched the St Martins community with a party – Natasha with her family, her waifs and strays who had come with her from London, and the newly arrived Polish family, Count Baranowski with his wife and son. They hadn't had much food, but the farmer gave them some eggs and Natasha had baked two cakes. There were Spam sandwiches, and cucumber sandwiches (the farmer again), and a single bottle of wine Natasha had found in the cellar amongst the empty bottles of Edmund's uncle's long, well-wined life.

It was just as they were thinking of getting the children off to bed that the telegram about Edmund had come.

★ ★ ★

Frances threaded her way past the cars turning into the Safeway car park for their Saturday shopping and drove the few extra yards to the station.

'I've always liked it,' said Gregor. 'An honest, dignified, nineteenth-century building.'

'Quite grand, really. I suppose Hereford was a wealthy provincial market town in those days. Yes, it has lovely proportions. Have you *seen* what they have done to Oxford station?'

'Remember, I don't have the same feelings about that as you have.'

Anya saw them standing together on the platform as the train pulled in to Hereford. They looked more at ease with each other than her mother ever did with Giles.

I suppose, she thought, Gregor is like another brother to Mum. They must have known each other since she was four and he was about seven. He's a pretty good uncle too. Safe. A bit more reliable than Hugh, who could be *anywhere* now, and I do think he might have come back for Natasha's party.

'Oh, dear,' said Frances, as Anya got out of the train. 'She's alone.'

★ ★ ★

Katya pedalled round by Glebe Lane on her way back to St Martins. She was riding Mabel's bike – a sturdy, old-fashioned upright, with sensible baskets for shopping. She reckoned that Mr Lacey would just about be leaving the vicarage, and she could walk up with him. Beyond the squat Norman church

56

with its soaring late mediaeval steeple, the vicarage sat in the middle of its garden like a prim spinster aunt amongst a crowd of unruly children.

The vicarage garden was to Richard Lacey what specimen cabinets for birds' eggs or fossils or skewered butterflies had been to his clerical predecessors. Richard's collection, however, was on a grand scale. He collected steam railway rolling stock. Not oo gauge, or even the child-sized versions that are sometimes to be found as amusements in the grounds of stately homes. Richard's trains were the real thing.

It had started nearly thirty years ago, before he had come to his present parish. After Beeching's cuts to the railways, he had discovered from one of his parishioners in Derby, where he was then incumbent of his first parish, that a particularly fine specimen of a 1920s narrow-gauge steam engine was being sold off for scrap metal. The parishioner (himself a scrap metal dealer) had agreed to buy it for Richard and deliver it to his house. The arrival of a steam locomotive on a trailer behind a huge lorry in a narrow street of terraced houses had caused some consternation, not only to the neighbours, but to his wife. Regretfully, he had had to ask the dealer to store the engine in his yard, where he visited it three times a week, painstakingly restoring and polishing.

This state of affairs could not be allowed to continue, particularly after he had also managed to obtain two carriages, one in the beautiful old GWR livery, and one that had regularly been used on the Flying Scotsman run. Richard began to look about for a rural parish, where the vicarage had a large garden.

When he had been offered his present parish twenty years ago, he had mentioned his hobby diffidently, but the Bishop (eighty-seven, and hard of hearing) had said, 'Splendid, splendid, my boy. Always been fond of steam trains myself.'

Muriel Lacey installed her furniture in the new vicarage and painted the dark brown walls of the lovely Georgian house in soft shades that brought it back to life again. The Laceys had no children yet, but she was still optimistic. Clunwardine Priors would be a delightful place for them to grow up. Twenty years later, there were still no children, but there were four more engines and seven more carriages dotted about the vicarage garden and orchard. There was also an engine from a Welsh colliery line, and a very early and valuable Victorian goods wagon. The room Muriel had set aside as a playroom for the children was spilling over with carriage lamps and station signs, huge metal advertising plaques for Oxo and Lipton's Tea, and two dozen leather money pouches for ticket collectors (1930s vintage).

Making the best of what God had seen fit to offer her, Muriel catalogued and arranged, and finally opened a museum of Richard's collection. It was she who wrote articles for railway journals and gave occasional lectures for the WI or local history clubs. Richard still liked best to exchange his dog-collar for a boiler suit and tinker with his engines until they were as glorious as the day they had first rolled out on the track.

'Good morning, Katya,' said Richard. He was standing just inside the vicarage gate, his hand thoughtfully stroking the rounded side of his favourite engine. He looked as though he might be planning to spend the morning there.

'Morning, Mr Lacey. Are you coming up to St Martins now?'

Richard stared at her blankly for a moment, then laughed at himself. 'Of course, of course. I was just on my way up. I want to check that everything is ready for the service at half-past eleven. Muriel can't come till the party proper, as soon after twelve as she can manage. She thought she'd better keep the museum open this morning, as she's planning to shut it this afternoon.'

They started up Glebe Lane together, Katya wheeling Mabel's bike.

'Down for long, are you, Katya?'

'Just the weekend,' said Katya sadly. 'School on Monday.'

'Of course, of course. It's beginning to look so sunshiny, I was thinking it must be the summer holidays. Are you coming down then?'

'Absolutely.'

'Mum and Dad both here?'

'Only Mum. Dad may come down this afternoon, after his rehearsal.'

'Ah yes, *Vet in Hot Water*. Muriel loves it. I've only seen it once or twice. It's the same night as my parochial church council meetings.'

'I think it's *stupid*. It's *gross*,' said Katya savagely. 'How would you like it if you had to go to school with people who have been laughing themselves sick at your father dropping his trousers and rolling in farmyard muck all over their television sets?'

* * *

The rehearsal was not going well. Penny, who had replaced the clever little Judy as Giles's assistant vet, was a lumpish girl who tried to play for coarse laughs. They had just had the statutory farmyard tumble, and she had tried to put in a bit of suggestive business of her own. Giles had complained, the director/producer had backed him up, saying that this was a family show, and Penny had sulked. When she was supposed to be helping him out of the pig trough (represented by an empty props basket) she had deliberately twisted his arm so that he fell painfully sideways and wrenched his back.

Giles lay on the floor, gasping a little with the pain.

'It's your own fault, you tub of lard,' Penny had hissed at him, so no one else could hear. 'If you'd lose some of that blubber round your middle, you wouldn't have accidents like that.'

Giles was so appalled, he could think of nothing to say.

'Take ten, darlings,' said the director. He walked over and looked down at Giles. 'You all right?'

Giles got painfully to his feet, and tried to flex his back. 'I'm OK,' he said shortly, though he was not. He couldn't risk crocking his back. 'Just a bit winded. Let's push on and do the farmhouse interior. Remember I've got to get away early today.'

'OK. By the way, there was a message for you.' The director freed it from his clipboard. 'Will you ring Nigel Laker when you have a minute.'

'Right,' said Giles, pleased. 'I'll go and do that now.' There was just a chance that Nigel might have something for him. He was putting together a new series, and had promised to keep Giles in mind.

Down the phone Nigel's voice was cheerful. 'I've got the go-ahead. I'd like to talk it over with you a.s.a.p. This afternoon.'

'Can't.' Giles's heart sank. You had to move in quickly with Nigel or his interest would shift to someone else. 'I've got to go down to this tremendous do in Herefordshire, my wife's old home. Fiftieth anniversary of the St Martins community.'

'Hey, I read about that anniversary party in one of the Sunday supplements. I was already interested in St Martins. Sounds quite a place.' Nigel's voice quickened with enthusiasm.

Hope jumped up in Giles's chest. 'Tell you what, Nigel. Have you got your car? How would you like to come down with me? We can talk on the way, and I can introduce you to the people there. All the former members are coming back – quite a few famous names.' He held his breath. Nigel was a notorious cultivator of famous names. This way Giles could avoid the train journey and weigh the scales a little in his favour while Nigel was still at the planning stage.

'Great. What time do you finish? I'll come and pick you up.'

'In an hour,' said Giles with determination. 'We'll have a pub lunch on the way down. If I phone St Martins now, I can fix you up with a room for the night.'

He was humming as he put the phone down.

★ ★ ★

On the way back to St Martins from Hereford station, Anya insisted that Gregor should sit in front. 'For your great long legs!' she laughed. She was resolutely cheerful. She perched in the middle behind them, ignoring the seat-belt and leaning forward with her elbows on the backs of their seats.

As the two women talked, Gregor allowed his mind to drift, and thought of all the people homing in on St Martins – now, and over the past half-century. He saw them, layer upon layer of time together, like migrating birds returning by instinct to the place where they belonged.

His own instinct had brought him back at the beginning of the eighties, after more than twenty years of temporary resting places in France, in Italy, in Sydney, in California. He had travelled light – one large suitcase and the bag carefully fitted out for his tools. Sometimes he stayed only weeks, sometimes months or years. He had been in California for five years, working and teaching. But wherever he lived – in rooms or motels, or the small flat overlooking Sydney harbour – he never unpacked his suitcase. He kept his clothes stored in it and could, at any moment, add his toothbrush and shaving kit, and leave.

At the end of the fifth year in California, when he received the letter renewing his teaching contract with UCLA, he took a bus out to a deserted part of the coastline he particularly liked, and went for a long walk. As a result of that walk, he sent a courteous reply to the letter, saying that he was returning to England but would be happy to come back and teach at the occasional summer school in future years. The next morning, ignoring the expense, he telephoned Natasha.

'Of course you can come home,' she said, not sounding in the least surprised. 'When you get here we will put our heads together. You must have a better studio, now that you are a so-famous international sculptor.'

Gregor snorted, and began to protest.

Natasha silenced him. 'I have an idea about the stables. We will talk.'

Gregor's instinct had been right. His experience of the world had been enriching in artistic terms, but now he needed time to rest, to assimilate, to come to terms with himself. He was past forty. He wanted to plan the rest of his working life, and he needed a place where his personal life was calm and stable, free from the clamour of society hostesses and nubile students. Apart from the occasional foray to open an exhibition, he became something of a recluse.

St Martins, he thought to himself, is a nourishment of the spirit. I cannot put my finger on it, but there is something about the place – not so much the physical place as the atmosphere – that provides sustenance. The experiment Natasha and Edmund set out on all those years ago has certainly borne fruit. He thought of the broken refugees like himself, after World War II, who had been made whole, and moved on, or stayed like Birgit and Peter. Of the musically gifted boy who had run away from abusive parents in the fifties and somehow found his way to St Martins. He was now the resident conductor of a famous German orchestra. Sally had come at the age of seven with her unmarried painter mother, played with Nicholas as a child, and later married him. There was the Romanian violinist. She had left just last summer, and her letters to them bubbled over with the excitement of her burgeoning career. Natasha could today look back on fifty years of great achievement.

Natasha. She was very frail now, and left the running of the domestic side to Mabel, although she still chaired the monthly committee meetings with the same decisiveness as before. Everyone still came to her for reassurance and advice. But reality must be faced. She could not carry on much longer. Gregor glanced sideways at Frances. Does she worry about her grandmother? he thought. Does she care about what will happen to St Martins when Natasha is gone? Is she really so bound up in the career of that husband of hers?

'Look!' cried Anya, waving frantically. 'There's Tony and Katya! Has there been a mix-up? Are they on the way to meet me?'

'No, Tony's new girlfriend, Alice. She's arriving at ten forty.'

Frances gave a toot on her horn as the two cars passed, starting a fit of barking from a gypsy dog at the encampment in the lay-by.

Chapter 4

ALICE TYLER, IN close-fitting white trousers and red blouse, with a white jacket slung over one shoulder and her hair tied back with a red silk scarf, paced up and down outside Hereford station. She had left a message the previous morning with Tony's flat-mate about the change in her train time, and he had promised faithfully to pass it on. Obviously he hadn't done so. She had already been waiting fifteen minutes, and was becoming irritated. Those two still behave like students, she thought impatiently. They are so *incompetent*.

Like Tony, Alice was an artist, but she worked in acrylics, not watercolour. She painted huge abstract canvases that appealed to forward-looking district councils and companies making take-over bids. Currently, she was artist-in-residence at a northern college newly elevated to university status, where she taught her students with vigour and severity. She painted almost entirely on commission, except when preparing work for a major exhibition, where her growing reputation would ensure that a quarter of the paintings would be sold at the private view, before the exhibition opened.

A car rounded the corner from the supermarket, but it was not Tony's. A good-looking, dark-haired man a little older than she got out and leaned over to thank the people inside before lifting out a small suitcase and closing the door. The car drove off, as the man gave a final wave. He did not, however, go into the station with his case, but looked about him, then crossed to a sign saying 'Taxis'. There were no taxis waiting.

After a few minutes, he said politely to Alice, 'Excuse me, but do you know if there is a bus I can catch to a place called

St Martins?' He had a slight foreign accent she could not identify.

'St Martins?' Alice was immediately interested. 'That's where I'm going, though my lift hasn't turned up yet. You are –?'

'Spiro Ionides. I was coming with Anya Kilworth, but I missed the train in Oxford. Fortunately I was given a lift by those kind people.' He nodded his head towards the direction in which the car had gone.

Alice held out her hand to him. 'Alice Tyler. Tony Kilworth is supposed to be meeting me.'

'Ah yes,' Spiro shook her hand, bowing slightly over it. 'Of course I have heard of you. I saw your exhibition last summer, just after I arrived in England.'

'You must be Anya's Greek.'

He coloured slightly, and Alice remembered that Greek men were reputed to be macho and possessive, but was merely amused that her own outspokenness should have disconcerted him.

'Don't worry about a taxi. I'm sure there will be room for you in Tony's car, if he *ever* – ah, this looks like it.'

Tony's car – a classic Triumph 2.5 that he had spent much time restoring when he should have been painting – swept up to the front of the station with a flourish.

'Hello, darling,' said Tony, kissing Alice, who did not return the kiss. 'Hope you haven't been waiting long.'

'Twenty-five minutes,' she said sternly. 'This is Spiro Ionides, who also needs to get to St Martins. Have you room?'

'How do you do,' said Tony. 'Hop in, there's just my kid sister.' He opened the passenger door. 'Katya, nip in the back and let Alice sit in the front.'

Katya regarded Anya's Greek with interest as he took the seat beside her. 'I thought you were coming with Anya,' she said.

Spiro gave her an attractive smile as Tony headed out of Hereford on the road back to St Martins.

'I am afraid I missed the train in Oxford. It was stupid of me, and Anya will be very cross.'

'Yes, she will be. But she's only just arrived. We passed her on our way in to Hereford. Mum picked her up at the station. How did you manage to get here, if you missed the train?'

'Hitch-hiked.'

Katya's eyes widened. Spiro was dressed in a pale grey Italian suit, an immaculately laundered white shirt, and a dark blue silk tie with matching handkerchief protruding just the right distance from his breast pocket. He did not look like a hitch-hiker, and her respect grew visibly. He wasn't at all what she had imagined – quite different from Anya's usual men, who dressed in baggy trousers worn at the knee and old sports jackets or hand-knitted jumpers. That such a man as this Spiro should resort to hitch-hiking in such a matter-of-fact way impressed her. She turned her attention briefly to Alice, who looked pretty fab, in a way Katya yearned to look, but dared not. Alice seemed to be having a restrained squabble with Tony in the front.

'I wouldn't mind if I hadn't specifically asked Bill to tell you, and he promised he would. I had to go to Birmingham yesterday to see a client, and I came on from there.'

'I'm sorry, really.' Tony seemed less than his usual suave self. 'No harm done, though – we wouldn't have bumped into Spiro if I'd been on time.'

'Are you a musician?' Katya asked Spiro. 'Or a painter?'

'No, I am an economist.'

Katya made a face.

'I am also,' Spiro grinned at her, 'a very good cook.'

★ ★ ★

After delivering Gregor and Anya to the front of St Martins and parking her car in the stableyard again, Frances put her head round the back door to see whether she was needed in the kitchen.

'Everything is under control, Frances,' said Olga. 'Go away and be quiet for a little. You have been up longer than any of us this morning. It's more than an hour till the service. Coffee in the drawing room beforehand, for anyone who wants some.'

Frances went out of the stableyard, along the path and past the chapel, pausing to pat her favourite gargoyle, who leaned out from the corner of the roof, just above head level. He continued to stick his tongue out at her. She returned the compliment, affectionately.

Harry, William's golden labrador gazed up to her from the flower border beyond the chapel, where he was lying disconsolately curled up, with a look of resignation in his eyes.

'Coming for a walk, then, Harry?' called Frances, and he burst out from under the lavender bush, sending a glittering shower of last night's raindrops in an arc over his head. He couldn't believe his luck.

'Poor old fellow,' said Frances, as he planted his muddy feet on her chest and blew lovingly into her face. 'I'm afraid Dad's not going to be able to take you for a walk for a long while yet, if ever. And I don't suppose anyone else remembers, or has time. Shall we walk up to the big meadow, then?'

At each mention of the word 'walk', Harry's excitement became more intense. He licked her chin, then bounded ahead of her across the garden, his tail aloft like a flag of victory. When Frances paused under the copper beech, he became anxious, and brought sticks for her to throw, to retain her interest. This had always been one of her special places at St Martins – this, and the den she had made under the rhododendrons, and the Ludbrook which ran on the far side of the meadow, and where she was now headed.

One of her earliest memories was of coming to St Martins when she was four. She had only the haziest recollection of their previous home in London, later flattened in the blitz. But she remembered being met at Stanway station, on one of the many pretty little rural branch lines that had been destroyed with the stroke of a pen twenty years later. A man had met them at the station with a horse and cart, because of the petrol rationing, and she had been enchanted, having seen few horses in London – only the brewers' dray horses, the milkman's horse and the poor sway-backed creature that belonged to the rag and bone man.

* * *

'Come *on*, Franny!' shouts Hugh, jumping down from the cart, ducking under Mummy's arm and tearing away across the lawn.

Frances allows the man to lift her down. The cart is miles above the ground and she is not as brave as Hugh. Natasha and Grandad kiss her. She is surprised to see them here, because she last saw them in London. Hugh is now rushing about on the grass, with his new grey shorts, bought big for school, flapping about his knees. He has his arms stretched out straight and is wheeling in great circles, making aeroplane noises.

She does not like aeroplanes. They remind her of the terror of air-raids, when they have to hide under the stairs or down in the hot, smelly underground station. She walks away from Hugh, across the lawn and under a huge tree that stretches up and up into the sky. Its branches reach out like a roof above her head, and its leaves aren't green, like the plane trees in their street in London, but a mysterious colour, like purple grapes. She walks on and on, and nobody tries to stop her. If she walked this far in the park, Mummy would get cross and shout at her. She looks back, a bit afraid. Miles away, Hugh is still racing about, and the grown-ups are taking the luggage from the cart into this strange house, which looks a bit like a castle and a bit like the pictures in her book of the Pied Piper.

Beyond the big tree there is a thicket of bushes with fat leaves, shiny and stiff like lino. Crouching down, she sees that there are hollows and tunnels amongst the bushes. She burrows in, and finds a perfect clearing in the centre, hidden from everywhere except the small circle of blue sky high above.

★ ★ ★

'So your Greek is not coming?' Natasha looked gravely at Anya.

'He isn't *my* Greek,' she returned crossly. 'I wish everyone would stop calling him that. He is just a friend I've been going out with, and he happens to be Greek.'

'Ah,' said Natasha. 'You have quarrelled.'

They were walking in the sunken garden, where Mr Dawlish was giving the flower beds a final quick hoe.

'I didn't say that.'

'It does not need the wisdom of a Solomon to deduce this.

You are cross and unhappy. Your Spiro does not come with you. You wish you had not come.'

Anya seized her great-grandmother's arm and squeezed it.

'Of course I am glad I've come. If Spiro doesn't come, that is his loss.'

She looked earnestly at Natasha, who was walking briskly without her stick and looked very bright-eyed and cheerful.

'Could I talk to you, Natasha?'

'Of course, my child. Come, let's sit on the old wooden seat under the arbour.'

When they were seated, well out of Mr Dawlish's hearing – although the rhythmic scratch, scratch, of his hoe sounded in the background – Anya poured out the jumble of Spiro's proposal and his idea that they should open a Greek restaurant. She contained her anger with difficulty. Natasha, listening, was struck not only by Anya's passion, but by the fact that she did not tell her story in her usual logical, structured way, but jumped about from one idea to the other. As she talked she picked off flakes of old paint from the seat.

'I see,' said Natasha at last. 'And it does not appeal to you, this idea of a restaurant?'

Anya raised angry eyes. 'Isn't that what I've just been saying?' She bit her lip. 'Sorry, Natasha, I've no right to take it out on you.'

'And you feel, I suppose, that because Frances never managed to pursue her academic career you must do it for her. Prove to her that it can be done.'

'I didn't say that. I never mentioned Mum.'

'Doushenka, I have known you all your life. You despise your mother. You feel she has thrown her life away.'

'I don't despise her,' said Anya miserably.

'Well – despise – this is perhaps too strong a word. But you feel she has wasted her life, and you do not want to do the same.'

Anya nodded mutely.

Natasha stared across the sunken garden to the edge of the lawn, where the school children would be giving their concert later on.

'Whether Frances has wasted her life or not is something only she can judge. You must remember that much of her time for the last thirty-five years has been devoted to you five children. Motherhood is not something mechanical, you know, as so many people suppose. In its way it is as much a creative art as painting or sculpture. Frances has always been an artist in people. And I know she would not be without you. Children are an enrichment of life. I always regretted that I had only one.'

'Life's so unfair.'

'Yes. But neither you nor Frances has ever suffered tragedy.' As Anya opened her mouth to speak, Natasha raised her hand. 'No, of course I do not wish you had. Only those who have not suffered talk about the *nobility* of suffering.'

She laid her hand on Anya's, and gazed thoughtfully out over the garden. 'Tell me, are you certain you want to go on as you are? You live on the fringes of the academic world, like a hungry child looking in through a window at a feast. Do you feel, truly, that the banquet is worth waiting for, perhaps many years, while your life stays – how shall we say? – suspended, holding its breath?'

Anya gulped unhappily. 'I don't know. I really don't know. I used to be so sure, but – somehow the meaning, the truth of it, seems to have vanished. The universities are starved of funds, and put under tremendous pressure to be 'vocational'. Everyone seems to have lost sight of their real raison d'être, as places where the human mind is exercised to its fullest capacity, regardless of material considerations.'

She began to wave her arms about. 'Nowadays it's all cost centres and quality audit and how many students you can process quickly through the machine. And instead of major, long-term research – things that really matter, things that will be remembered in the future – university staff are forced to focus on turning out lots of little bits of superficial things. It's just turned into a numbers game.'

She sighed. 'I'm not sure it *is* my world any more. Not the world I thought it was, anyway. But what else can I do? It's what I'm trained for. Where else can an academic economic historian find employment?' She tried to make of joke of it, but simply sounded sorrowful.

'Now that is no way to speak,' said Natasha firmly. 'What was I trained for? A life of parasitic ease. When that was taken from me, I looked about for what interested me. I had been taught to paint a little, as part of my education. I thought, I will make my hobby into a career!'

'You were younger than I am.'

'That is quite irrelevant, Anya. Don't make excuses. Of course, for me the need to eat was a wonderful spur. Imagine, please, that you are in a foreign city, without money, without friends, and you do not wish to starve to death. What will you do?'

Anya laughed. 'Take in pupils, I suppose.'

'This is what you wish to do?'

Instead of answering, Anya jumped up and began to stride about in front of the seat.

'No,' she said at last. 'No, I don't think I do. Some students I enjoy teaching, the ones I can fire with enthusiasm or who really care about learning for themselves. But they are very much in the minority. In the last year or so I've found teaching most of my students so dispiriting.'

She sat down again and took Natasha's hand. 'What do you suggest?'

'Let us review your talents. You have an artistic eye, but you have only used it, as far as I can remember, for embroidery.' Natasha pointed to the skirt Anya was wearing, with its twelve-inch deep band of embroidered wild flowers about the hem.

'I couldn't make a living by embroidering!'

'Perhaps. Perhaps not. Sally has a friend who produces the most beautiful work – done mostly on a sewing machine for speed, of course, but very original. She specialises in modern ecclesiastical embroidery. Why don't you talk to her? Find out more about it?'

Anya shook her head, 'Natasha, you are incorrigible. Every artistic goose is a swan in your estimation.'

'You are not a goose. Now, concentrate. What other interests have you?'

'Well – I like listening to music, but I'm no performer, as you know. I used to potter about in the garden when I was in Reading, but I suppose I'm not that committed to it because I haven't tried to rescue the wilderness behind the house in Oxford. You see, I'm quite useless.'

'You enjoy cooking.'

'No, Natasha,' said Anya warningly. 'Now you are trying to manipulate me. I do not want to open a restaurant with Spiro. It would be so – *demeaning*. Such a waste of all our years of education.'

'I think this could be great fun. Such fun as Edmund and I had in planning St Martins together. To make good food, for people to sit around a table and enjoy the company and the conversation and the eating – this is one of the oldest celebrations in civilisation. Not as important as motherhood, of course.' She smiled. 'But it, too, is one of the creative arts. And to work with the man you love, to build something together – you do love him, don't you, lyubushka?'

'Yes,' said Anya sadly. 'Yes, I do.'

★　★　★

Frances was sitting beside the Ludbrook, with one arm round her knees, and throwing sticks with the other hand for Harry, who was so grateful to her that he was exerting all the charms he possessed to keep her amused. He even dared the brook (he was not a brave dog) when the stick fell into it, and swam back like an intrepid explorer, keeping his nose well up. He presented it to her with anxious pride, and waited, tense, for it to be thrown again.

'The thing is, Harry,' said Frances, tousling his dripping ears so that the water from the brook spattered her skirt, 'the thing is, that I don't know what to do.'

Harry sat down, and looked at her attentively.

'Giles doesn't need me any more – holding him up, nursing his frail ego, *protecting* him.' She sighed. 'He's got what he wants now, success of a sort. He's a household name on the telly. Not what he originally hoped for, you know, but more than he has expected for some time now. And he has all his young women that he finds so attractive. I had a purpose, when the children were younger, he needed me for that as well, but even Katya is almost grown-up.'

Realising from the tone of her voice that the time for games was over, Harry lay down with his chin in her lap, and gazed seriously into her eyes.

'The trouble is, Harry, I think it is too late.' She laid her cheek on her knees and began to cry. She did not know what it was that she was too late for; she just felt an overwhelming sense of the void. The brook ran briskly over the stones, and the meadow grasses whispered behind her, until the tears dried up and she blew her nose crossly.

'I'm a fool, Harry, that's what I am. Time we got back to the party.'

★ ★ ★

Across the garden, from the door of the chapel, Peter Kaufmann saw Natasha and Anya talking. The small tables and chairs were now all arranged around the edges of the big lawn and some long trestle tables borrowed from the village hall were set up under the horse chestnut tree to hold the food. The green Scout tent had been erected at last, and leaned over drunkenly, waiting to provide shelter if it should rain. More than two hundred people were coming to the celebration, counting the school choir and the village drama group who were performing *A Midsummer Night's Dream* in the evening. By tomorrow the garden would be trampled and sorry-looking, but at least it was at its best now. It was a pity it was too early for any but the very earliest roses, delayed by the long cold winter and late spring, because over the years he had managed to build up a collection of old scented varieties that would fill the garden with fragrance in a month or so.

Before long he would have to put in an appearance for coffee in the drawing room, and from then on every minute would be filled. He felt the need for a time of quiet first. The chapel behind him was one of the oldest parts of St Martins, dating back to the days when the site had been occupied by a small hospice for travellers, under the care of a Norman priory twenty miles away. At that time the chapel had been a church, dedicated to St Martin, patron saint of innkeepers – the Roman soldier who had cared for the destitute. For years the priory hospice had provided safe lodging for those travelling along the old Roman road which lay north and south parallel to the Welsh border.

This road ran down from St Martins to become the main street of Clunwardine Priors, which had grown up around the old Roman thoroughfare as a huddle of Saxon cottages and eventually acquired its own church in the thirteenth century. With its rights of market and an annual fair paying dues to the priory, the village had prospered in the Middle Ages. Later, after the dissolution of the monasteries, the secular owners of St Martins, the Devereux family, had been both farmers and innkeepers, but gradually the travellers had taken themselves off to the better inns in the village, which provided staging posts for coach travel, and St Martins had grown from a farm to a small manor.

The railways had passed the village by, however, and it had fallen into decline throughout the nineteenth century, until the market and fair had been abandoned, and nearly a quarter of the half-timbered houses had either fallen in or been pulled down. In the last thirty years the fortunes of the village had changed again. A small and well-designed council estate had been built, screened by trees from the older part of the village, which was now a recognised stop on the black-and-white heritage trail. It had managed to retain its half-dozen shops, its bus service and its primary school. With the young married couples staying on in the village it was coming back to life.

It was fitting, Peter thought, that the St Martins community had been set up in such a place. From the bronze-age barrow on a nearby hill down to the new village community centre opened five years ago, this was a place that bore the imprint of history, without becoming frozen and dead, one of those model villages just for tourists and well-heeled couples retiring from London. He rather resented the tourists who came, as they did, to wander about its crooked lanes and photograph the old houses. But the tour coaches still had to yield to tractors backing into the working farmyards next to these houses, and manoeuvre their way with difficulty around the awkward corner with Trevor Davies's agricultural machinery yard on one side and the gates of the market garden on the other.

It was fitting, too, that St Martins had taken up again its old role as a provider of shelter and safety. He had never counted up how many people had stayed here. Some for just a few weeks, others – like Birgit and himself – for the remainder of their lives. The travellers who had come to St Martins in the last fifty years had been following a different road – a path within themselves, instead of the old Roman border road – but he found the metaphor satisfying.

Natasha had repaired the old chapel along with the rest of St Martins, and had it rededicated. It was now used occasionally for services – mostly interdenominational – and was particularly in demand for weddings and christenings. Those monks would not have welcomed me, thought Peter, wheeling his chair in over the threshold and allowing the heavy old door to sigh closed behind him. Infidel that I am, Jew, unbeliever. But he thought it cheerfully because he had always felt welcome here. The building was a simple nave and chancel, with no transept, and the squat tower over the west door held a single bell. Once used to ring the church offices throughout the day, it was now no longer robust and was used only for special occasions, like today.

The wheels of his chair made a soft swishing sound on the sisal matting that lay along the aisle, as he moved forward towards the altar. Most of the glass in the chapel was plain, but a small portion of a Virgin and Child, found when the rubble in the chapel was cleared, had been carefully fitted into the east window, otherwise unadorned. The south wall near the front pew held a simple brass plaque in memory of Edmund. Peter sat looking up at it, remembering the kindness of the older man before the war, when he and Natasha had kept open house in their London flat, always full of hopeful young artists and musicians. He recalled Irina as a gawky girl in her teens, stumping about, awkward and uncomfortable with her parents' friends, and following him around like an unlovely puppy.

'Fifty years of St Martins, Edmund,' he said. 'Wherever you are, you should be proud of Natasha. And I'm sorry I was so arrogant and high-handed when you offered Birgit and me a home with you both in London, back in the thirties. I would go my own way, wouldn't I? Thinking I must prove to the world that I could have as great a success in Berlin as in London. Well, I paid for it, my friend, I paid for it.'

* * *

Richard Lacey, coming quietly into the chapel to check that everything was ready for the service of thanksgiving at half-past eleven, did not at first notice Peter. He left his cassock and surplice in the tiny vestry, a curtained-off corner beside the door, where the bell rope also hung. A pile of service sheets had been laid out on the small table behind the back pews, and simple arrangements of the cottage flowers that Natasha preferred had been placed on the windowsills and in front of the plain oak pulpit.

He went forward and knelt in the front pew on the left, and was surprised to see Peter, sitting in his wheelchair below the memorial to Edmund. He acknowledged the other man with a smile and an inclination of the head, then addressed a few apologetic words to his Maker. Richard knew that he was neither a great churchman nor an evangelical hunter of souls, and this sometimes troubled him. His apology now was word-less and brief, for he knew he would be fretted over by Irina and Mabel if he did not turn up in time to drink coffee.

Richard fell in beside Peter's chair on the way down the aisle.

'I hope you don't object,' said Peter.

'Object?'

'That a Jew should come into your Christian chapel.'

'We are all,' said Richard gently, holding the door open, 'children of the same Father.'

'Yes,' said Peter. He began to wheel his chair along the path towards the house. Richard knew better than to assist him. 'I have never been a religious man, myself. An irony, perhaps, when one takes into account that I was imprisoned by the

Nazis for the faith into which I happened to be born, but to which I paid so little heed. For me, music was my faith and my creed. An international faith that knows no boundaries of race or religion.'

'That's very true. That is its power.'

'I thought, you see, that other men saw it in the same way, and I was proved wrong. In my old age, however, I have come to think about God more, as I am sure many of your parishioners do.'

Richard inclined his head.

'It has come to seem to me,' Peter went on, as though talking to himself, 'that all religions, like music, belong to a universal family, speak one language. That is, when religion is truly an experience of awe, of faith, of something beyond this material world, and not a partisan banner behind which the men of violence hide.'

'Men of doctrine would take issue with you, but I am not, myself, a man of doctrine. Faith, after all, is a matter of the heart and of the spirit, not of the logical mind. I think you are right – that an underlying belief in a Being, a Power beyond what our empirical senses perceive, is the root and branch of all true religions. As is the belief in good.'

'But is there an absolute good?'

'That's tricky ground. As soon as we start to define what we mean by good – love, honesty, loyalty, selflessness – and try to cite examples from human lives, we become tangled in arguments. Because goodness in daily life is so easily tainted by the not-good which surrounds it and overlaps it. But, yes, I do believe in striving after what is good. Not,' said Richard humbly, 'that I find myself very successful.'

'Come,' said Peter, neatly negotiating the sill of the french window into the drawing room. 'I did not intend to involve you in a theological discussion. Today is a day of celebration, even though for some of us it is tinged also with a little sadness in our memories.'

★ ★ ★

All of the present St Martins community, together with a few

76

close neighbours and friends, had gathered in the drawing room and were passing around cups of coffee and plates of biscuits made by Sally and Frances. Natasha, reluctant to admit that she felt a little tired after her walk with Anya in the garden, was enthroned on her high-backed chair just inside the window, talking to Jonathan Deerley, St Martins' most reclusive member. This was the first time he had been seen for a week. He lived, by preference, high in one of the attics, well away from the other members, with a gas ring for cooking and a window that opened on to the parapet, where he was sometimes seen walking at midnight. He was a shy man, whose plays – of an agonising complexity – were occasionally broadcast, very late at night, on Radio 3. Natasha was listening with kindly patience to his exposition of his latest work – he never talked of anything else. As his conversation was as tortuous as his prose style, this showed, Gregor thought, great forbearance on her part.

'How typical it is of Natasha, I always think,' he said to Frances as they came in together, 'that she prefers that high, hard Jacobean chair to all others. She has only consented to have a thin cushion on the seat in the last couple of years. To my mind that chair is a kind of symbol of her strength and endurance.'

Anya was determined to remain cheerful. Between mouthfuls of coffee she began to tell her mother and Nicholas funny stories about her Swiss and Swedish girls and their earnest pursuit of aristocratic husbands, which their romantic reading had led them to believe were to be found in great numbers in Oxford.

'Of course, there is an occasional conquest,' she said, 'when a well-endowed (in every sense) Swiss hotelier's daughter captivates an impoverished sprig of the lesser gentry. But really they're rare today amongst the students. Mostly they're as earnest and studious as any young men the girls would find at home in Berne or Gothenburg. In the end the girls go home disappointed, or settle for nice young men with no pretensions to blue blood. No doubt they're doing their bit for the greater unity of the countries of Europe.'

Sally came in flushed from the kitchen, carrying Sarah on

her hip. Fine strands of hair had broken free from her plait and stood out around her head like a rakish halo of red-gold frizz.

'Has anyone seen Bob? I can't find him anywhere. When last seen he was totally *filthy*, although I had him like a new pin this morning.'

'He ran off after Tony went to the station,' said Chrissie. 'He was cross, 'cos he wanted to go too.'

'I shouldn't worry,' said Frances, relieving Sally of Sarah, who immediately began to tug at her strand of beads with great absorption. 'I expect all the children will be covered in mud, grass stains and orange juice before we are halfway through the afternoon. Do sit down, darling, you've been working like a galley slave.'

Sally took a seat beside Lisa on the old, sagging, linen-covered couch and accepted a cup of coffee. 'How are you feeling, Lisa? You're looking a bit peaky. Why don't you skip the service and lie down for a bit?'

Lisa gave her a weak smile. 'I'm OK, really. It's just a bit overpowering in here, with so many people. I'll sit at the back of the chapel so I can slip out if I don't feel well.'

There was the sound of voices coming along the hall, and the clatter of Katya's football boots.

'That will be Tony back with Alice,' said Frances. 'I'm looking forward to meeting a woman who can unsettle our Tony.'

Katya flung back the door in her usual dramatic way.

'Look who we found!' she announced. 'Anya's Greek!'

★ ★ ★

It was Olga who discovered Bob, when they were starting on their second cups of coffee. Coming back along the hall from the kitchen with more milk, she noticed that the dining room door was slightly ajar. She set the jug of milk down on the marble-topped table in the hall and went to investigate. Her cry of outrage could be heard even above the level of conversation in the drawing room.

'Oh no!' cried Sally, as possibilities raced through her mind.

She beat Frances, Katya and Gregor to the dining room door by a short head.

Bob, red-faced and defiant, was standing with a spoon in his hand and liberal lumps of trifle dotted about his face and the front of his T-shirt.

'Bob!' said Sally in tones that drained away the defiance from his face, to be replaced with a down-turned, woebegone mouth. She seized the spoon from him and surveyed the violated trifle. 'Bob, how *could* you? You are *nearly seven years old.* You *know* you were not to touch anything in here.'

Bob shuffled his feet and mumbled that he was hungry.

'You should have come in with the rest of us — there were plenty of biscuits and flapjack, and juice.' Sally's voice shook. She was not only angry, she was very upset. She had just noticed the chunks torn from the galantine of chicken, the tumbled plates of sandwiches, and the grooves where fingers had been dragged through the icing on two of the cakes.

Bob looked around desperately for an escape route, but he was surrounded. 'Sorry,' he muttered, looking down at the spoon in his mother's hand, which he had no recollection of picking up.

'Watch out!' shouted Katya, and dived across to the other side of the table. 'Picasso and Seurat!'

Spiro, coming in behind them, looked about in astonishment on hearing this and saw two cats, a large randy black Tom and a multi-coloured tabby, leap from the table and streak between their legs and out of the door before anyone could catch them. The tabby had a chicken leg gripped determinedly in his jaws.

Olga sank down on a chair, put her hands over her face and began to cry. Bob, feeling there was safety in numbers, joined in with a howl. Sally looked wildly across at Katya.

'How much damage have they done?'

'It's difficult to tell.'

'We can't throw everything out,' wailed Sally. 'We can't! It's less than an hour till the party starts — it's almost time for the service. What are we going to do?'

Anya, coming along the hall to investigate the disaster, joined them. She had listened to Spiro's explanation of his unexpected arrival with outward coolness, but inner turmoil. She was still angry at his failure to catch the train, but her anger had been softened by the fact that, instead of waiting for the next train or abandoning the journey, he had been so resourceful in getting himself here. She had been keeping well away from him, however, talking to Mum and Nick and then to Peter Kaufmann and Richard Lacey.

'Let's start sorting it out – quick now,' she said. 'There isn't much time. Katya, help me move the things that are definitely all right along to the far end of the table.'

'OK,' said Katya. 'These cheese straws are fine. And the brownies – the cats won't have touched those, and Bob didn't get this far.'

They began to sort out the food, and Sally and Olga, pulling herself together, came to help them. Bob, seizing his chance, tried to wriggle out of the doorway, but was fielded by Gregor's long arm.

'You ought to be ashamed of yourself, Bob,' he said sternly. 'The least you can do is to help clean up the mess. Go and get a bucket from the kitchen, for the things that have to be thrown away.'

Bob ran off quite happily, thinking himself let off lightly. Frances smiled across at Gregor. 'I remember another little boy who used to find it difficult to keep his fingers out of the baking.'

He grinned back at her. 'I still do. Look, there are enough of us here. Why don't you go back and calm the others down. Natasha and Mabel will be fearing the worst.'

Quietly Spiro helped with sorting out the food. The damage was less than they had feared at first, but the amounts consigned to the bucket left the spread on the table distinctly thinned out. Sally and Olga were frantically reviewing what else they could provide for two hundred guests.

'I could go down to the village,' said Sally, 'and see what I can pick up. But there isn't usually much left by this time on a Saturday. There won't be any cakes and there's no hope of any more bread, and we only have a couple of loaves left in the freezer. I suppose we could make a few more sandwiches with those.'

'Drop scones,' said Olga. 'I could make some drop scones. That won't take long.'

'We could have crudités,' suggested Anya, 'if Gregor fetched in some more vegetables from the garden – bits of raw carrot and cauliflower and celery.'

'I can make a dead good dip to go with them,' Katya volunteered. 'You use yoghurt and a packet of French onion soup.'

'We do not have packet soups at St Martins,' said Olga with dignity.

'I do,' said Gregor. 'I drink mugs of the stuff when I'm working late at night. I think I might have some French onion, Katya. Good idea.'

Katya flushed with pleasure.

'If you will permit – ' said Spiro, diffidently.

They stopped talking and looked at him.

'Coming in, I saw that you have a orangery, yes? With a grape vine? If you have rice, sultanas and vegetables, I can make some *dolmades* – stuffed vine leaves, you know? Would this help? And if you have honey and almonds, I can make a very good Greek cake – '

'Wow!' said Katya.

'You mean you can *cook*!' exclaimed Sally. 'Come on then. And Katya, be sure to close the door after you.'

Chapter 5

IT WAS 11.25 and Mr Dawlish was ringing the chapel bell for the service of thanksgiving. Ten years ago he had appointed himself bell-ringer, verger, churchwarden and general factotum whenever services were held in the chapel. At St Paul's in Clunwardine Priors he was a mere sidesman, with occasional charge of hymn books, so that during services at St Martins' chapel he conducted himself with massive and remote dignity. The old bell had a peculiar sweetness of tone and rang out so clearly that it could be heard down in the village, even behind closed windows. It was this clarity of its note that Natasha had feared for when Mabel had raised in committee the recasting of the bell. Mabel was worried by fragile objects – glasses that might crack in the washing up, old fabrics that emitted the fine dust of disintegration – and longed to have the bell sturdily recast and rehung.

Natasha had proved surprisingly stubborn. 'The old bell will see me out, Mabel,' she argued, when the matter was raised again at Easter. 'Let us at least allow it that long.'

Mabel was made uneasy by references to Natasha's age. She bowed her head and dropped the suggestion. She had never felt quite secure at St Martins. Her original arrival with Irina and the children had been meant as a temporary stay, just until she took up her intended career as a teacher and moved out. At first they had all been too busy – scrubbing, painting, replacing windows, hanging curtains and blackout material – for anyone to think about what Mabel should do. After six months, when the house was passable and Mabel made half-hearted suggestions to Irina about finding a job, Irina panicked, insisting she must stay until the end of the war. Edmund's death had left his daughter fearful for William's safety as never before, and she could not think beyond the end of hostilities and his return to his family.

To quieten her conscience, Mabel managed to have herself taken on part-time at the village school to assist Miss Binns, who had come out of retirement for the duration and tired easily, but she found that she did not care for teaching as much as she had expected. She enjoyed the company of one or two children, but a roomful of them alarmed her. She did not move out of the house, as there was nowhere else to live in the village – all the spare rooms being occupied by evacuees – and in any case Natasha would not hear of her leaving St Martins.

The war ended and the regular village school teacher returned from her war work. Mabel could have stayed on in her part-time post, but did not care to, so she allowed the community to think that she had had to leave. She had no real right to be at St Martins, she knew. She was not a refugee or artist, musician or writer. She thought Natasha's paintings striking but did not care for them, with their bright colours and elongated figures against vaguely suggested backgrounds, in which the perspective was all wrong. She was tone deaf; her favourite reading was Ethel M. Dell. Knowing herself a misfit in what she regarded as the rarefied intellectual atmosphere of St Martins, she nevertheless felt a passionate love for the place that she could not explain. Fearing all the time that it might occur to Natasha and Irina that she was no longer needed, she set to work to make herself indispensable.

Irina, who had been accustomed to having a maid in London before the war, and who did not subscribe to her mother's belief in self-help and self-sufficiency, was only too happy to share housekeeping and child care with her younger friend. Natasha, watching with amusement as Mabel bustled about, visibly busy and important, said nothing until, in the autumn of 1946, she suggested to the committee that, as Mabel had taken over so many of the general housekeeping duties and had no other source of income, the trust should arrange to pay her a small salary for her services while she remained with Irina's family at St Martins.

When William was demobbed, he decided to join a solicitors' firm in Hereford instead of going back to London, and his family made St Martins their permanent home. Mabel stayed on, becoming even busier as Hugh and Frances grew up and went away to university. While Natasha lived, she knew that her position was safe. But the younger generation saw less need of Mabel's services, preferring to scramble along, cooking for themselves, cleaning and repairing on a casual rota basis. It was part of the trust agreement that members of the community should be able to remain at St Martins in old age if they wished; it was tacitly understood that younger and abler members would always help and care for the older and less able. The trouble, Mabel sometimes thought to herself, was that she had never exactly been a member. She had not exactly been an employee either. She still received her regular income, gradually increased over the years, but she had a worrying conviction that she no longer earned it. She was seventy now, though she felt ten years younger and was sure she could continue to be useful for some years yet, if they would allow her.

No, if everything continued as in the past, she would probably be safe enough. What she dared not articulate was: what would happen to St Martins itself, when Natasha was no longer there to lead it? Until his stroke, William would have been her natural successor. Of the next generation, Hugh and Frances had moved away. That left Nicholas, and he was surely too young, barely past thirty, and too busy forging ahead in his career.

Donning her decent navy felt hat, Mabel made her way to the chapel in answer to the summons on the bell, conscious of what, in vague terms, she would be praying for during the service, but not at all certain how the Almighty might see His way to answer her.

★　★　★

'You have your own *church*?' Alice was asking Tony in astonishment.

'It's just a chapel. It's part of the original buildings, which belonged to a priory. It isn't used all that often.'

84

They paused on the threshold. Alice took in the short sturdy pillars and the whitewashed walls, and the clean June sunlight falling through the windows across arrangements of foxgloves and cow-parsley and bluebells, whose names she did not know, but whose unassuming character was somehow non-threatening. Beyond the clear but elderly glass she could see the wavering images of trees and a few old gravestones, leaning gently into the earth. Unconsciously her mind began to arrange the shapes on canvas.

'Weird,' she said absently. 'But interesting.'

★ ★ ★

Sally banished everyone from the kitchen except Olga, Spiro and Katya. Bob was sent to his room for half an hour to reflect on his sins. Following Gregor out of the back door and around the corner of the stables to the chapel, Anya felt obscurely resentful. Spiro hadn't taken the trouble to turn up in time for the train, and now he was in the thick of things, while she felt – as she so often did – an outsider, in the way. That he should have been welcomed so warmly into the bosom of her family precisely because he had offered to cook made it seem that he was flaunting before her the very source of their quarrel, instead of trying to make it up with her.

'I'm really sorry,' said Sally, pulling out the baking tins which had just been washed and stored away. 'It isn't like Bob to be so naughty. Chrissie is the one who is usually up to mischief.'

'It isn't your fault, Sally,' said Olga gently. 'It was a terrible temptation to a little boy. We should all have been keeping a sharper watch. And I meant to shut the cats into the old dairy, but I simply forgot. They did as much damage as Bob did.'

Sally began passing down bags of flour, sugar and rice from the wall cupboards, and Katya lined them up on the big kitchen table.

'I just feel so guilty. You're all going to miss the service, and it's one of the highlights of the day, like *A Midsummer Night's Dream* this evening.'

'Don't worry,' said Katya. 'We're like an emergency service. They have to be on duty over Christmas. We're rescuing Natasha's party from disaster. That's more important than going to the service, everyone understands that.'

Spiro pulled a large basin out of the dresser. 'Can I use this? I'm sorry to miss the service, but if I can help here, perhaps Anya will forgive me for missing that train – she is still very stern with me!'

* * *

Gregor had gone off to fetch Frances, who had wandered across the garden and was leaning on the wall gazing at the meadow, with Harry frisking hopefully about her feet. Anya went into the chapel and knelt down in one of the back pews.

'Help me to see what I ought to do,' she prayed – to a God whose existence she did not believe in.

* * *

'I went down to the Ludbrook earlier,' said Frances to Gregor, slipping her arm through his. 'It's quite high, rushing along like anything. And the meadow is so beautiful, full of wild flowers at the moment. Did you know that old meadows like ours are becoming quite rare nowadays? We ought to have someone in to look at it, have it declared a site of special interest, or whatever it is they do.'

Gregor looked at her quizzically. 'I suggested that at the last committee meeting. Natasha is meant to be looking into it.'

'We always did that, didn't we? Read each other's thoughts.'

'You and Hugh did. I'm not sure that I – '

'Oh, you did. You can't have forgotten.'

Gregor looked away from her.

Frances drew a deep breath as they entered the chapel, which enshrined so many milestones of her own past. She had been married here, and all the children had been christened here, in the clumsy old font that some antiquarian friend of Dad's had said was possibly pre-Christian – a pagan sacrificial bowl – taken over and incorporated into the ritual when missionary priests had first come to these parts in Saxon times. 'Great political tact, they had, those fellows. Used the old pagan holy sites and artefacts and festivals whenever they could, so the poor benighted natives thought that Christianity was just an up-market version of their own faith. Very clever.'

She ran her fingers over the font's lumpy, familiar edge now as she passed. She remembered coming into the chapel on her wedding day on William's arm, as she came now on Gregor's. She remembered the ceremony with great clarity, but the rest of the day had faded and was lost to her.

★ ★ ★

'You all right, old thing?' asks William, as they stand alone in the drawing room, watching the guests making their way to the chapel. Irina, in sensible Crimplene, has disappeared through the ancient doorway. The room is quiet now that she is no longer fussing nervously with Frances's wreath of white freesias. Natasha, dramatic in something scarlet and pink, has kissed Frances and gone.

'I'm fine, Dad. Though to be truthful, I'll be glad when all this is over.'

'I thought it was supposed to be the greatest day of a girl's life.'

'Oh *that*,' Frances laughs. 'That's a bit old hat. Walking off into the sunset like a Hollywood film, you mean? Nowadays women have careers, just the same as men. Marriage isn't so important to us now, not as an end in itself.'

William looks doubtful. 'It's not that easy, old girl.' He lowers his eyes, embarrassed. 'After all, babies and things – '

'I can manage that,' says Frances confidently. 'Giles is in an OUDS production on the Edinburgh fringe this summer. We're going there straight after our honeymoon. That's where you get noticed, you see, by the West End producers. He's going to spend the next few months getting something lined up for when we graduate next summer. He'll soon be earning enough for us to have an au pair to help with the housework. Then I shall get on with my own career. I'm not going to have any babies for ages.'

Hugh comes to the french window. 'I think everyone is here. You could come across now.'

As Frances manoeuvres her wide skirts through the french

window he bends and breathes in her ear, 'Good luck, Franny. Take care of yourself.'

She cannot think why he is looking at her so sadly.

* * *

William, shuffling in behind them, supported by Nicholas, watched Gregor lead Frances to one of the front pews and sit down beside her. Their heads bowed forward in unison. He remembered that wedding, Frances and Giles. She looked so lovely, his gallant little Franny, subduing her tomboyish stride to her long skirts, glowing up at that fellow who even then looked smooth and untrustworthy. As a solicitor you got to recognise the signs. You could see it written all over his father, who was something high up in the City and had a chauffeur-driven Rolls. The mother was a mousy, nervous little thing who hardly uttered a word all day. He remembered that, because he had, of course, to partner her and look after her. Irina had been rather flattered by the excessive attentions of Giles's father.

I never liked him, thought William – or Giles. It was no surprise to me that the father failed so spectacularly the following year and just missed prosecution by a whisker. As for Giles, he's what we would have called a bounder when I was young. Good word. Describes him to a T. I can't understand why Frances has put up with him all these years. For the sake of the children, I suppose, though I'm not so sure that's as good a reason as some people make out.

Frances and Gregor, now, I always thought they would . . .

Groaning a little, William fumbled into a pew. And – praying – articulated in his mind words that his tongue could no longer find its way around.

* * *

Kneeling in the front pew, Frances closed her eyes and let the atmosphere of the chapel embrace her. She did not try to pray, or even to think very clearly. She could hear a pair of magpies squabbling outside on the lawn, and further off a lark, probably over the meadow. She had seen one tumbling high overhead as she had walked back from the brook. Eric had scythed the

88

grass round the gravestones yesterday, and the smell of mown hay drifted in at the door as people came in one by one, their feet muted on the matting in the aisle, then giving off a dull ring from the stone flags as they edged into the pews. Putting out her left hand she could touch the worn stones of a pillar, and under her knees the sturdy canvas of the hassock creaked gently. Gregor's jersey – darned at the elbow, as she had noticed earlier – brushed against her bare right arm, and she could feel the warmth of his arm through it.

I know where I am going *from*, she thought, but I do not know where I am going *to*. Perhaps if I am very quiet and listen, I will find out.

* * *

Lisa sat with Paul at the back of the chapel, in the pew nearest the door. I feel light-headed, she thought, leaning her head on her hand, with her elbow on the back of the pew in front, pretending to pray. Almost as if I were drunk. The baby has been very still since it kicked first thing this morning. Oh God, I hope it's all right. Why isn't it moving? Fear rose like sickness in her throat.

* * *

Irina had offered her arm to her mother, walking across to the chapel.

'Thank you, dear,' said Natasha sweetly, laying the tips of her fingers lightly on Irina's arm as once, long ago, she had laid them on the arms of young men escorting her to the Greshlovs' box at the opera, or up a sweeping staircase at a ball, or strolling beside an ornamental lake.

Humiliated, Irina held up her arm awkwardly, not knowing how to support the butterfly weight of her mother's hand. She walked stiffly herself, aware of the sciatica jabbing along her left leg. How *could* her mother float along so girlishly at her great age, when Irina would have been glad of a man's arm to lean on heavily, herself. They passed William and Nicholas sitting in a pew halfway down the aisle. William's eyes were shut, and he seemed to be mumbling silently to himself. Irina felt that burst of panic which seized her regularly now, ever since William's stroke. He had always been there – solid, reliable William – apart from those war years. Caring for her, tolerating her social ineptitudes with his kindly smile, understanding (and not minding) her inability to deal with people, admiring and encouraging her painstaking botanical paintings, which she had kept a secret from everyone else all her life. Now his illness had clapped down like a steel shutter between them. It frightened her that she could not even be sure if he was still *there*, behind the mumbling mouth and uncoordinated movements. The sight of him terrified her.

★ ★ ★

Poor Irina, thought Natasha, ashamed of herself, and allowing a little more weight to rest on her daughter's arm. I am most unkind to her. I am a wicked old woman and should not tease her as I do.

She sat down in the front pew on the right, across the aisle from Gregor and Frances, in a swirl of pale blue silk chiffon. This morning she had taken it into her head to wear the same dress as she had worn at the party they had originally held to launch St Martins. Her figure had grown more angular than it had been then, but the dress still fitted. She had never bought many clothes, but she bought the best quality she could afford and looked after them. Her wardrobe was still filled with frocks dating back over the last seventy years. She could remember having this one made, in 1936, when they were living in Chelsea. The flat-chested twenties look was out of fashion, and you were allowed to have some curves again. The dress had been beautifully cut, falling in softly draped folds across the bodice, with a skirt of separate panels that overlapped and rippled against each other as you moved. She had brought it out that day in 1944, defying wartime austerity, making a brave gesture against the knowledge that Edmund was out there, somewhere, on the beaches of Normandy, under fire.

As she sank gently forward on the hassock, she raised her eyes for a moment to the brass plaque on the wall just above her head. Then she dropped her eyes and talked to Edmund.

I hope you are pleased, doushenka, at the way our scheme turned out. Fifty years! Who could have imagined it? Are you pleased with me? Is it how you thought it would be? We have had our failures, of course. There was the flautist of absolutely *no* talent, my darling, who drank like a Moscow droshki driver and then played his appalling music all night. It was very difficult to get rid of him, he was always so ill and sorry in the morning. And there was a crowd of New Age travellers two years ago, who tried to occupy those fields we rent out to Alun Philips. I can't explain about New Age now, darling, there isn't time, but they were not what you would have liked. Not real gypsies – we still get those, and they are no bother, apart from one or two chickens disappearing. No, these other people, they were dealing in drugs, and they became quite abusive. Irina was very frightened, but the police dealt with them in the end.

Gregor – do you remember Gregor, doushenka? He was the little Polish boy who came just before you left, that last time. A tragic child. Such things he had seen. It reminded me of when I – No, better not to think about that.

Gregor is one of our successes. He did well at art school, then he became very unhappy and wandered round the world. I thought something had broken in him, perhaps those old memories taking him over, you know? I could understand that. But he came back at last, and has been like a grandson to me. We hardly ever see Hugh, except when he comes for a few months to write one of his books, shut away up in the attics. I'm afraid I don't even know where he is.

Now, my darling, I must stop talking to you, because Richard is about to start the service and it would be very unkind of me not to pay attention.

* * *

'Dearly beloved,' said Richard, as if he meant it, 'we are gathered together . . . '

* * *

Chrissie sat on her own in the pew in front of her father and Great-grandpa William, conscious of her dignity. She was the only person under twenty-five in the whole chapel, and she sat primly, with her sandals neatly together on the hassock and the 10p piece Daddy had given her for the collection clutched in her hand. Once, her collection money had slipped through a hole in the pocket of her dungarees and, as she struggled to find it when the plate came round, it had fallen out of the bottom of her trouser leg and gone rolling away under the pew in front. Mummy immediately passed her another coin, but the memory of the mortification still made her go hot.

She had had some very interesting conversations lately with Natasha about God. Chrissie wasn't quite convinced of the truth of some of the Bible stories, and had become very confused when a new teacher at her school introduced mixed religious teaching. As the only non-English family in the village were Christian Asians, all the primary school children were somewhat baffled, though they liked the opportunity to act out Muslim, Jewish and Buddhist festivals as well as Christian ones. You could count on something nearly every week, with special foods, and candles, and sometimes fancy clothes to dress up in. Miss Baxter was gratified by their enthusiasm and interest, which she reported back jubilantly to the headmaster, who had pointed out rather cynically that there might be some connection with the fact that the following lesson was invariably mental arithmetic.

On the whole, Chrissie thought, she liked the Jewish ceremonies best. She loved the candlestick with its curly branches and seven candles, and the music Miss Baxter played on the tape recorder. It was wild and haunting, and made shivers go up and down Chrissie's back. Diwali was fun too, but she was dubious about the Muslims. She hadn't liked the pictures of the women wrapped up like parcels so you couldn't see anything but their eyes – they looked creepy. The Orthodox Christians were nice. She was much taken with an icon hanging in Natasha's bedroom, of a very young Virgin with enormous oval eyes and a halo made of real gold leaf. The chapel was very boring compared with these riches, but she felt comfortable here. It aroused in her none of the sentimental religious fancies she sometimes indulged in, but it was a safe place, somewhere you could always slip into, to be quiet and alone.

Obediently, Chrissie knelt down, her money growing hot in her hand, and repeated, 'Our Father, Which art in Heaven . . .'

★ ★ ★

The service drew towards its close. Richard spoke simply but movingly of the spirit of St Martins and the many people it had helped. He touched lightly on Natasha's life, knowing that she would not tolerate a eulogy, and spoke rather longer of Edmund, whose death in Normandy they were also commemorating, and the crown of whose life was the founding of St Martins with his wife.

The blessing. A scraping of feet, and the congregation rose to sing the final hymn.

Gregor felt Frances's hand brush his as she reached for her service sheet, but he kept his eyes fixed on Richard, set apart in his gleaming surplice from the man who crawled about his railway engines in a dirty green boiler suit. So do our rituals and our garments shape us into different people – alter, subtly, our relationships. If Richard were to stand up in the pulpit before us in his boiler suit, would we listen with the same respectful attention to his words? Yet the man would be the same. And if I were to stand there, dressed as he is now, and deliver the same sermon, would they listen to me with the same respect? A man known as I am, these days, for sculptures that are – in Frances's words – brutalist? Sculptures that women like Irina find deeply shocking, and Frances finds distressing? Although I am saying in them many of the same things about the human condition as Richard is saying. Stripped, of course, of the comfortably familiar words and ritual.

Lift up your hearts! We lift them, Lord, to Thee.

Do we? Do we indeed, I wonder.

The small organ, sweet-toned but not powerful, rang out triumphantly, as Birgit played with her own particular dedication. When she and Peter had first arrived at St Martins after the war, emaciated skeletons from Auschwitz, she had told Natasha that she did not believe she could any longer count herself a Christian, after what Christian Nazis had done to her husband's people. Natasha had never pursued the subject, but in time, when the organ had been installed, it came to be understood that Birgit would play it.

Singing, in spite of himself, as enthusiastically as anyone, Gregor thought of the way certain places, the physical reality of them, had powerful associations for him, so that he could not, however much he tried, escape the past in them.

★　★　★

'This is the chapel, Gregor,' says Natasha in Polish, leading him in by the hand and sitting down on a pile of rubble near the door. Her brightly coloured cotton skirt, like a gypsy's, spreads out amongst the dust on the floor, like flowers trampled in a roadway. 'It has been neglected for years, and I am afraid it has been used to keep chickens in. Don't you think that is a dreadful thing to do?'

He nods. He has been at St Martins for over two months now, but he has hardly dared to speak. The habit of silence and fear has been so drilled into him that he cannot overcome it. He looks around. Part of the roof has fallen in. The floor is littered with straw and bits of broken stone and shattered pews. It reminds him powerfully of other ruins, still hot from the fires that have ravaged them, filled with the sweet stink of burnt human bodies, where he and Mama and Papa had to hide. He is rigid.

Natasha, who has been following the news reports of the recent Warsaw rising, wonders whether she should have brought the child here. Drawn to him by a shared experience neither of them can speak of, she longs to help, but cannot think where to start.

'Look,' she says, drawing him on to her lap, and lifting a ragged panel of glass from the top of a tea-chest. 'When Frances was helping me start to tidy up in here, see what we found.' She holds the panel up in front of him, so that the light flowing down the nave from the east window lights it up in intense shades of deep blue and crimson.

Gregor sees the Virgin and Child who used to look down

at him from the window above the family pew at home in Poland. He reaches out a finger to touch the dusty glass. 'Mary,' he whispers.

* * *

Standing in the very back pew, drawing himself away from the congregation of which he is obliged to be a part, Gregor looks down the aisle at the two figures in grey morning dress before the altar. Rage pounds in his head like physical blows. He understands, for the first time, that to see red is not a mere figure of speech. His vision swims in a blood-red haze, and he can barely draw breath. Hugh slips into the pew across the aisle and gives him an anguished look, but Gregor ignores him.

Frances comes into the chapel on William's arm. She pauses beside the first pews, adjusting her veil, allowing Olga, her bridesmaid, to spread out the train of her dress behind her. Through the smell of blood in his nostrils, Gregor can smell her. The scent she wears, *Je reviens*, and the flowers of her bouquet, orange blossom and freesias. As she moves forward, the skirt of her wedding dress brushes against him, but she does not look at him. She is abstracted, absorbed in the ritual.

He hates her so much he wants to hit her, there, in front of the whole congregation.

She has reached the altar. She hands her flowers to Olga. William steps back, the best man moves a little to one side. Giles bends towards her and smiles.

* * *

'Darling,' Lisa whispered now to Paul in that same pew at the back of the chapel, 'could we slip out, before we get caught up with everyone? I think I might lie down for a bit.'

* * *

As the congregation came out of the service there was a feeling of festivity in the air. Richard and Natasha stood together beside the door, shaking hands as people filed past. When everyone but Frances had gone, Natasha turned to Richard and kissed him on each cheek.

95

'I wish Edmund could have known you, Richard. You and your crazy trains – he would have loved that!'

Richard blushed and mumbled something. He would like to have known Edmund, if it came to that. He must have been quite a man, to have inspired such love in a woman like Natasha Devereux. It always seemed strange to him that he never thought of her as a woman so much older than himself. She still turned male heads in the street – he had seen it happen.

The hazy clouds were beginning to drift away as Frances and Natasha walked slowly back together towards the house. Chrissie came out of her family's front door and raced past.

'I'm going to see if Samira is coming!' she shouted.

'It's going to be fine after all,' said Frances. 'We won't need to use the Scout tent that Mabel has been agonising over. Did you pray for sunshine?'

'Not really. I was thinking about Edmund. Did you?'

Frances looked away from her, across the garden towards the rise of the meadow, before it dropped away to the Ludbrook.

'No, I wasn't praying. I wasn't even thinking. If I think these days I am too apt to work myself up into a state. So I just let myself go, on a tide of music and the beautiful language of the service. I'm so glad Richard is a traditionalist, at least as far as the texts are concerned. Though I'm relieved he supports the ordination of women.'

'Mum!' shouted Katya from the stableyard. 'Come and see! Spiro has done the most fabulous things!'

'Go on,' said Natasha, laughing. 'Go and see. It is good to see her full of excitement again, like a child. She forgets her teenage pose of boredom and angst.'

The kitchen was warm and spicy with the scent of cinnamon and nutmeg as Frances came in. Spiro and Sally were laughing while they put away baking tins, and Olga was humming to herself as she rinsed down the sink and wiped the table top that glowed with the sunlight slanting in through the open door. Picasso was washing his back legs nonchalantly on one of the assorted rush-seated chairs, having insinuated himself back into the kitchen while they were busy. Seurat had gone off somewhere with his chicken leg, probably deep into the shrubbery, and – being the more diplomatic of the two – had not shown his face again yet.

Laid out on the dresser were plates of egg and watercress sandwiches, buttered drop scones, a heap of chocolate muffins, and two particularly wicked looking cakes, sticky with honey, over which Sally had placed a net canopy, to the frustration of several wasps. Spiro opened the upper oven on the range and lifted out four large gratin dishes covered with neat rows of grey-green parcels, like fat sausages. The smell of roasted peppers and garlic billowed across the kitchen in a warm wave.

'I'm absolutely *starving*,' wailed Katya. 'Can't I have just *one*, Spiro?'

Spiro laughed at her and looked at Sally. 'Shall we permit her just one? She can tell us if they are all right.'

Before Sally could reply, Katya speared one of the *dolmades* on a fork and fielded it on a plate.

'Wow, it's fantastic,' she mumbled through a full mouth, fanning the heat away with her hand. 'Try a bit, Mum.'

Frances took the proffered forkful. 'Delicious, Spiro. What an inspiration! We've never thought of using the vine leaves. The vine is so old it doesn't produce any proper grapes any more, it's just ornamental.'

'Vines – they need proper care, of course,' said Spiro. He grinned, thinking of the cracked and broken panes of glass in the old orangery. The vine sprawled in every direction, its branches reaching out like the gnarled arms of some benevolent giant. Briefly he remembered the disciplined rows of vines in his uncle's vineyard in the Peloponnese. They seemed cowed and timid by comparison.

'Yes, we probably don't look after it as we should. Birgit and Peter are our flower experts, and Mr Dawlish is very good with all the standard vegetables – potatoes, carrots, tomatoes and peas, you know. But none of us has any expertise in the more exotic things.'

'You could grow much more in your orangery. Peppers. Melons. Figs.'

Frances laughed. 'I'm not sure whether Mr Dawlish would approve, but we'll have to get you to work on him. It would be fun to grow things like that – and helpful to the community's budget, if they did well.'

Sally ducked her head as she took off her apron.

'I quite fancy that. Luscious home-grown melon for breakfast. Nice juicy peppers, instead of the rather withered efforts from the village shop.'

'We could even sell peppers *to* the village shop,' said Katya, carried away with the idea. She looked at Spiro, Frances noticed, with enormous respect. He had shed his jacket and tie, and had donned the huge butcher's apron Gregor sometimes wore. His sleeves were rolled up and there was a dab of flour on his nose. What was even more interesting was that Katya had thrown off her poacher's jacket and several more of her layers, which now lay about on chairs and on the scullery floor. In her skirt, leggings and sleeveless T-shirt she was not conventionally dressed by Irina's standards, but she looked a good deal less odd. She was also bright with cheerfulness and excitement. Frances felt a rush of gratitude towards Spiro. And, in an odd way, towards Bob and the cats.

'Has anyone let Bob out of his confinement yet?' she asked.

'Heavens!' said Sally, 'I completely forgot. And I must go and see if Sarah is being a pest to Peter. I'd better give her something to eat before the guests arrive. They'll be here any minute.'

'You run along, darling,' said Frances. 'We'll muster the troops to move all the food outside. Spiro, could you round up Nick and Tony? There are crates of bottles to be carried up from the cellar and put out in the shade of the chestnut, next to those long tables. And,' she added quietly, as he was taking off his apron, 'you can't think how grateful I am.'

'This was nothing,' he said, laughing. 'I am enjoying myself. *You* can't think how grateful I am to get away from my books!'

★ ★ ★

Giles stole another look at his watch. In his view they had accomplished all that could usefully be done in this morning's rehearsal, and he was getting anxious about Nigel, who had arrived half an hour ago and was prowling about restlessly. It was absolutely essential not to offend Nigel. He held the key to Giles's immediate future, and it was important to clinch a deal quickly, while the reputation of *Vet in Hot Water* was still riding high. This morning's rehearsal had convinced him that his vague worries were more than justified. The second series, due to be screened in six months' time, was going to be panned by the critics.

It was always a risk, especially with a sitcom. A good idea could keep the team going for the first series, but if key members had to leave and the whole thing lost steam, the follow-up could just turn into a dying duck. With Max gone off to New York for a year as a comedy-writer-in-residence for a prestigious theatre workshop, and Judy doubtful about returning to play her minor part now that she was making a name for herself as a lead comic, the prospects for a third series were zilch.

He was getting a bit tired of it himself, frankly. He'd been so desperate for something that he'd agreed to the first series, and it had turned out to be great fun after all. But, let's face it, falling about head over arse in the muck in pop comedy was not going to do his long-term ambitions any good. He only had the vaguest idea what Nigel Laker was planning – he had been hugging it to his chest for weeks, not wanting the other channels to get a whiff of it. But Giles was pretty sure it was more up-market than this stuff.

The janitor walked in the door without knocking and jangled his keys.

'I gotta lock up. It's gone twelve. You're supposed to be outa here.'

He was an unpleasant, pimply young lout, chewing gum and leaning insolently against the door-frame. The director, having paid for the rehearsal room till twelve, was determined to get his money's worth.

'We have another five minutes,' he said fussily, looking at his watch.

Without answering, the janitor pointed indolently at the clock on the wall. It said one minute past twelve.

Giles intervened. 'Time we were off, I think.' He beamed

charmingly at both the director and the janitor, and lied, 'Good morning's work done. Let's quit while we're ahead.'

It took another fifteen minutes, even so, to sort out times for next week's filming schedule and to gather up his coat and suitcase.

'Let's get out of here,' he muttered to Nigel. 'God, I need a drink! Where's your car?'

'Just round the corner on the left. Let's get on our way and stop somewhere out of London for a drink and a bite. I know an acceptable hostelry about three-quarters of an hour from here. Nice little place where they serve real ale and quite decent food, not your usual bought-in bar lunch stuff.'

'Great.'

Nigel's Merc was parked on a double yellow line, and a parking ticket was stuck to the windscreen.

'Damn,' said Nigel. 'I was afraid of that. I thought I'd only be a couple of minutes.'

Giles's heart sank. 'Let me,' he said hastily, reaching out his hand for the ticket.

'Not on your life. I don't believe in handing over money to petty bureaucrats.' Nigel removed the ticket from its plastic envelope, tore it into tiny shreds and scattered them broadcast over the street. This seemed to cheer him up a good deal.

'Hop in,' he said. 'No talking about the new series till we get to the pub, then I'll fill you in.'

Chapter 6

'**W**E'LL NEED TO put all the rest of the cars in the field,' said Nicholas. 'We can only squeeze in one more here on the gravel.'

Mr Dawlish always wore a flat cap, whatever the weather, which he pushed back when speaking. By the end of a long discussion it would be hanging on for dear life to the wiry curls on the back of his head. He pushed it back now. 'Yes, Oi suppose. Mabee a bicycle might get, but nothing else. Oi'll get Miss Owens's sign, and move 'im, and open the fild gate.'

'Good thing Alun Philips was able to move his cows out of that field yesterday,' said Nicholas. 'I hope last night's rain won't mean the cars churn it up too much. I don't think we've ever had so many cars here before.'

Mr Dawlish heaved up the 'Parking' sign that Nicholas had earlier hammered into the grass verge, and trudged off down the drive to the point just before the field gate. Nicholas could hear him banging in the wooden support with a stone as the next car crunched up the gravel drive.

'Just go on round the house to the garden,' he said to the Patels from the village newsagent's shop, who were climbing out of a bright red Fiesta, the last car in the long row already parked. 'Refreshments over at the far end, by the big chestnut tree. Natasha is there somewhere too.' Samira, as Chrissie's best friend, led her parents off with an air of casual self-importance.

★ ★ ★

When Mia Patel had arrived in Bristol as a bride of twenty in 1974, chosen by Chanor's grandmother as suitable for marriage to her English-born grandson, she was determined that she would create a wonderful home for him and the children (who would come soon), modelled on what she found in *Good Housekeeping*, which at that time was her favourite reading. Mia was clever and ambitious.

'You must understand,' Chanor said, during their only meeting before the marriage, 'that England now is not like the days of the Raj. There are no servants.'

'No servants?' Mia smiled at him, polite but disbelieving.

'Truly, no servants. Except in families like – like the Queen's. Sometimes there is a servant who comes into the house a few hours in the day to clean, but that is all.' He cleared his throat. 'My mother,' he said, 'does not have a servant.'

'Not even of this daily kind?'

'No, not even that.' He did not want to admit this, though he was a good, honest boy. He had known at once that his grandmother had made a wonderful choice. Mia was the perfect wife for him.

'But in my grandfather's house,' said Mia, very puzzled, 'there are seventeen indoor servants and ten outdoor servants.'

'I know,' said Chanor sadly. Mia came from an old-fashioned household, where four generations of the family lived together in a rambling mansion.

'But,' he added hopefully, 'you will not need servants in England. I will buy you the very latest electric cooker, with built-in hob and oven, and a vacuum cleaner, and a washing machine, and a tumble-drier.' He paused. 'Even a dishwasher,' he added bravely. He was not quite sure how he would manage this, but he was sure that somehow he would find a way.

The marriage had proved a very happy one, although Chanor was not able to fulfil all his promises at once. Mia was determined that her house should be as unlike the cheerful but disorderly home of her Punjabi childhood as possible. There the instructions to servants would be changed and countermanded half a dozen times by different members of the household. The servants, being accustomed to this, postponed every task. If a meal was due to be served at noon, you could expect to sit down at two or – if it had been a hot day of short tempers – three o'clock in the afternoon. Every day was a drama. As a young girl she had tumbled about through this chaos with her brothers, sisters and cousins, without the slightest concern. When she was thirteen or fourteen, however, her innate sense of order surfaced. She had begun to be distressed by the muddle of her family life. Now she wanted to make for Chanor a home that was tranquil and ordered. When the children arrived, they would be brought up to be neat, polite and quiet.

At this point, Fate intervened. The children they both so much desired did not appear. Mia grew restive, sitting alone in her perfect house, and her ambition asserted itself. She began to attend evening classes at the local college of further education. She enrolled first for flower arranging (in the English style) and cake decorating. She went to French for beginners and elementary pottery, nouvelle cuisine, typing and Shakespearean tragedy. She avoided practical car maintenance (Chanor would not have approved), but progressed to intermediate French, practical mathematics, beginners' German, and American poetry. When at last Samira arrived, Mia had run out of courses at the college, and could have given instruction in most of them.

It was 1985 when Samira was born. Their business – a delicatessen selling mostly, but not exclusively, Indian foods – was flourishing in Thatcher's Britain. But before the baby was a year old, another Indian family in the neighbourhood had petrol poured through their letterbox and a match set to it. Eighteen months later a teenage boy they knew was badly beaten up in a racist attack and spent three weeks in hospital. Mia, who had always been so cool and in command, became – for the first time – hysterical.

'We cannot continue to live here,' she had said to Chanor, her face wet with tears. 'What will become of Samira when she has to go to school? Oh, what shall we do?'

Chanor was quite unnerved – both by the recent violent events and by Mia's loss of control. He promised immediately that he would look for a business in one of the nearby rural counties. When they discovered the newsagent's business for sale in Clunwardine Priors, Chanor was doubtful, but Mia knew with certainty that this was where they should make their home.

When she had first visited St Martins, as a result of Samira's friendship with Chrissie, she was appalled by the mess and the casual way artists' brushes were left amongst food on the kitchen table, or muddy gardening gloves lay on the tattered but lovely Georgian commode in the hall. The whole place, with its jumble of people, reminded her powerfully of her grandfather's house, although she had to concede that these people seemed to get on with their various kinds of work in a disciplined way. Gradually she began to see that even the domestic side was not as disordered as she had at first supposed. She was fascinated by the place, and attracted by the people, much as her daughter was, but for some reason they made her feel extremely shy (unusual for Mia Patel), with their lack of formality. She could not quite see on what terms she should be with them. While they for their part – although she did not realise this – simply accepted her as they accepted everyone else, and were unaware of her problem.

* * *

Natasha sat enthroned under the copper beech on her Jacobean chair, which had been carried into the garden by Tony. Guests had begun to arrive almost before the official start of the anniversary celebrations at noon – Natasha's parties had a certain local fame, and an invitation to one was much cherished. This anniversary, long discussed and eagerly awaited, promised to be a party to outdo all others.

'What *fun*, my dear!' cried Muriel Lacey, kissing Natasha. 'I am quite *blown* with cycling up the lane the very *instant* I closed the museum. Couldn't bear to waste a minute.'

'I'm sorry you weren't able to come for the service,' said Natasha. 'Richard did it beautifully. I was so pleased.'

'I was *devastated* not to be here, but there was this group from the Stanway Local History Society – you remember I did a talk for them last month? – well, they were going to be coming over either this Saturday or next Saturday, and I didn't want them to be disappointed by arriving only to find I was *shut* – it wouldn't have been kind, would it? – and it was a jolly good thing I did stay open because they *did* come and had a simply *marvellous* time and one old chap brought a 1910 grease can for the museum that Richard will be absolutely *thrilled* with – and, oh my dear,' said Muriel, without drawing breath, 'there is that *awful* man from The Poplars, you surely didn't invite *him*, did you?'

Seizing the moment when Muriel paused, Natasha said, 'Yes. Yes, I did. One must be neighbourly.' She smiled enigmatically.

'Natasha, you are *plotting* something. I know the signs. What is it he's called? Forrest? Bishop?'

'Frobisher.'

'Ah, yes, I knew it was something like that. *Dreadful* man! And as for his *wife*-!'

'Quite.'

'How he got planning permission for that house I *cannot* imagine. It sits in that lovely corner at the end of the village where there used to be nothing but apple and pear trees that were as old as *Methuselah* and it looks like a cross between a Tesco supermarket and a 1930s swimming bath with the mockest of mock Tudor beams stuck on all *over* the front. How did he get away with it?'

'He's a very clever man. That orchard was just outside the conservation zone of the village. It's a pity it wasn't included in the protected area, but I suppose people thought no one would want to build there, with the Ludbrook running right through the middle.'

'And now he has culverted the brook and quite *ruined* the view from Miss Bagshaw's cottage, she's so upset and says why wasn't she consulted or even *told*, and honestly I don't know *what* to say to the poor old dear – what do you think?'

Natasha, amused at this description of Miss Bagshaw, who was twenty years her junior, said, 'I don't understand the rules on planning permission, Muriel, but someone once told me that no one has rights to a view. I also know that Simon Frobisher has powerful friends and is a man of much influence. If he sets his mind on a thing, he will expect to get it in the end.'

'But what does he *do*? He seems to be about the place all the time, but he's much too young to be retired.'

'I understand that he has an office in The Poplars full of all this wonderful new computer equipment. I believe you can move millions of pounds around the world simply by using the computer and a telephone.'

'How terrifying! Is he a money man, then?'

'Amongst other things. His main business seems to be property development.'

'Do tell me,' said Muriel, her mind hopping to another subject, 'is there any chance of Hugh turning up?'

'I really don't know,' said Natasha a little sadly. 'We haven't seen him for two years, and that time it was only for a weekend. I told him that I was planning this party for the anniversary, but of course we hadn't arranged anything definite that long ago. At Easter I wrote to the last address we had for him. He was in Kashmir, where he went as a young man – but I don't know if he ever received my letter.'

* * *

William was also thinking about Hugh. He had never been able to understand what drove his son into the remote and difficult corners of the world where he had made a name for himself as an adventurer. As a child Hugh had been restless and daring, always getting into scrapes. And Frances, fifteen months younger, had tagged along behind, trying to jump as far and climb as high. He shuddered when he remembered teaching the pair of them to drive, on the farm tracks, when they were in their early teens. They were determined to outdo each other and – curiously, he thought, for he had fixed attitudes about the relative abilities of men and women – Frances had proved to be the better driver. She seemed to know instinctively how to handle a car, and would race along the tracks, but retain control. Hugh, determined not to be outdone by his younger sister, loved the speed, but did not have the skill to go with it.

He can't still be trying to go one better than Frances after all these years, thought William humorously, sitting where Mabel and Tony had installed him, in the dappled shade of the chestnut tree. Here he was close to the main serving tables and could watch the guests flooding into the garden, but was not so directly in their path to the refreshments that they would feel obliged to stop and speak to him.

Compared with Frances, Hugh's life has been full of drama and excitement, while she – as she puts it herself – has dwindled into a suburban housewife. I wonder whether he realises the agonies he puts us through. I shall never forget the time he was taken prisoner by that Indian tribe up the Amazon, and then reappeared weeks later in Peru. Or the time he was lost with his guide in a blizzard in northern Greenland, and the consul cabled to say that there wasn't much hope anyone could survive in those conditions. But of course he got another book out of it, to finance the next expedition.

I would like to see Hugh just once more. And if he doesn't come back soon, he won't have much chance of seeing Natasha again.

★ ★ ★

Chrissie and Samira, having filled paper plates to overflowing with food, had come into the stableyard where they could picnic away from the grown-ups.

'Would you like to see our puppies?' said Chrissie, when they finished. 'They're just two weeks old.'

'Oh, yes!' said Samira, who had been hoping Chrissie would offer.

'In here.' Chrissie led the way in through Nicholas and Sally's door, which opened on to a big family room occupying the whole ground floor of the old coach-house. At the far end a friendly sagging *bergère* suite was grouped comfortably around a wood stove, and a window – which had replaced the old shuttered opening – overlooked a corner of the garden and the meadow beyond. Beside the window was a lobster-pot playpen for Sarah, passed on to Sally by Frances when Chrissie was born. At the near end of the room, to the left of the front door, Sally had her own kitchen – with a window overlooking pots of geraniums in the stableyard, a modern electric stove, and a big scrubbed pine table where Chrissie's family usually had their meals. In a fraying dog basket near the wood stove Jeannie was curled up with her five puppies.

'The wood stove isn't lit in the summer, of course,' said Chrissie, 'but this is where she likes to be with the puppies. I s'pose it makes her feel safe.'

The two girls squatted down beside the basket. Jeannie eyed them, and licked a puppy with a proprietorial air.

'Would you like to hold one?'

'Oh yes,' breathed Samira, sitting down cross-legged on the rag rug and cradling the puppy with awe on her lap. Her home in the cottage behind and above her parents' post office and newsagent's was cleaned and polished to gleaming brightness, and she had to remove her shoes at the door when she came in. She regarded Chrissie's life amongst the happy casualness of St Martins with both envy and alarm. The puppy gave a small whimper, turned round and round a few times, then settled down to sleep. Samira stroked his fat pink tummy with longing.

'He's lovely,' she whispered.

'This is the one I'm going to have for my very own,' said Chrissie, lifting a female puppy competently. 'I haven't thought of a name for her yet. Harry's their daddy.'

Samira caressed the domed head of her puppy tenderly, and whispered in its ear. It burrowed more firmly down into her lap.

'Would you like to have one?' asked Chrissie generously. 'I don't think Mummy's found homes for all of them yet.'

Samira swallowed painfully. 'My mother would never let me,' she said.

'I know what,' said Chrissie, inspired. 'We'll get my granny to talk to her. She always says everybody ought to have a dog. Is that the one you'd like?'

'Oh, yes,' breathed Samira, laying her cheek against the puppy's head. 'He's so beautiful.'

★ ★ ★

Lisa was lying on top of the duvet, not wanting to look ill or to worry Paul by going properly to bed. She could hear the voices of the guests floating up through the open window, and two small tears of self-pity rolled down her cheeks. She brushed them away quickly, and said in a bright voice to Paul, who was standing moodily staring out of the window with his back to her, 'Who's come, can you see?'

'All the usual people from the village. Muriel Lacey was talking to Natasha for ages, but now the Patels are with her. Mrs Patel is wearing a beautiful sari – sort of peacock blue, with glittery gold bits.'

He craned round the window frame. 'It looks as though Gregor is being polite to that new teacher from the village school. Can't remember her name. And a whole crowd of Davieses have arrived. There's Trevor, and his brother who farms over by Stanway Bridges, and that other brother. They each have about six kids, don't they? Looks as though they could form the school choir on their own.'

'They do all have beautiful Welsh voices,' said Lisa, making an effort. 'Is Keith Howard here yet?'

'That looks like Sir Keith talking to Peter. He must have flown over from Germany specially. I was reading in the *Guardian* just last week about some important concert series he's conducting in the main towns of the old East Germany. Pretty good, eh?' Paul had never quite grown used to the sometimes exotic world of St Martins. He did not boast of it in the staffroom of the school in Worcester, where he taught biology and botany. Boasting was beneath his dignity – but he did just occasionally let drop a casual remark.

'Mr Patel is helping Nick and Tony bring out some crates of soft drinks, and the children are swarming around them like flies.' Paul chuckled.

'I do wish you would go and join them. I'll be fine here on my own. It'll be a pity if neither of us is there.' Lisa paused, looking at Paul's worried back. 'I don't want to upset Natasha,' she added cunningly. Natasha would not be upset, but Paul was always slightly in awe of her. 'Go on. I'll have a little snooze and come down later. I just didn't get much sleep last night, but I feel as though I could now.'

Paul turned round and looked at her, wrung with anxiety.

'But what if you want something? Nobody will hear you from down there in the garden, with people chattering like mad.'

'I've got that great bell Mabel gave us last night. I promise I'll clang that furiously if I need anything. We always used to have that if we were ill when we stayed at St Martins as children. It makes a terrific racket — you can hear it right out to the meadow and down the drive. Do go on.'

'Oh, all right then.' He stooped and kissed her carefully on the forehead.

As soon as he was gone, Lisa curled on her side as far as the lump that was the baby would let her, and said forlornly to it, 'What are you playing at? Just tell me that.' And then, because there was no one to see, she allowed two more tears to trickle down and soak into the pillow.

* * *

'This is Simon Frobisher,' said Natasha, 'My granddaughter, Frances Kilworth.'

'How do you do,' said Frances, extending her hand.

Simon Frobisher's grip was hard and assertive. Painful, even, Frances thought, for any woman whose handshake was less firm than her own. She looked at him thoughtfully. He exuded wealth and power as a tom-cat exudes its scent.

'Giles Kilworth's wife,' stated Simon Frobisher. He was a big man, with a charming smile, but he sounded as though he was used to making statements rather than asking questions.

Faintly annoyed, Frances did not reply, but held out her hand to the wife, a woman incongruously dressed in expensive tweeds — a Paris couturier's notion of English country dress — with spike-heeled shoes and too much make-up. She wore a Liberty scarf knotted over her hair, like someone trying to pose as the Queen driving a Land Rover round the Balmoral estate.

'Emileen Frobisher,' said Natasha.

The woman offered a hand like a limp rag to Frances, barely touching her fingers. She jangled with solid gold bracelets and was enveloped in a cloud of too much expensive perfume. 'Oh, we just simply love Giles Kilworth. I'm just devastated that the first series of *Vet in Hot Water* has finished. Is it true that there is going to be another?'

She had a curious accent. Frances, who normally had a good ear, could pick out traces of Birmingham, overlaid with Midwest America and a self-conscious gentility, but couldn't entirely pin it down.

'Yes,' she said. 'They've almost finished filming it.'

'Giles will be here this afternoon,' said Natasha, with the air of someone slipping a hare into a pack of hounds.

Emileen squealed. 'Oh my!' She seized Frances's arm. 'You will introduce me, Frances, won't you? Oh, I'd be just thrilled. Giles Kilworth, fancy!' As she grew more genuinely excited, she lapsed into what must be her native mode of speech, which was definitely laced with the flat vowels of the industrial Midlands.

Gently Frances disengaged herself, feeling unaccountably irritated at this woman using her first name, when she would normally never have given it a thought. Simon Frobisher, clearly aware of her reaction, gave one quick smile to himself, then stepped forward and set himself to charm her.

'I haven't seen St Martins before, Mrs Kilworth. Not properly. I wonder, would it be too much if I asked you to show me round?' He turned on her the full force of his personality, and smiled.

Frances, who was accustomed to professional charmers from Giles's theatrical crowd, nevertheless thawed slightly. 'If you like. Will you be all right, darling?'

'Of course.' Natasha seemed to be sizing them both up with her shrewd eyes. 'You show Simon around and Emileen can stay and talk to me. I'll tell her all about Giles.' As Frances bent over to kiss her briefly, she murmured, 'Don't be too nice to him, doushenka.'

'Now, Emileen,' Frances heard Natasha say, as she led Simon away, 'what would you like to know about my so-famous grandson-in-law?'

★ ★ ★

Frances took Simon round to the far side of the chestnut tree, where he could see the whole of St Martins stretched out beyond the copper beech, from the same angle as Tony's painting. She began to explain the different periods of the building, expecting him to become bored quickly, but he listened intently and asked intelligent questions. She noticed, as she was talking, that some of the roof tiles seemed to have slipped. One whole row dipped gracefully out of line. She couldn't remember seeing that when she had last been here.

From this vantage point, she started back towards the house and caught sight of William sitting in a basket chair under the outstretched branches of the chestnut.

'Have you met my father, Mr Frobisher?'

'How do you do, sir,' said Simon, taking William's trembling hand.

Frances saw her father wince as the other man squeezed.

'Simon Frobisher, Dad. I believe he's quite new to the village.'

William mumbled something she did not catch, so she smiled and nodded at him and said she'd be back later for a proper talk.

'I took Harry for a good walk this morning, Dad. All the way to the Ludbrook. He had a wonderful time.'

William's mouth twisted at one corner in a travesty of a smile.

'Come along this way, Mr Frobisher. I'll show you the main downstairs rooms, and the outbuildings where we have made the studios.'

* * *

For God's sake be careful, Frances, said William to himself. That man's a rogue. He may pretend he hasn't met me before, but he has. I handled the appeal against planning permission for his house four years ago – he defeated me then and that's why he is looking so triumphant now. And it was clients of mine in Stanway Bridges who managed to fight off his project to build an out-of-town supermarket and leisure centre just outside their village. What's he doing here? Natasha must have invited him, I suppose – but you be careful, my girl.

On their way through the house, Frances and Simon Frobisher came across Sally, checking that all the food from the dining room had been taken outside. She was chatting to Alice Tyler. Frances started to perform the introductions.

'Oh, Mrs Kilworth and I have met before,' said Simon. 'I commissioned one of her hangings for my house.' He shook her hand. 'Nice to see you again, Mrs Kilworth.'

'Sally, please,' said Sally. She did not look altogether happy at being confronted with Simon Frobisher, Frances thought.

'And Alice Tyler,' said Simon thoughtfully. 'Haven't I seen a painting of yours in the boardroom at Hever Chemicals?'

'Yes,' Alice said. She was not one to be coy about her successes. 'They bought that at an exhibition of mine a couple of years ago, and the CE later commissioned another for his private collection.'

'I thought it was very striking. I liked the tonal effects of the orange and crimson together.'

Oh, Lord, thought Frances, that's what he is, is he? A rich private collector who wants to talk about Art with a capital A. Well, I'm the wrong person for him then. Natasha needn't worry that I'll be too nice to him; I'm more likely to be too rude.

She was quite glad when Alice attached herself to the guided tour and monopolised Simon's attention.

In the stableyard she showed them the coach-house that had been converted into a house for Nicholas and Sally, and the run of outbuildings with elegant arched doorways, each of which was now a studio.

'Sally has one, and Natasha used to have another, but she doesn't really paint any more, so Desmond Fraser has it for his pottery. I think all the studios are in use at the moment. It always depends on who's living here. And the upper storey — which was once haylofts and quarters for grooms and coachmen — that's been made into music studios. I remember when I was a child the awful trouble they had getting a grand piano up there. Eventually they had to hoist it up on the old tackle that had been used for bales of hay. It spun round and round and we all held our breath, thinking it was going to fall. I think Hugh and I – that's my brother – half hoped that it would! It belongs to Peter Kaufmann and is probably priceless, but we ghoulishly wanted to see all its innards fall out, little savages that we were.'

'And those two doors?' asked Simon, pointing to the wall at right angles to the studios.

'The left-hand door is just a small barn, where everyone stores their bits and pieces. There are probably things left there from fifty years ago. It tends to accumulate easels with broken legs that someone is always going to fix, and half-full tins of house paint, and bicycles with one wheel.'

'And the other one?'

'That's Gregor Baranowski's studio, in the old stables. It extends all along that side of the stableyard. He needs a lot of space.'

'I would be most interested to see – '

'I'm sorry,' said Frances abruptly, suddenly tired of his prying, 'but I'm afraid I can't take you in there. Gregor wouldn't like it at all.'

'What wouldn't Gregor like?' He had come up behind them from the garden. For a big man he moved quietly.

'You wouldn't like me showing people round your studio.'

'No indeed. Mr Frobisher, isn't it?' Gregor put his large, strong hand under the other man's elbow and began to guide him back towards the garden. Simon, as tall though not as broad in the shoulder, looked as though no one had ever dared to do that to him before, but he did not raise any audible objection.

★ ★ ★

Frances is sitting on an upturned orange box in Natasha's studio, watching her paint a still life. The still life was Frances's idea, and she has set it up. Together they have carried out the small fruitwood table from the kitchen – to squawked protests from Mum and Mabel – and arranged on it a white cloth embroidered with red chickens that Natasha bought in Italy before the

114

war. Just off-centre, Frances has placed the green earthenware bowl she particularly loves. It has streaks and swirls of different greens, from a pale lime to a green that is almost black, and has reminded her, since she was very small, of the sea. It too came from Italy, and a small chip at the rim, from its long and busy life, shows the red earth of Umbria in the pottery beneath the glaze. She has piled up in the bowl (and allowed to tumble out of it) all the yellow fruits she can find – lemons, bananas, a grapefruit, and a bunch of very pale yellow-green grapes. Finally she has put a bunch of yellow ragwort, gathered from the hedge, in one of the plain glass kitchen tumblers, and stood it to the right and behind the bowl.

'Paint it crooked,' she suggests, 'from the corner.'

As she watches now, Natasha finishes laying out the underpainting and begins to mix more colours on her battered and paint-studded palette.

'You have a very good eye, doushenka,' says Natasha. 'It is a pity you will not paint.'

Frances smiles and hugs her knees. Natasha has tried very hard to make a painter of her, but she knows now, at fourteen, that she can never be good enough, and has abandoned it firmly. She does not want to settle for second-best. She will be famous in some other way, rather than hang on Natasha's coat-tails.

'It's going to be terrific, Natasha. I love the way you are handling the perspective – accurate but flattened out, if you know what I mean.'

'Yes. Artists began experimenting with perspective at the end of the last century – allowing you to see round the corners, you understand? Then Braque and Picasso took it further with analytical cubism. I like to use it some of the time, but I don't care for the extent of their fragmentation. If this turns out well, you can have it to hang in your room.'

'Can I really?' Frances is delighted. Natasha's canvases mostly have to be sold, for St Martins always seems to need money, however hard everyone tries. She will keep the picture always, if she is given it. It will remind her of this warm Saturday afternoon in autumn, with the leaves beginning to drift into the stableyard behind her, and the sound of Peter playing something exciting and crashing in his music room above their heads.

'I love the greens and yellows together, sort of fresh and spicy, and the bits of red embroidery adding little bits of warmth.'

'Perhaps you should think of a career in design – '

But Frances simply smiles again at Natasha's back, in its familiar paint-stained smock.

There is a clatter of boys' clumsy feet on the stone slabs and Hugh and Gregor darken the doorway.

'Light!' says Natasha imperiously, and they slink round the wall to Frances.

'We were sent to tell you it's teatime,' says Hugh. 'Iced buns from the village.'

'Some things, Hugh, are even more important than iced buns. The bloom on the grapes – that will be gone by tomorrow. I must finish them today. Sometimes, you have to seize the moment, or you lose it for ever.'

★ ★ ★

'Granny?' Chrissie tugged at Frances's sleeve.

'Hello, darling. Hello, Samira – are you enjoying the party?'

'Yes, thank you very much, Mrs Kilworth,' said Samira with her usual good manners. 'Thank you for inviting me.' She looked a bit tense, though, as though bursting to say something.

'Granny, you've got to help us!' Chrissie pleaded dramatically.

'What's the matter, have you broken something?' Frances smiled at them, both so earnest – Chrissie, fair, dishevelled, dungareed, and Samira, beautifully turned out, with white ankle socks that positively shone against her warm brown legs.

'Samira desperately wants one of Jeannie's puppies. I'm going to have one, and we could train them together, and take them for walks – '

'I'm sure she can have one. Sally's promised one to Miss Bagshaw. She says she'll feel safer with a dog, since that time the motorbike riders vandalised the bus shelter just along the road from her. But I don't think any of the others have homes yet.' (Miss Bagshaw, Frances recalled, had specified a *lady* dog.)

'My mother will not let me,' Samira burst out, love and

desire overcoming her habitual politeness. 'Oh, Mrs Kilworth, he is so beautiful!'

'*Please* would you help, Granny? He knows her already. Tell Mrs Patel that Samira's *got* to have him.'

'I certainly wouldn't say that, Chrissie. But I will try. I'll talk to her some time this afternoon. I'm sure Samira would look after a puppy very well.' And, she thought privately, a puppy is just what that dear girl needs, to bring her out of herself a bit. She needs a companion, she can't always be up here with Chrissie. And she needs something she can get into a mess with.

'I promise,' she said firmly. 'I'll do everything I can.'

★ ★ ★

Lisa had dozed fitfully and woken again, thinking that she detected some movement from the baby. She lay now, watching the motes of dust swirling in the sunlight that poured in through the window and listening to the sound of voices in the garden. Children were rushing about making that noise you heard on a beach, a sort of sustained happy scream. Last night Sally and Irina had had an argument about what to do with the younger children at the garden party. Irina wanted to shut them all away in a crêche set up in the old dairy, with a rota of volunteers to look after them. She was nervous of over-excited children, and worried about the damage they might do to themselves and the garden. Sally had been adamant that the party was as much for them as for the adults, and that they should be allowed to run about as they pleased. The rough grass on the lower ground below the ha-ha would come to no harm, she pointed out. From the sounds floating through the window, it seemed Sally had won.

Lisa remembered her mother talking about some of the scrapes she and Hugh had got into as children, and smiled. Perhaps Irina had a point. Though she herself would make sure that her own children had plenty of freedom and fresh air. She had always looked forward to the summer holidays of her childhood when Frances had packed them into the car and brought them down to St Martins. They had gone berserk, wild with stored up energy after a winter of confinement at the house in Reading, with its two medium-sized bedrooms and a single room like a cubby-hole, where she and Tony had for many years been squashed into bunk beds. When Anya left home for university, Tony had joined Nicholas in the larger room – previously divided with a curtain down the middle – and Lisa, at nine, had the tiny room to herself until Katya was born. She swore to Paul she would never put their children through the claustrophobia and lack of privacy she had endured.

'It's a wonder you are all still speaking to each other,' he had laughed. As an only child, much cosseted by elderly parents, he had no real understanding of what she was talking about.

Listening to the sound of the children, Lisa fantasised about coming to live at St Martins. Whenever she arrived, even now – grown-up and with a pleasant terraced house of her own – she felt herself relaxing into a state of contentment. Lucky Nick and Sally! If only Paul could get a job nearby – or if he would consider driving to Worcester every day . . . No, that wouldn't be fair to him.

She was half dozing again when there was a hesitant tap on the door.

'Yes?' she murmured sleepily.

Tony put his head round the door, followed, at ankle level, by Seurat. 'How are you doing?'

'OK,' said Lisa, heaving herself up, and surprisingly glad to see him.

'I thought you might like something to eat.' Tony disappeared into the hall again, then reappeared with a tray. 'I've brought a bit of everything I thought you'd enjoy. No cold sausages, I know you can't stand those. These *dolmades* Spiro made are great. And the honey cake is brilliant.'

He put the tray down on the bedside table and scooped Seurat out of the door. 'Oh, no you don't, my lad. You've had your share already.' He closed the door firmly on the cat and plumped up Lisa's pillows behind her head with more kindness than skill.

Looking at the food as he balanced the tray on her almost

vanished lap, Lisa felt suddenly greedy. 'Do you know,' she said, 'I'm starving!'

'Good. I'll stay and talk to you while you eat.' He perched beside her on the bed.

'How's the painting going? Have you sold anything recently?' Lisa asked, picking up some leaves from one of Sally's multi-coloured salads and nibbling.

Tony looked glum.

'Only one, about six weeks ago. If I didn't have that one morning's teaching a week at the art college, I'd be starving to death.'

'Thank heavens for teaching! Paul and Anya make their living at it. It keeps you off the streets, and without Mum's part-time lecturing we would all have been in dire straits years ago.'

'I don't think Anya really does make a living at it, you know. Grandad has been helping her out. Now he's had this stroke, I'm not sure what will happen. Nick has power of attorney.'

'He wouldn't hold back the money, would he, if Grandad wanted her to have it?'

'Oh no, but Nick's a great believer in self-reliance. He might put the pressure on her a bit, to get a viable job. I've had the odd lecture from him myself.'

'Has Grandad . . .?' asked Lisa delicately.

'No. He did offer. But like Mum I'm a bit pig-headed, I suppose. I said I was determined to make my own way. He was always there as a back-up, of course.' He grinned, and picked bits out of Lisa's cheese. 'Mum's giving up her lectureship at the poly – at the end of this term. Katya told me in the car, coming down yesterday. Did you know?'

'No!' Lisa stopped eating and stared at him. 'I never thought she'd do that. I suppose Dad must be making a lot more money now, with that sitcom thing.'

'You know Dad. Easy come, easy go. I'll bet he's spent most of it already. Savile Row suits, lunch at the Savoy Grill, a few crates of expensive bottles.'

'I thought Mum liked to have some money of her own anyway, even when Dad is doing all right. It gives her some independence.'

'Lisa, you are an idiot,' Tony said tolerantly. 'She's spent every penny she earned on all of us. She's been keeping us off the breadline for years. You didn't really think she's ever saved anything up for herself, did you?'

'I don't know. I suppose I never really thought about it. She always seemed to have enough to see us all through college or university, and get us started. What about Katya, though? She's got another five years at school. And university afterwards — she's bound to want to go, whatever she says now. She's brighter than all the rest of us put together. That's been her big problem at school.'

'Mmm.' Tony chewed on a stick of celery. 'You're right. I don't know what Mum's planning to do about Katya. Someone needs to do something. She's pretty miserable at the moment, poor thing. I don't know about you, but I've been feeling a bit guilty lately.'

'Guilty?'

'Yeah.' He began to plait three spring onions together. 'When you and I both cleared out four years ago, I never thought about Katya being left behind. The last one of us. And you remember . . . There were always tensions. Dad and his tarty women . . . '

'She'd be better away from that awful school. I wasn't ever happy there, but at least I was boringly inconspicuous.'

'It's got a lot worse since we were there. It's really tough — bullying, drugs, you name it.'

'Poor Katya. She'd be happier in a nice quiet, non-confrontational school. Paul might have some ideas.'

'Yeah.' Tony looked at her sideways. 'But Mum — what do you make of her? Mid-life crisis? Change of life?'

'I wouldn't know,' said Lisa primly. 'Maybe she's had enough, now most of us have left home.' She couldn't imagine herself ever reaching such a state, but Mum was middle-aged — over fifty. Confidently Lisa knew that she would manage her own life better. 'You see her more often than I do, living in London and scrounging meals the way you do.'

'Well, why not? I've only mastered beans on toast and scrambled eggs, though Bill does an acceptable omelette. We eat out sometimes, but mostly we can't afford it. Our own cooking gets pretty boring.' Absent-mindedly he began to nibble one of the dolmades, dribbling bits of filling on Lisa's duvet cover. 'Mum does seem to have been in a funny mood lately. Restless and a bit short tempered, which isn't like her, is it? You know how she always used to be able to drown herself in a book, even when we were all crashing around, fighting and roaring. She can't even seem to read now. Just keeps jumping up and fiddling about. There's a kind of atmosphere about the house. It's worse when Dad's there, of course, especially when he brings his arty-farty friends.'

Tony, who knew he had genuine talent, even if he lacked the drive to make the most of it, had long been contemptuous of most of his father's theatrical crowd. 'I'm not surprised Katya's being so difficult lately. It must be awful, being the only one, with the rest of us gone.'

He had finished art college – commuting to London daily – a few weeks before Lisa had married. They had moved out of the mean little house in Reading in the same month. Now Lisa had a house bigger than the one she had grown up in, and his own big airy studio flat, though having to be shared with the amiable Bill, gave him a great sense of freedom. He felt nothing but pity for Katya. And for Mum, of course.

'I haven't had a chance to speak to Alice yet,' said Lisa. 'Are you two serious about each other?'

'I'm serious,' said Tony, gloomy again. 'She thinks I'm a bit wet because I can't get my act together. We both had two years off after A Levels, but she went round the world while all I did was bum around doing part-time jobs in cafés and night-clubs. Now, four years out of art school and I haven't had a single one-man exhibition yet.'

'She's terribly successful, isn't she?'

'Yeah. She's got this creative artist fellowship, and she's had annual exhibitions for the last five years, ever since she left college. One of the posh Sunday supplements even did an article about her.'

'She's older than you are.'

'Only a year.'

'And she's got commercial sense. That doesn't mean she's the better artist.'

'Maybe not.' Tony was honest about this. 'But she's always going to be more successful than I am.'

'She certainly looks terrific. She makes me feel like a barrage balloon.'

'That's part of the trouble. All these millionaires keep falling for her. Right now she's in a huddle with that awful new man in the village – Simon Frobisher. I might as well not exist.'

'Poor old Tony.' Lisa had first been through a scene like this with Tony when he was fifteen, but the elegant, detached pose he had acquired at art college had meant that in recent years it was usually the girls who were in pursuit of him. This time he sounded as though he was in a bad state about this Alice. Privately, Lisa thought she looked a hard-faced woman.

She licked the honey off her fingers. Spiro's Greek cake was delicious, but something was troubling her insides. Perhaps she shouldn't have wolfed all that food down quite so fast. A sharp pain rose in her back, spread round her stomach like gripping hands and then subsided.

'Maybe you shouldn't look at her quite so much like Harry asking to be taken for a walk?' she suggested. 'Play a little hard to get. It's always worked in the past.'

Tony turned to her with a look of real misery. 'I've tried. I can't pull it off. It's all I can do not to follow her around with my tongue hanging out.'

Lisa gave a small gasp as another pain hit her.

'You all right?' asked Tony. 'Finished with the tray?'

'Yes,' said Lisa in a tight voice. 'I think I've stupidly given myself indigestion.'

'Bad luck.' Tony moved the tray on to the bedside table and patted her shoulder absently. He walked over to the window. Down in the garden, Alice was still talking to Simon Frobisher. He had hoped that his visit to Lisa might have made Alice miss him, but she didn't even seem to have noticed. From behind him, he heard another gasp from Lisa. As he turned around, she said in a small voice,

'Tony, you'd better get Paul. And ask Mabel to phone for the doctor. I think the baby might be coming.'

Chapter 7

'THE GREAT ECCENTRICS,' said Nigel, crumbling his garlic bread. 'That's the working title. 'Gives me plenty of scope. But the approach is going to be serious. An in-depth study of the social relevance of eccentricity in English cultural development over the last four hundred years. Part history, part art and culture, part sociological documentary. None of this galloping about taking a cutesie look at funny buildings and telling gushing anecdotes. This will be the first time the significance of the socially non-norm-oriented behaviour of the so-called eccentric will have been examined and given a public airing on prime-time television. Ten two-hour slots.' He could not keep the triumph out of his voice, although it jarred with his usual pose of nonchalant indifference.

'Do you have anyone lined up yet?' Giles asked casually, taking a pull at his beer. Nigel was right. He was a wine man himself, but this was really something, this beer.

'I've got a list of experts as long as your arm. I'm just starting to approach them, but that won't be a problem. They'll jump at it.' Nigel began to eat his *salade aux fruits de mer* with rapidity. 'You know what they're like, these academics. Queuing up to get their names on the telly. I don't need to pay much attention to what they say, I just want their names in the line-up, to lend the whole thing weight. This is my baby, and I'm going to make it the way I want. I'm directing and producing, with Jack Witherspoon as my number two.'

That was good, thought Giles. Jack was 100 per cent top quality. Where Nigel had the creative flair and the ability to raise the funds, Jack would ensure that each production was meticulous and everything ran smoothly. He couldn't, however, quite see where he himself would fit in. He was beginning to hope – just a very faint whisper of a hope – that Nigel was going to ask him to front the series, to do a Michael Wood. For a brief moment he felt almost dizzy with excitement, then he reined himself in. Surely Nigel would be wanting to do that himself?

'This is going to be the series that gives me the world ratings, old boy,' said Nigel, who affected a dated slang along with his bow-ties and collar-length hair. 'Remember *Civilisation*? Well, this is going to do for cultural eccentrics what Clark did for mainstream culture. We're already in negotiation with companies in the States and Europe, but that is all completely hush-hush at the moment, so not a word to anyone. I want to get the deals sewn up before I release the news to the press – the BIG story all in one go.'

He's definitely going to front it himself, thought Giles.

'Here are some of the personalities and places I've roughed out.' Nigel pushed aside his half-eaten salad and pulled several folded sheets of paper from the inside pocket of his golden calf-suede bomber jacket. 'Cast your eyes over those.' He took a jaunty gulp of his beer.

It did look good. Giles ate with one hand and grasped the notes in the other. He had to hold them some distance away from him, because he had left his reading glasses in the pocket of his overcoat, which was lying on the back seat of Nigel's car.

'This is brilliant,' he said, truthfully. There was a lot of interesting stuff here. Handled properly, it could make a fantastic series.

'Like the other half?' Nigel got up without waiting for an answer and made his way to the bar. He was the kind of man for whom crowds gave way. Despite the Saturday lunchtime press, he passed straight through and was served immediately by the barman.

Halfway down the second page of the notes, Giles saw 'St Martins: commune for artists and musicians. Pre-dated sixties movements by nearly twenty years. Leading eccentric: Natasha Devereux, Russian archduchess. Survival of the aristocratic patron. Prime site for visuals. Sculptor/recluse: Gregor Baranowski. Works found in major collections world-wide. Exclusive interview??? Peter Kaufmann, Auschwitz victim. Totalitarianism and art??? How commune run. How out-lasted sixties. Free love???'

Nigel set the beer down on the table and looked at Giles. 'Well?'

Giles took a drink to give himself time, and started again on his steak and kidney pie.

'It looks really fantastic, Nigel. Great stuff. But it's a good thing you're coming down to see St Martins for yourself!' He gave a laugh, to take away the sting. 'It isn't quite like that.' He pointed with his knife at the papers.

'OK, fine. Give,' said Nigel imperturbably.

'Well, it isn't a commune in the sixties sense, it's a residential trust. Everyone pays rent according to their means into the trust funds. It's all very organised, with a committee and proper trust documents. Natasha's husband Edmund set all that up before he was killed in the war.'

'OK. I buy that.' Nigel was scribbling in a notebook.

'Also, Natasha is a princess, not an archduchess.'

'Same thing,' said Nigel dismissively.

'And she doesn't like people to make a thing of it.'

Nigel shrugged.

'She's also pretty hard up. She's more of a leader and guiding light than a patron. She had to make her own way, you know, as a painter. In post-World-War-I Paris.'

'Yeah, I knew she painted.'

Giles felt a slight twinge of doubt at Nigel's offhand tone. How well had Nigel done his homework? One did not say of Natasha that she had just 'painted'. She had been famous between the wars, a leading figure in the art world – and even more famous afterwards, if it came to that. His own interest in Frances had first been aroused because someone had told him whose granddaughter she was.

'Also, it may be quite difficult to get interviews with either Gregor or Peter. They're both very wary of publicity.'

'Ah, but with you on the inside –!' Nigel flashed him a brilliant smile.

Giles swallowed. 'Well, naturally, I'll do my best. But I felt I had to warn you.'

'Sure, sure.'

'And absolutely no free love.' For a brief, wild moment, Giles tried to envisage Irina and Mabel in the context of free love, and snorted some of his beer down the wrong way. Nigel thumped him sympathetically on the back.

'You're right about the visuals, though,' said Giles, when he could speak again. 'It's an amazing place. Practically every architectural period from the Middle Ages to the end of the eighteenth century. And because the family has never had a great deal of money, most of it's stayed unaltered, apart from the Georgian façade slapped on to the front of the sixteenth-century house. There's a vast, rambling garden that Frances and her brother ran wild in when they were children. Kids love it. Ours used to howl like anything when we brought them home from holidays there. You could get some brilliant wide-angled shots of the house across the grounds. Birgit and Peter Kaufmann laid out the gardens in the fifties, with different areas to represent different periods of St Martins – a Tudor knot garden, a formal parterre, and so on. You could do something with that – marry them to the corresponding bits of the house. Aerial shots, too – coming up over the meadow from the Ludbrook and swinging round over the chapel and the house.' Giles found he was getting quite excited himself.

'There's a chapel? Great!' Nigel scribbled again. 'What about the studios?'

'Old barns and stables. Very cleverly done. Natasha designed them herself, and did the whole conversion with the help of one local joiner and the founder members of the community. It was pretty amazing, I suppose, given post-war austerity. The acoustics in the music rooms are supposed to be very good. You could use that. Have a shot of a quartet, maybe, rehearsing in one of the studios.'

'Right. You said 'community'?'

'Yes, it's never been called a commune. That would give the wrong impression altogether.'

'I'm thinking of using St Martins for the lead programme. It has all that variety – architecture, gardens, music, painting, sculpture, ceramics, and so on. A microcosm of what we'll be covering throughout the series. Except – the piece I read didn't mention any writers.'

Ah, thought Giles. He's only read that piece in the Sunday supplement about the fiftieth anniversary. He hasn't researched it at all yet. That gives me a bit of an edge.

'Writers haven't been a major factor. There was someone, I believe, who was part of the verse drama movement in the fifties, but that was before my time. He went off to be a professor at an Australian university, I think. There's another dramatist there now, Jonathan Deerley. You'll know his stuff, of course.' Call his bluff, thought Giles.

'Sure, sure,' said Nigel gracefully, without batting an eyelid. 'He'll do. We'll just have a few excerpts from his work – background material.'

'Not sure he's very suitable,' said Giles, thinking of Jonathan's turgid and impenetrable prose going out to the prime-time TV audience. 'Of course, we could always use other Herefordshire writers.' He noticed that he had used 'we', unconsciously allying himself with the project.

'Good idea.' Nigel scribbled. 'Er – Housman.'

Giles bit back the urge to say, 'No, that's Shropshire.' Better not risk getting up Nigel's nose. He contented himself with a noncommittal grunt.

He had noticed an omission from Nigel's notes. 'Of course,' he said, calmly, 'there's Hugh Appleton.'

'Hugh Appleton? *Hugh Appleton* has some connection with St Martins?'

'Yes,' said Giles, sitting back and looking complacently at Nigel. 'He's my brother-in-law.'

'Holy Moses,' said Nigel reverently. 'Any chance we could get an interview with him?'

'I'll see what I can do.' Giles waved his hand airily. 'I may be able to fix it for you.'

Having played this trump card, he waited to see whether Nigel was going to reveal what, exactly, he had in mind for Giles. He was conscious of being on firmer ground now.

Nigel made further notes, then laid down his pen and drank some more of his beer. 'Now, I expect you'd like to know how you fit into the picture.'

Giles nodded, with the right mixture of interest and unconcern.

'I see this as a very *visual* series. Lots of subtle camera work. Even with the face-to-face interviews, I plan to have quite a lot of it happening off camera while the visuals reinforce the verbals – a *layered* feel to it, a kind of metaphor for the whole deeper significance of the meaning I am planning to convey.'

Get on with it, thought Giles. Stop waffling about. He smiled knowingly and nodded.

'So I want you for the voice-overs,' said Nigel.

Voice-overs. Giles felt as though he was sagging in his chair like a punctured balloon. To hide this from Nigel, he took up his knife and fork again, to finish his pie. It was difficult to be sure whether rage or disappointment had the upper hand.

'Voice-overs,' he said neutrally.

Nigel watched the other man clinically. He was ten years younger than Giles, and looked after himself. He could (and did) pass for thirty-nine when he chose. How could an actor let himself go like that? Couldn't the old fool see what a chance he was being offered? He'd never be more than a mediocre actor. This latest thing he'd done had brought him to the attention of the public, which was one reason Nigel wanted him, but it was a flash in the pan and wouldn't be sustained. Chums in the business had told him the second series was going to flop. But Giles had a great voice, one of *the* great voices around at the moment. Look at him – ageing, balding, *fat* – who did he think he was: Gielgud or Olivier at thirty? Stuffing himself with all that animal grease and fat. Nigel's ascetic lip curled slightly. But he wanted that voice, so he became persuasive.

'I've never understood why you haven't done it before, Giles. With *your* voice – you should be fighting the punters off.

Look at all the top names doing voice-overs for cultural series nowadays: Anna, Tony – all the people with the top-rank voices.' To put the fellow at his ease he picked daintily at a king prawn covered with a rocket and lovage dressing.

'Well . . .' said Giles. He was thinking furiously. Nigel was right. There *were* some top names in the business doing this kind of voice-over narration now. You got a major credit line. And the studio work, building the narration around the edited tapes, could be fitted in with other commitments. It was going to be something really big, Nigel's series. It gave you a kind of status, doing that sort of thing. One of our senior actors. Great names of the theatre. He rolled the phrases around in his mind, seeing the reviews in his mind's eye. He had, with difficulty, let go of his image of himself as a glamorous leading man when he had agreed to *Vet in Hot Water*. But he wasn't entirely at ease with the notion of himself as a sitcom man. He'd always been a serious actor, damn it!

Culture, with a touch of humour, looking at eccentrics. But – not to be on camera!

He tried out his voice inside his head – rolling, sonorous, with an underlying warmth. This man, the viewers would feel, knows a thing or two about life.

'Well,' he said again, consideringly. 'It certainly sounds interesting, Nigel. Of course, I'm not quite sure how things are going to work out with *Vet*. We may be doing another series,' he lied manfully. 'I'll need to have a word with Peregrine, see what else he has lined up for me.'

'Actually,' said Nigel, gathering up his belongings and standing up, 'I've already had a quick word with Peregrine. He seemed very keen, but he wanted me to tell you all about it myself. So you'll come on board then?'

'Yes,' said Giles. Then, not wanting to sound churlish, 'Great. Really great. I'll look forward to it.'

*   *   *

'Definitely contractions,' said Dr Porter, winding up his stethoscope and packing it away into his bag. 'As your waters haven't broken yet, it might just be a false alarm, but we'll get you into the maternity unit where we can keep an eye on you. Your blood pressure is up a bit too.'

'It has been up for a couple of weeks,' said Lisa. 'My doctor in Worcester said it wasn't enough to worry about.'

'No more it is, but you'll be better going straight into hospital now. Is there someone who can drive you, or shall I phone for an ambulance? You'll be quicker by car.'

'My husband can take me.' Lisa drew her breath in suddenly, with a sharp hiss, between her teeth. She was determined not to make a fuss about this business of giving birth, but the pains clutching her were worse than anything she had ever experienced or imagined.

'No rush,' said the doctor calmly, as Paul came back into the bedroom. He was used to dealing with first-time fathers and their panic reactions. 'Just pack an overnight bag for your wife and get her gently down to the car. I'll phone through to the maternity unit, then I'll drive into Hereford behind you and see you safely installed. Take your time. It may all come to nothing – another four weeks, did you say, till baby is due? Even if he's decided to put in an appearance early, these things always take much longer than you might suppose, especially first babies.'

At the bottom of the wide old staircase Frances was waiting for him. They were old friends. Jim Porter had seen all her children through illnesses and broken limbs on their childhood visits to St Martins. They looked at one another.

'Not a false alarm, is it, Jim?'

'Could be, but I doubt it. All yours were early, weren't they? I remember, Frances, the scare you gave me when you started to produce Katya down here on my patch – what was it, fourteen years ago?'

'Thirteen. I remember it well. You hadn't had an over-forty mother before.'

'Scared me to death, but you took it very calmly.'

'I was so pleased that she was going to be born here, right at St Martins. My old doctor in Reading had retired and I didn't like the new man. I was pleased as Punch she decided

131

to arrive when she did. Probably the only time in her life Katya's ever been early for anything.'

'Three hours flat. We *could* have got you into hospital, you know. There would have been time, but you were so stubborn.'

She smiled serenely. 'I knew everything was going to be fine. I'd already had four, remember. I could just feel things were all right.'

'Luckily for us both, they were. Look, could I use your phone? I want to alert the maternity unit.'

★ ★ ★

I can feel myself floating, thinks Frances. She has politely but firmly refused all forms of painkiller and the portable gas machine. I've managed without before, she says. I can do it again.

With Anya, the pain had been terrible. How can something so natural tear you apart? Why should the giving of life be accompanied by this terrible, devastating pain? No wonder the authors of Genesis felt compelled to find a logical explanation for it. 'In sorrow thou shalt bring forth children.' Old *male* patriarchs. She wept with the unfairness of it during the thirty-six hours of hell Anya put her through, but her determination not to lose control of her body, to manage the pain, made her refuse any relief for it.

'*Pregnant!*' Giles had shouted. 'You're pregnant? God, you've really cocked things up, haven't you?'

Her own first thought had been, *We've* really cocked it up. She counted the months. The baby would arrive only a few weeks before her final examinations. Would she be allowed to sit them? The college had made enough fuss about her marrying. It was against college regulations. Eventually they had made an exception, but how would they react to this? She was half appalled and half elated at the thought of the baby, still unde-tectable but alive there inside her. But at Giles's reaction she was immediately upset and on the defensive. She cried a good deal, uncontrollably, unlike herself, and eventually he calmed down and accepted the situation.

But having survived Anya's birth, she knew that she could

manage any physical pain life chose to throw at her afterwards. When Nicholas was born two years later, she was prepared. It was an easier birth, perhaps because she was more relaxed, but took almost as long. With Tony and Lisa, it was each time a little easier.

Now she is floating above the cloud of pain, in her own childhood bed in St Martins. That is somehow fitting. She feels she has come full circle from the time she first slept in this room, during the last year of the war, amazed at being given a full sized, grown-up bed and a room to herself. The room has never been redecorated since, for money is always tight at St Martins. Along the wall under the window are the Peter Rabbit pictures she cut out and glued up without permission. Over the fireplace, rather faded from the sun, is the poster of Monet's water-lilies given to her by Gregor and pinned up in her Impressionist phase. The drawing-pins are still in place, pushed in by her seventeen-year-old fingers, more than half her lifetime ago.

It is curious the way she is outside her own body. It has never felt like this before, giving birth. Somewhere she read about a near-death experience, where a man described floating above his body and looking down. And there she can see herself, lying on the bed, with the doctor and the midwife bending over her. That is myself, thinks Frances, down there. And yet I am here. And the pain is quite separate from the me who is here. The pain is outside me, down there. I can feel it, and yet I do not suffer it. How strange, and fascinating.

She smiles.

There is a sudden thin cry, like a cat.

This, she knows, will be a special baby.

*   *   *

Katya and Gregor sat companionably side by side on the ha-ha, with their legs dangling over into the rough grass verges beyond. Gregor had spent an hour being polite to the guests, which was as long as he felt he could cope with at one stretch. He had also managed to speak to Keith, who was still physically recognisable as the terrified child who had turned up on the doorstep all those years ago, when Gregor was about fifteen. He was as tall as Gregor now, but painfully thin, as though that childhood deprivation had left its permanent mark on him. Otherwise, he had blossomed into a warm, confident man, with a shaggy bush of badly cut hair, and such a consuming passion still for his music that he could hardly bear to speak of anything else. Germany suited him quite well, he said. He had no worries over funding, and the quality of the orchestra was outstanding. But he thought that when this contract came to an end, he would not stay on. He wanted to bring music to the countries struggling to find their feet after the collapse of communism in Eastern Europe.

'They've no money, of course,' he said to Gregor. 'And so many of the opera houses and concert halls are in a terrible state of repair. But at least they haven't been pulled down to make way for office blocks or inner ring roads. I don't need any money for myself. I have more than I know what to do with already. I don't want anything.'

Gregor observed that Keith's suit was as worn and baggy as the one he himself possessed, hanging in solitary state in his wardrobe.

'What about the orchestras?'

'Well, there are problems, of course. With the collapse of the centralised bureaucracy, there's often no one to pay their salaries, and some of the players – with dependants to support – have drifted away. And inflation just shoots through the roof. But I'll think of something. I'd like to start with an orchestra that still has a core of good people and build it up. Do some foreign tours to earn the hard currency, say six months in every year, then spend the rest of the time giving concerts in small towns – or villages, even – for tiny prices. Not free – people tend to despise what is free, or in that part of the world, distrust it. But, say, for the price of a couple of glasses of beer.'

'It sounds a great idea, if you can pull it off.'

'Oh, I will,' said Keith with conviction. 'I will.'

Someone else had claimed Sir Keith then, and Gregor had found himself waylaid by a terrible woman, all clanking brace-

lets and thick lipstick, who had cornered him in the herb
garden.

'Oh, Mr Baranowski – *is* that how you pronounce it? – I'm
so thrilled to meet you at last! We've been in the village for
over a year now, and I've never been so *close*.'

She stepped a little nearer. Gregor tried to retreat, but found
he was backed up against the box hedge.

'I'm Emileen Frobisher,' she said, giving him her hand, which
he felt obliged to take and then found difficult to get rid of.
She leaned against him.

'I've seen you driving past, of course, but never thought I'd
get the chance to meet you. Then when we got the Princess's
invitation, I was so thrilled, you have no idea!'

Gregor was temporarily baffled by this. He could not, for
the moment, think who she was referring to. The woman
reminded him powerfully of certain Californian matrons who
had the same habit of backing him into a corner and then
standing too close to him. He looked around, slightly panic-
stricken, for a means of escape.

'Gregor!' Katya was shouting to him from the other side of
the herb garden. 'Can you come and lend a hand?'

'If you would just excuse me,' he muttered to the woman,
giving her back her hand, which fluttered for a moment on his
arm, causing more panic. 'I must go.'

As he dived along the camomile path to Katya he heard
Emileen Frobisher saying in a loud stage whisper to another
woman, 'Of course he's a *genius*, you know. He has works in
the Metropolitan *and* the Getty.'

'Thank God, Katya,' he said on reaching her. 'Who sent
you?'

'Personal rescue mission,' she laughed, grabbing his hand and
dragging him away to the wilder end of the garden. 'I could
see that woman had her talons into you, so I thought I'd better
beam you out.'

They ensconced themselves beyond the orchard, above the
rough ground turned over to the younger children. Katya had
some cake wrapped up in a paper napkin, which she shared
with him. 'Made it myself,' she said carelessly.

'We ought to be back there, being polite,' said Gregor, without much guilt, as they sat on the ha-ha, picking the bits of fruit out of the cake.

'Phooey,' said Katya. 'I've done my bit for the moment. Helped cook the food. Helped serve the food for nearly two hours. Mopped up the messes the kids have spilt on the tables all round the garden. Mopped up the kids. Taken a zillion of them to the loo when they've drunk themselves silly on orange juice. I deserve a break. So do you. We can't have our resident *genius* wearing himself out.' She imitated Emileen Frobisher and then dissolved into giggles.

'You mind your manners, young woman,' he said, punching her on the shoulder. 'I'll genius you.'

She punched him in return, then leaned back and plucked a juicy grass stem to chew. 'You are a lucky beast, Gregor. I wish I could live here, and do what I please, and be totally happy and contented.'

'I do *work*, you know,' he said equably, selecting a piece of flat grass and whistling through it.

'Yeah, but it's fun work. I loathe everything I have to do. I loathe school. I loathe Reading. I loathe Mum and Dad.'

'You don't really, you know. That's all just part of being a teenager. Happens to all of us.'

'Yes, but you didn't *have* any parents when you were a teenager.' She rolled over on her stomach, suddenly appalled and contrite. 'Oh, I'm sorry, Gregor. I didn't mean it. That was a stupid thing to say.'

'It's all right. I do understand the point you're trying to make. Because I lost my parents while I was still a child, I never went through this period of stress with them that you're going through. Trying to make them see that you are growing up, that you're a separate person, with a separate life.'

'You sound as though you do understand. I wish Mum did.'

'Oh, I think she does. She was just the same. Only, of course she had to rebel against St Martins, to get away from here,' he plucked thoughtfully at the grass. 'Which was not, in the long run, the best thing she could have done.'

'But you didn't have anyone to rebel against, did you?'

'Oh, yes, I did! I had lots of substitute parents, you see. Natasha and Irina and William and Mabel and Birgit and Peter, all trying to make it up to me that I had lost my own parents – and what made it worse was that I couldn't ever forget how grateful I was to be here at all. I was very mixed up, I promise you.'

'But your life is great now. You've had everything. All that time you spent going round the world, living in Europe and Australia and California. And being famous. And now living here. You're so lucky. And you're the most peaceful person I know, next to Natasha.'

'Am I?' said Gregor, sadly. 'There are a lot of things missing in my life, you know. I'm not a very complete person.'

'What's missing, for heaven's sake? You've got it all.'

At first Katya thought he was not going to answer her. He was pulling the seed heads off the long grass in a distracted way, then he turned to her.

'What's missing?'

He began to lay the seed heads in a line on the ground between them.

'Wife,' he said, counting on the seed heads. 'Sons. Daughters. Posterity. Someone to talk to in the long cold hours of the night.'

She stared at him, then looked down at the grass heads. 'But you chose that,' she mumbled uncertainly. 'You chose not to marry or have children. You chose your art instead. Didn't you?'

'Did I?' he said.

He gathered the seed heads up into his hand and looked at them. Then he crushed them together in his fist and threw them into the long grass verge.

★ ★ ★

Frances climbed slowly up the spiral stone staircase to her old room, which was located at the top of the square tower tacked on to one end of the house. There was an unresolved scholarly dispute about this tower. Some experts argued that it had been added when St Martins had fallen into the hands of a minor landowner after the seizure of church lands, at the time of the Reformation. Others, having more recently examined the building in detail, maintained that it was part of the original monastic structure. Although its purpose was clearly defensive, they assured Natasha that this was perfectly in accord with the fact that St Martins was only two miles from the Welsh border and vulnerable to attack in the late Norman period. Even religious houses needed to be defended.

Whatever the truth of the matter, the tower had always seemed ancient to Frances. When she had first come here as a small child, she had been too young to have any true conception of time, but as she had grown older the tower – with its staircase worn hollow by passing feet and its narrow window slots at the lower levels – had conveyed to her a sense of generations of former inhabitants, stretching back deep into time. The top room, her room (and the only tower room regularly used), was quite spacious, filling the whole of the highest floor. Its windows too had been enlarged at some time several centuries before, so that they afforded views in all four directions. Whatever the time of day, it was filled with light. It also caught the wind and rain when a storm was blowing. It had given her a special delight to sit up here alone on a stormy night, feeling as though she were at sea in a tall ship. Hugh used to tease her about it, calling it her crow's nest.

This morning she had only had time to leave her small suitcase and run a quick brush through her hair before she was caught up in the preparations for the anniversary. But now, after seeing Paul and Lisa off on their way to Hereford, she was suddenly overcome by fatigue, and had escaped here for a brief rest before the village school children gave their concert on the lawn by the sunken garden. It was only natural she should feel tired, she argued with herself, after her early start, her car journey, and the party preparations, but the weariness seemed to go deeper than that.

'Mum,' Lisa had said, clinging to her briefly. 'Oh, Mum.'

'Let me come with you, darling.'

'No,' Lisa said firmly, getting into the car. 'I'll be fine. It's probably nothing. I'll send Paul back to report. You must stay here for the party.'

Paul had driven away, with infinitely slow care, followed by Jim Porter, who leaned out of the window calling, 'Don't worry. Everything's under control.' He disappeared around the bend in the drive, waving his hand above the roof of the car.

Frances sat on her bed, on the old Amish quilt Natasha had brought back to her flat in Chelsea after an exhibition of her paintings in Philadelphia in 1932, before the modern passion for patchwork had pushed the price of antique quilts so high. Natasha had told Frances once that she had given $5 for the quilt in a little back-street shop. 'That was equivalent to about £1 in those days.'

The quilt was a modest one, in decent pieces of navy print on white, white print on scarlet, and scarlet on navy. The interlocked loops formed a traditional pattern which was called 'Wedding Ring', she remembered. She traced the curved shapes, so painstakingly fitted together with tiny, nineteenth-century stitches, and wondered whose wedding trousseau it had once belonged to. She gazed round the room fondly. The well loved Beatrix Potter pictures were still stuck below the window, their edges frayed with age and some of their corners curling away from the dried-up glue. What a monster I was, she thought, cutting up those beautiful books. What can have possessed me? She could not now remember a time when she had not respected, even revered, the integrity of books. The Monet poster had faded to an almost uniform blue-green shade, with the original picture looming out of it like a ghostly face seen through mist.

She kicked off her shoes and drew her feet up on to the bed, wrapping her arms around her legs and laying her forehead on her knees.

I am so disorientated, she thought. I don't seem to belong anywhere any longer. I'm sure, I'm almost sure, that if I'm ever going to sort myself out I must leave Giles.

She had thought this before, more than once, but she had always before been racked with feelings of guilt and pity. What was different this time, what she found so disconcerting, was that she no longer seemed to feel anything. She could take out the image of Giles in her mind – Giles as he was now, and the many facets of him over the years – and he seemed to be totally disconnected from her. Worse than a stranger. With a stranger she might feel interest, a need to explore a new personality. But for Giles she had no sense of anything but a massive indifference, a paralysing boredom.

There must be something different about me, she thought. For Giles is unchanged. He is older, heavier, less discreet than he once was about his affairs, but not changed in essentials since we were first married. He is more pleased with his career than he has been for a long time, I suppose. Perhaps that is why I no longer feel the need to sustain him.

She was filled with an undefined yearning for something. Tears pricked in her eyes, but she had no reason to cry. Except that her life was so empty. She wanted to shout out, in a great rage, Is this all there is? All my life is ever going to amount to? She had her children and grandchildren, but her life stretched ahead and behind like a grey wasteland.

I hate people who indulge in self-pity, she thought with loathing. It is one of the areas of Giles's character which has undermined our relationship over the years. And yet here am I, no better than he, wallowing in it. I wish I were Katya's age again. I wish I could start all over, with the experience and clarity of sight I have now, and make a better job of things.

'Life is not a dress rehearsal.'

She had read that somewhere recently, and it haunted her. Most of her life she had behaved as if it were.

★ ★ ★

Nicholas hesitated outside Frances's door. It was closed. This was so unlike her that he considered going back down the stairs without knocking. All through his childhood he remembered open doors. At night, padding across the landing after a bad dream, he would know he could walk straight in and be reassured. Or in the daytime, even when she was marking essays on a corner of the dining-room table, she would always stop to comfort an injury or adjudicate a quarrel. The only time he could remember closed doors was when she was occasionally crippled with migraines and lay utterly silent in a darkened room, which had always rather scared him. He had wanted to go in and shake her, make her come out and be her usual steady self. He had never done so, of course, being a quiet, responsible boy, the eldest after Anya, the eldest son, the man of the family, as he felt himself to be from the age of about ten.

He had followed her now across the garden and up to her room, thinking she had only gone to fetch something. Up in her room at the top of the tower, he hoped he would be able to see her quietly alone for a little while. There were things he needed to speak to her about, away from the others.

There was a sound of movement from inside the room. He heard the creak of the bed, and then the pad of stockinged feet across towards the south window. No migraine, then. Curiously shy, he lifted his hand and knocked.

'Come in,' Frances called, in a subdued voice.

'Mum?' Nicholas put his head round the door. 'I'm not disturbing you, am I?'

'No, of course not, darling. I was just a little tired. It's already been a long day, and I felt like a break from the crowds.'

She looked pale, he thought.

'Could you spare me a few minutes? For a quick chat?'

'Of course. You take the chair.' She indicated the old Lloyd Loom chair, padded with two large and faded cushions. She crossed back from the window, and perched on the bed, gathering her skirts about her drawn-up knees. Nicholas was disconcerted by how young she suddenly looked, curled up on the bed of her childhood room.

'How is Lisa?' he asked. 'I didn't realise what was going on until Tony found me just now. Is she all right?'

'Jim Porter seems to think so. It may just be a false alarm, but he's taken her into the hospital, just in case. I wasn't surprised, really. You arrived as early as this – four weeks ahead of time.'

'Did I? I didn't realise. All of our three have been late.'

'Was it Lisa you wanted to talk about?' she asked, steering

him, as she had so often done in the past, back to the point. Nicholas's mind would so often wander off into by-ways. Homework that should have lasted half an hour would be unfinished two hours later as he lay on his stomach in the crowded sitting room in Reading, following up intriguing side-lines in encyclopaedias and textbooks. 'Learn to focus yourself, Nick, or you will never get anywhere.' But she would laugh, too, and say: But what is it that is so fascinating about conger eels? Or the internal combustion engine, or the origins of the signs of the zodiac, or whatever hare he was pursuing.

He clasped his hands between his knees now and looked at her steadily.

'I need to talk to you about St Martins, Mum. We have major repairs to do. And I don't think Natasha can be expected to go on running things much longer. And the trust is very nearly bankrupt.'

Chapter 8

THE CHILDREN'S VOICES rose, shrill and confident, over the sound of birdsong. They had been arranged where the lawn sloped gently down towards the sunken garden, elevating them sufficiently above their audience to give the impression of a stage. Most of the guests had gathered to hear them, some bringing their chairs across to the paths between the flower beds, others standing in groups and chatting between songs. Miss Baxter, who was deeply committed to her job as a teacher and who longed to become a part of village life, had suggested the concert to Natasha as the school's contribution to marking the anniversary.

'St Martins has done so much for the school over the years,' she said earnestly to Natasha. 'The headmaster has told me about the splendid talks that members of the community have given to the PTA and to the children, and about the musical and artistic help you have all given. And I believe you yourself led the campaign in the seventies that saved the school from being shut down.'

'I am,' said Natasha, 'a great believer in the value of village schools. My own grandchildren and the other children from the community have been very happy there.'

'I do so agree with you,' said Miss Baxter, smiling warmly with all of her rather large teeth. 'About the value of village schools.'

'Without a school, a village becomes moribund,' said Natasha.

'Oh yes!' said Miss Baxter, not quite sure what moribund meant. Then she suggested the concert. Nothing too elaborate or ambitious. Just the children spontaneously singing some of the old folk songs that were so important, weren't they?

In the end Natasha had felt obliged to agree, as it would have seemed ungracious to refuse. The result had been weeks of intensive preparation that might have made the children resentful, except that they were now so stuffed with food and lemonade that their T-shirts strained over rounded stomachs, and their faces presented a mosaic of jam stains and cake crumbs.

Twas on a Monday mo-orning that I beheld my da-arling,
She looked so neat and cha-arming, in every high degree.

They sang lustily and relatively in tune. Johnny Dawlish, Mr Dawlish's grandson, and a boy of remarkable charm and wickedness, pulled the ponytail of the girl in front of him in time to the music, so that her head jerked backwards at every stressed syllable. Miss Baxter, perched on an upturned wooden crate to conduct, observed the jerking. She frowned, shook her head and smiled at Melissa, to indicate that she quite understood such enthusiasm, but it was not necessary to express it in movement. Melissa rolled her eyes and gave Miss Baxter an agonised look, trying to indicate Johnny Dawlish without turning round. Johnny raised an angelic face to Miss Baxter (who had not yet known him long) and continued to tug.

Between verses Melissa said out of the side of her mouth, 'I'll get you for that, Johnny Dawlish, see if I don't.'

The local amateur dramatic group (Clunwardine Priors and Stanway Bridges, known as the Priorbridge Thespians), having heard of the school's contribution to the anniversary, had been determined not to be outdone. For the last two months they had been rehearsing *A Midsummer Night's Dream*, which was to be presented at half-past six on the terrace. This had appealed to Natasha, since the date of the party was close to midsummer and the Thespians had a generous portion of talent in their ranks. Sally, Olga and Eric all belonged to the group. Sally, their treasured wardrobe mistress, produced costumes which gave the Thespians the outward appearance of a professional company. Olga had a walk-on part tonight as a courtier, in addition to her regular duties as stage manager. Eric, a silent man in ordinary life, was a more than competent actor. Tonight he was to be one of the rustic mechanicals, Peter Quince. To her great secret excitement, although she feigned indifference, Chrissie was playing the fairy who encounters Puck in the forest.

Frances had walked across from the house to hear the singing and came up behind Mabel standing at the far end of the sunken garden, as the children were finishing their first song.

She put her arm around Mabel's waist and dropped a kiss on to the plump cheek. 'You can't imagine how good it is to be back,' she said.

'You've no call to stay away so long,' said Mabel gruffly. 'It's nearly four months since you were here. Natasha needs you around sometimes, you know. So do your mum and dad. So do I, if it comes to that.'

'Oh, Mabel,' said Frances, 'I do love you. You're so dependable. Solid as a rock.'

'Get along with you,' said Mabel.

★ ★ ★

They run through the dark streets to the wailing of the air-raid warning. Mummy is ahead with Hugh. Her face is a horrible greeny-white. Frances saw it in the hall light before they shut the front door and began to run. Her gas-mask bumps up and down painfully against her chest and she wants to cry but doesn't have the breath for it.

'A stitch,' she gasps, 'I've got a stitch. I can't – run – any – more.'

Mabel, who has been running with her, holding her hand, stops at once. Mabel is Mummy's friend and came to live with them a few days ago. Her hair was full of white dust when she arrived on their doorstep, and she didn't have anything but some clothes tied up in a bundle with a bit of string.

'It was all I could find in the rubble,' she said to Frances later, in the room they shared. 'I had two new pairs of silk stockings I was saving for something special, and there was nothing left of them but little wispy ribbons.'

Now Mabel bends down and scoops Frances up in her arms. 'Don't you worry, lovey,' she says. 'Mabel will carry you.'

The ARP warden shepherds them down the steep dark steps into the underground station just as they hear the bang of the first bomb exploding. It is very near. Frances hates the underground and clings to Mabel's neck like a baby monkey. It always smells funny down there, and now that it is used as an air-raid shelter it smells worse. Hugh likes it. He likes the singing and the jokes, and all the strange people herded together by the war. 'It's an adventure, Franny,' he says. But Frances hates it. She feels trapped, and imagines everything above her in London falling down on top of her – the houses and the gardens and the buses – so she will never be able to get out.

Mabel finds a clear corner for the four of them and spreads out the travelling rug she has been carrying over her arm. She takes Frances on her lap and cuddles her. She is a much more cuddly person than Mummy is. Mabel starts to sing softly to Frances.

Two, two, the lily-white boys, clothèd all in green-I-Oh!
One is one and all alone, and ever more shall be so.

What a funny song, thinks Frances, her head cushioned on Mabel's plump arm. I don't know what it means.

* * *

A slight disturbance interrupted the singing. The neat rows of children quivered and broke, and there was a squeal from somewhere in the middle of the group.

'Johnny Dawlish,' said Natasha.

'I don't think so,' said Irina, straining to see. 'There's a yellow-haired little girl with a ponytail – she seems to be hitting someone.'

'Johnny Dawlish will be the cause of it,' said Natasha with certainty.

'Oh yes, you're right, Mother, he's there. But it's Johnny Dawlish who's being hit.'

'He will have started it. An enterprising and clever child, but he misapplies his talents. He reminds me of Hugh.'

'Hugh? Hugh was never as naughty as that scamp!'

'Irina, he was never out of trouble. Full of high spirits and

146

inquisitiveness. Just as he is now. He's never grown up to this day, doushenka, and you know it.'

Irina sighed. They were sitting together on the old wooden garden bench where Natasha had sat talking to Anya that morning. The bench had been in the garden at St Martins when they had first arrived, and Irina had always been fond of retreating on a sunny afternoon to this quiet corner.

'I do think it is time Hugh settled down, Mother. We could do with his help here. I think he's very inconsiderate, the way he stays away for so long. Anything might have happened to us – he never gets in touch.' Her voice took on the injured tone that Natasha had always felt was her daughter's greatest failing. She laid her hand on Irina's.

'My dear, you will never change Hugh now. You must know that. You might as well try to cage the eagle.'

The children were singing again, 'The Nut-Brown Maiden'. When they had finished, Natasha turned to Irina again. 'Frances looks tired, don't you think? And not very happy.'

'I don't think she's ever been happy with that man. But that was her choice. I don't think she looks any unhappier than usual.'

Natasha was silent, then said, 'Usually, she contains herself. She achieves – how shall I say? – a contentment, a balance in her life. But now she is upset and restive. I have never seen her like this, not since she was in her teens.' She paused again. 'She is as unsettled as Katya.'

'Mother – don't be ridiculous!'

'Yes, she is moody and unsure of herself, like an adolescent. And as well as being unhappy, she looks so young. She looks vulnerable.'

* * *

'Have you seen Anya?' Frances asked Mabel, as they hurried back to the house to replenish the tea urn before the rest of the audience returned from the children's concert.

'No,' said Mabel. 'No, I haven't. She was serving on the main table when people first started arriving, but I've been so busy myself I lost sight of her. She'll be somewhere about, talking to her friends from the village, or helping Sally, or with that boyfriend of hers, the Greek boy.'

'No, she's not with him. That's why I asked. I've just seen him over there with Desmond Fraser and Chanor Patel. In fact I haven't seen them together all day.'

'He seems a nice boy,' said Mabel, holding open the back door for Frances to follow her into the kitchen.

'Yes. Yes, he does. I liked the way he started straight in and helped, as soon as he got here. Not many young men would have done that. Our big family usually frightens people off. I quite took to him.' Frances gazed around the kitchen, where Olga was squirting washing-up liquid into a sink full of hot water. 'Oh dear, Olga, were you going to tackle this all alone?'

'I don't mind,' said Olga, with her shy smile. 'We need more dishes and glasses, and there isn't time to run the dishwasher. Mrs Dawlish is coming to help in a minute, when the concert finishes.'

'We'll help too,' said Frances, unhooking Gregor's striped butcher's apron from the back of the larder door and pulling it over her head. She plugged in the tea urn to heat up. 'Have you seen Anya anywhere?'

'I'm here,' said Anya, following them in with a large tray precariously loaded with piles of miscellaneous dirty plates.

'Olga and I can do this,' said Mabel. 'You two take out those extra cakes we've been hoarding in the pantry, then come and get the tea urn when it's ready. People will be dying for a cup of tea after the concert, and the children will be panting with thirst.'

* * *

'I think he's super, your Spiro,' said Frances.

They had restocked the refreshment table and had now paused for a moment with cups of tea and pieces of Olga's sponge cake, sitting at a small table at the end of the lawn near the ha-ha.

Anya made a slight, impatient gesture. 'Your Spiro' was almost – though not quite – as bad as 'your Greek'.

'What is it that's the matter, darling?'

So Anya told her, as she had told Natasha earlier, about Spiro's idea for a restaurant, and the row they had had. Frances listened in silence, making no comment. So Anya went on and told her about her own sense of failure in her career.

Frances bowed her head and began tracing patterns in the cake crumbs on her plate. Still she said nothing.

At last Anya could stand it no longer. 'Well?' she said challengingly. 'Well – can't you say something, Mum?'

When Frances looked up at her, Anya saw that her eyes were distressed, and immediately felt ashamed. She opened her mouth, but before she could say anything, Frances began to talk.

'When I was seventeen,' she said, 'I fell in love. I suppose that whatever age you are when you first fall in love, it is an overwhelming experience. But if you are older, you understand yourself better. You have a little more control over things. At seventeen it takes over every moment of your waking life.' She paused. 'In many ways I was very young at seventeen, living here at St Martins.'

'Only half my age,' whispered Anya. 'Only *half* my age.' Frances did not seem to have heard her.

'We had a love affair. Yes, I think you could say it was a love affair. It coloured everything for me – for him too, I suppose – that one long summer.' She sighed, and smiled briefly. She raised her eyes and looked at Anya. 'It was so innocent. Nothing *happened*. Not what your generation, jumping in and out of bed with each other, would even think of as an affair. But perhaps, because of that, it meant all the more. I sometimes think that the freedom you have is a poor thing, compared with what you have lost. Even a touch, a time alone together, a simple kiss, was so significant for us.'

She laughed a little at herself. 'I sound positively Victorian, don't I? But I do think something has been sacrificed. Was it the sixties? Was it some kind of post-war need to smash what had gone before, because people – my generation, I suppose – thought that what they were going to put in its place was going to be so much better? Some things *are* better, of course. In many ways, women have a better deal – but not in all ways. And I think a tenderness has gone out of life.'

She was silent for so long that Anya felt compelled to speak.

'It wasn't Dad, was it? I mean, you didn't meet him till Oxford – and that would have been later – that winter?'

'Yes. That winter.'

She began to draw patterns in the cake crumbs again.

'I was out of my depth at Oxford. It seems odd to me now, looking back, that I should have been so gauche, so socially naive. After all, St Martins has always been full of interesting and creative people, coming and going. But in a way that had always been happening in the background of my life, not involving me directly. And everyone was so relaxed and easygoing. I've realised since, of course, that that is the mark of true professionals. They simply get on with things. It is those who are trying to impress – and who don't have much to be impressive about – who make the most show and noise.'

She sighed suddenly, sharply. 'I was so impressed with Giles. And his friends. And terribly flattered to be taken up by them. Coming from my rather bookish rural grammar school, to find myself amongst the well-heeled London social set was very seductive. They made a great fuss of me, and I was too naive to see that they were also making a fool of me. They treated me like a kind of mascot.'

'You didn't get married till the end of your second year, did you?'

'No. I don't think Giles was serious about me that first year. But when we came back after the summer, he laid siege to me, and I was too inexperienced to resist. Not that I wanted to. At least, I don't think I did.'

'And he – I mean, the other man – was it all over by then?'

'No.'

Anya waited.

'Not for him. I realised later – a few years later – that it hadn't been over for me either, but by then it was too late.'

'This love affair, when you were seventeen – '

Frances interrupted, speaking almost to herself, as though Anya wasn't there. 'I was seventeen. He was older, of course.

He was twenty. He seemed to have grown up so much, that last year at art college. It was a kind of awakening for me. Suddenly I felt alive all over. Life was positively burning in my fingertips. It had a curious kind of forbidden excitement about it too, almost like incest. Yet here was this stranger, so big, so adult, so male.'

Anya looked at her, her mouth parted in astonishment. 'Was it –?'

'Yes,' said Frances. 'It was Gregor.'

* * *

'Granny!' Chrissie was plucking importunately at Frances's sleeve. 'Have you spoken to Samira's mummy yet?'

'Not yet, darling, but I haven't forgotten, I promise you.'

Samira stood behind Chrissie, rubbing the toe of her right shoe on the back of her left leg.

'Oh, please, Granny!'

'What is it?' asked Anya.

'They want Samira to have one of Jeannie's puppies. Mrs Patel isn't keen on dogs, so I've promised to be a go-between.'

'Tell you what, Chrissie,' said Anya. 'If you go and look in my duffel bag – I brought you a present.'

'What, what?'

'Go and find it. My bag is hanging up in the cloakroom, and your present is in the front pocket, wrapped up in yellow paper.'

The two girls dashed off.

'I may just have made it worse,' said Anya ruefully. 'I've brought a collar and lead for Chrissie's new puppy. I hope it doesn't make it more painful for Samira.'

'Well, *I* hope I can persuade Mrs Patel. She is a very sweet person, but she is fearsomely tidy, and dogs can't help making a bit of a mess. Hairs on the upholstery and muddy feet. But I do like that child. It's the least I can do, to speak up for her.'

They sat in silence for a moment.

'Mum, thank you for telling me.'

Frances looked at her, troubled. 'I'm not sure that any of what I said is much use to you. I suppose I have been brooding on it myself just recently. It's so easy to lose your way, where matters of the heart are concerned. I was misled by unfamiliar glamour, you see, and failed to understand the value of what I had with Gregor. Our relationship was confused by our having grown up together. In some ways we knew each other too well. There was no mystery about him. And yet, and yet . . . '

She sighed. 'When Giles came along, *he* seemed so strange and glamorous. I realise now, of course, that Gregor is much more of a mystery than your father will ever be. With Giles, everything is on the surface, even if the surface can be adapted to the needs of the passing moment. Gregor has depths and hidden places I haven't explored even now, after all these years.' She thought of Gregor's new sculpture, the Venus Rampant, that he had shown her that morning, then she caught herself up. 'I'm sorry. I shouldn't speak to you about your father like this.'

'It doesn't matter. I think I understand Dad pretty well. I've always wondered – ' Anya looked embarrassed.

'What?'

'Well, what you saw in him. I realised a long time ago that you were the much more complex character. I've never been able to figure it out, your relationship.'

Frances shook herself. 'What we were really meant to be talking about was your relationship with Spiro. And what I think I was trying to say, in my confused way, was that you shouldn't let yourself be distracted by the surfaces. It isn't whether Spiro opens a restaurant in Wales or goes back to his university job in Greece that is important. It is what you feel about each other at a much deeper level that matters. And that is quite separate from your career. Of course eventually they affect each other, but the issues are different. You have to try to disentangle them in your mind. Think about what you want to do about your career. And think about your feelings for Spiro. Then try to see if they can be fitted together, if that is what you want. What it comes down to, in the end, is what really matters to you in your life. Where do you want to be in ten years' time? Perhaps you and Spiro both need more time to think, anyway. Don't rush into marriage with him, if you aren't sure. Let him open his restaurant. See how you feel about it then. Try to sort out your career – to stay on in Oxford doing what you are doing at present, or to try something different. Perhaps you need to get away from Oxford. It seems to be having a bad effect on you lately. Make a fresh start.'

She put her hand on Anya's. 'The one thing I am sure of, darling, is that you need to do something positive. You can't stand still and agonise any longer. You need to take charge of your life.'

★ ★ ★

Across the lawn Gregor was waylaid by Muriel Lacey, whose voice lapped round him warm as bathwater, and about as meaningful. But he was watching Frances and Anya talking. He did not listen to Muriel, straining instead to hear what Frances was saying to her daughter, although the whole lawn and most of the guests were between them. Suddenly she looked up and their eyes met. He looked away.

★ ★ ★

Frances and Gregor had gone out for the day in the MG, with a picnic. Usually Hugh was with them; the three of them had always gone about together since they were children. Frances could barely remember now – and only as something dreamlike and unreal, like someone else's story – the time when it was only Hugh and herself, and then the shameful time when they had excluded Gregor. It was a wicked thing they did to him, the shy dark boy with the terrified eyes, who could not speak. Sometimes they heard him whisper a few sounds to his mother, but they thought it was nonsense, gobbledygook. So when they got him to themselves, in a corner of the garden or fields remote from prying grown-ups, they would dance about him shouting: 'Yashee goshtocksee yiddle diddle booshda.'

He never said a word to them, but stood silently shivering, with his arms crossed over his head, as if to ward off blows. They never touched him, and he never cried. This must have gone on for weeks, and then suddenly they tired of it, and simply ignored him. He would follow them around, and gradu-

153

ally he began to speak, and he spoke in English. 'Water,' he would say, pointing at the Ludbrook. 'Dog' – old Ranger, great-grandfather of Harry. 'Bread. Sky. Table. Shoes.' The words came faster and faster, and for Frances it became a game.

'What is it?' she would demand, pointing with her plump childish finger.

'Chair. Grass,' Gregor would reply with mounting excitement, as the barriers around him began to fall. 'Wood. Cup. Book. Paint. Stone. Frances. Hugh. Gregor.'

After that, it was always the three of them together, larking about down Glebe Lane, past the vicarage and church on the way to and from the village school. Climbing trees in the woods. Scratching their arms and legs into bloody tattoos as they gathered blackberries in the farm lanes. (Gregor always came home with most – he had the longest reach, the most staying power, and the greatest self-control about eating them.) Taking long cycle rides around the Herefordshire lanes and over the Welsh border to Hay-on-Wye and Clyro or (labouring and panting) up Hay Bluff.

Sometimes they went off for a week or more on cycling holidays, staying at the primitive little Welsh youth hostels with their smelly outdoor privies that made even St Martins' old-fashioned plumbing seem luxurious.

It had been a long, contented childhood, that seemed to stretch back and back unchanged in Frances's mind to that dimly remembered time when she and Hugh first arrived at St Martins. But slowly, insidiously, things had begun to change. First, two years ago, Gregor had gone away to art college. Because of his disordered schooling he was only a year ahead of Hugh. They missed him, she and Hugh, but they were busy themselves, travelling by bus every day into Hereford. Hugh, in his last year at school, was working for his Oxbridge entrance and his A Levels – she, in the Lower Sixth, about to do the same the following year. Gregor would turn up at least once a month from London, having hitch-hiked to St Martins. But the three of them were slipping apart, pursuing their enlarging lives. Then last year Hugh had gone off to Cambridge, and

Frances, the only one of them left at home, had studied furiously.

This summer, the summer of 1957, they were all at home, and Frances had the MG – of which the two boys were understandably envious. Several times a week the three of them would pile into it and venture out into a widening circle from St Martins, further than they had ever attempted by bicycle. They would take a picnic, and eat it on the bank of a river or on top of a hill, or else stop at a pub for a drink and a pie (greatly daring, for Frances was still under age).

On this day, this particular August day, drowsy with heat, buzzing with bees and heavy with the scent of ripening fields, Hugh had gone off on the train to Gloucester to meet a friend from Cambridge, so Frances and Gregor had packed a picnic as usual and driven off in the car alone.

They drove with the top folded down and Frances's dark hair beat like a brown flag in the wind. Gregor's tight black curls vibrated and pulsed with the air and the speed of the car, which Frances sent flying round the loops of the road and up the rising ground into the Cotswolds beyond Cirencester. Gregor had been finding it more and more difficult, going out with Frances and Hugh these last weeks since they had all come home for the summer vacation. Everything was changing. He had finished his basic course at college, though he planned to go back for some additional optional courses. He wanted to start working seriously, saying the things he needed to say in stone and clay and bronze, but he was uncertain whether he had mastered enough of the techniques. Nothing that he had shaped into solid form had yet managed to capture what he could see and feel inside his head. And Hugh was growing away from them. His aspirations had widened at Cambridge. Gregor sensed that soon Hugh would be off for good, leaving Frances and him behind.

And Frances. He was afraid of her going away to Oxford at the end of this summer. And he was afraid to be alone with her in the car like this.

When the three of them travelled in the car, Gregor had always, naturally, taken the back seat. He was, after all, the third member of the trio, the outsider. And sitting in the back he escaped the potent nearness of Frances beside him. Though if he leaned forward her hair whipped in his face and he could open his lips and catch a strand of it between them, crunching it lightly between his teeth. It tasted of soap and the heat of the summer sun.

Now, however, he was sitting in front beside her, and the roll of the car round the bends pressed their thighs together. It was almost more than Gregor could bear. He wanted to reach out and touch her, but he did not dare. He did not even venture to lay his arm lightly along the back of the seat as he would once have done, when the gesture would have been wholly casual, without significance for either of them. Now for him it would vibrate with meaning, and he was afraid that if he touched her, he would lose control. The touch of her thigh he counted to himself as a happy accident, a gift of the motion of the car, and not his responsibility. He had no idea whether these random brushes of their bodies together meant anything to her. She showed no sign. But she did seem to be driving faster and more recklessly than usual.

They had come as far as they could with the car, where the country lane petered out at the last farm gate. From here they would have to climb. Gregor lifted the picnic basket from the back seat, and Frances folded the old, rather moth-eaten plaid rug over her arm. To reach the path up to the top of the hill with its prehistoric long-barrow, they had to cross a stile. Gregor climbed over first, then turned and offered his hand to Frances. She hesitated, above him on the stile, looking down at his upturned face. She had never since she was five years old been helped over a stile. Then she placed her hand in his and sprang over.

They continued to hold hands as they climbed the hill. Neither wanted to make the gesture of withdrawal. But they did not speak until they reached the top, with its wonderful view over the pieced and folded landscape.

'Up here,' said Gregor, drawing her up after him to the top of the barrow, remote and sleeping on its hilltop.

They stood for minutes, their sides pressed together, looking blindly out at the view, with her hair blowing across his throat. There was a slight declivity in the top of the barrow, sheltered from the wind, and Frances spread out the rug here while Gregor unpacked the picnic. They ate their lunch in a silence full of powerful unspoken meaning.

'Sandwich?' said Frances.

'Mmm. Have some more cider.'

★ ★ ★

The sun is directly above them, its heat trapped in this hollow where they sit, the view hidden from them by the soft turf-covered humps of the barrow's sunken roof. Gregor puts out his hand and touches Frances's bare arm, and she shivers slightly. Unconsciously, unwillingly almost, he slides his arm around her waist, and she relaxes against him, her head turned into the curve of his shoulder. His hand moves up and delicately cups her breast. She shivers again, violently. Then he cannot help himself, he is kissing her and she puts up her hands to cup the back of his head, and she is kissing him wildly, inexpertly, back.

'Oh God, Frances, I love you,' he cries out, as if in pain.

'I love you,' she says, kissing his chest where his shirt is open, the hollow of his neck below his ear, his eyelids. 'I love you. I love you.'

Her hair is spread out on the grass, and the yellow pouches of wild orchids bob on their slender stems between the strands of it, making a frame for her face.

★ ★ ★

'What shall we do about the nature ramble, if Paul doesn't come back?' Nicholas asked Natasha.

'Could you? No, I don't suppose you could,' Natasha laughed.

Nicholas looked slightly put out. 'I've always been interested in natural history, Natasha,' he said stiffly.

'But in books.'

'Yes, well,' he admitted, 'I suppose I'm not a field botanist, like Paul. Still, if the worst comes to the worst, I can take the kids round and point out some trees to them. And wild flowers

157

in the meadow. Mum's pretty good at those. We could do it together.'

He looked at his watch. 'Quarter to three. We've nearly three-quarters of an hour. He'll ring, surely, if he can't make it.'

★ ★ ★

'There's nothing you can do at present, Mr Fenway,' said the ward sister firmly. 'Mrs Fenway is resting at present, and doctor will examine her again in an hour, but it seems to be a false alarm.'

Paul started to protest, but she cut him short.

'This is not at all uncommon, you know,' she said quite kindly, seizing a few moments from her hard-pressed day to reassure him. 'I expect doctor will want to keep her in overnight, just for observation, but she will probably be able to come home again tomorrow.'

'We're not at home, exactly,' he explained yet again. 'We are out at St Martins. For the anniversary.'

'Yes, so I understand.' She flashed him a smile, looking nearly human for a moment. 'How splendid! I do envy you.'

'Now.' She began to walk him firmly towards the glass swing doors. 'I think your wife would relax better if you went back. She's rather distressed about both of you leaving the party and is anxious for you to return. The best thing for her just now is to get some sleep.'

She held the door open for him.

'Why don't you ring us some time after six, and see how she is doing? I expect doctor will be able to tell you then whether she will be able to go home in the morning.'

With the skill of long practice she moved behind him, making it impossible for him to get back into the ward without pushing her aside. Paul found himself effectively ejected and on his way across the car park before he knew what had happened.

On the drive to the hospital Lisa had said that the pains seemed to be diminishing.

'I'm going to look an awful fool if it's a false alarm,' she said ruefully.

He unclenched his left hand from the steering wheel and patted her knee.

'And you're supposed to be taking the children on a nature trail round the estate at half-past three,' she reminded him. He had completely forgotten. He groaned.

'I'll be fine,' she said later, propped up against the grey iron railings of the hospital bed-head, with a cup of soupy hospital tea going cold on the bedside locker. 'Do go back, please, Paul. I feel so bad about all this. Go back and carry on as normal. I don't want things spoiled for Natasha. If the pains start up again, the doctor promised me there would be plenty of time to fetch you. Off with you.'

So here he was, working his way out of the Saturday afternoon traffic jams, trying to remember what he had planned to do on this wretched nature trail. He'd prepared some worksheets and photocopied them. Those must still be in his case in the bedroom. One on birds, one on trees, one on plants, and a sort of mystery guessing game one, that he found always went down well on the first field trip with the Form I pupils at school. Nothing to worry about. He could do this standing on his head, if he could just wrench his mind away from the hospital, and the greenish look of Lisa before Dr Porter arrived.

He hadn't done a sheet on fungi, but they were always popular. Little boys in particular were fascinated by poisonous toadstools. Little girls, in his limited experience, shrieked and made faces, though he suspected they were just as intrigued. But perhaps this lot would be too young. He didn't want any of them larking about, doing something silly.

Odd, when you thought about it. Here he was driving towards St Martins, having left his wife, Hugh Appleton's niece, about to have a baby in that hospital, all because of a similar talk on botany when he himself was a schoolboy.

* * *

'Any questions?' asked Hugh Appleton, grinning at them conspiratorially from the table where he had perched, swinging one leg idly. This alone set him apart from the usual Friday evening lecturers, who stayed behind the lectern for safety, gripping it rigidly and staring out over the heads of the boys.

It was Paul's second term at boarding-school, and he was wretched. He had somehow failed to make friends, a situation that was unfamiliar to him. The work was demanding, though not impossible, but he had become overpoweringly indifferent to it. His mind was focused on the piece of paper he kept under his mattress on which he was crossing off the days until the Easter holidays.

Someone – a big prefect with an alarming man's voice and incipient moustache – asked a question from the back row. Hugh Appleton answered clearly, gesturing with his hands, making a neat quick drawing of a tree on the overhead projector transparency. This gave others the courage to ask questions. Soon the explorer – so celebrated they had not expected him to look like an ordinary man at all – was laughing and fielding questions from all over the hall. Paul's hand crept up nervously and then retreated, several times.

'One last question,' said the Headmaster, benign at having secured such a speaker for the school. He intended to let it be known at the next headmasters' conference.

Hugh Appleton's eye fastened on Paul. He smiled straight at him. 'You there, in the third row – you've been trying for ages.'

Paul got trembling to his feet and cleared his throat. 'Could you tell us, did you see *Meconopsis betonicifolia* in its natural habitat? And was it monocarpic?'

The boys around him rolled their eyes, and pulled mocking faces, but the explorer beamed at him. 'Well done!' He looked at Paul with real appreciation. 'Now, I can tell you a very funny story about *Meconopsis* . . . '

After the vote of thanks from the Head Boy – a splendid figure, whose blazer was covered in gold braid – there was a great roar of clapping and stamping from the audience, who had never supposed a lecture on the flora and fauna of the Himalayas could be so interesting, though they would have come to hear Hugh Appleton if he had chosen to speak about dustbins.

Amid the orderly shoving as the boys disgorged from the hall, a hand plucked Paul's sleeve.

'The Head wants you, in his study.' A prefect was looking at him appraisingly.

Paul was terrified. What had he done? He had never been face to face with the Headmaster since he arrived.

'Come in, Fenway,' said the Head jovially. 'Mr Appleton wants a word with you.'

Hugh Appleton looked him up and down. 'So you already know something about botany?'

Paul mumbled something about always having been interested. His ears were burning.

'Here's my card. Mind you, I'm not often there, but it's the nearest thing to a permanent base that I have. When you're in your last year at school, write to me, and I'll see if I can fix you up with a field trip somewhere before you go up to university. That will give you a head start.'

Paul looked at the pasteboard rectangle. 'St Martins', somewhere in Herefordshire. From that moment on, Hugh Appleton was his hero.

★　★　★

No one was now directing cars in the driveway. Latecomers made their own way into the field and parked where they could. The beautiful silver Mercedes, nosing over the gravel paused doubtfully, then rolled on. Clearly no one could expect it to be accommodated amongst those muddy ruts and plebeian Fords and Vauxhalls. There was one gap in the row of cars parked in front of the house, but it had clearly been occupied previously by a much smaller car.

'Turn left through this archway,' said Giles, relieved to have arrived intact. The Merc had been doing 100 m.p.h. on the motorway. 'There will probably be room round at the back in the stableyard.'

The Mercedes hesitated fractionally.

'Don't worry,' Giles smiled broadly. 'No horses. Only the studios, and the entrance to my eldest son's house. I'm sure we can fit in there. Ah, yes, just beyond Frances's Cavalier.'

Like an aristocrat slumming, the silver car slid condescendingly into the space he indicated, partially blocking the door to Gregor's studio, and the two men got out. Nigel looked quickly around, noting the arched doorways Giles had told him about.

'The studios?' He raised an enquiring eyebrow.

Giles nodded. 'Painting, sculpture and so on below, music above.'

The back door of the main house swung open and a gawky young girl came out, dressed in a man's grey T-shirt and some nondescript layers of black below. She was struggling with a large tray heavily laden with dishes.

'Hi, Dad,' she said, thrusting the tray at him so that he was forced to take it from her. 'Who's your friend?'

Giles closed his eyes briefly. 'My daughter,' he said resignedly. 'Katya.'

Chapter 9

'MAY I PRESENT Nigel Laker, Natasha?' Giles bowed gravely towards Natasha, seated again in her Jacobean chair. 'Nigel, this is my wife's grandmother, Natasha Devereux, the artist. And, of course, founder and guiding light of the St Martins community for half a century.' The persona he had assumed for the scene had the hushed gravity of a Richard Dimbleby, with a touch of Peter Ustinov's Slav exoticism. He had considered introducing Natasha as the Princess Natasha Greshlov, but thought better of it when she turned her sardonic eye on him. He was convinced that she had seen him thrust the loaded tray into Sally's surprised arms as he passed her.

'Speak to you later,' he mouthed to his startled daughter-in-law.

'Ah, Giles,' said Natasha gracefully, playing the scene back to him. 'How good you were able to come.' Her Russian accent was a shade more noticeable than usual, and she lifted her hand, palm down, in the gesture of her girlhood.

Totally upstaged by her, Giles was obliged to raise her hand to his lips.

'And Mr Laker. I was told you would be coming with Giles. They brought me word he had telephoned.' Suddenly behind her there seemed to be a shadowy throng of ghostly servants standing, in gorgeous livery. 'I welcome you to St Martins, Mr Laker, and our little celebrations.' She lifted her hand again, and Nigel, who had instantly fallen in love with her, kissed it with far more fervour than would have been permitted in the Romanov court.

'You are one of Giles's *theatrical* friends, I believe?' There was a certain shading to her tone on the word 'theatrical' – a musical rise and fall – that made it sound at once racy and slightly disreputable.

Nigel, usually so suavely in command of every situation, found himself bowing slightly.

'Television, Mrs Devereux. I haven't worked in the straight theatre for fifteen years.'

'Everyone,' she said, with a sweep of her fine eyes over the crowded garden, 'calls me Natasha. Except my daughter Irina, who feels obliged to call me Mother, in order to make a distinction.'

'I should be honoured,' said Nigel, feeling that he ought to sink on one knee, as if he were about to be knighted, and wondering how long he could keep this up.

Suddenly she laughed, a full-throated, appealing, girlish laugh.

'Off you go, Giles,' she said, in her normal tone of voice, 'and see your neglected family. Mr Laker can stay and talk to me.'

'Nigel, please.'

'Certainly. Nigel.'

Giles looked as though he was about to protest – he wanted to keep his finger on developments here – but changed his mind. Natasha was a very clever woman. She would know exactly how to handle Nigel. It might be better to leave them alone.

'Do sit down – Nigel,' said Natasha as Giles left them. On her lips the name sounded faintly absurd, and he coloured slightly, recalling certain uncomfortable episodes of his school-days. With a nod of her head she indicated an upright and not very comfortable-looking dining room chair placed at right angles to her own. He sat, obediently.

Natasha set herself to amuse this young-middle-aged friend of Frances's husband. She had sensed immediately that Giles had some urgent reason for bringing him down, and knowing the precarious state of Frances's finances, Natasha was prepared to humour him if it would help. She had decades of experience at this sort of strategic conversation masquerading as party chatter, and this well-groomed, slightly precious man was no match for her.

She began to entertain him with anecdotes of her life in Paris and London between the wars, throwing in the occasional scandalous story. Nigel adored her. He wished that he dared take notes, for her reminiscences were the very essence of his work in television, but instead he set himself to file them away in his capacious memory. As he grew bolder, he put questions about some of the more famous names – Picasso, George Bernard Shaw, the Bloomsbury set. Perfectly aware of what he was doing, Natasha answered him tranquilly, with no more and no less than the truth. An experienced interviewer, he could recognise the rich authenticity in what he heard. This was wonderful – the St Martins programme began to take shape in his mind. He had intended that it should form only the first half of the first programme, but now he was beginning to wonder how he could confine so much material to a mere two hours.

Having laid her bait, Natasha now began to reel in her fish. She asked him about his work in the past, his plans for the future. Like everyone in his profession, Nigel loved nothing better than to enlarge on such fascinating topics. He found himself telling her about his first fumbling steps in the theatre, after he had failed his degree through spending too much time with the university dramatic club. He told her humorous tales of his time as an ASM with a provincial repertory company and later at a down-market London theatre. These stories had often been a success – told with wit and salaciousness – when poured into the ears of suggestible girls hoping for a television career and willing to sleep with him as part of the price. He felt that they fell somewhat flat after Natasha's own tales, although she listened with flattering attention and inserted keen comments that somehow enhanced their interest.

At some point he was handed tea and a plate of sandwiches and cakes by a young woman. He noted merely that she looked troubled, and bore a very faint resemblance to Giles, before he dismissed her from his mind. He was leading up to the import-ant part now, his plans for *The Great Eccentrics*.

Just in time, and with great self-control, he stopped himself mentioning the provisional title for the new series. It had suddenly occurred to him that this remarkable lady – he could not think of her simply as a woman – was way out of his class, and might not appreciate being thought of as an eccentric. Indeed, now that he had met her, her whole career seemed to him not eccentric at all, but a wonderful flowering of a rich talent for life. He felt, to tell the truth, somewhat humbled, and drunk with the fascination of her.

Natasha, however, was too quick for him. As he described his new series, his enthusiasm shaped it before her.

'I do not,' she said, 'watch a great deal of television, apart from drama and some of the nature programmes, which I feel television does so well. It seems to me, however, that this series you are talking about could be very appealing.'

He felt as if she had given him a present.

'You have a title for it, yes?' She cocked her head to one side and smiled at him. 'Something like *The Great Eccentrics*, perhaps?'

Damn it, he thought, is she a witch?

'Well – er,' he stammered, 'perhaps something along those lines. But –,' he rallied, 'I would be using the term according to its root derivation. Meaning people who have been "off-centre" because they have been the explorers, the innovators, the ones to push back the frontiers of new ideas and modalities.'

Natasha winced slightly.

'And did you,' she asked innocently, 'think of using St Martins in this series?'

He threw up his hands in a gesture of surrender.

'I am found out!'

She smiled at him quite kindly, as if he had been Johnny Dawlish caught scrumping amongst the lichen-covered apple trees in the orchard.

'It might be a good subject for you. Whether it would be good for us – this is another matter.'

'Everything would be done with the greatest care. I am aiming very much for the upper end of the market. *Civilisation*?' he murmured, reminding her of what he had said earlier.

'Ah, yes.' She hadn't been so entertained for a good while. The parry and thrust of their discussion, despite her unequal opponent, reminded her of negotiations over exhibitions in the past, and the many dragons she had had to slay in setting up St Martins in the first place.

'And where does Giles fit into this? Or was he simply used to provide an introduction?'

'Oh, not at all,' he protested. 'St Martins was on my list from the outset. But I didn't realise until this morning that Giles had any connection with St Martins. I am hoping to use him as the narrator, in voice-overs. That was what I rang him about.'

Natasha considered.

'And how did he react to that?'

Nigel gave her a measuring look. 'Not too well. I think he was hoping to be asked to front it. But I'm not going to use anyone on camera. Too intrusive. Too apt to create a cult figure. And Giles – '

'Quite. Poor Giles no longer quite has the looks for it. But his voice – '

'Exactly,' he cried in delight. 'His voice. It's a wonderful resource. I really want to have it for the series. And he has agreed.'

Suddenly he noticed the cup of cold tea he was holding in his hand, and the plate of uneaten food balanced on his knee. He began to nibble at the edges of a cucumber sandwich. It was excellent.

'Would you be willing for us to use St Martins?'

Natasha steepled her fingers together and propped her chin on them.

'I will need to consider this. And talk to my granddaughter, Frances.'

'Not Giles?'

'Oh, no. Giles has nothing to do with St Martins. We will speak again this evening – or else I will get Frances to talk to you.'

'Thank you.' He took a gulp of the cold tea, and regretted it.

'One other thing,' he said.

'Yes?'

'I believe Hugh Appleton is your grandson.'

'He is.'

'Would there be any chance I might interview him? Is he here? Will he be coming to the anniversary?'

'I am afraid I really do not know,' said Natasha.

★ ★ ★

'I'll have a vodka and orange,' said Hugh Appleton, 'and bring me some of those smoked almonds.'

The stewardess, who had recognised him at once without looking at the passenger list, came back, simpering slightly, with his drink and nuts on a tray. A large American businessman, whom she had bypassed, made protesting noises and glowered at her, but she whisked past his outstretched hand. She prolonged the arranging of glass and plate on Hugh's tip-down table, and the pouring of his drink, as long as she could. Then she leaned forward confidingly towards the ear so enticingly framed by the wavy dark brown hair and asked for his autograph, for her younger brother – she said.

Hugh, who was accustomed to the effect his appearance and his fame produced on women, and regarded it as a great joke, gave her a pleasant smile and complied, writing his name on the back of a Russian railway timetable he had in his breast pocket.

'You won't need this again?' she asked deferentially.

'Not at all. I have plenty of other fiction with me to read.'

To make his point he pulled out of another pocket a volume printed on poor-quality paper – but boldly for all that – of miscellaneous stories and essays in Russian, which would have secured any of the authors a life sentence in the gulags of Siberia just a few years earlier. The stewardess tiptoed reverently away, to attend to the importunate American.

Hugh turned the open book face down on his lap and struggled to tear open the recalcitrant foil packet of nuts sitting so incongruously on one of the porcelain plates reserved for first-class passengers in the front of the plane.

What would that girl have thought if she could have seen me a month ago? he thought. Unshaven, dirty, and smelling like a rank goat from the uncut pelts used as bedding in the cave up in the mountains of Kashmir. It had been a sobering trip. He had not visited the area for nearly twenty years, and this time had found few of the old friends from his youth still alive. Or at any rate admitting to it. The area was dangerously divided, politically, and the old, remote, mountain simplicities had been overtaken by events in India, in Pakistan and in the broken Asian fragments of the old Soviet Union. Religion, once a fateful but calm certainty in the tribesmen's lives, had been tainted by a nasty cocktail of fanaticisms. It's always a mistake to go back, he thought, and I was driven by no more than nostalgia. Much better to go on. To find somewhere fresh, a new perspective. He sipped pensively at his vodka, and thought humorously: Though I am rather running out of new and unexplored places. Bhutan, now, I've never been there. And there are certainly a few areas deep in the African interior that offer possibilities. And there's the Siberian expedition.

He picked up his book, and began to read.

* * *

'Peter,' said Frances, 'could we have a talk? Just for a minute before I round up the children for the nature trail?'

She had found him on the terrace, dead-heading flowers in the tubs and urns that framed it. He swung his wheelchair towards her and cocked an eyebrow.

'Of course. Provided you help me with this. It's been over-looked in all the fuss, and I don't want the terrace to seem neglected when people gather here for drinks before the play.'

Frances looked at the lavish displays cascading over the sides of the containers and grinned. 'Oh, I don't think it will seem neglected, but I'm happy to help.'

She bent over the nearest urn and began to pinch and pluck, remembering how Peter had taught her to dead-head when she had first taken an interest in gardening, at the age of about seven. In those days she had preferred growing things she could eat, and quickly, like mustard and cress and radishes, but he had assured her that the time would come when she would prefer the beauty of gardening to its utility. He had, of course, been right.

'Potatoes and cabbages,' he had said with some contempt, 'are all very well for peasants, but an artist grows roses and a philosopher grows oak trees. For the future.'

Then he had laughed, and added, 'But potatoes and cabbages are useful also to the artist and the philosopher, who without them would starve.'

They worked now in companionable silence for a few minutes, and it was Peter who spoke first.

'What was it you wished to speak of, Frances?'

'Nick has been talking to me.' She hooked her hair behind ears as she used to do when she was a child. 'He's told me about the worrying financial situation here at St Martins, and the work that needs to be done on the house.'

'Yes.' He wheeled himself over to a big rectangular trough of marble, where the blurred faces of putti peeped out from behind rings of grey-green lichen. 'It is very serious, Nick thinks. You know that I am no good with money, Frances. Birgit always used to try to save a little, but we never seemed to manage to hold on to much.'

Frances, who knew of his many private charities and sponsorships over the years, made a quick gesture. 'I wasn't talking about you personally, Peter, but the trust.'

'I know, my dear, but I would like to be able to pay more into it. Unfortunately I only have the state old age pension and the royalties my recordings still earn – we sometimes get a little bonus when one of them is reissued on CD, but it doesn't amount to much.'

'I realise that. Mum and Dad don't have a lot either – Dad's done so much for my children.'

She began to count the members of the community off on her fingers.

'Natasha only has the money from the farm, and she's never charged a realistic rent for that. Nick is probably paying all he can afford for the moment. Jonathan, Desmond and the others don't have much disposable income. Jonathan's plays won't ever earn him real money. It's possible Desmond's pots might catch the eye of a buyer for one of the big London shops, but he's never going to be rich! Who else? Eric's silk-screen printing . . . '

'What it needs,' Peter interrupted, not looking at her, 'is someone to take charge. See whether there is some way to raise the money for the repairs – Nick thinks they'll be in the order of £100,000.'

'Oh, no! That much? He didn't mention the amount.'

'Oh, yes.' He turned to face her. 'Natasha cannot be expected to go on, you know. We are all so accustomed to leaning on her, and she is so unusual a person, that I think we forget her age.' He laughed. 'Natasha and the Queen Mother – it must have been an exceptional vintage year, 1900!'

'But – raise the money? How?'

'I don't know.' He turned back to the marble trough. 'How did Natasha raise the money she needed in the early days? I know your grandfather didn't inherit much money with the house, and Natasha found, after she had been here a few months, that there were rotted joists that had to be replaced. And there were the studios. I know most of the work was done by the community – Birgit and I helped too after we arrived – but the materials must have cost something.'

He paused. 'I do remember that when we decided to renovate the Edwardian generator, so we could make our own electricity, it cost nearly a thousand pounds, but that was cheaper than having mains electricity put in. That time we gave some concerts and Natasha sold three large paintings, just for the generator fund. That was in 1953, I think.'

'I remember. I remember the first time we switched on the lights. It was very exciting, though I've always felt a bit sorry we had to say goodbye to the oil lamps. I loved their soft light.'

'Not so good to read music by, when your eyes are getting worn out,' said Peter crisply.

'And of course the electricity was a great boon for the fridge and then the freezer. And now I don't suppose we would think we could manage without washing machines and dishwashers. It was a good thing you had the generator restored, because it wasn't until – what was it? – 1984 that they brought the mains electricity up here.'

'That's right.'

'But – these repairs. A concert, you think? It would need to be in Wembley stadium for that kind of money.'

He shrugged. 'I don't know. How do people raise money these days? Sponsored marathons?'

Frances laughed. 'I don't see any of us running in a marathon.'

'Talk to Natasha,' he said.

'But you see, Peter. It isn't really my business. I don't live here any more.'

He gave her a penetrating look. 'Don't you? Well, perhaps you should.'

* * *

Giles was enjoying himself. He had been moving about amongst the crowds, bestowing his wonderful smiles about him, like coins. From a discreet distance he had watched Natasha and Nigel talking, and was reassured that they seemed to be pleased with each other's company. He had spoken to Nick and Anya, heard from Tony about Lisa's hasty departure to hospital, and managed to avoid Katya, who frankly scared him these days. He hadn't yet seen his wife, but she would be somewhere about.

St Martins was looking very beautiful in its crazy, haphazard way, the stone warmed to soft straw colour by the early summer sun and the half-timbered portions bulging pleasingly out of true. He hadn't often spent time in the garden, not being an outdoor man himself, but he saw now what presence the place had – its proportions, the spaciousness of the buildings and grounds, the sheer, majestic height of the old trees. He had forgotten the ha-ha, with its rough ground beyond, where there were sometimes sheep but which today was full of children. He wasn't sure he had even known there was a meadow. For a full five minutes he leaned on the crumbling wall that divided the garden from the meadow, gazing over it with real pleasure. Amazing. Amongst the feathery waving grasses it was full of flowers – tiny blue stars on thin stems and great vigorous heads of yellow and flat red flowers as thin and crumpled as tissue paper, which he thought might be poppies. Frances would know all their names. As, of course, would Hugh. Briefly he regretted that he had been raised in a service flat in Mayfair, his childhood visits to the country being confined to picnics around Cannes, when his parents made their regular summer visits to the Côte d'Azur.

He had begun to feel lately that there were a lot of things he had not taken proper account of in the past. Frances and her family, and all this, for a start. Perhaps he and Frances should try to spend more time down here, recharging the batteries. The discussion with Nigel over lunch, about his planned series and his view of St Martins, had started Giles thinking that he might quite fancy being a country gentleman. It would have been impossible when Frances suggested it all those years ago, of course, but now that he was established . . . He imagined himself into the role of country landowner, in plus-fours, with a gun over his arm and a pair of dogs at his heels. He didn't like dogs, of course. Strange dogs approaching him in the street had made him nervous as a child, and he had never quite shaken off the nervousness as an adult. He had absolutely banned dogs from the house in Reading. But for the image he was building up in his mind, some dogs about the place would be necessary. Not allowed into the house, of course, as Harry and Jeannie were at present.

He would stroll about, keeping an eye on things. Perhaps exchange a few comments about the crops and the weather with Alun Philips. Have his morning coffee in the sunken garden and a G. and T. on the terrace in the evening, with a few distinguished house guests invited down from London for the weekend. He had a brief, unsettling vision of a pert house-maid serving the drinks in a white frilled cap and an apron worn over an abbreviated black dress that tipped up, as she leaned forward, to reveal frilly white lace knickers. Of course, that was the farce he had been in, years ago – his first West End part. He had played the young love interest, the son of the house who was engaged to a frightfully nice girl but kept falling about in the bushes with every other female in the cast

173

except his mother and an old dowager. It had been good fun. That was when Frances had insisted they invest the money in a house, and he had wanted to stay on in the rented London flat.

She'd probably been right, he had to concede. Life with five children would have become intolerable in that flat, and they could never have afforded to buy it. Whereas he'd made enquiries recently about the value of the Reading house, and been agreeably surprised. Sell that, invest the money for a tidy little bit of income, and move to St Martins. Natasha didn't need the main part of the house any more, it was far too much for her in her old age. They could make a little granny flat for her on the ground floor of the east wing, which wasn't much used at present. Or better still, they could find her a nice retirement home, where she could be looked after properly. As long as it wasn't too expensive.

The image was taking on a very pleasing shape. He hadn't been happy, approaching middle age, and had fought against it, in his mind, for a long time. Looking at his contemporaries in the theatre, he wondered that most of them could accept it so calmly – the men, at any rate. As for the women – well, actresses in their forties and fifties, even a few in their sixties, seemed to manage to stay so much younger and more vital looking these days. For Giles, the arrival of his fifties had seemed like a trick, a nasty, subversive attack. He couldn't stop himself fancying girls in their twenties, still thinking of himself as the same age. But many things had been nudging him lately – the sitcom role, his thinning hair, his slight deterioration in health, a kind of weariness with life which wasn't like him at all.

About a month ago he had had an unsettling conversation with an old friend, a contemporary at Oxford who had gone on the stage at the same time as Giles. Rupert had had a highly successful career – including seventeen years in Hollywood. He had been through three divorces in fairly quick succession, but on returning to England at the age of forty had married a Kentish farmer's daughter and fathered three cheerful, uncomplicated children. His marriage was blissful, and he now took only those parts he really wanted to play – mostly on television, he said, because the working conditions were so much more civilised than the live theatre. He played middle-aged and elderly (often very elderly) parts with great charm and subtlety, and was regarded as an enormous prize by any casting director.

Giles had been invited to Sunday lunch at Rupert and Mary's small farm near Goudhurst – a proper, old-fashioned affair (roast beef, Yorkshire pudding, three veg, and a summer pudding with cream). Quite unlike the meals his set in London consumed these days. The whole family (and Giles, who was expected to help) had cleared the table and washed up in the big sunny kitchen where they had eaten. Everyone seemed to be talking at once, and yet it had been, oddly, great fun. It had reminded him of his infrequent visits to St Martins before his marriage, but in those days he had despised the big family meals round the kitchen table, the sheer casualness of it all.

When the dishes were done, Giles had been lent a pair of muddy wellingtons and been taken off by Rupert and his younger son to admire the goats, who had three new kids. Mary made goats' milk cheese and ice-cream, and to Rupert's great delight had won several prizes.

Full of excellent lunch and a sense of benevolence, Giles had told Rupert how lucky he was, how he envied him.

'I don't have anything you couldn't have yourself, old man. You have a beautiful wife and a fine family of children. Grand-children too, you lucky sod.'

'Don't!' said Giles, as he would in London, and shuddered. 'I don't admit to being a grandfather.'

'Don't be a fool,' said Rupert, smiling at him tolerantly. 'Best period of one's life. I envy *you*, as a matter of fact. Being a grandfather while you're still young enough to enjoy it. I'm a late starter, so I can't hope even to become one till I'm past sixty-five.'

Giles leaned on the gate to the goats' field and watched one of the kids feeding, with its ridiculous tail whisking round and round.

'I don't feel like that myself,' he said gloomily. 'It's death in our profession, once you reach middle age. And I don't know how all the time has slipped away. Where have they all gone, those years? I don't feel as though I've got anywhere.'

'That's how I felt when I came back from the States. Nearly twenty years of so-called success and money-making. But the films weren't of the lasting kind. My personal life was a total mess. And the money had all gone in divorce settlements. I decided to start all over again. Stop thinking about being a glamorous young star and concentrate on parts that gave me personal satisfaction – and believe me, it's the older parts that have real depth to them. Made up my mind to live quietly within my means. Then I met Mary, and everything just seemed to come together. I've never been as happy as this in my life before, never. For heaven's sake, man, stop trying to be young! Enjoy the age you are – it's the prime of life! Otherwise, you'll turn around one day and find you are old, without having had the pleasures of middle life.'

Amazed by this outburst from Rupert, who had once been so elegant and arrogant a young blood, Giles could only grunt noncommittally.

'We all envied you Frances, you know,' said Rupert, grinning. 'That beautiful, intelligent girl – can't think why she fell for you instead of me. And the astonishing thing is, she's more beautiful than ever now. Motherhood and middle age obviously suit her. Can't think why you live this life, semi-detached from her. And still chasing bits of skirt who can't hold a candle to her. Honestly, Giles – why don't you grow up?'

* * *

'Happy?' Gregor asked unexpectedly, meeting Frances by the tent, where she was herding together the children for the nature trail.

She stood quite still, for a moment, half turned towards him, her arms full of cardigans and jerseys pressed on her by children as the afternoon grew hotter.

Happy? What an odd thing for him to say to her. She had arrived this morning torn by doubts, guilty at not feeling guilty about Giles. She was worried about Katya and Anya, even a bit concerned about Tony. Dad's helplessness was so distressing she tried not to think about it. And now, this afternoon, this new worry about Lisa. The premature contractions might mean something had gone wrong with the baby. She couldn't get that out of her mind. And there was this blow about the £100,000 needed to repair St Martins, and Nick's and Peter's certainty that she would find a way to solve their problems.

How could she feel happy? Yet she realised that she was strangely light of heart, standing here in the middle of the garden party, with the children swirling around her and the parents entering a sleepy mid-afternoon phase.

Gregor was looking at her as he had done several times that day, as though he was trying to peer inside her, and read her thoughts. There had been a time when they could always read each other's thoughts, like twins. She smiled at him uncertainly.

'Happy? Yes. Yes, I'm happy. And you?'

'Oh yes.' He lifted the pile of jerseys out of her arms and set them on the grass beside the tent.

★ ★ ★

And Frances herself, thought Giles. His casual affairs had begun to pall recently. There was something tawdry about them, he had to admit. There had been a lot of truth in what Rupert had said. And through it all Frances had remained faithful to him. He didn't deserve it, he knew. But there had always been a straightness and honesty in her character. She would never have betrayed him behind his back. If she had had enough of him, she would have said so, openly and to his face.

Rupert thought her even more beautiful now than when she was a girl. Such a thought had never entered Giles's head, attracted as he was by the bland, characterless faces of his usual girls. He had stopped looking at Frances a long time ago. Frances was simply there, familiar and comfortable as a favourite armchair. Something to come back to when you were tired and wanted soothing.

He caught sight of her now, over by that awful green tent someone had put up. Children were dancing about her like gnats, and she was talking to that fellow Gregor, the sculptor, who had been brought up as a sort of adopted brother to

Frances and Hugh. Giles found he was seeing her properly now, quite suddenly. Her dark brown hair fell forward over her cheeks as she leaned down to speak to Chrissie. There were some grey hairs in it, he knew, but only a few. You couldn't tell that from here, and it was as thick and glossy as ever. She was wearing one of the long flared skirts she had always favoured, because, she said, they gave you freedom of movement. It was a knitted fabric of cream printed with soft blues and greens. She wore a cream blouse with a collar that turned up at the back, and she had rolled the sleeves up to the elbow. She looked serene and composed, and totally remote from him.

As he watched, she grew suddenly still. Gregor had said something that startled her. With his actor's aptitude for reading body language, Giles could see that as clearly as if he had been beside them. He saw her suddenly smile at Gregor, her whole face alive and eager. My God! thought Giles. She is *beautiful*. I never realised.

He saw Gregor lean across and take a pile of something – clothes it looked like – out of her arms. He placed them carefully on the ground. Then he touched Frances's bare arm. It was an oddly intimate gesture.

★ ★ ★

Nicholas had managed to escape from a couple who lived at Stanway Bridges and who were clients of the law firm in which he was the junior partner. They had cornered him half an hour before, trying to get some free advice about a dispute they were involved in with a neighbour who had built a fence encroaching on their property. He felt rather indignant about this, wanting to point out that he would not come to the husband in the middle of a party and expect him to mend his car. (The husband owned three garages in the neighbourhood.) However, he had not yet devised a way of wriggling out of such situations politely.

He wished he could ask William's advice about the best way to deal with this recurrent problem, but conversation with his grandfather was embarrassing and agonising these days, as the old man strained to form the words of simple sentences. Nicholas had noticed Mabel helping him off a little while ago for an afternoon rest, so he would be fit for the evening's events. Some of the guests were drifting away too, those who lived nearby, to put younger children down for naps while the older children were entertained on the nature trail. There would be a general lull now, until drinks were served on the terrace as they all gathered again for the play.

His mind was full of the things he had to do – take charge of the nature trail with Mum if Paul didn't turn up within the next ten minutes, help Sally and the others lay out the costumes in the small sitting room and Natasha's bedroom, which were being used as dressing rooms. In fact, the more he thought about it, the more he remembered they still had to do before the play. He needed to fix that loose hinge on the step-ladder before he could tack up the drapes at the back of the terrace. Help! He looked at his watch. Only three hours before it started, and he was sure Chrissie and Samira hadn't pinned the flowers to the grassy bank. He needed to talk to Eddie Pembridge about some of the scene changes too.

Nicholas hurried across the garden towards the house. Simon Frobisher fell into step beside him.

'A splendid event, Mr Kilworth,' he said suavely. 'Allow me to congratulate you.'

Nicholas made the usual mumbling disclaimer that such a remark provokes.

'It must be difficult for you,' Simon continued smoothly, 'so much responsibility. All these old people depending on you – Mrs Devereux so frail and aged, the other ladies not getting any younger (though managing so splendidly today), Mr Kaufmann confined to a wheelchair, your grandfather so tragically struck down. It is a lot of responsibility for a young man just making his way in his profession, with a wife and three young children too.'

Nicholas, only half attending to him, mumbled again. He hardly knew the fellow, and considered his remarks intrusive and offensive. He would not demean himself by pointing out that the older members of the community, though no longer as physically robust as they had once been, were all still mentally as keen-edged as ever. Including his grandfather, he suspected. A speech therapist had started to work with him, and Nick was confident that William's quiet, unshowy determination would win back his speech. He did not in any way feel that the leadership of St Martins fell on his shoulders. He and Sally were still very junior members of the community.

'I believe you are faced with some very serious repairs to the property,' Simon Frobisher was saying. 'Worrying, worrying, trying to keep up these old properties. Constant drain on the purse.'

Suddenly Nicholas was listening. Where had the fellow found that out? Very few of the community even knew about it – himself, Natasha, Peter, Gregor. Peter had probably told Birgit, but she wouldn't have discussed it with anyone. Of course, they had had some initial estimates done, and this Frobisher had his finger in the building trade, as well as his various other interests – so Nicholas had heard. Perhaps he had picked up some rumour from his connections amongst the local tradesmen.

Nicholas stopped and turned to the other man.

'What makes you think that?'

Simon made a deprecating gesture. 'Oh, just something I heard.' He smiled at Nicholas. He had a wide, hearty smile that did not touch his eyes, which were shrewd and fixed intently on Nicholas.

'I might have a possible solution for you. I spoke to Mrs Devereux yesterday, and made a suggestion. You might care to discuss it with her. And perhaps I might call on you at your office in Hereford – at three o'clock on Tuesday.' It was a order, not a request.

It was difficult not to be bulldozed by the sheer force of this man's personality, but Nicholas took a firm grip on himself. He said, in a tone which would have made Natasha proud of him, 'I'm sorry, Tuesday afternoon is out of the question. The only time I have available next week is on Thursday. At half-past eight in the morning.'

Simon Frobisher looked amused, as if a very small dog had yapped at him. 'Very well,' he said, in a humouring voice, 'half-past eight on Thursday.'

* * *

Paul's car slithered to a halt at the front of the house in a cascade of gravel. He leapt out of it and started running. He galloped upstairs to the room he had shared with Lisa last night, and started throwing things, uncharacteristically, out of his suitcase and on to the floor. There, laid at the bottom of the suitcase under the clothes to keep them flat, were the handouts he had prepared for the nature trail. He hung his field glasses around his neck, stuffed his compass, some string and a handful of pencils in his pocket, and burrowed in the pocket of the suitcase for his field microscope.

Then he shot out of the door, along the landing, and jumped down the stairs two at a time. Mabel came out of William and Irina's room looking cross, with her finger to her lips. As soon as she saw that it was Paul, she pressed her hand instinctively to her mouth.

'How is Lisa?' she asked urgently.

Paul paused long enough to pat her shoulder.

'Fine, fine. They think it's just a false alarm. I'm to phone this evening and see whether they want to keep her in for observation overnight.'

'Oh, thank heaven! You scared me, leaping down the stairs like that.'

'I was getting the things I need for the nature trail. They haven't had to start without me, have they?'

'No, no, I don't think so. A few minutes ago Frances and Gregor were marshalling all the children over by the marquee. They hadn't found Nick yet. He and your mother were going to try to stand in for you, but they'll be glad you're back. They weren't at all sure what you had been planning to do with the children.'

'I'll get over there straight away, and set their minds at rest.'

Paul bounded through the drawing room and out on to the terrace. As he ran across to the tent he called out in reply to questions, 'Yes, she's fine. She's resting a little at the hospital. She's fine.'

Frances had paired the children off ready to set out on

the nature trail, and Nick arrived just ahead of Paul, looking flustered.

'Yes, fine,' said Paul again. 'They're going to let her come home tonight or tomorrow.'

Frances had a cherubic boy with red curls firmly by the hand. 'Johnny Dawlish is very interested in your nature walk, Paul. I'm sure you'll let him stay with you at the front.'

Paul sized up Johnny with a glance. He knew a good deal about the species boy. 'Of course,' he said, taking him over from Frances with a swift grip. 'Right, kids, let's be off.'

Chapter 10

NATASHA LAY ON her bed, with the curtains half drawn against the strong afternoon light, having been persuaded by Mabel to rest a little before the evening party. She had been unwilling at first, but seeing the way that the party was resolving itself into two parts – an exploration of the woods, the meadow and the brook for the children and a period of napping or basking in the sun for the adults – she agreed at last to retire to her room for an hour or so.

'I'll bring you a cup of tea at five,' Mabel promised. 'So you'll have plenty of time to beautify yourself before drinks at six. I'm going to lie down myself, like the rest of the oldies. The young ones are getting things ready for the play.'

Natasha winced at Mabel's categories, but interpreted them without difficulty.

'Which classification do Frances and Gregor fall into?'

'Oh, well – ' Mabel never minded being teased. 'Neither, I suppose. Middlies?'

'And what are they doing?'

'Gregor has gone sneaking off to his studio to do some work. Says he's had enough partying to last a lifetime.' Her tone was a mixture of exasperation and affection. 'He has *promised* to reappear in time for drinks. I'm not sure where Frances is. She was going to chat to her father till she found he'd gone to lie down. Last time I saw her she was at the top of the lane.'

'Could you ask her to come and see me here, at about half-past five? I want to have a quiet word with her before all the evening's entertainment starts.'

'Will do. Now you lie down and have a proper rest, Natasha, and stop gadding about like a twenty-year-old.'

When Mabel had gone off to her own room, Natasha took off her blue dress and hung it carefully in the wardrobe. She thought she would dress formally for the evening, to honour the Thespians, and to round off the evening with proper solemnity. The young ones, as Mabel called them, were planning a barbecue to follow the performance of *A Midsummer Night's Dream*, but she intended to stay well away from that. From a distance a barbecue had an intriguing, nostalgic scent, recalling summers' meals cooked over open fires at the family dacha, or whole boars roasted at Papa's hunting lodge. But this modern barbecued food was poor stuff, charred on the outside and raw in the middle. The young men liked to preside at such events, wielding long-handled implements and no doubt obeying some atavistic hunting instinct, but their skill at cooking fell well short of that of the Greshlovs' lowliest kitchen boy. She would allow them to serve her one small cutlet, and eat one mouthful of it, and honour would be satisfied.

Her silk dressing gown lay across the foot of the bed. Mabel must have laid it out for her. Natasha slid her arms into its cool folds and tied it round her waist, feeling a little guilty about Mabel. She knew that she often mocked Mabel – in her mind, if not out loud – but where would St Martins have been all these years without her? She was sometimes self-important and bossy, but she held thing together on the domestic side, as Irina could never have done, and this had left Natasha free to run the trust and the creative side of the community. She was grateful to Mabel, truly she was, and she ought to show it more. When the war ended and Mabel had pretended she had been obliged to give up her job at the village school, Natasha had known the truth of the matter, but she had stayed silent, intrigued to see how Mabel would contrive to remain at St Martins. She had watched with amusement and admiration as Mabel had wound herself firmly into the community.

Irina and Mabel – she had never been kind enough to them. Her daughter had been a great disappointment to Natasha, when in her own impatient twenties and thirties. From childhood Irina had never shown a scrap of artistic talent, and she was gauche and difficult in all social situations. As the years had passed, Natasha had come to accept this, reluctantly, remembering that Edmund had said that Irina was very like his own mother, whom Natasha had met only once before her death and who had struck her as lumpish and boring.

Irina, however, had given her Hugh and Frances, who had made up to Natasha for their mother's deficiencies, and then from Frances had come a whole stream of talented descendants for her. This late enrichment of her life had wrapped her round, lapping her against the desolation of her girlhood tragedy. She felt warm and protected against the isolation she had once felt, as sole survivor of her line.

She lay on the bed, propped up with her back against the high-piled pillows in their cases trimmed with antique hand-made lace. Her feet rested on the old-fashioned honeycomb cover over proper blankets. These she insisted on, in the face of Mabel's persuasive arguments in favour of duvets filled with hollow-fibre polyester with their easy-wash poly-cotton covers. She took up the book she was reading at night – a modern novel set in Baltimore by an American woman novelist, whose she work she loved – but could not settle to it.

Instead, she reached out and lifted down from the wall above her bed the exquisite fourteenth-century icon of the Virgin, and held it lightly and lovingly between her hands.

★ ★ ★

They have come to Budapest for two reasons, Natasha and Edmund. The first is to oversee the opening of an exhibition which Natasha is sharing with two fellow artists from Paris. It is 1925 and Natasha's career has begun to take wing. Edmund has been able to arrange a fortnight's leave from his diplomatic duties at the embassy in order to come with her. Natasha laughed at this. She who walked alone most of the distance from Petersburg to Paris, in rags, begging or stealing her food on the way – not to be able to look after herself in the distinguished capital city of Hungary! But Edmund has been firm – he cannot bear to be apart from her, and he also has some secret fears (of which he does not tell her) that there might be agents of the Bolsheviks in Budapest, who would not scruple to slip an assassin's knife into a woman now publicly known – since her fame has grown – to be distantly related to the Romanovs.

It is Edmund who has arranged everything. He has booked the tickets on the Orient Express, arranged rooms at the Gellért Hotel overlooking the Danube, and persuaded the wife of one of his colleagues to look after five-year-old Irina for a fortnight (without difficulty, because apart from an occasional tendency to whine she is a quiet, trouble-free child).

There is a second reason for this visit to Budapest, of which they have barely dared to speak to each other. Edmund has discovered, through devious diplomatic channels, that a number of Russian aristocrats have recently turned up in Budapest, coming by mysterious routes out of the heart of the closed and forbidding Soviet Union. Natasha has no hope of her immediate family, but there might be someone who has news of her great web of cousins and second cousins and third cousins. Or of friends, believed lost. Such things are still happening, even eight years after the bloody slaughter of the Revolution. It is a tiny flame of hope, and Edmund is determined to use every connection he can find through diplomatic colleagues to help in the search.

They have been over a week now in Budapest. The exhibition is ready, and the private viewing for the notables of the city will take place the next evening. Their search amongst the Russian émigrés has proved fruitless and disheartening. Those they have managed to interview have mostly been former shopkeepers or household servants, while others – known to be in the city – have simply melted away into the Hungarian countryside when it is known that they are being sought.

Edmund insists on a day's holiday, and they take a boat trip up the Danube to Margaret Island. Natasha, who has been more keyed up with anxiety than she wants to admit, relaxes with the peaceful motion of the boat and the gentle views of the passing shores. They return in the early afternoon and disembark in Pest, a little distance from the hotel and on the other side of the river, planning to stop at Café Gerbeaud in

Vörösmarty Ter to drink coffee and eat cakes before returning to the hotel to dress for dinner at the British Embassy.

'Look!' says Natasha. They are walking hand in hand along a narrow lane leading to Váci Utca, Budapest's smartest shopping street. Here, in this side street, the roadway is barely wide enough for a cart to pass, and a few dark shops peek out amongst the elaborately scrolled ironwork of the doors leading to flats. They are passing a tiny shop with a window no more than two feet wide crammed with antiques and works of art. It is clear at once that these are the sad little family treasures of exiled Russians, smuggled out hidden inside shirts or corsets, and sold off one by one as a hedge against destitution.

They peer into the window, whose glass is smeared and grimy both inside and out, and Edmund feels Natasha stiffen at his side.

'The icon,' she whispers.

'It's lovely,' he says. It portrays a very young Virgin, wide-eyed, not unlike Natasha herself, but with the great sad eyes of Byzantine art.

'It is mine,' she says flatly.

'Yours?'

'Papa gave it to me when I was born. It has been in my family for generations. It hung always above my bed.'

'Can you be sure?'

'Doushenka, each icon is unique. I prayed every night for seventeen years before my Virgin.'

The shopkeeper is shifty-eyed and pretends he has no knowledge of English or French, and very little German.

No, he does not know where the icon comes from. No, it was his assistant, not he, who bought it. He knows nothing about it. He shrugs, spits, and names the price, which is outrageous.

Edmund buys it. He would have paid any price the dirty old rogue asked. He would do anything that might help Natasha escape from the screaming nightmares that grip her still when the old terrors return.

Natasha bears the icon of the Virgin back to Paris like a living child. It has hung over her bed ever since.

Natasha held the icon between her hands, tilted slightly towards the window so that the sun falling slantwise between the curtains caught the gold leaf of the Virgin's halo, making it burn like flame. The serene eyes looked out of the face straight into the eyes of the viewer, no matter where you stood. A soft smile played about the girl's lips – secret, proud and shy. Natasha had always known that her Virgin had received the visitation of the angel, but as yet she had confided in no one. She was still pondering these things in her heart. As a child, she had felt the Virgin was her private friend, a girl not much older than herself, to whom she could confess her misdemeanours without fear of being misunderstood. The Virgin was loving and approachable, unlike the fearsome black-gowned and bearded priests, who in Natasha's childish mind were confused with a huge grey-bearded patriarch, also black-gowned, enthroned, and frowning terribly, which was her clear image of God.

When that terrible thing had happened to her, that bitter winter day in 1917, and she had fled from her defiled home in nothing but her shift, she ran through the snowy streets, crying out in her head to her Virgin of the icon: How could you betray me like this?

Finding the icon in Budapest with Edmund had been a miracle, but a small one compared with the miracle of finding Edmund, of having survived long enough to find him, of having become a new person with a new life. She had lost her faith for ever, watching her family being butchered before her eyes, little Petya last of all, holding out his arms to her. But she had rescued the icon as one might rescue a dear friend, and she looked at it now with love.

Material objects meant little to Natasha. She had learned early the bitter lesson of their impermanence. Only people mattered to her now. Although she loved to be surrounded by beautiful objects, she felt no possessiveness about them, and would as happily give them to friends as keep them. This was the only object about which she felt differently, and it was rather because it was the only link now left with her family than because of its beauty.

However, she would discuss the plan she had in mind with Frances, who was the only other member of her family to whom she had told the story of the icon.

★ ★ ★

William lay flat on his back, looking up at the ceiling. Irina's steady breathing from the other bed, interrupted occasionally by the small gasps caused by her asthma, told him that she was asleep. He was pleased. He knew that today was a sore trial to her, desperately shy as she was of outsiders, and it was a relief that some of it could be veiled over with sleep. Probably she had slept very little last night, although she had put on a brave face for him this morning. He felt very tender towards her, his poor Irina, so afraid all her life, so ashamed that she could not live up to her famous mother.

She never seemed to be able to realise her own gifts, and he had never succeeded in persuading her of their value. She had been a very loving mother, taking the orphaned Gregor to her heart as well as their own two children, despite her earlier doubts about the Baranowski family. Yet she did not readily show her feelings. And she had always given William such a deep, unquestioning love that it had raised his own feelings for her – which had started as pity – into a passion whose strength he rarely revealed, but which had underpinned his life. He wished that her sense of her own lack of worth had not held back her artistic gift. He was the only person who knew that since girlhood she had painted beautiful and meticulously accurate botanical watercolours. She kept them hidden in portfolios at the back of the wardrobe, and worked on her new pieces secretively. William could appreciate their fineness, but could understand her reluctance to show them to Natasha, whose bold and innovative canvases had brought her world-wide fame before she was thirty. Natasha would probably think Irina's work paltry and old-fashioned, but William was fascinated by her understanding of the delicate mechanisms of the plant world, and her ability to give her paintings a luminous, almost spiritual quality. When she was working on one of her paintings, all her everyday complaints and anxieties would fall away, and she would be the steady, observant, rich person he alone appeared to know.

It had amused him, watching his children and grandchildren grow up, to see how many characteristics of Irina emerged in them. Hugh, the professional botanist, and Frances with her amateur love of wild flowers and her steady failure to reach her potential, were truly Irina's children. Anya suffered from her grandmother's social gaucherie, although her upbringing had helped her overcome much of it. Tony had her skill with watercolour, and her inability to make the most of his artistic talent. Lisa had married a botanist. Nick was more like himself, but had inherited Irina's tendency to worry. Katya? Well, he couldn't quite be sure about Katya yet, she was still in the making.

He shut his eyes and imagined his own and Irina's blood and genes spreading out like the delta of a great river into a network of interlaced streams, creating their descendants. He was so thankful to Frances for having a large family. He had tried whenever he could, and in the teeth of her resistance, to help with the expense of the children. He had wanted to say to her – he never had, and now might never be able to – that it was not anything as cold as responsibility or duty that moved him, but an almost overpowering sense of gratitude.

Despite the fatigues of the day, he did not feel like sleeping, preferring to lie still and ponder. He had discovered that one consequence of losing his speech was the greater time he had to think – an advantage he was quite sure that the members of his family (so tense and anxious to help) were unaware of. It was so much easier to think, to live inside his head, than to make the grotesque effort at speech. He felt oddly liberated, after his stroke, able to distance himself from those around him and from his own body, watching its antics with detached amusement. Of course he would regain his speech, eventually. He practised his exercises carefully and in private, but at present he took a certain guilty pleasure in retreating behind his glass screen of non-communication. He also understood, for the first time, just why Peter grew so wild when people began to treat him like an imbecile after he was confined to a wheelchair.

Towards William this attitude was even more pronounced, but he had come to see it, humbly, as a gift, a chance to feel life as others must feel it. Did autistic children feel as he did now? Or those who were the victims of some mental handicap? Perfectly lucid and ordered within their own worlds, but unable to communicate?

As a young man during the Normandy invasions in 1944, William had become separated from the rest of his company during the bloody chaos of the first few days. He had found himself at a remote farm, down a narrow country lane that looked like the twin of any English country lane across the Channel. In a field he had come upon a toothless old man hoeing turnips. He might have been any English farmer, too elderly for conscription and carrying on alone. Never much of a linguist, William had tried out his half-forgotten schoolboy French, asking for directions. The old man had at first stared at him, then – recognising his uniform – had seized his arm and begun to pour out a perfect torrent of incomprehensible sounds. Later, looking back, William realised that the man's lack of teeth and a strong local patois had contributed to the difficulty. At the time he had felt as though he was drowning in a flood like black treacle – clearly warm and welcoming, but stifling in its lack of meaning. He often thought of that man now when he forced his lips and tongue through the hideously complicated motions of speech.

Frances had said that she would come later and talk to him. For Frances he would make the effort, and try not to shame either of them by gaping or dribbling. It was only his daughter, he knew, who would have thought to take his poor confused dog for a walk. If he could lean on Frances's arm, and didn't attempt to go too far, he almost felt he might manage himself to walk with old Harry to the top of the meadow rise and back.

★ ★ ★

Frances found Mrs Patel talking to Muriel Lacey beside the neglected pond at the lower end of the ground below the ha-ha. This pond had been the creation and enthusiasm of a long-departed member of the community, a sculptor who had worked during the sixties – unsuccessfully – with bricks and objects retrieved from municipal tips. Even in those times, so cherishing of the untalented, he had been unable to achieve any recognition for his bizarre artefacts. He had consoled himself by turning the old natural duckpond into a small ornamental lake, and for some years it had graced the rough ground and attracted frogs and dragonflies over from the Ludbrook.

Common sense and the chance to return to a safe job with the council had enticed him away from St Martins in the early seventies, and since then the pond had been neglected. Birgit and Peter had never much cared for it; their taste was for more formal gardens. Mr Dawlish had some mysterious and unexplained hostility to all garden pools. When asked about it, he would simply shake his head and shift away from the subject. So the pool was drifting back to a state of muddled nature: unkempt, unattractive – and probably dangerous when there were children about. Although it dated from the period after she had moved away from St Martins, Frances had always been rather fond of the miniature lake, with its water-lilies and flag irises, and the island a third of the way along its length which supported a small rowan and a colony of nesting ducks. The children had adored the place, retrieving frog spawn from it to take back in jam jars to their bedrooms in Reading – where Frances had unpleasant memories of rescuing bold tadpoles who had managed to crawl out of their bowls and start off across the carpet, and of trying, sickeningly, to separate the cannibalistic ones from their tasty siblings.

Now she found herself longing to change into jeans and waders, and get into the pond to rake out the weed that was smothering the surface and strangling the lilies. The lower bank, she thought, could be cleared of weeds and filled with bog plants. And the water irises were in desperate need of being lifted and separated.

Muriel and Mrs Patel were sitting on the seat that had been placed for viewing the pond. It was not particularly comfortable – just some boards supported on two low brick pillars – but it stood under the edge of a weeping willow tree, providing a secluded and pleasant place on a hot afternoon.

'Don't get up,' said Frances to them firmly, as they tried to make room for her on the seat, which was only large enough for two. 'I'm going to make myself useful and do a bit of tidying.'

She found a long thin branch which had come down from the willow during the winter storms, and thrust it into the pond. Then she began to wind up the weed like spaghetti, drawing it to the side of the pond and scooping it off the stick into the long grass.

'Very clever,' said Muriel.

'It was Nick who worked out the method, when he was about fifteen. It's surprisingly effective.'

'Samira,' said Mrs Patel shyly, 'is so fond of his daughter.'

'We love Samira too,' said Frances, scooping away at the weed, with her back to them. 'I think she and Chrissie are really good friends – it's lasted five years now, and that's a good basis for a lifetime's friendship.'

'They both often come and help me in the museum,' said Muriel. 'They're very *useful*, not like some children. Chrissie arranges and dusts the exhibits, and Samira likes to do the metal polishing. I always give them old shirts of Richard's to wear as overalls. I do hope Samira doesn't come home *too* dirty.'

'Sometimes children need the chance to get dirty,' said Frances. 'Especially little girls. They're always being told to wash their hands and brush their hair and tidy themselves up. Little boys, of course, quite rightly ignore all this. They go out and have a gloriously creative time making messes. The pressures are greater on little girls to conform to some tidy image, aren't they? Even nowadays.'

She turned round, a cone of weed like drowned green hair dripping across her arm. 'But I think we should encourage our girls to enjoy their freedom while they're young, don't you?' She gave Samira's mother a wide conspiratorial smile.

'I – I'm not sure,' said Mrs Patel, hesitantly.

'They need the chance to develop their potential, without having to be miniature adult women. Heaven knows they'll spend so much of the rest of their lives caring for other people, doing what other people expect of them – conforming.' Frances made a face. 'Of course, it's a good thing for all children to develop a sense of responsibility, not to think that they have special privileges and will always be waited on.'

'Yes. You are right, of course,' said Mrs Patel.

'I remember,' said Muriel, 'when I was eight I longed for a guinea pig. My mother said I could have one, but only on condition that I took on the entire responsibility for looking after it myself. Of course I promised glibly, having no idea what was involved. I soon learned! I *hated* cleaning out the cage, but as he lived in my room, I had to put up with the smell if I didn't! And once I forgot to give him fresh food for two days. When he nearly died I was so upset I really understood what it meant, to keep a pet.'

Bless you, Muriel, thought Frances.

'I always think a dog is the best pet for a child,' she went on, innocently. 'There isn't all the cleaning up you have with a caged pet – dogs don't really make a mess. Looking after the feeding is a responsibility, but not too troublesome. Then taking a dog for a walk, and perhaps going to obedience classes, is good healthy exercise. And I always feel,' she said, rounding off her case, 'that a child with a dog is a lot safer from danger than a child on her own.'

She shook the wad of pondweed decisively off into the grass.

There was a little silence, while Mrs Patel thought this over.

'I've just had a *splendid* idea,' said Muriel. 'Sally will be wanting homes for Jeannie's pups, won't she?'

'Yes. One is promised to Miss Bagshaw, but that's all. And of course Chrissie is to have one. They felt it was time she took on responsibility for her own dog.'

'That means there will be three left,' Muriel cried with shining eyes, turning to Mrs Patel. 'Why don't you ask Sally if you could have one for Samira? Harry and Jeannie's pups are always *lovely* dogs, very intelligent and well behaved. Do ask her!'

'Oh, I couldn't possibly! But perhaps you are right. Perhaps she should have a dog. We could get one at a pet shop.'

'No, no,' said Frances firmly. 'You really wouldn't know what you were getting. I'd be very happy to ask Sally. Shall I?'

'Yes,' said Mrs Patel, suddenly deciding that she liked the idea. 'Yes, if you please.'

★ ★ ★

Mia fully understood that she had been manoeuvred by Frances in the matter of the puppy for Samira, but she had allowed it to happen. Partly because the suggestion had taken her completely by surprise and partly because she was amused by Frances's naive English attempt at deception. It would have been so hopelessly out-matched by the wiles of her own mother or grandmother negotiating with a fruit-seller or workman over prices and services in her own village. She found it entertaining that Frances thought she had been taken in, but she liked Frances and managed to keep her own face straight.

★ ★ ★

It was cool in Gregor's studio, after the sun in the garden. To let in the breeze and some light he opened the tops of two of the old stall doors, where horses had once poked their heads out into the yard, but closed the big main door behind him, shutting out the view of the pretentious silver Mercedes parked outside. He had told Mabel he was going to do some work and allowed her to think that meant his Venus. But in truth the Venus was all but ready to ship, apart from a final rub over.

He stood with folded arms, looking at the huge, angry piece with its pendulous breasts and ravenous mouth, and remembered the stricken look on Frances's face when she had seen it that morning. He had come to hate it himself, and had nearly abandoned it in disgust, but a sort of guilt about leaving any task unfinished, however distasteful (probably inflicted on him in childhood by Mabel), had kept him going to the end. He would make arrangements to ship it off to Texas next week, and that would be the last of it.

With a dismissive shrug, he turned and climbed up the spiral staircase that led to his quarters above the stables. When he had returned to St Martins from California the stables had been only partially converted – the ground floor level being used as overflow studios when they were needed, while the upstairs – reached by an interior door from the music rooms, now blocked – simply served as storage space. Gregor had built the spiral staircase himself, and it now provided the only access to his private part of St Martins. Natasha had insisted that Nicholas and Sally should have a proper family home, but the other members of the community, apart from Gregor, all lived together in a happy muddle, sharing the kitchen and two bath-rooms, and using Natasha's drawing room whenever they wished. This arrangement only worked because they all respected each other's privacy, but even so Natasha knew that Gregor would be happier with his own domain.

He had made the row of lofts into one large space, lit from both east and west by windows – at one side set into the old trapdoor for the hoist and at the other replacing the broken remains of a dovecote. His bed consisted of a slatted platform (again made by himself) and he had built cupboards by boxing in the wedge-shaped space created by the slope of the roof. There had already been a cold stand-pipe in the stable, for the use of the grooms in the old days. Natasha had had this extended upstairs for him and a small water heater installed over the sink, which served him for cooking and washing. When he wanted a shower he went over to the main house, but his near self-sufficiency pleased him. He could always retreat here when he wanted to be alone and quiet.

He rinsed a dirty mug now under the tap – his normal labour-saving method of washing up – and plugged in the electric kettle. When it boiled he put coffee, sugar and milk all in the bottom of the mug and poured the hot water over them. Ignoring the lumps of undissolved coffee floating about on the surface, he carried the mug over to his one ancient armchair by the east-facing window. The mug had been given to him last Christmas by Katya – cheeky monkey – and said in big careless letters on the side: 'Sculptors do it in clay'. She said she had had it specially made for him by a college friend of Tony's who was down on his luck. Gregor felt himself both repelled by it and fond of it. He used it for his coffee every day.

He drank some of the coffee, then set the mug down on the floor by his feet and leaned his head back against the chair, with his eyes closed. In the last few years he had begun to feel he was settled for life. This bare spacious room provided all his physical needs, the studio below – together with his work – all his spiritual ones. He had envisaged himself growing old with vigour and grace, like Natasha, amongst people he loved, in the place he preferred before anywhere else in the world. His secure reputation brought him more commissions than he could handle; because he worked slowly and painstakingly he would never become a rich man, but he had more than sufficient for his needs.

Now, it seemed, there was a snake in his Eden. The news Nick had broken to him, along with Natasha and Peter, had stunned him. He accepted, humbly, that he was not in many ways a practical man. He was good with his hands, whether he was working at his sculpture or mending a chair leg, but he never bothered his head with household budgeting. He paid his rent and his share of the running costs into the trust by standing order, and never gave them another thought. He was ashamed that Nick had had to take on the worry over the repairs, but he felt helpless himself when confronted with the prospective cost. He would see what he could do to raise some money towards it, and he felt awkward about two commissions he had recently turned down because he wanted time to work on his new piece, a bronze, which he was doing for his own satisfaction and would not sell.

His mind reeled at the amount – £100,000. How could they possibly raise that much? None of them was rich. Nick said the repairs to the roof must be done before the winter, or the rain and snow would start to come in, causing more damage. The repointing of the tower could probably be left till next spring. The dangerous state of the wiring – well, it depended how far they were prepared to risk their lives.

'We could go back to oil lamps,' Gregor now said defiantly out loud, 'and disconnect the electricity.' But that would mean no hot water for him, and only the wood stove in the studio to heat this great volume of air – no storage heaters on both levels as there were now. He could sleep downstairs by the stove. He himself and Nick's family could all eat in the big kitchen with the others. Thank God they had kept the old solid fuel range. But he saw that all this could only be a makeshift arrangement. They had managed in primitive conditions in the first few years of the community, but there had been no elderly people to keep warm then. Peter, stuck in his wheelchair, had difficulties with his circulation. William would need special care for a long while yet. Natasha was over ninety.

Oh God, he groaned, what are we going to do?

And although he tried to keep the question of the money at the front of his mind, as the most urgent, there was this other problem. St Martins might cease to be his concern, because for the last six months he had been thinking that he might have to leave.

When he had returned to St Martins – more than ten years ago now – he had known that Frances was safely living in Reading. It was all so long ago. He was well over it. She . . . well, she had shown how she felt by her betrayal of him. At her wedding reception Gregor, for the first and last time in his life, had drunk himself silly, then spent the whole night after they had left for their honeymoon wandering around the estate, being sick into the bushes every hour or so. He had not originally intended to stay for the wedding. After his fight with Frances in the wood-shed the previous Christmas he would have liked to walk out of St Martins, but he was taking his second optional year at art college and felt that he could not let Natasha down by dropping out. Since the wedding was to take place the weekend after his summer term finished, he decided that to leave before it would be a sign of weakness – it would show Frances how much he cared – so he had waited until she had departed on her honeymoon and then announced to Natasha that he was going to Italy. She had not been surprised, only grieved.

She had said simply, 'You have your work, Gregor. Many men do not have that.'

Coming back after his years of travelling and occasional desultory affairs, he was sure that Frances's visits to St Martins with her children would cause him no pain. He had put behind him any thought of marriage and children; celibacy seemed in keeping with the solitary nature of his work. Reaching this decision had brought him a sense of release, a cool, clean feeling of independence.

By the end of the first day of the first visit of Frances and her children to St Martins, he realised that his feelings for her were not as cool and detached as he had supposed. Their long separation had left him confused and ambivalent. After that, he tried to avoid her when she visited – pleading work, skulking in his studio – but this discovery about himself did not change his resolve. He got on well with the children, rather to his surprise. They seemed to have little of Giles in their make-up, apart from some physical resemblances in Anya and Tony. Perhaps it came of their being brought up so much by their mother. When he had been home about a year, Mabel let drop the true situation between Frances and Giles: his string of affairs, carelessly flaunted; her loyalty (misplaced, in Mabel's view).

Gregor became an honorary uncle to the children, although Anya and Nick were adults by then. But it was with the baby, Katya, that a particularly close relationship had grown up. He would have liked a daughter like Katya, awkward though she could sometimes be nowadays.

In the past few years he had found ways of coping with Frances's visits. She, for her part, was courteous but distant, as though she was holding back even from that other kind of friendship they had once had, before the summer of their love affair. Thinking of it now, he felt his hands grip the arms of his chair, and a hot pulse beating in his neck. But he could cope.

Then they had come down for Christmas six months ago, all of them except Giles, who was doing a show in the north.

★ ★ ★

It is Christmas Eve 1993, the cooking preparations are all taken care of, and there will be a watch-night service in the village church, to which most of them have decided to go.

Three hours need filling in between their Christmas Eve dinner and the time they must leave for the service, and Tony, Lisa and Katya have put their heads together.

'We're going to play parlour games,' says Lisa, pretty and flushed. She has just announced her pregnancy. 'We have appointed Tony as Master of Ceremonies, so you all have to do what he says.'

They play charades first – very successful, though abilities are mixed.

Then Pelmanism. Mabel is hopeless. Gregor and William, closely matched, have to have a sudden death play-off.

Hide-and-seek – everyone is getting into the spirit of things now. Chrissie wins by climbing inside the grandfather clock (it runs irregularly for weeks afterwards).

Forfeits. Some complicated version Tony has learned at college, which involves the loser having to be kissed by the winner, whatever their age or sex. (Gregor, remembering his own days at art college, suspects this is a watered-down version of the game.)

Mabel loses to Peter.

Bob loses to Tony. ('Yuck,' says Bob.)

Katya loses to Natasha.

Frances loses to Gregor.

He ought to have seen it coming, but there is no escape. He marches her out to the obligatory bunch of mistletoe in the hall and takes her briskly by the shoulders. Then he makes the mistake of looking at her, something he usually manages to avoid doing. She is frightened. And suddenly the anger and pain that he thought he had left behind rises up, blurring his vision. If the others had not been crowded into the drawing-room door, cheering him on, he would have let go of her and fled back to his studio. Instead he kisses her roughly, carelessly, on the mouth. ('It must be on the mouth,' says Tony. 'No good otherwise.') He can feel her under his hands. His old desire for her is still there.

★ ★ ★

Gregor picked up his cold cup of coffee, unattractively skinned over, then gathered together his long legs and got up wearily from the chair. He felt bone tired. He poured the coffee down the sink and washed away the residue with a spurt from the cold tap. There was still time to do a little work before he had to put on his public face again.

The new piece stood at the back of the studio, with its damp sacking hiding it from view. As Gregor lifted the sacking and laid it aside, the light from one of the stall doors fell on the figure, making iridescent rainbow pools on the wet clay.

He studied it thoughtfully. It represented an entirely new direction for him, yet it was in a classic tradition, reaching back through Rodin and Michelangelo to the sculptors of the Golden Age of Athens. He dampened his hands, and ran a loving palm over the curves of the figure. That scamp with her mug! 'Sculptors do it in clay.' He laughed out loud.

★ ★ ★

Paul had completed the tour of the meadow. Between them the children had managed to find twenty-seven different varieties of wild flower, and proudly filled in their sheets. They had spent even longer at the Ludbrook, looking for sticklebacks (none found), identifying water-loving plants (seven), and analysing the bottom of the stream. Melissa had half fallen in, wetting the unsuitable skirt her mother had forced her to wear, under protest, to the party, and been wrung out by Samira and Chrissie, who had gathered huge untidy bunches of wild flowers for the play scenery. Two other children had got their shoes wet, and one child, wading in barefoot and careless, had stubbed his toe painfully on a large stone. Not too bad a record of injuries, Paul reckoned.

He was hurrying them now through the wood, aware that he was running out of time but wanting to help them complete the sheet on trees. The group had begun to disintegrate since they had left the brook, and he had lost hold of Johnny Dawlish earlier than that – before Melissa had fallen in. About six of them were still grouped close to him, and he could see perhaps ten others dodging about amongst the trees playing tig.

'Come along now,' he called. 'We'll just count up how many varieties we have, then we'd better get back. It's nearly time for more food!'

These magic words enticed most of the children in. They came bearing their leaves and bits of beech mast and sycamore seeds. Paul never went out on a nature walk without counting noses first. He counted quickly again – twenty-one. Drat! He was two short. And one of them was Johnny Dawlish.

'Has any one seen – ' he was just beginning, when from deeper in the wood there came the splintering noise of breaking wood, a shriek, a loud thud, and then a mighty howl.

A small boy came breathlessly crashing through the trees towards them.

'Sir, sir,' he cried, school manners automatically reasserting themselves, 'Sir, Johnny Dawlish has fallen out of a tree, and I think he's dead.'

Chapter 11

O F COURSE JOHNNY Dawlish was not dead. The sound
that filled the wood suggested a stuck pig, but a healthy
one. Still, it had given Paul a bad moment. He set off at a run
in the direction of the noise, the other children following him
eager as hounds on the scent. Johnny was sitting at the foot of
a beech tree, beside a branch with a torn and shattered end,
nursing his right ankle in both hands. As soon as he caught
sight of Paul, he redoubled his yells.

The children grouped themselves around him with
expressions of detached interest or sympathy, with the exception
of Melissa, who did not try to hide her delight. 'See! That's
what happens,' she hissed, through the gaps where some of her
second teeth were still coming in. 'Serve you right.'

Johnny gave her a look of loathing and continued to yell.
The performance was beginning to sound a bit mechanical.

Paul knelt down in the dried leaves of last autumn and felt
the ankle. 'Nothing broken, I think, Johnny.'

'Oh, do shut up, Johnny,' said Chrissie in exasperation. 'You
are a sissy.'

Johnny transferred his glowering look from Melissa to Chrissie, but he let his yells die away. His throat was getting rather
sore.

'Right,' said Paul, standing up and brushing the leaves off
the knees of his trousers. 'Time for a little first-aid practice.
I'm going to take off Johnny's shoe and sock, in case his foot
starts to swell and gets stuck. Then I'm going to make a simple
bandage with my handkerchief. It isn't really large enough, but
it will give the ankle a bit of support. There may be nothing
more than bruising, but we're going to assume it's a sprain.'

This began to look more promising even than the nature trail. Johnny assumed an air of heroic suffering while Paul eased off his shoe and peeled down the grubby sock underneath.

'Pee-uu!' shouted all the other children together, grabbing their noses.

Paul made his handkerchief into a small neat bandage round the ankle – which was showing no sign yet of swelling – and handed Johnny's shoe and sock to one of the other boys to carry. He held it at arm's length, holding his nose ostentatiously with the other hand.

'Right, now, Johnny.' Paul stooped down with his back to the boy. 'Get your arms round my neck and I'll give you a lift back to the house where we can get a proper look at that ankle and decide what to do with you.'

The excited procession started back from the wood, led by the Shoe, with Melissa, Chrissie and Samira bringing up the rear, whispering amongst themselves and giggling.

★   ★   ★

Mia, Frances and Muriel reached the kitchen just ahead of the excited party of children from the nature trail. Paul lowered Johnny Dawlish into one of the rush-seated chairs, where he sat with his leg sticking out like Long John Silver's wooden leg.

'Johnny,' said Paul, 'fell out of a tree. I haven't discovered how he came to be up a tree in the first place, when they were all forbidden to do anything so silly, but there you are. I don't think it is anything serious, but I'm no expert.'

Frances and Mia knelt down by Johnny's chair. Frances gave a quick thumbs-up sign to Chrissie and Samira, who were crowded with the other children in the doorway, then unwound Paul's handkerchief.

'I'm not an expert either,' said Frances. 'Only the usual excitements of child-rearing have come my way – broken collarbones, front teeth knocked out, things like that.'

'Perhaps I can help, Mrs Kilworth,' said Mia.

'I do wish you'd call me Frances,' she said, without looking up.

'Thank you.' Mia swallowed. 'My name is Mia.'

'What a pretty name!' Frances lifted her head and smiled at her. 'Do you know about this sort of thing?'

'I did a course in first aid,' said Mia shyly. 'When we were living in Bristol.'

'I wish you'd take over, then.'

Within five minutes Mia determined that there was no break, and not even a sprain. Johnny's entire performance had been designed to elicit sympathy and divert attention from his own crime in climbing – and breaking – the beech tree. His shoe and sock were restored to him amidst much mockery from his friends, and the children ran off.

'Thank you, Mia,' said Frances. 'Let's all have a cup of tea before the next round of celebrations. Muriel, tea for you?'

'Oh, Frances,' said Mabel, hurrying in, 'are you making tea? Would you take a cup to Natasha? I'm late with it, and she was wanting to see you. There's something she wants to talk to you about.'

* * *

Hugh's plane was circling over Heathrow. Incoming flights were stacked up, and they had already been waiting twenty minutes.

'If I look out one more time and see Windsor Castle going past underneath again,' said the woman sitting next to Hugh, 'I think I shall scream. This seems to happen to me every time I come into Heathrow.'

She was a university professor from the Midlands, a woman of about his own age, also returning from Russia, where she had been arranging student exchanges with her opposite number at the University of Moscow.

'The problem,' she had explained to Hugh, 'is the imbalance in the numbers. The Russian students all have passable English and would kill to get on to the programme and spread their wings abroad. But our students are such poor linguists. They have perhaps scraped through GCSE French, and immediately forgotten it. Russian is quite beyond them. They fancy a year in Russia, but only if they can take all their classes in English.'

'What is your subject?'

'I'm a historian – and in my day that meant you had to have

205

good Latin and French, and possibly German. Nowadays I'm director of a school of European studies, which we've recently been extending to include Eastern Europe. But during those awful financial cuts of the eighties, the university lost its modern languages department. I ask you! How parochial this country has become!'

'Yes, I had to have Latin and French to get into Cambridge – even for science.' He grinned. 'In *my* day. But I've always loved languages, and they seem to come to me easily. It's been very useful to me.'

'Yes,' she said briskly, 'I know who you are, but I'm not going to embarrass you by asking for your autograph, like that flirtatious stewardess.'

Hugh laughed. 'Fine. Tell me more about your programme. Why don't you make it a condition that your prospective exchange students attend a crash course in Russian?'

They had had an enjoyable discussion as the landscape unrolled beneath them, but the delay in landing was annoying for them both. Hugh could see that he had now lost his chance of catching the train he had intended. Professor Hughes said that her husband would be cursing at the way the car park charge would be mounting up.

'He didn't need to drive down and meet me, but he's very sweet about it. He never seems to worry about the cost of the petrol, but he becomes quite wild about car park charges, especially at places like airports, where he feels you are a helpless victim of profiteering.'

'Ladies and gentlemen,' said a man's voice over the intercom, 'this is your chief cabin steward speaking. I'm afraid we will be experiencing a few more minutes' delay. We will shortly be serving complimentary drinks from the bar.'

'Trying to buy us off with alcohol,' said Professor Hughes.

The stewardess, whose smile had become as fixed as her lacquered hair, hovered beside them. 'No thank you,' said Hugh. 'Nothing for me.'

'I will have a mineral water,' said Professor Hughes. 'With a slice of lemon. And plenty of ice.'

* * *

Gregor stood back from the figure, considering. Yes. He felt it was finished. He didn't want to over-work it and lose the spontaneity. He laid the damp sacking carefully over it, and carried his tools over to the sink. It was the original china clay sink of the stables, used by grooms and stable-lads in the days when the Devereux family had kept both farm horses and carriage horses in these stables. He often thought of those men and the beasts they cared for when he turned on the same tap as their hands had once held. This whole area in the back corner was just as it had been. There was only a cold tap, no hot water, and the sink rested on four brick legs. At one side was a cupboard once used to hold simple remedies for the horses and the stablemen's gear — saddle soap and linseed oil, thread and bits of spare leather for mending tack. When Gregor and Natasha had cleaned the place out after he returned from California, they had found a rotting ball of oiled thread, and a bottle covered in dust and cobwebs, with a dark purple residue in the bottom.

'Gentian violet,' said Natasha. 'I remember the grooms using it when I was a girl. They painted it on small wounds, where one horse had kicked another, or a horse had knocked himself on a gate. When I was little I used to be very frightened of it — the treatment looked much worse than the wound! But old Sergei swore by it.'

On the other side of the sink was a wooden draining board. This had been thick with sticky dirt when Gregor had moved in, but he had sanded it down carefully and then rubbed it over several times with oil. The wood had warmed to a beautiful dark red, probably pitch pine. He kept it regularly oiled now, and cleaned his tools meticulously. Although he cared little for his clothes, preferring the comfort of shapeless trousers and old baggy jerseys, he could not bear untidiness in his work.

* * *

'You can't go off looking like that!' said Frances. They were all three at Hereford railway station. Frances and Hugh had their bicycles, strapped all around with gear for the two weeks they were going to spend cycling from Cheltenham through the Cotswolds, and on as far as Stratford-upon-Avon.

'Why not?' said Gregor aggressively. They always seemed to be quarrelling this summer, he and Frances. She had begun to find fault with everything he did or said, and he reacted like a sleepy bear suddenly prodded beyond endurance with a stick. He saw himself that way – a clumsy hibernating Polish bear, who had been poked out of his dreams by vicious little boys.

'You have perfectly respectable clothes to wear to your course in London,' she said. 'You don't have to shame us all by turning up in down-at-heel shoes and a threadbare duffelcoat. Honestly, Gregor – can't you make a little effort?'

'Leave off, Franny,' said Hugh in a pacifying voice. He didn't know what was the matter with the other two this summer. Last year, the summer before Frances went up to Oxford, they had wanted to be together every minute, and he had taken himself off discreetly on several occasions so they could be alone. Now, for the first time ever, Gregor had refused to come with them on their cycle tour. He was going to spend a month at his college in London, getting some extra tuition himself and paying for it by teaching on a summer course for amateurs.

'It's different at art school,' said Gregor patiently, trying to keep his tone level. He had explained all this before. 'People don't expect you to dress up. In fact, they'd despise you if you did.' He drew a deep breath. 'Not like your swanky Oxford friends.' He couldn't hold it back.

'Don't you dare speak about Oxford like that! It just shows how ignorant you are – your ideas haven't moved on since the nineteenth century. Nowadays people have to *work* to get in. They don't get in because they're rich or titled.'

'It helps if you've been at an expensive school,' Hugh put in mildly.

'For the men, perhaps,' Frances flashed at him. 'Not the women.'

'OK, OK!' Hugh held up his hands in a gesture of surrender. 'I think Gregor was talking about the men – your London friends. And, if it comes to that,' he grinned wickedly, 'Gregor has a title.'

'Don't be daft,' said Gregor crossly.

Frances bit her lips. There were tears on her eyelashes. 'I'm sorry, Gregor. I suppose you know best how things are at your college. It's just . . . '

'Leave it,' said Hugh. 'Here's our train. We'll see you in a month, Gregor, when you've finished beating your sculpture students over the head with a mallet. I hope they know what they are letting themselves in for.'

'Don't get blisters on your bum,' Gregor rejoined. He was cheered by Frances's change of tone. 'You've been getting soft all winter.'

Hugh began loading the bicycles into the guard's van. Frances and Gregor stood uncertainly, looking at each other.

'I'd better go and check the platform for my train,' said Gregor. They both knew it would be leaving from this same one. 'Well, goodbye, then. Have a good time.' He held out his hand formally.

Frances made a sudden, suppressed noise, then she leaned forward and kissed him quickly on the lips. 'Goodbye,' she said in a small voice.

He stood watching as their train pulled out, not waving. Then he turned aside and touched his lips once with his fingertip.

★ ★ ★

'Let's just help ourselves,' said Giles to Alice Tyler. He had come across this attractive girl being monopolised by a large, powerful man of the type Giles always thought of contemptuously as 'City gent'. A most unexpected guest at Natasha's party. Pin-striped suit. Very white, very new shirt. Dark thick hair, just beginning to grey in the right places to make him look distinguished (not thinning on top like his own). Heavy gold signet ring. Discreet tie-pin. He was the sort of man, Giles thought, who would attend the opera because it was currently in vogue, not because it gave him pleasure. He would take care to be seen at the plays which were being discussed in the right circles, but would not have the imagination to understand a creative new interpretation of a classic Shakespeare or Chekhov play. His only reading would be company reports and the *Financial Times*.

He might, from his appearance, have been the product of the same social class which had produced Giles himself (and his father, whom the man somewhat resembled) but Giles's fine-tuned awareness of voices detected something wrong in the man's speech. The merest underlying trace of something at once alien and tougher than the language amongst which he had himself grown up. There was also about the man a slight hint of menace, as if – should you oppose him in some crucial matter – he might become threatening.

The girl was extremely attractive. He liked a girl who could wear tight white trousers which continued all day to look neither creased nor strained at the seams. The open neckline on her hot red blouse was deep enough to be provocative without being vulgar. And unlike most of the girls who came his way, she did not gush or press herself upon him, exuding desire (real or feigned) like a scent of musk. This girl – Alice, he discovered her name was – seemed rather cool and distant towards him, although perfectly courteous, and her smile held a hint of amusement which was suggestive. He found himself stirred and attracted by her all the more because of this slight withholding of herself.

Alice was quite relieved to be rescued from Simon Frobisher. It had been a useful contact to make, and she had set about selling herself and her work with her usual skill. This had become almost second nature to her now, so that she could keep up the mixture of mild flirtatiousness and shrewd business talk while thinking about other things, such as what to do about Tony, whom she liked and was exasperated by in about equal measures. However, by half-past five she felt she really had devoted enough time to Frobisher, and was wondering how to get rid of him without endangering the prospect of a commission. She was surprised, too, that he had stayed with her so long. He must have wished to, for he was the sort of man who would simply walk away when it suited him, not caring whether he caused offence or not. She decided that he lingered at her side partly because he was attracted to her – often an important factor in her business negotiations – and partly because he seemed to be waiting for something to happen. From time to time his attention would wander, and she would become aware that he was gazing beyond her towards the house or some other part of the garden. This sense of expectancy began at last to unnerve her, so that she welcomed Giles's arrival, although she took good care not to show it.

The covert fencing between these two middle-aged men Alice found entertaining. She knew who Giles was, though it was immediately clear that he did not know who she was. And the two men did not know each other. Alice imagined that Simon was a man whose life was too occupied with more important issues for him to find the time to watch anything so trivial as *Vet in Hot Water*. And unless he was a devotee of the theatre – which he showed no sign of being – he was unlikely ever to have seen Giles on stage. (Alice had seen him only once herself.) She knew from Tony that Giles rarely came to St Martins, so it was not surprising he had never met Simon Frobisher. Alice always enjoyed being in possession of more knowledge about the people around her than they had themselves, and this added spice to the manoeuvrings of Giles to cut her away from Simon. Giles was a skilled operator, who must regularly capture girls like this, but he would not have succeeded if Simon had not been willing to let her go. She saw Simon suddenly make a decision, as though his waiting was over, and then he excused himself, saying that he needed to make some business calls. He had a phone, he said, in his car.

'Thank goodness we've got rid of him,' said Giles, placing a hand under her elbow and drawing it very intimately to his side. 'I can't stand that money-grubbing type of fellow. Creatively dead from the neck up.'

Alice contemplated responding, in order to provoke him, 'But not from the waist down.' She decided, however, that it would be more entertaining to allow Giles to take the lead in their initial exchanges, so she merely smiled.

Desmond Fraser was helping Olga and Katya lay out bottles

and glasses on a side table on the terrace, and Chrissie and Samira appeared, both carrying large trays of cocktail savouries with elaborate and nervous care.

'I have to go and get changed now,' said Chrissie, with a touch of self-importance. 'The performance is starting in just over half an hour.'

'Yes,' said Olga, 'come along. You can help me fix my ruff properly, and I'll help you with tying your points.'

'Points?' said Alice to Giles, who was pouring a spritzer for her and a gin and tonic for himself.

'The laces that hold your hose on to your shirt. Each one has to be tied separately. Crazy method of dressing – can't think why men put up with it so long. Absolutely bane of one's life in a Shakespeare play where the producer is aiming for authenticity. I'd have thought the village group would have settled for stretch tights.' He spoke tolerantly, with a little gentle amusement at the antics of such amateurs. 'Here you are, then. Cheers!'

'Cheers,' said Alice. 'I've heard they're rather good – the village players,' she said innocently.

'Oh, well, I suppose it helps to pass the long tedious winter evenings in the country. But at this time of the year I would have thought they would be stooking the corn, or whatever it is they do.' He gave the phrase the exaggerated Mummersetshire accent of slapstick comedy.

'I believe they do that later in the year. I should think haymaking happens about now, though I couldn't say for sure. I'm a city girl myself.'

'Ah yes, haymaking. Rural romps in the hay barn, eh?' Giles's eyes gleamed briefly. 'Look, I feel a bit silly standing here on the terrace drinking alone before anyone else arrives. Let's slip away into the garden.'

'If you like,' said Alice. Really, she thought, this is so predictable.

He guided her to a corner of the shrubbery, where earlier in the afternoon he had noticed a very private seat screened both from the house and from the rest of the garden. Alice sat down and he sat next to her, so closely that their sides brushed.

They sipped their drinks.

'And what do you do, my dear?' asked Giles, setting down his glass on the seat and resting his arm along the back, behind her shoulders.

'I'm an artist. Acrylics. I have an artist-in-residence post this year, which might be renewed for another year.'

'Well done,' said Giles kindly, taking another sip of his gin. 'I could see at once that you were in one of the creative arts. I'm a man of the theatre myself.' He said it with his pretend little-boy modesty, never doubting for a moment she knew who he was. Indeed, she had already shown it by her question about tying points.

'Oh, yes, I know!' Alice put just a touch of adolescent awe into her voice, playing up to him. It amused her to think that – from what she had heard from Tony – she probably earned twice what Giles did and (apart from this recent TV success) was better known, at least in the right circles.

'Ever had an exhibition?' he asked carelessly. He wasn't really interested. It was just part of his usual lead-in. He could feel the familiar warm, fluid excitement stirring in him. He leaned towards her as though interested in her answer. This gave him a clear view down inside her blouse. As he suspected, she wore nothing under it. Very nice.

Alice, who had dealt with this routine many times before, neither moved away nor raised her hand to button her blouse higher. She simply relaxed back against his arm and looked up, flatteringly, into his eyes, her lips parted slightly.

'Well, yes. I have been exhibiting every summer for the last five years. Since I graduated. At one of the top Bond Street galleries. I'm very fortunate – I am doing quite well.'

Giles should have been listening to her. He should have paid attention to the slightly jarring note of emphasis in her words, which did not quite match her really very suggestive physical presence.

'Ah,' he said, 'splendid' – hearing nothing. He circled her shoulders with his arm and drew her towards him, slipping his hand, in one practised movement, inside her blouse to grasp her breast. The other hand slid up the inside of her thigh.

She tilted her head back as his open mouth came down towards her, and the smell of his gin flowed over her face. She smiled coolly, but made no move to struggle. She said simply, 'I am also considering marrying your son.'

* * *

Frances set down the tray of tea and biscuits on the small round table beside the french window in Natasha's bedroom which, like the two windows in the drawing room, opened directly on to the terrace. It stood ajar to admit a little air. These south-facing rooms had grown quite hot during the afternoon. Natasha came in, carrying her sponge bag.

'Ah, there you are, Frances. I thought I would have a quick shower to give me energy for our busy evening. And you've brought tea and biscuits, good. Has there been any word of Lisa yet?'

'Paul is just going to ring the hospital. I'd like to have done it myself, but I don't want him to think I'm interfering.'

'You are worried about her, aren't you?'

'I know I shouldn't be.' Frances fiddled absently with the teacups.

'She's strong and healthy, and there haven't been any complications in the pregnancy. I think you should try to be calm. Even if the baby is coming – early births run in the family.'

Natasha tidied away things from her dressing table and sat on her usual chair in the window, a low seated balloon-backed Victorian chair upholstered in dark gold velvet. Her movements were not as quick and decisive as they had been in Frances's childhood, but they were surprisingly spry for a woman of her age. The stick she had needed to use after spraining an ankle last winter seemed to have been discarded altogether, and apart from a certain concentration when she stood up from a chair, she had more vigour than many women twenty-five years younger.

'What is your secret, Natasha?' asked Frances, pouring the tea and handing a cup to her grandmother. 'How do you manage to stay so young?'

Natasha did not laugh or brush the question aside, but gave

it serious consideration. 'I suppose it is because I have always been too busy to notice that I have grown so old. There has never been a time in my life to sit down and mourn the passing of youth. Probably, if I had led a normal life I would be decrepit or in my grave by now. But I have been preserved by my active life as an English eccentric – as the good Nigel Laker would say.'

'Nigel Laker?'

'Have you not met him? He drove Giles down from London. He wants to make a television documentary about St Martins as part of a series about eccentrics and their contributions to culture.'

'No, I've not met him. If it comes to that, I haven't seen Giles either, except in the distance.' Frances took her own cup and sat, as she had always done, on the stool beside Natasha's chair. 'Would it be a good thing, this television programme, or a bad thing?'

'Ah, there you put your finger on the exact point. I think, if we can ensure that we supervise it carefully, it might be a very good thing. It might make our work more widely known, give some of the members of the community – like Desmond – a little welcome publicity. Some of his pots are quite beautiful, you know, but he hasn't received much recognition yet. And perhaps others will be inspired to follow our example and offer a home and encouragement to creative artists.'

Natasha took a sip of her tea. 'Ah, good, I was ready for that. I find increasingly that tea is both more comforting and more stimulating than alcohol. How some of my friends in Paris in the old days would have been scandalised.' She smiled, recalling those days with fondness but no regret.

'The television programme might, however, be a bad thing,' she went on, 'if this Nigel is rather less sincere than he would have me believe. We could be held up to ridicule. Or things might simply be inaccurate and distorted.'

'As they often are.'

'As indeed they often are. The money would be useful, of course.'

'They would pay, would they? Did he say?'

'They would pay. I made sure of that. No amount has been specified yet, of course, and that would need to be negotiated with firmness.'

Natasha paused, then began again delicately. 'I want to discuss something with you. Do you remember a conversation we had, a long time ago now – wasn't it 1980? That Christmas when you had just discovered you were pregnant with Katya?'

'Oh yes, I remember that very well.'

* * *

Frances sits on the stool beside her grandmother's bedroom window, looking out over the terrace where the low early morning light catches the frost on the lawn and the last dried-up leaves of the plants in the tubs and pots. After a quarrelsome drive down with the children last night – Giles has a Christmas engagement in Wimbledon and will not be coming to St Martins – she has slept badly and awoken to another session of retching miserably over the loo, with Lisa pounding on the door, shouting at her to hurry up.

She has just told Natasha her news. What she thought was a bout of gastric flu is an unplanned and unwanted pregnancy. The temporary locum doctor in Reading – filling in until old Dr Carmichael's replacement arrived – was young, female and sympathetic. She discussed, practically and without fuss, the element of risk inherent in post-forty pregnancy, and the option of abortion. Frances, confused and angry, has said she will think about it.

'Don't think too long. Come and see me when you get back after Christmas.'

'I don't know what to do,' says Frances, looking out at the frost. 'When I was younger, I was quite cold-blooded about abortion. I didn't see why a woman shouldn't get rid of a baby she didn't want. But I think once you've carried a child, felt it growing and moving inside you, then your views change. Mine did, anyway. You realise the baby is a person in its own right, much earlier than you could ever have understood before.'

'But why should you not keep it? Are you worried it might be handicapped?'

'Of course that is a consideration. Of course it is. But it is really something quite different.'

There is a long silence, then Frances blurts out, 'I was going to leave Giles. I had definitely decided. Anya and Nicholas both have their university lives now. They hardly come back to Reading, and I can't say I blame them. I was going to ask you if Tony, Lisa and I could come and live at St Martins, at least until they go to college – then I would take myself off, out of your way.'

'Of course you can come, doushenka, always. You know this.'

'I had the offer of a job, you see, a couple of months ago. Working full-time as an editor with a small firm publishing books on local history and based in Worcester. This was before I got pregnant. I was prepared to go on trying to hold the marriage together, but I really wanted this job. It was something fresh, a new opportunity to do something I was interested in. The salary wasn't huge, but it was very much better than the pittance I get from the poly and from odd bits of coaching. And of course it offered all the things I've never had in the part-time jobs I do – company pension scheme, paid holidays, sick pay.'

'But Giles didn't want you to take it?'

'No.'

'You know, Frances, I think he feels threatened whenever you show him what he does not want to see – that you are more talented than he is, that you could walk into lots of different jobs and make a success of them.'

'Well, he certainly shouted and raged. I suggested we move to Worcester – I've been waiting all these years to move away from the London commuter belt, and he keeps promising, but it never comes to anything. He won't contemplate moving, though he's hardly ever at Reading. He wants me to earn money – we couldn't do without it – but he doesn't want me to have a proper job. It would turn me into a real person with a life of my own, instead of a prop to his life. That's what it comes down to. He said some hateful things, then he went off

217

slamming the door – off to his latest girlfriend – called, will you believe, Bootsie Fabersham.'

'I don't know why you endure it. Why you didn't leave him years ago?'

'I had this idea that children need both parents. I think I still do. Anyway, I was in a state, thinking that the children are nearly grown up now, so they don't really need him any more. Wondering if I should just take the job and leave him. Then this Bootsie telephoned – telephoned *me* – to announce that she was having a baby, and Giles was going to leave me for her. I thought: Right, that settles it then. I'll take the initiative and leave him first. I could bring Tony and Lisa down here and commute to Worcester, and there would always be room for Anya and Nick to come in the vacations – they prefer to spend them here anyway.'

'But I don't understand. What went wrong?'

'Giles. That was what went wrong. Pleading with me, swearing that Bootsie was only trying to use him. Being very loving, as he can be when he tries.'

'And so you became pregnant.'

'And so I became pregnant. I can't take the job now. They need someone who can start in March and spend the next two years working flat out producing a new series of pocket-sized county histories. There's no way they could give me maternity leave, even if they were willing to, and of course no obligation on them if I had only just started working for them.'

'Come anyway. We will find you something to do at St Martins.'

'I can't.' Frances lays her forehead against Natasha's skirt. 'I still feel this obligation to let the new baby know its father.' She pressed the palms of her hands to the sides of her head. 'I feel so trapped, so suffocated. I need to escape, or I'll go mad – but I can't. I'm drowning under a weight of people and responsibilities. I'm so *tired*.'

Natasha caresses the bent head, feeling helpless. What can she do for Frances, who is so hopelessly entangled in her own sense of obligation to other people, and has always, for years, put herself last?

'Yes,' said Frances, 'I remember that conversation very well. You said: Come anyway.'

'And you would not come.'

'No. And I still don't know whether I did the right thing or the wrong thing, but that's all in the past now. It's curious you should mention that time, because I've been thinking about it myself today, and wondering how different things might have been if I had left Giles then. I think the younger children might have been happier, growing up away from the tensions and constrictions of that horrible house in Reading.' She looked up at her grandmother. 'You cannot imagine how much I loathe it – it has become a prison for me.' She paused. 'And of course then, when I was only forty, I could have found a job, some sort of job, back in the eighties, when the whole country was beginning to flourish. I would have managed somehow while Katya was a baby, and Tony and Lisa could have finished their schooling in Hereford or Leominster. Why didn't I do it? Why was I so weak?'

'But you are not weak any longer. Is that what you are saying, doushenka?'

Frances nodded, looking out at the summer garden, so different from the delicately frosted one thirteen and a half years ago. She saw Giles, Alice and that man – what was he called? Simon Frobisher – walking across the lawn towards the terrace.

'I am leaving Giles.' She got up and crossed to the window, and pulled it closed. She turned and stood with her back to the window, facing Natasha. 'I haven't told him yet, but I think I will do so tonight. I don't think I could share a bed with him again. And the curious thing is that I feel nothing. I don't feel guilt, or sadness that everything went wrong, or even a sense of relief. I'm numb. But I've come to some point of crisis in my life. I don't feel I can go on living in a state of untruth.'

She came back to the stool and sat down again, taking Natasha's hand.

'The problem is, that I don't know how I shall be able to live. I'd find it difficult to get a job now. I suppose I would be able to claim the dole, but that would mean I wouldn't be able to contribute much to the trust, and I know how difficult things are at present. Possibly I could get some teaching locally, enough to keep me and Katya.' She sighed bitterly. 'All those vaulting ambitions I had – do you remember? I was going to be so famous, for *something*! And now I just want to be able to earn enough to put meals on a table for a woman and a girl.'

'You are forgetting,' said Natasha gently, 'that it was I who wanted to see *you* about something.'

'I don't want charity, Natasha.'

'But how could I be offering you charity, when you have only just told me this? No, I want to discuss with you something about St Martins.'

'Is it something to do with this £100,000 you have to find?'

'You know about that?'

'Both Nick and Peter have been talking to me about it.'

'Not Gregor?'

'No,' said Frances, looking down and pleating her skirt between her fingers. 'Not Gregor.'

'There is no reason he should. He is the only other person who knows. But I expect he did not want to worry you. He is always very protective of you – even now.'

Frances looked up swiftly. 'What do you mean, even now?'

'You know exactly what I mean,' said Natasha sweetly. 'Now, this money. It will not be easy to come by. But our so-generous neighbour, Mr Frobisher, has come up with a solution.'

Frances was watching Giles and Alice through the window. Giles was leading Alice away towards the shrubbery. Suddenly she felt nausea rising in her throat. Not again. Not here at St Martins. Not with Tony's girlfriend. She barely heard what Natasha was saying.

'Simon Frobisher?' she said vaguely. 'That dreadful man – the one you told me not to be too nice to?'

'Precisely.' Natasha drew a long breath. 'Not a dreadful man at all, of course,' she said ironically. 'The deus ex machina. The genie out of the bottle. He has offered to buy the meadow from me. For £100,000. So that he can build little box-like houses all over it, packed as closely together as he can get them.'

Frances stared, her attention fully caught now. 'Not the meadow! Not our precious meadow, which dates back to the Domesday Book! Natasha, you can't possibly.'

'No,' said Natasha. 'I can't possibly. Do not worry, doushenka, your beloved meadow is safe. I know how much you treasure it. No, I have another plan.'

She got up rather stiffly from the chair, and crossed to her bed, gathering the silk folds of her dressing gown around her protectively. She paused, and then reached out slowly and took down the icon of the Virgin.

– 'We also have this, of which Mr Simon Frobisher knows nothing. He thinks, of course, that he has me in a blind corner, unable to refuse his offer because I have nowhere else to turn. You notice that he offers me the exact amount that we believe we will need for the repairs. How does he know this? He is like Machiavelli's prince. He has informers carefully placed in the building trade, he spies out the position at St Martins himself. He has been here before, you understand, paying a visit of courtesy. I believe he has desired our meadow since he came to live in Clunwardine Priors, probably even before. If it were not absurd, I would believe that he arranged for the roof to deteriorate, the mortar to fall out and the wiring to fail. But he is not a black magician, just a ruthless and determined man.'

She came back to Frances, and placed the icon in her hands.

'I have made a few discreet enquiries, by telephone, of old friends. I believe my Virgin will be worth enough to save St Martins.'

Chapter 12

SPIRO FOUND ANYA down by the pond. He was sure she had been avoiding him all day, and couldn't decide whether it was better to leave her alone, and wait for her to come to him, or whether he should make some move himself. They had barely exchanged a dozen words since he had arrived, and Anya seemed to be seeking the safety of other people's company, to avoid being alone with him. But when the members of the community and their guests began to gather again on the terrace for drinks before the play, and the Thespians had hurried off anxiously to change into their costumes, Anya was nowhere to be seen.

Finally Spiro approached Gregor, who was just coming out of his studio with a streak of clay on his cheek and an abstracted look in his eye.

'Have you any idea where Anya might be?' Spiro asked, judging that Gregor would not ply him with questions, or even pay much attention.

'She's always liked the corner down by the pond,' said Gregor at once. 'If she's gone off on her own somewhere, that's where I'd look if I were you.'

He pointed out the path down to the far end of the rough ground, and the clump of trees that hid the pond from where they were standing.

'I'd take heart,' said Gregor thoughtfully – who was not as abstracted as Spiro supposed – 'from the fact that she seems to have taken it so badly. If she didn't care, see, she'd be going briskly about in her usual way. I should go and have it out with her. Now.' He paused, and seemed to Spiro to be studying the barn door. 'It's much better to bring these things out into the open, not hold back through fear and delicacy. You're neither of you agonised adolescents, after all.'

He grinned and clapped Spiro lightly on the shoulder.

Spiro followed the path he had pointed out. Beyond the trees he caught a glimpse of water, and then of the embroidered cotton skirt Anya was wearing. She was standing at the edge of the pond, tearing a handful of wild flowers to bits and dropping the fragments into the water. A disapproving male mallard, who had hoped for something to eat, was cruising about in front of her. As Spiro watched, she threw out her hand, scattering the last of the petals.

Without saying anything, Spiro went up to her, and put his arms gently around her. She turned and buried her face against his chest.

'I'm sorry,' she said, her mouth muffled against his shirt. 'I've been horrible to you all day.'

'And I'm sorry I missed the train this morning,' he said, resting his chin on the top of her head. 'And I'm sorry about the way I rushed you the other day. I don't care whether we open a restaurant, or go to Athens, or stay in Oxford – or go and live like tramps on the beach and cook snails off the rocks over a driftwood fire. All that really matters to me is that we should be together.'

'Me too,' said Anya incoherently, crying into his shirt front.

'I would like to marry you.' He cleared his throat and tightened his arms around her. 'That is what I want for us – a life together until we are a bent old couple too deaf and blind to notice each other. But if you don't want to make that commitment . . . perhaps you would prefer to live together?'

'Let's talk about the options, Spiro,' said Anya, leaning back against the hard grip of his arm and grinning up at him damply. 'And as you've seen, I come from a very long-lived family, so you need to think very carefully before you put your head in the noose.'

'They're serving drinks now on the terrace, but I think we do not need to join them yet,' said Spiro. 'Not until the play starts. We have half an hour. Why don't you show me the stream – the Ludbrook, is it called? We can walk there and talk quietly for a little.'

★ ★ ★

'You are not going to sell the Virgin,' said Frances emphatically. She was pacing about Natasha's room, to prevent herself from shouting. 'I know how much it means to you. It is the only thing you have left of your family.'

'My darling Frances, I am surrounded by my family.'

'Your Russian family. Your past. We all need a past, each one of us. Without a past one is rootless, like a tree that has been torn away from the ground.'

'I carry my past inside my head. I have my memories. I do not need the Virgin. I love her, but I do not need her. As you grow old you find that you need less and less. For me St Martins is far more important than the Virgin. It has been my life's work, that and my painting. St Martins must be saved, for the future of the community and for the family.'

'We could sell the meadow to Simon Frobisher instead,' said Frances hesitantly.

'No. If the meadow is turned into a housing estate, that too would ruin St Martins. The whole purpose has always been to offer a quiet place for work and creative growth. I do not think this could continue if the whole place is turned into a – a suburb. And that is quite apart from the value of the meadow itself as a place of such history and interest.'

'There must be a way,' said Frances. Her stomach was clenched tight with this new problem. Natasha had asked her to handle the sale of the icon, since she had better contacts in London nowadays than her grandmother, and had the physical strength to travel and negotiate. Frances felt as though she had been asked to commit an act of betrayal.

'There must be another way. I know it wouldn't be as straightforward as selling the meadow or the icon for the whole of the money needed, but – this television programme, that will bring in some money. And Peter was talking about the concerts you held when you restored the old electricity generator back in the fifties. Concerts. And exhibitions – why not exhibitions? We could get all the former members of the community to rally round. Perhaps Keith could organise a benefit concert – something really big – he'd know how to go about that. And an exhibition – if we could time an exhibition to coincide with the television programme Nigel Laker wants to make . . . I wonder whether there might be a chance in the future of hiring parts of St Martins to be used as the occasional setting for television drama? I think they pay quite reasonably for that. It would mean disruption for a few days, but not for long.'

Natasha looked at her with fond amusement. 'You see, already here is a job for you – you who thought it was too late for you.'

'Anyone could do this. And we must do it, Natasha. Look, I would be very happy to be your lieutenant, if you like – your chief dogsbody. Would that help? I could do all the running around – we could work together on this.'

Natasha looked down at the face of the Virgin. The icon was now resting on her lap, and Mary smiled up at her, like a fellow conspirator.

'Very well, we are agreed. When you have told Giles, you and Katya will come to live here in St Martins, and we will work together to raise the money. Katya will be so happy.'

'I know, I know. She is miserable in Reading. She has always belonged here at St Martins – from the day she decided to be born here.'

'There are three things more I would like to ask you, Frances.'

'Yes?'

'First, will you tell Simon Frobisher that our answer is no? I feel a little tired to cope with him this evening. Tell him before he leaves, and make it quite clear that it is no use his trying to persuade or threaten any further. Will you do that?'

'Yes, of course. And . . .?'

'I think it would be best too if you spoke to Nigel Laker. You understand the world of the theatre and television. You will know better than I how to handle this matter of the programme he wishes to make.'

'Yes, I'm quite happy to do that. I'm not an expert, of

course, but I know people within that world whose advice I can ask.'

'Good. And I will talk to Peter and Keith about concerts, and to Gregor and Sally, and one or two others about a possible exhibition.'

'I think we'll make an excellent team,' said Frances vigorously, and she dropped a kiss on Natasha's cheek. 'You said there were three things?'

Just then there was a brisk knock on the door. It opened and Mabel bustled in.

'Come along, you two. Everyone has gathered for drinks on the terrace, and they're asking where on earth you both are. Do hurry. The play's due to start in fifteen minutes, once Sally's put Sarah to bed. People are starting to panic, and Theseus's ruff has just fallen apart.'

'Later,' Natasha murmured, touching Frances's arm lightly as she got to her feet.

★ ★ ★

'Here you are, Natasha,' said Gregor, leading her to the carved Jacobean chair placed like a throne in the front row of seats facing the terrace. The table of drinks had been carried away by Richard and Nick, and the simple scenery set up. It consisted of nothing more than two chairs similar to Natasha's, indicating the throne room in the palace of Duke Theseus of Athens, together with some swags of rich but faded fabric draped around the outside of the french windows leading from the house. Olga had found some old curtains bundled away in the attics, and Sally had pieced them together so they gave an impression of luxurious damask from a few yards away. Outside the window of Natasha's bedroom Titania's grassy bank was represented by an old ottoman from the vicarage, covered with a sheet screen-printed by Eric to look like grass. To this Chrissie and Samira had pinned their clusters of wild flowers.

'I feel like Queen Elizabeth,' said Natasha, 'attending a performance at court.'

'That's who you're meant to be,' said Katya, curling up on the grass at her feet and leaning her back against the side of

Natasha's chair. 'No one is allowed to laugh or applaud unless you do.'

'A fearsome responsibility.' Natasha smiled and stroked the curly dark head.

Katya affected to ignore this, and leaned across to talk to the Davies twins from the village.

'You don't know how lucky you are,' she said. 'There's always something interesting going on here in the village – open-air productions of plays, fêtes, bell-ringing competitions, ploughing matches, vintage car rallies. There's never anything like that in Reading.'

'Have you ever noticed,' said Natasha quietly to Gregor, who had taken the chair on her other side, 'that they always refer to 'Reading'? None of them ever says 'home'. And yet I would say that Frances is a natural home-maker.'

Gregor grunted unintelligibly.

'I haven't been there for more than ten years,' she went on pensively, 'but it always seemed to me a mean little house, with pinched rooms and ungenerous windows.'

'I suppose it was all they could afford at the time,' he said, looking down at his hands, loosely clasped between his knees.

'Yes, it was. Poor Frances. Perhaps she never could make it feel like a home, especially when St Martins was exerting so powerful a tug in the opposite direction.'

Gregor lifted his chin and looked at her in surprise. 'What makes you think that?'

'Oh Gregor, for an intelligent man – who can catch human emotions so powerfully in your work – you can be very stupid sometimes! Frances has never really left St Martins any more than you did. You both need this place – it's where you belong. She won't be happy until she comes back.'

He eyed her warily. 'Do you think she might?'

Natasha pressed her lips together and glanced away to where Frances was standing on the very edge of the audience. Beyond her Tony's girlfriend – what was she called? – came sauntering out from behind the shrubbery with the easy, stalking pace of a female panther. She was followed by Giles, who could be seen, even at this distance, to be breathing fast, and who wore a look of barely controlled fury. She turned back to Gregor.

'It wouldn't surprise me. It would do us all good to have Frances here.'

Gregor noticed her stress on the word 'all' and had opened his mouth to say more, when Mr Peters, whose Scout tent had given so much trouble in the morning, stepped out of the french windows, resplendent in a herald's tabard, and blew a fanfare on a trumpet. The chattering amongst the audience died away. Bob, heavy-eyed after the excitements of the day, climbed up into Mabel's lap and settled there with his head resting on her arm.

> *Now, fair Hippolyta, our nuptial hour*
> *Draws on apace: four happy days bring in*
> *Another moon: but O, methinks how slow*
> *This old moon wanes! she lingers my desires,*
> *Like to a step-dame, or a dowager,*
> *Long withering out a young man's revenue.*

Theseus was played by Eddie Pembridge, who owned the Green Lion in the village. He was a big man, with great presence, and his bass voice, trained to carry across a crowded public bar, rang out over the garden. Even Giles paused and raised his head. Ena Pembridge, coming in on her husband's arm as Theseus's betrothed queen, Hippolyta, was as statuesque as he. Her voice had an undertone of provocative sexual banter:

> *Four days will quickly steep themselves in night:*
> *Four nights will quickly dream away the time:*
> *And then the moon, like to a silver bow*
> *New-bent in heaven, shall behold the night*
> *Of our solemnities.*

They're very good, thought Frances, as Egeus entered to complain about his daughter Hermia's disobedience in falling in love with the wrong man and refusing to marry the husband of her father's choice. The complex courting dance of the play began, with Demetrius and Lysander vying for Hermia's love,

Hermia in love with Lysander, and Helena, Hermia's friend and the spurned love of Demetrius, full of bitterness – betraying friendship and trust because of the violence of her own rejected passion.

Nothing changes, thought Frances with a wry smile, as Helena decided to reveal the escape of Hermia and Lysander to Demetrius, hoping for no more reward than his thanks for being able to pursue his new love. You would think we would learn what cruel sport love makes of us, but each generation has to discover it all over again for itself.

Not bad, thought Nigel, relaxing a little in his chair two rows behind Natasha. He had planned to avoid the amateur theatricals, but had found himself talking to Peter Kaufmann over drinks, and could not easily escape as the pianist directed his wheelchair down the ramp to where chairs had been arranged in rows. Kaufmann had been very pleasant, not difficult at all, and had agreed to perform a short extract for the opening programme of Nigel's series, 'Provided,' he had said firmly, 'an acceptable fee is paid into the St Martins trust funds.' Nigel had immediately agreed a generous fee, and was now prepared to sit out the play, which looked as though it might be quite bearable. As long as the producer allows old Will to speak for himself, he thought, you can't go far wrong, and they have some talent, these people, for a group of amateurs from the provinces.

Giles stopped a few yards behind Frances, on the fringes of the audience, and tried to get a grip on himself. He used his familiar stage technique to steady his angry breathing, and forced himself to relax, but inside he was still seething with humiliation.

'I don't really fancy fat old men,' Alice had announced coolly after she had calmly declared her relationship with Tony, just when he had thought he was going to make it with her. 'Oh, I know some girls are turned on by sugar daddies – and fair enough if you need a bit of financial security. But frankly, Mr Kilworth' – she made his name sound like an insult – 'I am right out of your price bracket. And I like my men lean and lovely, not flabby, with seedy skin and an alcohol flush in the nose and eyeballs.'

He, Giles Kilworth, smooth and experienced escort of innumerable beautiful women, had been left quite speechless. She had removed his hands, frozen in a grotesque mockery of seduction, and risen to her feet with a smooth, cat-like motion. After a few moments he had followed her out of the shrubbery, stumbling over his own feet like a stage clown.

That will ask some tears in the true performing of it, said Bottom on stage. *If I do it, let the audience look to their eyes: I will move storms: I will condole in some measure. To the rest — yet my chief humour is for a tyrant. I could play Ercles rarely, or a part to tear a cat in, to make all split.*

Katya wrapped her arms round her legs and rested her chin on her knees. She could feel the warmth of Natasha's leg against her side. Some time ago she had thrown off her heavy boots and socks, and the cool grass curled up deliciously between her bare toes. The town craftsmen were leaving the terrace by the french windows, calling out to each other their arrangements to meet the next night in the wood for a rehearsal of their play. A play inside another play, thought Katya. No, with its own prologue, it's almost a play inside a play inside a play inside reality. As if everything is a series of images in mirrors that reflect each other, getting further away and harder to reach. But sometimes I feel as though I am inside the image, and reality is far away, back down the tunnel of mirrors. Perhaps if I were clever enough, I could learn to manipulate the images and the mirrors, so that I could live inside the image where I feel at home, and force reality to become the shadow in the mirror. Perhaps that's what people do when they grow up — if reality becomes unbearable, you just turn it upside down. She stole a glance towards her mother. Frances looked very still and remote, as though she were listening to something underneath the words of the play.

A soft shivering passage sounded on a flute from somewhere behind the audience. A figure in a tight bodysuit of moss green, under a floating transparent tunic, approached the terrace, coming up from the garden towards the steps and playing that strange wild thread of music. From the other side of the terrace a small figure in grey gossamer like spiders' webs skimmed up the steps, meeting Puck halfway. Chrissie's voice was as pure and clear as a choirboy's:

> *Over hill, over dale,*
> > *Thorough bush, thorough briar,*
> *Over park, over pale,*
> > *Thorough flood, thorough fire,*
> *I do wander every where,*
> *Swifter than the moonës sphere:*
> *And I serve the Fairy Queen,*
> *To dew her orbs upon the green.*
> *The cowslips tall her pensioners be,*
> *In their gold coats spots you see:*
> *Those be rubies, fairy favours:*
> *In those freckles live their savours.*
> *I must go seek some dewdrops here,*
> *And hang a pearl in every cowslip's ear.*
> *Farewell, thou lob of spirits: I'll be gone —*
> *Our queen and all her elves come here anon.*

Puck and the fairy spoke of the quarrel between the king and queen of fairyland, then drew aside as the two processions approached and confronted each other. Oberon was played by a new teacher at the village school. He had arrived that Easter, and had not previously appeared in any production by the Priorbridge Thespians. He had just the right touch of mischievous arrogance for the part, Frances thought. Kate Fellowes, daughter of a farmer living halfway between Clunwardine Priors and Stanway Bridges, was Titania. She had been acting with the Thespians for fourteen years, since the age of six, and now, with one more year to go at RADA, would have graced any professional production. She was wearing her great cloud of copper-coloured hair loose on her shoulders, and it whirled about her, rippling above the gauzy layers of her costume, as she spun round and confronted her husband.

> *What, jealous Oberon! Fairies, skip hence –*
> *I have forsworn his bed and company . . .*
> *I know*
> *When thou hast stol'n away from fairy land,*
> *And in the shape of Corin sat all day,*
> *Playing on pipes of corn, and versing love,*
> *To amorous Phillida. Why art thou here,*
> *Come from the farthest steep of India?*
> *But that, forsooth, the bouncing Amazon,*
> *Your buskined mistress and your warrior love,*
> *To Theseus must be wedded; and you come*
> *To give their bed joy and prosperity.*

* * *

In the Cambridge theatre, the Marlowe players are giving a performance of *A Midsummer Night's Dream*. Frances sits between Giles and his Cambridge friend, John Rafael. They have driven over from Oxford to attend the May Ball at John's college, preceded by the trip to the theatre and dinner.

A room has been booked in a hotel for Frances and John's girlfriend, an arrogant deb called Cecilia, who looked at Frances's ball gown with undisguised disdain as they changed and put on their make-up. Frances is relieved that they will probably not make any further use of the room until they change again tomorrow morning. The ball lasts all night and they are to punt up to Granchester for breakfast. She does not feel she wants to share girlish confidences with Cecilia in the dark.

She turns over the pages of her programme, tense with excitement. She has never been asked to a Commem at Oxford or a May Ball at Cambridge before. In fact, apart from the modest affairs sometimes held in the village hall, she has never been to a dance at all, something she was rash enough to admit to Cecilia in the first few moments of their acquaintance, before she realised the wisdom of holding her tongue. Her head swims at the thought of dancing all night with Giles in this magical place – somehow more magical than Oxford, loved but familiar as it is. Cambridge is strange to her, and seems to float in a gilded cloud of its own river mist.

Carelessly scanning the names in the cast list, her eye is arrested by the sight of one she recognises. She remembers the girl from the Oxford interviews eighteen months ago. They talked long into the night, immediately establishing the intimacy of old friends. It was both comforting and exhilarating for Frances, whose natural shyness with people means she does not easily make friends. She was sorry to discover later that they had chosen different universities. Now here the other girl is, playing Titania.

> These are the forgeries of jealousy:
> And never, since the middle summer's spring,
> Met we on hill, in dale, forest or mead,
> By pavéd fountain, or by rushy brook,
> Or in the beachéd margent of the sea,
> To dance our ringlets to the whistling wind,
> But with thy brawls thou hast disturbed our sport.
> Therefore the winds, piping to us in vain,
> As in revenge, have sucked up from the sea
> Contagious fogs: which falling in the land,
> Hath every pelting river made so proud
> That they have overborne their continents.

The musical voice conjures up the vision of a land sick and ill at ease, nature fractured. Frances jumps, startled from her absorption in the play as Giles slides his hand into her lap and leans over to nibble her ear.

★ ★ ★

Two different interpretations of the part, thought Frances now. This Titania of the 1990s is all mystic air and fire. The Cambridge one, dark haired and square jawed, was passionate woman, defying an overbearing husband, as human as the human characters in the play – back in the early days of

233

the feminist movement. She smiled ruefully to herself. That Titania had gone on to become a distinguished novelist. Odd how things turn out. When we sat in that Oxford room, drinking coffee and mapping out our ambitions and dreams to each other, we can't have been so very different.

She felt her arm gripped from behind.

'I need to talk to you,' said Giles.

She looked round at him in irritation. 'I want to watch the play,' she whispered.

He sighed. 'In the interval, then.'

★ ★ ★

Paul had telephoned the hospital in Hereford just before the play started.

'Your wife is fine,' a soothing female voice said. 'She is still having some contraction-like pains, but doctor thinks they are likely to pass. We'll be settling her for the night soon.'

'She needs to stay in overnight, then?'

'Much the best thing. Give us a ring about nine tomorrow, and we'll see how things are.'

'You will let me know if – well, if anything starts to happen?'

'Yes, of course, Mr Fenway. Goodbye.' The voice was cheerfully dismissive.

Paul tried to concentrate on the play.

Titania was speaking of her human friend, mother of the child Oberon wanted to take from her.

> The fairy land buys not the child of me.
> His mother was a vot'ress of my order;
> And in the spicéd Indian air, by night,
> Full often hath she gossiped by my side;
> And sat with me on Neptune's yellow sands,
> Marking th'embarkéd traders on the flood;
> When we have laughed to see the sails conceive
> And grow big-bellied with the wanton wind;
> Which she, with pretty and with swimming gait
> Following – her womb then rich with my young squire –
> Would imitate, and sail upon the land,

To fetch me trifles, and return again,
As from a voyage, rich with merchandise.

It was true, thought Paul. Lisa's profile, which he found so distressing, did resemble a sailing ship blown before the wind. As a scientist he had little time in his life for poetry, but Shakespeare did manage to put his finger on things with amazing accuracy. To compare a pregnant woman with a merchant ship laden with the treasures of the Indies made it more acceptable somehow.

But she, being mortal, of that boy did die.

Paul clenched his fists and turned away. It is quite different nowadays. Women hardly ever die in childbirth.

* * *

Hugh Appleton leaned back in his hired car and closed his eyes. The driver, fortunately, was a silent fellow. The fatigue of the last few weeks of travelling was catching up with him now that he was back firmly on English soil, being borne effortlessly on towards St Martins, to the only place he could think of as home. His easy familiarity with many people and places would keep him away for years at a time, and then suddenly – quite without warning and curiously disconcerting – the feeling would overwhelm him that he could not be at peace until those familiar scenes surrounded him again. The plane from Moscow had been hopelessly late at Heathrow. He had phoned ahead from Russia and arranged to be collected and driven to Reading railway station, where he could catch a train for Hereford, but now he had missed the last possible connection. The driver, after checking with his office, had said he was willing to drive Hugh all the way from Heathrow to St Martins. It was an extravagance, but he must not let Natasha down altogether. He would be late enough as it was.

Something rustled in his pocket as he turned to make his head more comfortable. He patted his pocket and smiled. Then he slept.

★ ★ ★

Oberon was instructing Puck about the magic flower he was to fetch from the other side of the world, which had the power to make people fall in love.

> *It fell upon a little western flower;*
> *Before, milk-white; now purple with love's wound —*
> *And maidens call it Love-in-idleness.*
> *Fetch me that flower, the herb I showed thee once.*
> *The juice of it, on sleeping eyelids laid,*
> *Will make or man or woman madly dote*
> *Upon the next live creature that it sees.*
> *Fetch me this herb, and be thou here again*
> *Ere the leviathan can swim a league.*

Puck leapt from the terrace in one swift movement, then paused for a moment, crouched on the grass like a runner at the start of a race. He called back over his shoulder to Oberon:

> *I'll put a girdle round about the earth*
> *In forty minutes.*

Time, thought Frances — how clever Shakespeare is with time. He draws our attention to his artifice in *Henry V*, when he has the Chorus persuade us to suspend our disbelief and imagine that events taking place over many years and many miles are truly represented within the wooden O of the theatre. But in fact he is doing it all the time, in all his plays. Puck reappears almost at once, not within forty minutes. How long would it take for a whale to swim a league? Would it take forty minutes? It would surely take longer than it takes Puck to re-enter carrying the herb. Wouldn't it? Yet he plays these games with time, and we accept them.

It is one of those themes he keeps coming back to, like the qualities and duties of a king, the corruption of power, and the confusion between shadow and substance, imagination and reality. There's that speech about the seven ages of man, put into the mocking mouth of Jaques in *As You Like It*, but I'm sure he means us to see that there is an underlying truth in it. In Jaques's scheme of things I would be too old to start again, to make a new life. But things are different now. Well, not different, but the boundaries extend further. People live longer. Look at Natasha. And although Oberon treats Titania badly in this play, on the whole Shakespeare was surprisingly strong in defence of women. What can Giles possibly want to talk about? He hasn't uttered a word to me since he arrived; now he wants to disrupt my enjoyment of the play.

Puck laid the magic potion on the eyes of the wrong lover, forcing the enchanted Lysander to abandon his true love Hermia and pursue the outraged Helena. The knockabout of the craftsmen's rehearsal ended in their flight when they saw the ass's head on the luckless Bottom's shoulders, and Titania, awakening from her sleep on the grassy bank, was besotted with the monster. Oberon chided Puck for his mistake and sprinkled the potion into Demetrius's eyes. And so the play reached its central knot – the ordered world reduced to total disorder. Hermia, once loved by two men, now abandoned and reviled by both. The scorned Helena, now pursued by two lovers, weeping at their cruel mockery. Titania, the ethereal queen of enchantment, forced to lie in the arms of a monster, a foolish braggart of a man with an ass's head, instead of reigning as queen and maintaining order and balance in the parallel world she ruled with her consort.

The players left the stage, and Mr Peters, playing the herald with his trumpet, declared an interval of twenty minutes.

Frances found her elbow gripped again firmly by Giles. He began to steer her away from the audience without any further word of explanation, and she could not resist a slight dig at him: 'Are we going into the shrubbery?'

His hand jerked and he veered suddenly to the left.

'We'll go into the walled garden,' he said, abruptly but with a conciliatory note in his voice.

They found a place where they could sit on the worn old bricks surrounding the raised beds in one corner. The heat of the sun, which had been building up in the encircling Georgian walls all day, made this angle of the garden warm and sheltered.

'I wanted to tell you about the offer I've had for a new series – from Nigel Laker. You saw I'd brought him down?'

Frances gritted her teeth. 'You haven't introduced him to me, but I did receive your instructions that he was to have a room for the night. I made up a bed for him in one of the ground-floor rooms of the east wing.'

'Good, good. Sorry I didn't introduce you.' He waved his hand dismissively. 'But you all seemed pretty busy.'

'Pretty busy, yes. I would have liked to meet him all the same.'

'Oh, you will, you will. It's going to be big, this series, and I'll be seeing a lot of him.'

'*The Great Eccentrics*? Yes, Natasha told me about it. You're to do the voice-overs.'

'Ah, yes.' He looked briefly disconcerted. 'I didn't realise you'd heard about it. Well, of course, I'll be involved in a good deal of the planning, you know. Ran my eye over Nigel's preliminary ideas when we had lunch and gave him a bit of advice.' He sounded pleased and confident.

'I'll be dealing with him myself,' she said quietly. 'Natasha has asked me to act for her in the negotiations about the programme he wants to make on St Martins.'

'Yes, yes. We'll both need to look after that.'

Frances looked at him steadily, but did not answer. The bricks under her hands were soft and warm, crumbling slightly with age. As she gripped them to stop herself speaking out angrily to Giles, her fingers dug into the dark brown soil of the bed behind her. This was where Gregor had dug up carrots this morning, and the soil was the colour and texture of rich Muscovado sugar. The garden wall beyond the vegetable bed was crowned with ivy, which had climbed up the outside and cascaded down against the inner face. Its relentless advance had sent out tough parasitic tendrils that were working their way insidiously into every cranny of the tender warm brick. I must see that ivy is cleared, thought Frances with great clarity, her mind stepping smartly to one side of Giles. It will destroy the wall.

The black bitter reek of the ivy mingled with the fertile scent of the earth under her fingers.

Giles had assumed the look of a scholar, a man of wisdom and vision, who could impart great ideas to the eager masses gathered to hear him. 'I have decided we need to make a few changes in our life-style,' he said. His tone was pitched a little lower than usual, with a fruity resonance. He is practising his voice for the new series, thought Frances.

'Oh? Have you indeed?' She clenched her fists over handfuls of St Martins soil and clung to it, like a shipwrecked survivor clutching at the land.

'Yes. I've decided we should sell the Reading house and move to St Martins. I'll keep the London pied-à-terre, of course. But I think it's time we took over here, turned it into a proper home. It will be great for entertaining. I've reached that point in my career when I need a big country place. All part of the image. Doesn't do me any good, not having a place where I can entertain people like Nigel. I need to be able to demonstrate that I've arrived. Success breeds success, you know.'

He glanced sideways at Frances, but she was gazing away from him, across towards the wooden gate which they had left open, and beyond which the audience could be seen drinking cups of coffee and walking about the lawn. She was crumbling handfuls of dirt between her fingers, letting it fall like fine rain back on to the vegetable bed. He raised his eyebrows in surprise.

'It's unfortunate that it's such a long way from London,' he went on, pursuing his thoughts. 'Kent or Oxfordshire would have been better, but the price of places the size of St Martins in those areas would be right through the roof.'

He pondered. He had been thinking about this all afternoon, but by putting it into words he could fill in the details, see the whole thing taking shape delightfully before him.

'I'll probably need to get a better car – a Daimler, I think – for travelling back and forth. The trains aren't to be thought of, and flying is too complicated. Bristol's the nearest airport.'

'You've been banned from driving.' It was her first response, and her voice held nothing but a detached interest. Watching him, listening to him, was like watching a play.

239

'Oh, I'll have a driver. Or rather, a general manservant. He can act as a dresser too, and odd-jobs body.'

Still she did not react. His voice took on an injured note.

'Well? Aren't you pleased? Isn't this what you've been wanting to do for years? All those holidays with the children down here? All those complaints about the house in Reading?' His face flushed. 'For God's sake, Frances, I thought you'd be pleased.'

'Pleased? Well, I'm *surprised*.' She turned to look at him. 'After all these years when you've sneered at St Martins and all it represents. You've mocked my family. Derided the very idea of living in the country. And in any case, I can see several flaws in your plan.'

'Such as?'

'St Martins doesn't belong to us, it belongs to Natasha. We could live here if the trust committee agreed, but it could never be *our* grand house in the country, as you seem to think.'

Giles's eyes slid away shiftily. 'It might be possible to come to some arrangement.'

'No,' said Frances firmly. 'My grandfather tied the trust up very firmly indeed. Natasha only controls ultimate ownership of the property, not its usage. The ownership, of course, she can bequeath to her heirs on whatever terms she wishes, within the general constraints of the original trust agreement.'

Giles opened his mouth as though he was about to protest, then closed it again.

'And this idea of a – what was it? a Daimler? And a driver? And house parties? Where do you suppose you would get the money for those? I'm sure Nigel's series will pay well, but it won't make you a millionaire.'

He smirked. 'Ah, now there I'm ahead of you. Had a chat with a fellow called Frobisher while you were watching the stage-struck villagers. He's keen to buy that field for a very handsome sum.' He gestured expansively in the direction of the meadow.

Her temper flared up at last. 'Can't you grasp this one simple idea? That meadow doesn't belong to you any more than the house does. It belongs to Natasha, and the trust has use of it in perpetuity.'

'Be reasonable, Frances. The meadow is useless to St Martins as it is now. Frobisher will pay well for it. I'm sure you can make Natasha see sense. And that is family property. The trust doesn't make any use of it.'

Frances stood up, letting the last fragments of rich brown soil trickle back on to the bed. She said nothing for a moment, then drew a deep breath and looked at him squarely.

'There is no point in continuing with this conversation, Giles. You won't be coming to live at St Martins. But Katya and I will. I'm leaving you.'

He gaped at her. 'But why?' His voice was injured, outraged. What, for God's sake, had he done? Suggest that they leave Reading and come to Herefordshire. Wasn't that what she'd always said she wanted?

'Why?' She withdrew her gaze, looking inside herself. 'Perhaps you should ask: Why never before? For years our life together has been a pretence. Your whole life is a pretence. You don't even know yourself who you are. Sometimes I'm inclined to blame your profession, but when I look back I can see that it was already there when I first knew you. You have been acting a part so long in your private life that nowadays you seem more real to me when you are on stage.'

She drew another long, shuddering breath, and her voice broke. 'I did love you once. At least I think I did. I thought you believed in the same things as I did. But at the heart of you there is nothing but a great emptiness, and I'm tired of trying to fill it. And I – well, there are things I want to do before it's too late.'

'Frances,' he said, suddenly aware of panic gripping him, 'you can't do this. Be reasonable, please . . . '

Frances looked at him with pity. 'I think we have just become a habit with each other, you and I. There is nothing else holding us together. Your career is taking off so well, and I'm glad of that. The children are grown, all but Katya. You don't need me any more.'

'Oh, Frances, please.' He was pleading with her. For the first time in his life, perhaps, sincere.

She cut him off, turning on her heel. 'There is nothing more to be said.'

She walked back along the brick path and through the archway on to the lawn. Only when she was hidden within the crowd did she pull out her handkerchief, and blow her nose. She had long practice in holding back tears.

The herald sounded the fanfare for the second half of the play.

Chapter 13

FRANCES FOUND A seat next to her father. After his rest William looked brighter, and managed a near-smile as she sat down. She took his hand in hers.

'I've been trying to catch up with you all day, Dad. But when I haven't been helping with the party, you've been resting. How are you?'

'Better.' He was able to shape the word, though the 't' sound was slurred.

'Mabel says the physiotherapy and the speech therapy are doing wonders. We'll soon have you back to normal.'

William looked at his daughter tolerantly. He knew, even if she didn't, that this was unlikely, but he was prepared to go along with the pretence. Her eyes, he noticed, were unnaturally bright. Had she been crying?

'You?' he said.

'Me? Oh, I'm fine,' she answered automatically. Then she smiled ruefully. Dad had always been able to see through her polite deceptions. 'Well, no, to be honest, I'm not fine. But I will be. I've just told Giles that I'm leaving him. Katya and I will be coming back to St Martins to live.'

William's whole frame gave an involuntary jerk, then his face flushed and softened. The twisted muscles at the side of his mouth relaxed and he beamed at her.

'I'm glad. Franny, I'm glad.' His voice sounded almost normal. 'Sounds selfish, but I've never been happy. About that marriage of yours.' He took a deep breath. 'Wonderful to have you both here.'

She squeezed his hand, and the tears spilled over and ran

down her cheeks. She brushed them away impatiently with the back of the other hand.

'Listen to you! You're speaking as well as ever.'

'Joy,' said William, 'is a powerful medicine.'

★ ★ ★

> *My lord*, said Lysander, *I shall reply amazedly,*
> *Half sleep, half waking . . . but as yet, I swear,*
> *I cannot truly say how I came here . . .*

The tangled plot of the play began to unwind. The lovers paired off, and the mortals left the magic wood for the pleasures of the court and the marriage celebrations. And the 'hard-handed men that work in Athens' found they were chosen to perform before Duke Theseus, who chided Hippolyta's sarcasm about them, pointing out:

> *Love, therefore, and tongue-tied simplicity*
> *In least speak most, to my capacity.*

Nigel leaned back in his chair with his hands in the pockets of his calfskin jacket and smiled contentedly as Eric, playing Quince, spoke the prologue of the inner play with its comically disordered punctuation. Wall marched stiffly on stage wearing a harness over his shoulders supporting pieces of hardboard in front and behind, roughly plastered over. Moonshine carried an old candle lantern from the stable and led Harry, who had been cast as the man-in-the-moon's dog. The audience rocked with laughter at the mincing Thisbe, with his wellingtons and bass voice. Nigel cheered along with them. During the interval Gregor Baranowski had agreed to do an interview for *The Great Eccentrics* – stipulating, like Peter Kaufmann, that a fee was to be paid into the trust funds. All in all it had been a very productive day. He just needed to see Frances Kilworth to schedule a further visit, this time with his assistant Jack and the chief cameraman he planned to use. They would settle terms then, and organise a filming schedule.

On stage Bottom as Pyramus ranted and swaggered, then discovered the bloody mantle dropped by Thisbe and pawed

by a very charming and gentle Lion. He drew his sword and
waved it about so that the audience could see it was made
of cardboard loosely covered with kitchen foil, bending and
wobbling in his hand.

> Come, tears, confound;
> Out, sword, and wound
> The pap of Pyramus:
> Ay, that left pap,
> Where heart doth hop . . .

He thrust the cardboard sword under his left arm and began
to stagger wildly about the stage, bouncing off the flower
troughs and teetering on the very edge of the terrace, as though
he was going to fall into the laps of the front row of the
audience. The children sitting cross-legged on the grass in front
of the chairs shrieked with excitement.

> Thus die I, thus, thus, thus . . . .
> Now am I dead,

he collapsed on his back at the front of the stage, with his legs
sticking straight up into the air.

> Now am I fled,

he groaned dreadfully.

> My soul is in the sky.
> Tongue, lose thy light!
> Moon, take thy flight!
> Now die, die, die, die, die.

His final twitching convulsions were greeted with a great
cheer from the audience. Thisbe, tiptoeing on stage in her
wellingtons to find her lover, was revealed – now without
her mantle – to have a thick ginger beard. She grieved over
her dead lover:

> These lily lips,
> This cherry nose,

These yellow cowslip cheeks,
Are gone, are gone:
Lovers, make moan:
His eyes were green as leeks.

As befitted a true romantic heroine, Thisbe hunted for Pyramus's sword but – failing to find it – stabbed herself daintily with the scabbard. She arranged herself delicately across the body, showing a good deal of hairy leg.

'Give over,' said Pyramus in a loud stage whisper.

The roar of applause at the end of the mechanicals' 'palpable-gross play' drowned the sound of a car drawing up at the far side of the house, before the front door. As the cheering died away Katya raised her head and listened. She thought she could hear the sound of a car driving away down St Martins' lane, but she hadn't noticed anyone leave. She glanced around. Her father had been standing over near the stableyard, dissociating himself from the amateur play-acting. He didn't seem to be there now, but he wasn't allowed to drive. She shrugged and turned back to Puck and the other fairies, dancing in Theseus's hall, led by Oberon and placing candles all around the edge of the stage so that it began to glow in the fading light.

Now, until the break of day,
Through this house each fairy stray.
To the best bride-bed will we:
Which by us shall blesséd be:
And the issue, there create
Ever shall be fortunate:
So shall all the couples three
Ever true in loving be:

Frances felt William's hand warm in hers. The laughter had caught her up, and the tears had dried on her cheeks. Suddenly she felt an unexpected and unfamiliar sense of happiness welling inside her. She glanced around and caught Gregor's eye. He smiled at her. Over his shoulder, she could see a figure, blurred and indistinct in the long shadows cast by the setting sun, approaching from the stableyard. Puck was speaking the epilogue:

> If we shadows have offended,
> Think but this, and all is mended,
> That you have but slumb'red here
> While these visions did appear.
> And this weak and idle theme,
> No more yielding but a dream,
> Gentles, do not reprehend.
> If you pardon, we will mend.
> And, as I am an honest Puck,
> If we have unearnéd luck
> Now to 'scape the serpent's tongue,
> We will make amends ere long:
> Else the Puck a liar call.
> So, good night unto you all.
> Give me your hands, if we be friends:
> And Robin shall restore amends.

A tall man stepped out of the shadows just below the terrace and led the applause. The light of the candles on stage fell across him, lighting up a thick head of dark hair peppered with grey.

'Uncle Hugh!' shouted Katya.

'Hugh,' breathed Frances, squeezing William's hand.

A smile lit up Natasha's face. Now we are complete, she thought.

★ ★ ★

As twilight fell over St Martins, a kind of wild excitement seemed to take hold of the party-goers. *A Midsummer Night's Dream* had been a success beyond anyone's expectations. The stranger who had come up from London with Giles Kilworth turned out to be a television director, and he was seen going about shaking the actors' hands, congratulating everyone. He thought he might be able to introduce Kate Fellowes to a few useful people before she finished at RADA, talked about getting them to do a scene from the play in some TV programme he was planning to make about St Martins, and hugged Chrissie, telling her he had never seen the fairy played with such panache. All the actors were drunk with achievement.

Chrissie threw herself on Hugh. 'Did you see me? Did you see me?'

But before he had to admit that he had arrived too late for her major scene he was borne off by Katya and Nick. Sally captured Chrissie and managed to rescue her filmy costume before it was ripped to tatters. Clad in jeans and a pullover – for the evening was growing a little chilly – Chrissie raced off to find Samira.

'Let's go and see our puppies,' she said. 'Have you thought of a name for yours yet?'

'Not yet,' said Samira. 'I still can't believe he's mine.'

'Let's show the puppies to your mum while they are getting the barbecue ready. When she sees them she'll understand why you just had to have one.'

They ran together across the grass and into the stableyard.

'Here, you two,' called Anya, coming with Spiro out of the kitchen, carrying a tray of plastic boxes full of sausages and chops. 'Come and give us a hand.'

'Can't,' said Chrissie cheekily. 'We're terribly busy.'

'Monkey,' said Anya. 'There'll be no putting up with her after that play.'

Spiro dropped a kiss on the top of her head, as his hands were full. 'I see that all the women in this family have very strong and difficult characters.'

'I warned you.'

Mia Patel, sitting with Muriel, Richard and Chanor at a folding picnic table near the barbecue and buttering a great mound of hamburger rolls, suddenly found her lap filled with two sleepy puppies who squirmed in confusion. With a small shriek she dropped the buttery knife. Samira leaned on her shoulder, gently caressing the head of one of the puppies.

'This one is mine. Isn't he beautiful?'

Mia looked at the puppies nervously, her hands hovering in the air above them. Chrissie's puppy turned round a few times, then sank down to sleep, her nose tucked between her paws, but the other puppy ducked from beneath Samira's hand and planted his forepaws firmly on Mia's chest. He had a slightly worried expression, and his little bright eyes looked intelligently into hers. Then he butted his head into the hollow of her neck before touching her chin with the tip of his nose. He gave a small sigh, then he too circled on her lap and settled to sleep, curled up against his sister.

'Yes, well,' said Mia, unable to suppress her smile. 'He certainly has a very appealing face. I'm sure we will get along very well together. But now, girls, you must take them away – we can't have the dogs near the food.'

'Chrissie,' said Frances firmly, as she put down another tray of rolls, 'I think we've all had quite enough of those puppies for one day. Take them back to Jeannie and wash your hands.'

The two girls obediently picked up the puppies, and as they headed back to Chrissie's door she winked at Samira.

★ ★ ★

Hugh's dramatic arrival had been seen by everyone both on the stage and in the audience, and for half an hour after the play finished he felt like a parcel being passed round from hand to hand. At last, however, he found Frances and seized her in a bear hug.

'Surprised?'

'No, not really.' She laughed and hugged him back. It was wonderful to feel the solid reality of him again. Sometimes, when he was away for years at a time, she almost wondered if she had imagined the existence of her brother.

He pulled a face. 'That's putting me in my place. After all the exclamations of joy and astonishment from everyone else.'

'It's not that. This morning I did wonder whether you were going to manage it, and I was so worried for Natasha's sake. But just before you appeared, I knew you were here. I felt you. Just the way we used to know, when we were children.'

'Yes.' He grinned and ruffled her hair. 'You may be my kid

sister, but I've always felt that was an accident – I'm sure we were meant to be twins. Gregor will be glad to have us both here. I've got the feeling he isn't too happy at the moment.'

'There's something very odd happening to his work.'

'We could always tell, couldn't we?'

'Poor Gregor. I was thinking earlier today about how horrid we were when he first came.' She sighed.

Hugh looked at her shrewdly. 'He soon got over that, as soon as we did. It was the things that happened later that were more serious.'

Frances turned away from him abruptly, but he put his arm round her shoulders.

'You've finished with Giles, haven't you?'

She stared at him. 'I really can't believe you sensed that without being told. You must have been speaking to Dad or Natasha. They are the only ones who know.'

'No, they haven't said a word. Two things. Giles went off in my taxi – which struck me as a bit odd. And then you – ' He held her at arm's length and studied her. 'You look somehow – shiny. Bright and liberated.'

'Idiot!' she said affectionately. 'In fact it upset me far more than I had expected, telling him I was leaving. You can't just snuff out thirty-five years of your life with no sense of regret, no sense of failure. But – I do feel liberated.'

'Come on,' he said, steering her towards the lawn overlooking the rough ground below the ha-ha, where Nick, Tony, Anya and Spiro had the barbecue lit and the food ready for cooking. 'Mabel has got Dad sitting over there at a table for four, and has gone to find Mum. Let's just sit with the parents for a bit, and let all your offspring and guests look after themselves for a while.'

★ ★ ★

Irina could not think why she should feel both so tearful and so joyous. She sat between Hugh and William, and the scent of charcoal and sizzling meat filled the evening air around her. Hugh kept giving her little hugs, with his arm round her shoulders, and every time he did, the tears welled up in her eyes. She tried to be fierce with him.

'Why haven't you been in touch? We haven't heard from you for months. Don't you know how much we worry about you when you go off on these dreadful expeditions?'

'Shut up, Mum,' said Hugh cheerfully. 'There are no nice red pillarboxes in the Hindu Kush. Nor yet on the upper reaches of the Yangtze Kiang. Nor in the high plateaux of Kashmir. That's where I've spent most of the last two years.'

Irina sniffed. 'You can't hoodwink me with your romantic tales. They probably have satellite TV in all those places now.'

Hugh laughed. 'Well, I confess, Mum – in the towns they do. But I'm not in the towns. I'm off up the remote valleys and into the mountains. Or following footpaths through forests. Honestly, it's very difficult to get messages back. But I do admit that I occasionally pass through civilised places and I haven't been as thoughtful as I should have been about sending word.' He crossed his heart elaborately, licked his finger and drew it across his throat. 'I promise I won't be so unkind again.'

'You won't be going off again?' Irina looked mournful and dubious.

William laid his hand on her knee.

'Our Hugh,' he said. 'You know him. Wouldn't be our Hugh if he didn't wander.'

This time Irina's tears did spill over. She did something quite out of character. She turned to William and buried her face against his shoulder. 'Oh, William, I've been so afraid. I thought you had slipped right away from me. But your speech – it's coming back. It's a bit blurred. But you're really speaking again.'

Frances wondered why William looked a little ashamed.

'Been practising my exercises,' he said gruffly. 'Been afraid to try in front of all of you. You can thank Frances for giving me the jolt I needed.'

'Frances?' Irina looked across the table at her daughter.

'Later, Mum. Look, here comes Spiro with some food for us.' She smiled as Spiro put a dish down in the centre of the table with a flourish. 'That smells delicious – I'm sure our barbecues have never smelt like that before.'

Spiro laughed and laid a napkin over his arm with a flourish. 'I made a little marinade, you understand,' he said, mimicking a stage waiter with a thick Greek accent, 'for the pork chops – garlic, olive oil, red wine. And then I put rosemary on the charcoal. This makes the difference.'

As he hurried back to join the other young people grouped around the barbecue, Hugh grinned at his sister. 'Am I right? He is the prospective son-in-law?'

'I hope so,' said Frances, tasting her chop. 'I certainly hope so.'

★   ★   ★

'Where's your girlfriend?' Anya asked Tony, as they turned the new batch of chops on the grid of the barbecue.

'Don't know,' said Tony glumly. 'I should think I'm finished there. Apparently our esteemed father tried to seduce her in the shrubbery.'

'Oh, no!'

'Oh, yes.'

'God,' said Anya savagely, 'that really is the limit. Why couldn't we have had a nice normal father, like other people. You know, one of those who went off to work in an office with a rolled umbrella and a bowler hat.'

Tony gave a snort of laughter in spite of himself. 'I suppose we might have felt more secure, but it would have been more boring.'

'I'm not sure I ever felt insecure,' said Anya, pricking the skins of another pound of sausages – real sausages made by the butcher in the village, not bought in a plastic packet. 'With Mum always there, I think I always felt safe. But – Alice . . . Surely she doesn't hold you responsible for Dad's behaviour?'

'I don't know. I don't suppose it makes the prospect of any involvement with me more attractive, do you? Apart from which . . . ' He groaned. 'Oh, I don't know.'

'Come on, spit it out.'

'Well, she was so cool and indifferent about it. And, well, *coarse.*' He looked suddenly embarrassed and youthful. 'She said,

"Your father tried to get me to spread my legs for him" – oh, I don't want to repeat it all.'

Anya patted his arm kindly with her hand in its oven glove. 'Maybe he's done you a favour. After all, she spent the afternoon chatting up that awful smarmy developer man. And I've just spotted her again. She's looking very intimate with the famous TV director.'

Tony jutted out his chin. 'To hell with her then. What do I care? Watch out, those other sausages are getting charred. Bung them on this plate and I'll go and feed them to the teenagers who are snogging over there in that dark corner. They won't notice.'

★ ★ ★

Frances pushed away her plate. 'I seem to have eaten more today than I usually do in a week. My skin feels like those sausages – overstuffed and splitting.'

Hugh laughed. 'Well, I was glad of it.' He helped himself to another blackened potato and some salad from a wooden bowl. 'I can't remember when I last had a meal – apart from the plastic stuff they give you on the aeroplane.'

'You said your plane was late into Heathrow, but you didn't say where you were coming from,' said Frances.

'Weren't you in Kashmir?' asked Irina.

'Yes, till about a month ago. But I came home via Russia.'

'Russia!' Frances's eyes swung round to the table where Natasha was sitting with Gregor, Mabel and the Kaufmanns.

'Yes.' Hugh's eyes followed hers. 'Extraordinary going back. I haven't been since the Berlin Wall came down, you know. Didn't much care for it before. Hedged around with bureaucracy, no chance of getting out into the wild places that I like to explore. All that has changed now.'

William cleared his throat. 'Did you. Explore?'

'This time? Not in the sense you mean. But I've made some contacts. I'm going back in the spring and meeting up with a fellow who can take me into the interior of the Siberian forest.'

Irina made a small involuntary noise.

'Quite safe now, Mum. And a really beautiful place. I plan

to stay at St Martins till then, if you'll have me. And work on a book. That'll be nearly nine months.'

'In what sense,' asked Frances, 'did you explore?'

Hugh looked at her. 'I promise I'll tell you all about it, but later. I want to talk to Natasha first.'

'Something I have to do,' said Frances, getting up and making a face, 'is to speak to Simon Frobisher. I promised Natasha I would, and I expect people will start leaving soon.'

'Who is Simon Frobisher?' Hugh stood up as well.

'A developer who has offered Natasha a hundred thousand pounds for the meadow, so he can build nasty little houses on it.'

'A hundred thousand pounds!'

'Yes. Which just happens to be what we need to stop St Martins falling down.'

'You're not going to accept!'

'No, I'm going to refuse. And I don't think it will be a very pleasant experience. Simon Frobisher looks like a man who expects to get his way. All the time.'

'I'll come with you,' said Hugh.

* * *

Simon Frobisher was not pleased. He loomed threateningly over Frances against the darkening sky, so that she nearly took a step back. She was glad to have Hugh beside her.

'Not worth your while, Mr Frobisher,' said Hugh smoothly. 'We already have matters in hand to have the site declared a protected area. As I am sure you are aware, the number of unspoiled mediaeval meadows in the country is tiny. This site is unique for a number of reasons. It is the only known location of one species of wild orchid, and it is also the habitat of a species of butterfly found in just three other places. Even if we agreed to sell, you would not be allowed to build.'

Frances glanced up at him with gratitude. She wasn't sure whether he was inventing the orchids and the butterflies, but no one would question Hugh Appleton's authority – certainly not this man of the urban jungle. She could actually hear the snap of Simon Frobisher's teeth as he tried to control his fury. Where he had hoped to drive like an earth-mover over the artists and elderly people who made up most of the St Martins community, he found himself confronted by a man who, for more than thirty years, had been taking on officials, army officers, and dictators in some of the toughest countries in the world, and winning.

Hugh flung that expansive arm of his around Simon Frobisher's shoulders and steered him towards the terrace, where the candles had been left burning and the table of drinks set up again.

'I know you are interested in St Martins,' he was saying. 'Now this wouldn't make you a profit, but it could be set off against tax. Have you considered the possibility of marking your support of the work of the community? Perhaps by establishing a travelling scholarship for young artists, to be administered by the community? The Frobisher Award? And there is part of the east wing that is almost derelict. It could be done up as a new centre – perhaps an arts centre for the use of local people. Those who haven't the exceptional ability to be full-time artists or musicians, but who are talented amateurs. You've seen this evening how good the local dramatic talent is, but they have nowhere proper to rehearse and perform. You could really do some good in the community, and do your business some good at the same time.'

They walked off together, and Frances watched them go, not even trying to suppress her smile. Simon Frobisher was a very tough proposition for Hugh to take on, but it wouldn't altogether surprise her if he was successful. The Frobisher Award! She gave a muffled chuckle.

'You're looking pleased with yourself,' said Anya, coming from the house.

'So are you.'

'Yes, I am.' She threw her arms briefly around her mother and kissed her. 'I am indeed.'

Frances did not need to ask questions. She had been watching Anya and Spiro together since the play had finished.

'Why are you waving that walking stick about?' she said.

'Natasha asked if I would get it for her. I think she's a little tired. No, don't look so worried. She seems very cheerful. It's just been a long day.'

'What's the time?' Frances tilted her watch towards the light from the terrace. 'A quarter past nine. Not much longer to go. To tell the truth, I'm a bit tired myself.'

'Poor old thing, not up to the high life any more?' Anya teased.

'Don't be impudent! I left the house at five this morning, when everyone else here was still sound asleep in bed.'

'Why don't you go and put your feet up then?'

'I just might do that.'

★ ★ ★

Hugh did not leave Simon Frobisher until he had extracted the promise of a meeting the following day to discuss ways in which one or more of the Frobisher businesses might invest in the work of the St Martins community. As Simon went off to find Emileen and make his escape from the party before someone else tried to extract money from him, Hugh started down the steps of the terrace, whistling softly between his teeth.

Gregor emerged from the shadows. 'You're a crafty devil, Hugh. How did you manage that?'

'Been listening have you, boyo?' said Hugh, punching Gregor affectionately on the shoulder.

'Came to get myself a beer and overheard the end of your persuasive arguments. Kept out of the way so I didn't cramp your style.'

'He was being a bit threatening to Frances when she told him we wouldn't sell him the meadow, so I thought I'd take him on, just for the devilment of it. I'll count it one of my greatest successes if I can persuade that killer shark to put some money into promotion of the arts.' Hugh gave a bark of laughter. 'Or how about the Frobisher Meadow Preservation Trust?'

'Wouldn't put anything past you.'

They walked companionably back towards the supper tables, where members of the community and their guests were sitting quietly talking, nibbling at the last crumbs of the cakes and finishing the coffee.

'Something you ought to know, Gregor,' said Hugh quietly.
'What's that, then?'
'Frances is leaving Giles. She told him today.'
Gregor stopped dead. 'Truly?'
'Truly. She and Katya are coming back to live at St Martins at the end of Katya's school term.'
Gregor stood with clenched fists, every muscle tense.
Hugh touched him lightly on the arm. 'Strange, isn't it, how things happen? Perhaps it will all work out after all, the way it should have done.'
'I wouldn't count on it,' said Gregor harshly.
Frances, still standing by the archway to the walled garden, where she had met Anya, saw them in the distance walking away from the terrace. Hugh and Gregor. The three of them had once been so close that Natasha had said you could not slip a sheet of paper between them. But the passing years had pulled them apart, scattered them, destroyed that strange mental closeness they had once felt. I've become so disillusioned as I've grown older, she thought. It seemed that I must have imagined the way things used to be. But I'm not so sure. Today I feel as though it has come back again. Not so strongly. There are so many other influences at work on us now – their careers, my children, other people, other pressing concerns. But underneath everything else, it's still there, that closeness.
At the edge of the light from the terrace, and still outside the circles of lamp-light from the supper tables, she saw the two men stop suddenly. They seemed to be talking earnestly. She saw Hugh lay his hand briefly on Gregor's arm, and then both men glanced in her direction, though they could not possibly have seen her, standing still and silent in the dark shadows of the ivy-covered wall.

★ ★ ★

On Christmas Eve, 1953, Frances went out for a walk by herself. There had been a fall of snow in the afternoon – not heavy, but enough to blanket the garden and fields and lay a ridge of snow along every branch and wall. The bushes in the shrubbery crouched like fat polar bears, and when she reached the Ludbrook she found a lacy fringe of ice along the edges of the stream, delicate as fine glass, beneath which the stream hurried dark grey and sinister. The grasses and water weeds rising through the ice were sheathed in transparent tubes that tinkled together in the breeze like a ring of chimes.

She had come out soon after lunch, but already the sun was sitting like a tired red ball on the horizon. It looked elliptical, as though it had been squashed, and the rest of the sky, menacingly dark, was tinted faintly over its surface with the blood red reflected from the sun sinking behind the Black Mountains, as if it were burying itself in Wales to hibernate for the winter.

The house was full of rustling paper and secrets. Frances had been well organised this year, buying her presents one by one as she saved enough from her pocket money and her newspaper round in the village. The most important presents were Hugh's and Gregor's. In a magazine in the newsagent's she had seen a brass compass – it was waterproof, with a heavy-duty case and a special kind of gimbals to hold it steady. It was very expensive, but when she had saved enough to buy it, she persuaded Dad to get it for her on one of his business trips to London.

'Hugh will love it, Franny, but are you sure you can afford it?'

'I'm putting all my money towards Christmas, Dad.'

'No crisps? No paperbacks? No nice new notebooks?' He knew her weaknesses.

'Nothing.' She grinned. 'Christmas is much more important!'

Gregor's present was not as expensive, but took more time. A craft shop in Hereford had bought in a stock of a new kind of modelling material which could be fired in an ordinary oven. Frances had seen Gregor looking at it longingly from the time it arrived, but he never seemed to be able to save his money the way she did. With Christmas on the way he had nothing to spare.

One afternoon after school, Frances sneaked off and went into the shop. There she discovered that you could buy a whole range of modelling tools, beautifully made out of smooth, pale wood. Each was double-ended. Some were rounded, some square, some pointed. Some had serrated edges. Some were pronged. The shopkeeper showed her the catalogue which pictured all the different tools, and got out the four types he had decided to buy. Immediately she knew that she must buy Gregor the whole set, as well as the modelling material.

'Could you get the others for me?' she asked.

The shopkeeper shook his head. 'I would have to order at least twenty of each.' Her face fell. 'But, tell you what. I'll give you the name and address of the company, and you can write to them yourself.'

She bought all the tools the Hereford shop could supply, and wrote to the manufacturer. No answer came for three weeks, then when they replied they said they did not deal with private customers – however, they were enclosing a list of local suppliers. Apart from the Hereford shop, the only one she could possibly reach was in Worcester.

The following Saturday she made an excuse to go into Hereford, and caught the train to Worcester. It took her a long time to hunt for the shop, but at last she found it, down a small side street, in the opposite direction from where she had first been directed. The kindly old lady who ran the shop shared her enthusiasm for the delicate wooden tools.

'Beautiful, aren't they?' She ran her finger along the silky wood. 'Almost seems a shame to use them for modelling and get them dirty! I couldn't resist them. I ordered the whole range, though it was daft – I'll never sell them. And you've come all the way over from Herefordshire, have you? Did you say they're for your brother?'

'Yes. Well, he's a sort of adopted brother. He's from Poland – he escaped during the war.'

The lady made clicking, sympathetic noises, and said she thought that as Frances was buying so many of the tools, she might manage a discount. Then she found a very attractive black leather case that had once contained a slide-rule.

'I never could bear to throw this out. I knew it would come in useful some day. *My* brother, now, he's a surveyor, and the slide-rule he kept in this case got broken once on site. I rescued the case and it's been lying in that drawer for twenty years at least. Look – they'll just fit nicely inside, and you'll have room for the ones you've already bought.'

Frances thanked her gratefully. The pale wood of the tools gleamed against the black velvet lining of the case. As the lady said, they looked almost too beautiful to use.

All her presents were wrapped now and hidden in her tower room, ready to bring down this evening and put under the tree. She shivered suddenly. She had been standing still too long. The sun had disappeared completely, and as she turned back to the house, she felt snowflakes brush against her cheek.

By the time she was crossing the lawn towards the terrace, the snow was falling heavily. The air was very still and the flakes tumbled down straight from the sky in great billowing cascades. It reminded Frances of a nursery rhyme book she had when she was little, where Mother Goose was shown shaking out feathers from pillows, which changed to snowflakes as they reached the earth.

The curtains in the drawing room were still open, so she could see the tree – nearly eight feet tall – standing just inside one of the french windows. For the first time ever there were electric Christmas lights on it, twinkling amongst the branches. The work on restoring the generator had been finished two months ago, in time for the winter, but Natasha had decreed that for Christmas, at least, they would still use the oil lamps and candles.

'It is very practical, I know, to have the electric light,' said Natasha, 'but I have grown used to the softer light here in St Martins. For Christmas, I think we will all be better without electric bulbs.'

Looking through the window now, Frances could see that the fairy lights were the only electric lights switched on. There was a big log fire burning on the hearth, and oil lamps on the mantelpiece and side tables. Mum was knitting, Mabel mending, and Dad reading the paper. At the far end of the room Natasha was talking to Birgit, who sat, as she always did, a little back from the group around the fire. On her lap she held Keith, the silent little boy who had turned up at St Martins a year ago. After long negotiations the authorities had allowed him to stay, and he followed Peter around everywhere. Stephen Howlett, one of Natasha's artist friends from the early St Martins days, had come back for Christmas and was standing on a stepladder fixing a bunch of mistletoe to the new electric light fixture hanging from the ceiling. Peter was perched on another ladder, tapping in a nail to hold one end of a swag of greenery.

'Be careful,' Mabel called. 'Don't damage the beam.'

'Don't worry,' Peter mumbled through a mouthful of nails. 'They're small, and I'm putting them in the joints, up out of sight.'

Gregor and Hugh were lying on their stomachs in front of the fire, toasting crumpets, then buttering them and piling them up on a large platter. The glow of the fire lit up their faces and shone on Hugh's hair, dark brown, clasping his cheeks, and Gregor's, black and curly.

Frances came in through the french window, stamping the snow off her boots and brushing flakes from her eyelashes.

'It's snowing again for Christmas,' she said. 'Are any of those crumpets for me?'

★ ★ ★

'So you've been in Russia,' said Gregor.

'Yes. I'll tell you all about it when we can have some peace.' Hugh studied him thoughtfully. 'Have you ever thought of going back, Gregor? Visiting Poland, going to see your old home? Some people are even trying to reclaim property that was confiscated during the war.'

Gregor shook his head. 'I don't think I would ever want to go back. And I certainly don't want to reclaim our property. Too painful. Ever since you and Frances accepted me I have thought of this as my home. Nothing changes that.'

'I do understand, you know.'

'Of course you do. Off you go and see Natasha now. Look, the Laceys are leaving.'

Hugh walked slowly across to Natasha's table. He had to be exclaimed over and patted by Muriel, who was genuinely delighted to see him, and he promised Richard that he would come to matins the next morning and then have a tour of the railway collection.

When they had gone, he sat down with a sigh of contentment, and stretched out his legs in front of him.

'Tired?' asked Natasha.

'Mmm. A bit. It's the change of time zones too. It may be . . . ' he looked at his watch, 'not quite ten o'clock here, but for me it's nearly one in the morning. I expect you're tired yourself.'

'Yes, but only happy-tired. It has been a wonderful day. I'm not too tired to hear your news.'

He looked at her sideways. She is remarkable, he thought. Her carriage is as upright as ever, her eyes unclouded. Her skin, perhaps, looked a little thinner, more fragile, than when he had last seen her, but that was all. He drew in his legs and sat forward, taking both her hands in his.

'I want to tell you,' he said, 'about my trip to Russia.'

Chapter 14

A SLIVER OF light showed under the door of Frances's tower room. Katya was sitting hunched up on the bed, dressed again in some of the layers of clothing she had been wearing in the morning, although she was still barefoot. She glowered at Frances as she came in, over the lumps of black and grey cloth clutched between her folded arms. One ear of a tattered teddy bear could just be seen peeping out. Frances avoided looking at it, sparing Katya her dignity.

'Hello, darling. You're looking rather glum.'

'Hasn't Natasha spoken to you then?' said Katya challengingly.

'Spoken to me about what? We've spoken about a lot of things today.'

'Obviously she hasn't.' Katya said witheringly.

'What is it, Katya?'

'Everything is just so horrible, but what do *you* care?'

'Horrible? I thought you looked as though you were enjoying yourself all day.'

'Oh, *that*. I'm always happy here. That's just the *point*.'

Frances suddenly felt very tired. She realised now what Katya was talking about, but she had not planned to have this discussion until tomorrow, when they would both feel less exhausted. She wasn't sure she could face it now.

'Oh,' she said, sinking wearily down on the old Lloyd Loom chair, which gave its familiar and comforting creak. She kicked off her shoes and looked at her feet. Her toe was coming through the right foot of her tights, and there were grass stains in a line above where her shoes had reached.

She drew a deep breath and tried at the same time to gather her wits together.

'You mean – about coming to live at St Martins?'

'She *has* spoken to you, then?'

'As a matter of fact, I was the one who raised it.'

'You?'

'Yes, me. I know you aren't happy in Reading. Would you like to come and live at St Martins?'

Katya sat bolt upright, and her bear popped up under her chin like a magician's rabbit out of a hat. 'Do you really mean it? Can I really?'

She flung herself across the room and on to her mother's lap. The weight – and astonishment – hit Frances like a stone, but the unexpected joy of holding her youngest daughter on her lap, big as she was now, was just as powerful.

Katya planted a large kiss on her mother's cheek, then she looked a little ashamed. 'It's not that I don't want to live with you, Mum. It's just that I don't want to live *there*. Couldn't you come to St Martins too?'

'I am coming.'

'*Really!*' Katya shrieked. 'But that's fab! What's going to happen to the house in Reading?'

'I expect it will be sold. But that isn't all, Katya.' Frances put her arms around her daughter and laid her cheek against the dark curls. 'Your father and I are separating. I am leaving him.'

'Oh,' said Katya quietly.

'I'm sorry, darling. I feel I've let you down.'

'Let *me* down?' Katya squirmed around and looked at her in astonishment. 'Don't be daft. More than half the people in my class have divorced parents or unmarried mums.' She looked grave. 'I've seen it coming, you know,' she said with dignity. 'I don't know why you didn't leave him years ago. I wouldn't stick with a bloke who was always having it off with other women.'

'Darling!'

'Oh, Mum, I'm not a child.' Katya threw out her arms expressively and her bear sailed across the room and landed by the door. They both began to laugh.

'Poor old Ted,' said Frances. 'I wondered where he'd got to.'

'He prefers living here too.' Katya smiled radiantly. 'Can we just stay on here after the weekend, and get a removal firm to send our stuff?'

'No, we cannot. You must finish your term at school.'

'Oh, Mum!'

'Oh, Mum yourself. You must do your end of term exams and tie up all the loose ends. It's only just over a month. Then I'll need you to help me pack everything up in tea-chests. Perhaps Tony will be able to give us a hand too.'

'OK. Can I tell people?'

'Just family for the moment.' She hugged her daughter briefly. 'Whatever you say, I do feel as though I've let you down. Marriage shouldn't be undertaken lightly, and when it fails both partners have to share the responsibility for the failure. I don't want your father blamed. I expect I was never the right person to be his wife.'

She bit her lip and looked beyond Katya, her eyes full of the past. 'Theatrical marriages are put under more strain than most – except perhaps marriages in the armed forces.' She sighed. 'I want to do this with dignity, and I hope that your father and I will be able to remain friends. If we achieved nothing else, we achieved five children, and we are both very proud of all of you.'

'I think you're super, Mum,' said Katya awkwardly. 'And I'll do everything I can to help. I know I've been a pest sometimes, but I really feel I can be a better person if we come to live at St Martins.'

Frances smiled and smacked her gently on her thigh. 'I expect we both can be. Come on, we ought to go down and help tidy up. You'd better put something on your feet. And I'm going to take off my tights and put on some trainers.'

'Have you got some shoes I could borrow? I think I'm going to give up my boots – they're a bit tacky.'

As they came into the main hall of the house the telephone

was ringing, but Mabel, coming through from the kitchen, reached it before them.

'Yes . . . yes certainly. I'll fetch him.'

She laid down the receiver and called over her shoulder to Frances and Katya as she hurried back to the kitchen: 'It's the hospital. They want to speak to Paul.'

'Oh, Mum,' Katya looked conscience-stricken. 'I'd forgotten all about poor Lisa. Do you think she's all right?'

'Of course she's all right. They are probably just ringing with the latest bulletin.'

Paul shot out of the back passage drying his hands on a tea towel.

'Yes, this is Paul Fenway here . . . What! Already? . . . I'll be there in under half an hour.' He threw the receiver down and turned to Frances.

'Apparently she really is in labour and there isn't long to go. Why wouldn't they let me stay before? Why didn't they let me know sooner? God, I wanted to be with her all the way through.'

'Give me that,' said Frances, taking the tea towel out of his hands and passing it to Katya. 'Go and get your coat. I'll drive you – you're in no fit state.'

'I'm fine.'

'Just do as you're told, Paul. They can manage without me here. There's lots of people to help with the clearing and washing up.'

'I'll go and help,' said Katya. 'Tell Lisa I said to keep her chin up.'

Paul ran obediently upstairs for his coat and Frances unhooked hers from the cloakroom on her way out to the car. The keys clinked in the pocket. As she was unlocking her car she saw Nigel Laker coming across the stableyard with Alice. Neither seemed to be helping with the clearing up. But I suppose they are guests, she told herself severely, even if they are staying in the house.

'Mrs Kilworth,' said Nigel, startled, 'are you leaving?'

'No, just driving my son-in-law to the hospital. His wife's

baby is on the way. I'm not sure how late it will be when I get back, so I'll say good-night.'

'I was going to ask you when we could have another meeting, to arrange a schedule for the shooting of the programme.'

'How about the weekend after next? A fortnight today? Fine. Down here.'

Paul came clattering out of the kitchen door and jumped into the passenger seat.

As Frances got into the car she could hear Alice as she and Nigel turned away toward the house: 'Babies, yuck! I can't stand them. Especially new ones.'

'Don't worry, Paul,' said Frances as she pulled out into St Martins lane. 'I know this route better than the back of my own hand – which I can't say I've ever paid that much attention to! At this time of night it will only take us twenty minutes.'

Paul wove his fingers together and stared out into the night, which was blacker by far than it would be at home in Worcester. Apart from time spent on field trips, he had always lived in towns, and the denser darkness of the countryside never failed to surprise him. He tried to relax, and lowered his window so that he could look out at the stars.

'They always seem so much nearer in the country, don't they?' said Frances, as though she had read his thoughts. 'When I was a little girl and first came to live here from London I couldn't get used to the night sky. There must have been times during the blackout in London, when there wasn't a raid on, and you could see the stars, but I was probably tucked up in my bed then. The only nights I can remember were full of searchlights and fires and explosions. The quiet when we came to St Martins – it frightened me. And the huge stars – I thought I could reach out and touch them. I don't know what I was doing awake in the night. I was only four. But perhaps the unfamiliarity kept me awake. I remember watching the stars from the windows of my tower. I would pad round from one window to the other, looking out in all four directions at the different stars, and talking to them. I gave them all names.' She chuckled. 'I must have been quite mad.'

Paul smiled at her weakly. 'Probably the first sign of a scientific mind. I'm surprised you didn't become an astro-physicist.'

Frances gave a snort of laughter as she turned on to the back road from the village to Hereford.

'Heavens, I didn't give them scientific names! I thought they were people, looking back at me out of windows in the sky. I always wondered why I couldn't see the windows during the daytime. Not long after that I discovered an old book of Greek and Roman myths in the drawing-room bookcase – it had belonged to my grandfather, Edmund Devereux, Natasha's husband. You know, of course – he was killed in the war, shortly after we moved to St Martins to escape the blitz. It was a beautiful book, published at the end of the last century and bound in dark red leather tooled with gold. Now I come to think of it, it probably belonged to one of his parents. There were wonderful illustrations, each with a tissue paper sheet to protect it. I'd never seen a book like it, and it opened up whole new worlds. A lot of the myths, of course, relate to the stars – Perseus and Andromeda, for example, and Orion the hunter. The stories reinforced my own imaginings, and in a way, I suppose, started me on the road to becoming an historian.'

'Is the book still there?'

'Yes, I think so. It certainly was the last time I looked.' Frances reflected briefly that it was quite natural that it had not occurred either to Natasha or to herself to consider selling Edmund's books, which were probably worth double the money needed to do the repairs.

'I'll have to look it out, so I can read the stories to our baby.'

'Of course you must. There are a lot of beautiful children's classics there. It's a shame children have to put up with paperbacks and small print these days. I think a child finds a good solid book with thick paper and clear print so much more satisfying.'

The road wound away underneath them, swooping round the sleeping fields and past the RAF base. The town was empty of traffic and just under twenty minutes after leaving St Martins they were pulling up in the hospital car park.

'You go on in, Paul,' said Frances, 'and find the maternity

ward. I'll just check that it's all right to leave the car here and then I'll catch you up.'

'Right. Thanks.' He gave her a shaky grin.

The hospital was very quiet. Although it was Saturday night the casualty department was almost deserted. The usual drunks and fist-fights of Saturday must already have been and gone. Frances's rubber-soled trainers made no sound on the lino floor as she followed the directions the girl on reception had given her. The group of rooms that formed the maternity suite had been painted in cheerful colours, and the empty waiting-room had a play corner for children awaiting the arrival of new brothers and sisters. Frances sat down and took up a magazine. She began to turn over the pages without looking at them. There was no sign of Paul. On the wall opposite her, a mural had been painted. It depicted a rather crude fairyland in bright harsh colours. The elves and gnomes were faintly grotesque, and the characters from fairy tales who peopled its improbable landscape were a poor imitation of Disney. She got up and took another seat, so that she was facing the blank uncurtained windows instead. The whole place felt weirdly deserted. No one else, it appeared, was having a baby tonight.

'Mrs Fenway?' A nurse had approached on silent feet, and Frances jumped, startled.

'No, Mrs Kilworth. Lisa Fenway is my daughter.'

'Oh, yes, of course. Mr Fenway did say you were his mother-in-law.'

'Is she all right?'

'Yes, mother and baby are splendid.' The nurse spoke in that clinically cheerful tone that always makes one suspect the worst. 'Mr Fenway just arrived in time,' she added brightly.

'We did expect you to let us know sooner,' said Frances, rather grimly.

'I'm sure we did send a message. Perhaps Mr Fenway didn't receive it. I understand he was at a party.' The public mask slipped slightly. The nurse's tone was accusing.

'It was a fiftieth anniversary party given by my ninety-four-year-old grandmother, the artist Natasha Devereux,' said Frances, rising to the provocation, and thinking: This is ridiculous, why should I feel I have to justify him? Just because I'm tired I mustn't let her upset me.

She went on firmly: 'Lisa was very anxious that Paul should not disappoint her great-grandmother. And no message was sent to us until the last moment.' She drew a breath to steady herself. 'May I see my daughter, please?'

'Yes, of course,' the nurse looked slightly mollified. 'Please come this way.'

As Frances followed her along a corridor, she decided she would wait and let Lisa and Paul tell her whether it was a boy or a girl. They turned into a small ward holding four beds. In two, the humped blankets showed where the women were asleep; in the third a young black girl was sitting up reading. She smiled at Frances as she passed. Lisa was propped up in the furthest bed, looking rather pale, with damp tendrils of hair clinging to her forehead. Paul got up to let Frances sit down beside the bed, and in the hospital cot she could see a small red face with eyes screwed shut and spiky black hair. Frances leaned over and kissed Lisa.

'How are you feeling, darling?'

'Sore!' said Lisa, 'And a bit tired, but otherwise I'm fine. It was all quite fast in the end.'

'And you've saved yourself a whole month of pregnancy.'

'Brilliant, isn't it? And she's fine – six and a half pounds.' She called softly across to the nurse: 'Nurse, could my mother hold her new granddaughter?'

The nurse lifted the solid little bundle and put her into Frances's arms. The baby moved her head, turning away from the light, and made little sucking motions with her lips.

'She's very like you,' said Frances. 'Same shape of head. And your hair was just like that when you were born.'

'Was it? I think she has Paul's chin.'

Frances studied the small square chin and looked across the bed, where Paul was standing with a smile of great self-satisfaction on his face. 'Yes, definitely Paul's chin. He looks as though he did it all himself.'

Paul laughed joyously. 'Sssh,' said the nurse.

'Have you thought of a name yet?' asked Frances.

270

'Oh, no question,' said Lisa, smiling up at Paul. 'It has to be Natasha.'

'Absolutely,' he said.

'She'll be very pleased,' said Frances, laying her cheek for a moment against the spiky hair, and feeling the strong pulse of the baby's new life beating. 'I wonder what the world will be like when she is ninety-four.'

'It's almost unbelievable, isn't it?' said Lisa, reaching out and laying her hand on her mother's, where it cupped the baby's head. And for a moment Frances saw before her the chain of women linking this Natasha to the other, and then back into the past, to all those other generations of women, who had laboured and brought forth. She had a fleeting sense of the great sisterhood she shared with all those women.

'Paul and I had better go now, and let you get some sleep,' she said, getting up and starting to lay the baby back in her cot. The nurse bustled over officiously and intervened, taking the baby from Frances and putting her down again. Lisa and Frances exchanged glances.

'My mother-in-law has five children of her own,' said Paul stiffly. Frances shook her head at him.

'Oh, I'm sure,' said the nurse in a disbelieving tone. 'But things have changed since those days.'

Frances managed to get Paul out into the corridor and halfway down the stairs before he exploded.

'Well, honestly, Frances – what an awful woman!'

'She was very young,' said Frances mildly. 'She got under my skin at first, but when I saw how young she was – perhaps it's her first night in charge. She's just protecting her dignity and her professional position.'

Paul snorted. 'Well, I hope she knows what she's doing. I can't wait to get Lisa and Natasha out of there and bring them home.'

Natasha. The name hung oddly in the air between them as they got into the car and started home.

★ ★ ★

'I was in Kashmir about five months,' said Hugh. He got up

271

and moved two more lamps over to the table where he sat talking to Natasha. There was hardly anyone else left outside now. For the last quarter of an hour the final guests had been coming up to Natasha and saying good-night, enthusing over the party. 'It will go down in the annals of Clunwardine Priors,' Richard Lacey had said as he was leaving. 'I'll write something up to go in the parish records. I don't suppose there has been a grander party in the history of the village.'

'You are very kind, Richard, but you exaggerate,' said Natasha. 'I am sure in the eighteenth century there were some very grand parties here indeed.'

'Well, then, it has been the grandest in the Irish sense – the most wonderful, the most fun.'

At last everyone had gone, and Mabel organised her squad of helpers to start clearing up.

'You stay put, Hugh,' she said firmly when he offered to help. 'You've come the furthest and you are the most longed-for guest, so just you stay and sit with Natasha. Only – wouldn't you both rather move inside? It's getting quite dark even with the lamps.'

'We will do very well here for a little longer,' said Natasha. 'And look, there's a moon coming up.'

'Well, just don't catch a chill. We all know that you are as strong as a horse, but it has been a very long and tiring day.'

'I promise,' said Natasha solemnly, with her eyes dancing, 'that I will not deliberately catch a chill.'

They watched the last of the dishes being cleared away, then Natasha turned to her grandson.

'Now, doushenka. You spent five months in Kashmir.'

'Yes. It was a sad experience, really. I was last there about seventeen years ago, and of course, as you know, Kashmir was my very first expedition, back when I was a student, when you financed me.' He smiled at her fondly. 'I'm sure you only did it because I was jealous of Frances's MG.'

'Not at all. They were both, in their way, gifts of freedom. You both needed to stretch your wings. Just because you had been brought up in the St Martins community it didn't mean you would necessarily want to spend the rest of your lives here. So I gave you each the chance to escape.'

Hugh looked at her in surprise. 'I never realised that was your reason. How subtle of you. But rather sad, I suppose, that we did both leave.'

'Frances is coming back. Has she told you? Of course she has.'

'Yes, she told me almost at once. And I hope to spend more time here. There are still some places I want to visit – did I tell you about the trip to Siberia? But I've been feeling more and more that I need to get the essence of my experience down on paper. I know I've been writing pretty coffee-table books for ages. Yes, that's what they are, Natasha, don't protest. But now I want to try to distil something more worthwhile out of all these years of travelling and meeting people from the world's hidden cultures. So I plan to be around for longer periods, if you will have me.'

'What nonsense, of course we will have you. But,' she prompted gently, 'you were saying that Kashmir was a sad experience.'

Hugh gathered some cake crumbs into his hand and began rolling them into a ball. 'Yes. Quite a few of my friends from way back were alleged to be dead. Some of them really were. Others were in hiding, and refused to see me. There is so much hatred and mistrust now, the country is spoiled for me, and I used to love it.'

He sighed, and flicked the ball of crumbs into the shadows.

'Anyway, I travelled from Kashmir back to Delhi, then I flew to Moscow. I had heard about a fellow who might be willing to act as a guide for me on an expedition next spring, just before the snows melt, into the remoter parts of the Siberian forest. The idea is to stay right through the short summer and study both the flora and fauna, and also to assess whether the exploitation of other parts of Siberia is having any effect on that area.'

'This you will enjoy. I have seen on the television a film of Siberia. So strange it seems, after all the years of the gulags. And before, when I was a girl, one thought of Siberia as one might now think of the dark side of the moon.'

273

Hugh nodded. 'Even to someone of my generation it seems strange.'

He hesitated before he went on, and studied his grandmother in the light of the lamps. He was not sure how much he should say.

'I found that the man I wanted to meet – Potopov – wouldn't be available for a fortnight. He was off somewhere, Georgia I think. So I had a couple of weeks to fill in. I haven't been in Russia for – what? – nearly twenty years. And then it was only to give a paper at a conference. Surrounded by KGB men masquerading (very unsuccessfully!) as academics. Looking behind me every minute, wondering whether a hand was going to drop on my shoulder and I was going to be led away to the Lubyanka. It's very different now. I decided to do a bit of exploring for myself in Mother Russia. And that's what I want to tell you about.'

★ ★ ★

Hugh had travelled from Moscow to St Petersburg by train in the company of a Canadian journalist, Charlie McGregor, whom he had known for at least ten years.

'You're right,' said Charlie. 'Things sure have changed in Russia. Mostly for the better, but, Jesus!, the rise in the crime rate is scary. In a totalitarian state you have state-run crime, but private enterprise is strictly a no-no. Since the collapse of the Soviet Union the fastest growth industry has been organised crime. Mafia-type bosses – home-grown or imported – are getting a grip on commerce, distribution, you name it. And of course the drug trade. Alcoholism was always a problem – it's getting worse. On top of that, food supplies from the satellite countries have dried up because the Russians can't take them by force any more, and don't have any currency to pay for them. Their own farms are inefficient, but a large proportion of what they do produce is rotting away because they have no understanding of how to organise a distribution system.'

'Yes,' said Hugh. 'It's upsetting to see emaciated old ladies in the streets begging for food. And it's summer. The winter doesn't bear thinking about.'

'They just die,' said Charlie bluntly. 'A lot of people are starting to say that things were better under the communists. Mostly the old people, and parents with a lot of children to feed. Many of the young, however, are grabbing their opportunities. Either to become legitimate entrepreneurs, or to operate on the fringes and beyond the law. Take this guy I'm going to interview. Ex-KGB. But he's only about twenty-six, twenty-seven. So he's not going around beating his breast and bemoaning the past. He's set himself up as a private detective. Employs two of his former colleagues and a woman who left the police in rather mysterious circumstances. He uses his know-how and his contacts still in post to get hold of information, and he makes a very lucrative living, so I understand. Mind you, he may be just a bit too clever by half. He works for private clients – OK, divorce, missing persons, all that. But he does little jobs for the police and little jobs for some of these shadowy men who have got very rich very suddenly. It's possible that one of these days the latter will find out he is shopping them to the police and he will end up at the bottom of the Neva.'

'Sounds like Chicago during Prohibition,' said Hugh.

'You'd better believe it. Though I understand St Petersburg isn't quite as bad as Moscow. Anyway, I'm in a hurry to do my interview with this Ivan Brelov before the Mafia beat me to him.'

Hugh took a pull from the small bottle of vodka they were sharing, and nibbled without enthusiasm on a dry sandwich he had bought in the station.

'Any chance I might come with you?'

'He's not your sort of person. Young Ivan has no interest in wild life outside the streets of St Petersburg, or in cultures other than the new capitalism.'

'No, I don't suppose he does. But I might have a job for him.'

'You? Now watch it, Hugh. These people are strictly for keeping at arm's length.'

'Oh, purely as one of his "private" customers, as you describe them. I am trying to trace someone.'

'Who?' Charlie's interest was caught.

'Well, not one specific person. My grandmother came from St Petersburg. She escaped during the Revolution, and walked – literally – almost the whole way to Paris, when she was in her teens. The rest of her family was murdered by the Bolsheviks, but I know where she lived. At least I know the name of the house. And I thought I might be able to find someone who remembered someone – perhaps who worked for her family. There won't be any of her contemporaries left. She's ninety-four.'

'She's still alive!'

'Very much so. She's the painter, Natasha Devereux.'

'Jesus, Hugh, I never knew that before.' Charlie pulled a dog-eared notebook out of his pocket and began scribbling. 'But Devereux isn't a Russian name.'

'No, no, that's her married name. It's an English name, even though it sounds French. Not too uncommon in Herefordshire, where my grandfather came from.'

'So what was her maiden name?'

'Greshlov. She was the Princess Natasha Greshlov, but she dropped the title after she got to Paris.'

'This is fascinating. Maybe I could do a story on it?'

'Maybe. We'll see. I am doing this very much on the quiet. I don't want my grandmother upset. But if you want to help me in a bit of sleuthing, and you've got some useful connections . . . '

'You're on.'

The next morning in his office – with its expensive imported Italian furniture, its computers, and its smart secretary bringing coffee in English porcelain – Ivan Brelov showed himself a model of courtesy, although he gave the impression of a man with meetings booked end-to-end for the next eighteen months, who was fitting the two of them in by forgoing his workout in the gym with his personal trainer. He reminded Hugh of the young financial whiz-kids who rose and then fell so spectacularly in the City of London in the eighties. Hugh, introduced by Charlie as a colleague, had been accepted without question by Ivan, though Hugh noticed that he exchanged a glance with the secretary. Throughout the interview he listened quietly to Charlie as he skilfully drew out the ex-KGB man. It reminded him of the skill needed to track and photograph a wild animal. Slow, innocent, cautious – then the quick flick of the shutter and the quiet move on before the quarry was alarmed. No doubt this particular quarry had a good grasp of Charlie's tactics, but he did not take fright. From time to time he would look at his computer screen and tap a few keys, but otherwise he gave his undivided attention to the newspaper man.

Charlie moved smoothly from his last question to introducing Hugh's proposition of a small private investigation in St Petersburg.

Ivan smiled. 'Ah, Mr Appleton, I wondered why you were here. Our city is too old and too civilised to be of much interest to you for one of your expeditions, is this not so?'

Hugh and Charlie exchanged startled glances.

Ivan laughed out loud, like a small boy proud of his cleverness. 'There is no mystery, my friends. This is my business. You would not think much of me if I let anyone who pleased come and go. My attractive secretary – whose legs I noticed you both admired – so delightful, is it not that the short skirts of the sixties are coming back? – my secretary is in fact one of my investigators. Former police detective, Lyudmila Sergeyevna Babin. She has sent through to me on our computer network all the details she has been able to discover about you while we have been having our pleasant chat.' His English was flawless, if a little old-fashioned, and spoken with an American accent. He smiled like a happy shark and rotated the computer screen so they could read it.

Hugh's date and place of birth, the address of St Martins, educational details, list of publications, list of television programmes, countries visited, and date and time of arrival in Moscow and St Petersburg were all set out neatly on the screen.

'Given a little time, she would, of course, ferret out a good deal more. Your sexual liaisons, for example. Your drinking habits. Your relatives and your associates over the last – say – thirty years. Your security clearance in Britain, the United

States and here in Russia, both before and after the end of our late lamented Soviet Union.'

'You have made your point, Mr Brelov,' said Hugh, who had encountered secret police before, but still found it an unsettling experience. 'I am sure, given time, you could tell me what colour pyjamas I was wearing on Christmas Day in 1961. Are you interested in doing a small job for me, or not?'

'Certainly, Mr Appleton,' said Ivan, feigning contrition. 'You must forgive my little games. Tell me what you want to know.'

So Hugh outlined what little he knew about Natasha's family and the location of the house, and explained that, if it still stood, he would like to photograph it. He also wanted to discover any people who might have had a connection with the Greshlovs, however remote.

'My grandmother is very old, Mr Brelov, and she will never return to Russia. But she went through a terrible time when the whole of her family was murdered before her eyes and she escaped into the streets in nothing but her shift. I feel that she would be glad to lay, so to speak, those old ghosts to rest. There was one servant who helped her – a young man a little older than herself – but he would be dead by now. It might be possible to trace his family. And she was troubled for many years, not knowing what became of the rest of the servants. There was an old nanny she loved dearly. I realise it is a long time ago, but any scraps of information – they would mean a great deal to her.'

'I like it!' said Ivan. 'And yours is not the first such case, my friend. Almost every week I have letters from America, from France and Germany and England – descendants of Russians who fled all those years ago. And almost all of them related to the Romanovs – is not that interesting? So many people wanting to claim this palace or that – or a golden cup in the Hermitage – or a share in the Romanov fortune. Surely *your* grandmother was indeed a princess, but all you want is photographs and a few words with the grandson of the third stableboy.' He roared with laughter. 'I am sure we can help you, my friend.'

Hugh had learned long ago to ignore this kind of baiting,

so he merely smiled politely and waited until Ivan had finished playing games. Suddenly the detective decided to become businesslike. He pressed an intercom button on his desk.

'Lyudmila, my darling, will you come and join us?'

It was Lyudmila who did most of the work. Her looks were one of her professional assets: people took her for an empty-headed beauty, whereas in fact she was a graduate of Moscow University, with a PhD in criminal psychology and eight years' experience as a detective in the St Petersburg police. She was quite frank about why she had left the force.

'The male pigs who hold all the power are never going to let women into their privileged positions.' Her English too was excellent, and her accent was not New York but Oxford. 'You have this too, I believe, in your countries? "You sleep with me, Lyudmila, and I will see you get promotion." ' She gave a growl of disgust. 'I spit at them and their methods. I know other women who have been trapped like this. The first part of the bargain is kept, and then – what? – oh, dear, no promotion is possible. And when I refused this little favour to a very senior officer, he tried to rape me – there in his office, with his secretary turning people away because he was occupied. I hit him with a glass ashtray. I wish I had hit him harder. Then I resigned, before he could invent some case against me.'

In Ivan's organisation Lyudmila used her intellectual talents with ferocious determination, but it was her natural gift for playing the naive blonde that enabled her to get past the natural wariness of post-Soviet Russians. Two days after their visit to the office, Hugh and Charlie met Lyudmila in a café near the centre of town.

'I have found the house. It survived the siege by the Germans during the last war – it was some distance out of town, away from the battle lines. Since then the suburbs have spread, and there are many houses around it, but part of the grounds are now a municipal park. I thought this was the building, but now I have made sure.'

279

'And the house is still standing?' Hugh beamed. 'What is it used for?'

'Part is now an orphanage. The rest is a municipal school of music. The inside, you understand, will be much changed – the rooms will be partitioned, much else destroyed. But the outside, I think you will find, has not been altered.'

'When can we go and see it?'

'Now, if you have finished your coffee. My car is in the next street.'

They drove for half an hour in Lyudmila's Lada, then turned in through eighteenth-century wrought iron gates. The park looked much like any other city park. Mothers and grand-mothers walked with children. Down on the lake a large group of men and boys were racing model yachts in what seemed to be a club regatta.

'Natasha said there was a lake.' Hugh had a strange sense of déjà vu. He had formed a mental picture of the place which proved to be partly accurate. But to be entering in reality what had always seemed to be a part of history, long dead, had a dreamlike quality about it.

Lyudmila parked in front of the house. It was vast, about four times the size of St Martins, and the fabric of the building was shabby. Gutters were split and rain had run for years down the face of the building, leaving waterfalls of green slime. The front steps were chipped, and the pillars supporting the great portico had lost the mortar that should have secured the separate drums of stone. Hugh ducked with instinctive nervousness under the heavy lintel with its elaborate cartouche. They were allowed to peep briefly into the entrance hall. Worn brown linoleum covered the marble floor, and a flimsy partition wall divided it down the middle. There was a great stone fireplace, still, which looked as though no fire had burned in it for half a century.

'This is where they were killed,' said Hugh quietly to Charlie. 'In front of that fireplace. There were swords and axes and all sorts of weapons hanging on the wall, but the servants had run off, and Natasha's father was the only man left in the house. He was killed on the threshold, and then his wife and children here by the fire – all except Natasha. They killed her little brother Petya last, then they all raped her in turn, before the man who helped her managed to get her away.'

Lyudmila was listening to him intently. 'She was a brave woman, your grandmother, yes?'

'She still is. But I think that even now she feels guilty. Because she survived and the others did not.'

Hugh took one photograph of the hallway, but thought he would probably not show it to Natasha. Then he used the rest of the roll of film photographing the outside of the house from every angle, and taking pictures of the model boat races on the lake, and of a group of children playing on swings near the remains of the old orchard. They drove back to the centre of town in silence.

Lyudmila had no more news for them for a week. Then the day before they were due to travel back to Moscow she telephoned Hugh at the hotel.

'I have had luck, Hugh. I have found a man who was a boy servant of the Greshlovs. He is now a watchmaker here in Petersburg. I will take you to meet him this evening.'

Hugh waited impatiently for the day to pass. He had wanted to go at once to meet the old man, but Lyudmila had said that it was not possible until the evening.

'He is old, you understand, and his eyes are no longer good. So he must work when there is daylight to see the watches and clocks that he repairs. The hours of daylight are gold to him. It is not convenient to visit him until after dark.'

Feeling ashamed, Hugh said that he understood, and went off to pass the day as best he could. Charlie was having a second interview with Ivan Brelov, and then planned to do some sightseeing. Hugh felt too restless to join him. More than a few days spent amongst the crowds of a large city always made him uneasy, and he would be glad to be leaving. His own family connection with the place seemed too slight to awaken any sense of belonging here. For a time he wandered along the river, then he sought out the shop belonging to the watchmaker, which Lyudmila had told him was not far from his hotel. For a time he lingered on the opposite side of the street, watching. It was a small shop, neither grand nor poor, with a freshly painted front and one large window. Behind the window he could see the shadowy shape of a man sitting at a table, with a jeweller's glass screwed into his eye. This, he supposed, must be the old man who once polished Natasha's boots in those long-gone days.

Lyudmila collected him at the hotel at eight o'clock. Charlie was busy writing up his story, and said he would not come with them.

'No need to overwhelm the old boy with three of us. We'll have a drink in the bar when you get back, and you can tell me all about it.'

'He lives in two rooms over the shop, with his widowed daughter,' said Lyudmila, as she knocked on the door of the darkened shop. 'Her husband was killed in the siege. There are grown-up grandchildren, married and living here in St Petersburg and in Moscow. He seems quite clear in his mind, you understand. I have spoken to him on the telephone at his shop. And he is still working. I was told that he is about eighty-five or eighty-six, and a little crippled in one hip, but otherwise very strong.'

The door was answered by a sombrely dressed woman with white hair drawn back into a bun. Lyudmila explained in Russian who they were, and the woman led them silently up a flight of narrow steps into the room above the shop. It was very crowded with furniture – a heavy table and dining chairs, bookcases, and two armchairs. In one corner, partially curtained off, was a high, old-fashioned bed covered with a feather-bed and a coverlet which had once been patterned in bright reds and greens, but was now faded to muted shades. At the back of the room was a door, ajar, leading to another, smaller room, which seemed to be almost entirely filled with a bed and a large chest. To the right of the door a small cooking area had been made, with a bottled-gas stove, a sink with a single cold tap, and a hanging food cupboard on the wall.

The woman who had answered the door sat down at the table and took up her mending. Hugh turned and looked at the old man, who was sitting in a worn armchair beside a tiled stove which, in winter, would have provided the only heat in the place but which was now unlit during the summer months.

'Fyodor Petrovich,' Lyudmila began in Russian, 'this is the gentleman from England who is the grandson of the Princess Natasha Greshlov. You remember that you told me you worked in the home of the Greshlovs when you were a young boy.'

The old man fixed Hugh with a pair of exceedingly sharp blue eyes that seemed to weigh him up and find him, for the moment at least, satisfactory. 'Please sit down,' he said, indicating the chair opposite him.

'He says . . . ' Lyudmila began in English.

'Thank you,' said Hugh to the old man, switching to Russian. 'Thank you, Fyodor Petrovich, for agreeing to see me.'

Lyudmila gaped. Hugh had not revealed his knowledge of the language before. Then she took a seat at the table, and watched them with curiosity.

'Lyudmila Sergeyevna has told me that you are the grandson of Natasha Greshlov,' said the watchmaker. 'But how do I know that this is true?'

'I have here my passport,' said Hugh, passing it over. 'My father is William Appleton, an Englishman. My mother was born Irina Devereux. Lyudmila Sergeyevna can confirm this – she has checked with the embassy. Irina is the only child of Natasha Greshlov who married an Englishman, Edmund Devereux, in Paris in 1919. This too can easily be confirmed.'

The old man handed back the passport and studied him thoughtfully. 'You have something of the look of Natasha about you. Perhaps your story is true. I can, of course, have it checked.'

'Certainly,' said Hugh. He felt dizzy. There was something wrong here. The books, the cultured voice. Would the former boot-boy speak of his mistress as 'Natasha'? Was this some trick of Ivan Brelov's? Perhaps he should have insisted on Charlie coming with him. The air in the room felt close, but he kept his voice calm.

'I have no proof, of course, that you ever worked for the Greshlovs or knew my grandmother.'

'The Princess Natasha Greshlov,' said the old man, speaking carefully, as though he realised his earlier slip, 'had a small scar on her left temple, very tiny, like a crescent moon. It happened when she climbed a tree to rescue her little brother, who could not climb down by himself. He was frightened, and by accident he kicked her face as she climbed. The heel of his boot cut her temple. At the time he was five and she was thirteen years old. She did not even scold him, or tell their parents, and he was both ashamed and grateful.'

Hugh drew a long breath. Then he reached into the inside pocket of his jacket and drew out a folded letter. It was the letter from Natasha reminding him about her anniversary party, which had caught up with him in Delhi. He handed it to the old watchmaker.

'This is the most recent letter from my grandmother. I am afraid it is in English, but her signature is at the end.'

The old man's head snapped up, then he reached out with a trembling hand. He seemed almost unable to speak. In agitation, he stood up.

'She is still alive?' His voice shook.

Hugh stood up, reaching out to grasp the man's arms with his hands. 'She is still alive.'

'My God, my God,' said the old man.

'Who are you?' cried Hugh.

The man looked at him wildly, then he said, 'I am Pyotr Ivanovich Greshlov.'

They stared at each other in silence.

'You are Petya,' said Hugh.

Chapter 15

'HE WASN'T DEAD,' said Hugh. 'Unconscious, but not dead.'

They were both silent.

'If only I had known,' said Natasha. Her hands twisted together briefly in her lap, then lay still.

'As I piece it together, from what both you and Petya remember of that night, the men who broke into your house were more interested in amusing themselves than in killing. They weren't revolutionaries – just a crowd of louts excited by what was happening in Russia at that time – excited and out of control.'

Hugh paused. 'In my experience, whenever trouble boils up in a country there is always frustration and a sense of injury seething below the surface. Men who – in normal circumstances – would go quietly about their daily business suddenly turn violent. On that night it was amusing for a while to kill the aristocrats from the big house, but by the time they got to Petya they'd grown a little tired of killing and they botched it. He must already have been so traumatised that he passed out when they started stabbing him – he expected to die. Then they got the idea that they would have a different kind of fun with you. And then they thought of the wine in the cellar.'

He was watching Natasha closely, but she was regarding him calmly, her hands resting quietly in her lap. If she was reliving the horror of that night she gave no sign of it.

'When Petya regained consciousness it was pitch black. He could feel the bodies of the rest of your family around him in the darkness, and he could hear the men singing and crashing about in the distance. He thought, of course, that you were

285

lying there dead in the dark with the others. He realised after a time that he was still alive, and could move, and was just wondering if he could manage to crawl away when he got a terrible fright. The door of a cupboard beside the fireplace began to open.'

'The wood store,' said Natasha.

'Yes.' Hugh pulled the packet of photographs out of his pocket and laid one in the pool of lamplight which fell across the table where they were sitting. 'It's still there.' He looked at it wonderingly. He had noticed the small door in the entrance hall of the music school, and thought nothing of it. He passed the photograph to Natasha.

'Fyodor Petrovich, the boot-boy, had hidden there in terror when the men first attacked the house, before your father went to the front door. He watched everything that happened through a gap at the side of the cupboard door, and he was as terrified when he heard Petya moving as Petya was by him. As soon as they recognised each other, they slipped out of the house as quickly and as quietly as they could. I suppose you can't have been much ahead of them.'

He laid his hand on hers, but although she bit her lip, she remained calm.

'Petya was badly hurt, but not fatally. He had been stabbed several times in the chest, but clumsily, and once in the throat – and that blow had glanced off his collarbone. Either the men had bungled the business or they had grown ashamed when it came to killing a child. Once the two boys were outside the gates and in the streets, they hid in a doorway and bound up Petya's injuries with strips torn from their shirts. Then they started the long cold walk to Fyodor's parents' home on the other side of St Petersburg. Fyodor helped Petya along, half carrying him some of the time. He was about a year older, but still only a child. No one paid any attention to them. It took them two days. The streets were full of fighting and dead bodies, and they kept hiding, but I don't think anyone was interested in a couple of young lads. Petya was so dirty and tattered by now that he looked like a beggar child.'

Hugh smiled. 'Fyodor's parents nearly went mad with joy

when they turned up. They had heard that everyone in your house had been killed. They took Petya in and nursed him, keeping him hidden in case anyone in their street might betray him. Then – you remember the terrible influenza epidemic that spread everywhere at that time? Poor Fyodor died of it. Despite the wounding Petya was a strong and healthy boy, and although he caught the flu, he survived. They grieved for their son, Fyodor's parents, but they took Petya to their hearts, and reared him like a child of their own, poor as they were. They pretended to the outside world that he was Fyodor, and he took on the dead boy's identity – his papers all state that he is Fyodor Petrovich Chapaev. There was an uncle who was a watchmaker with a small business. He saw that Petya was a bright boy, willing to learn, and he took him on as an apprentice. Only those three people knew that Fyodor Petrovich was really Pyotr Ivanovich Greshlov – and they have all been dead for many years now. Even Petya's own wife and family didn't know who he was. His daughter was there when he told me all this, and I'm not sure she believes him even now. But he told me things only Petya could have known.'

Natasha shifted in her chair, and he realised that she had been sitting rigidly, as if frozen. 'So all this time he has been alive – still there – in St Petersburg.'

'He couldn't believe that you had survived. But I told him how you escaped, and showed him the letter you had written me about the anniversary celebrations. When he saw your signature, he knew I was speaking the truth. We talked until dawn the next morning.'

'Is he well? Is he strong?'

'He seems very well. His arthritic hip gives him pain, particularly if he sits still too long. Then he gets up and moves about to ease it. He's still working, because he enjoys it. He likes to meet the people who come into the shop to gossip. He is an artist too, in his way.'

'It is very difficult to take this in, doushenka. Petya still alive. An old man with a family. I saw him last, nine years old, lying in a pool of blood.'

Hugh gripped her hand firmly, and tried to divert her mind.

'Look at all these other photographs I took – the house, the children playing in the park, the model boats on the lake. I asked about the other servants too, as well as Fyodor. He knew nothing of them, apart from the fact that they had run away. Except for your nanny, your Nianyushka. The men found her later, hiding in the nursery – long after they were thoroughly drunk. They teased her for a bit – dressed her up in your mother's clothes – but they didn't hurt her. She came to Fyodor's father for help, but Petya didn't see her. He was hidden away. Fyodor's father found a carrier who was willing to give her a lift on his cart to her son's house in Povenets. As far as Petya knows she lived out the rest of her life quite safely there.'

Natasha gave a sigh, a small escape of air, but she seemed more relaxed. Hugh pulled out a second packet of photographs. 'I took pictures of Petya and his daughter, Marinka. Here they are. And he gave me some family photos. These are his twin grandsons when they were boys. Marinka married very young – only fifteen. This is the family of one of the grandsons, taken last year. He is a lawyer in Moscow. And the other one, with his wife and three daughters. They live only two streets away from Petya. He is a doctor. So they have both done well. The whole family suffered a good deal during the war, of course, in the siege.'

Natasha took up the pictures one by one, studying them intently. 'This one, the doctor, he looks like you.'

'I suppose he does. It is so strange, isn't it?'

'And you saw Petya when, exactly? Which day?'

'Three days ago. On Wednesday.'

'On Wednesday.'

'Unfortunately I had to be in Moscow on Thursday and Friday, to meet Potopov. I managed to have the photographs developed at my hotel in Moscow. Then I caught the plane back here. But I spoke to the two grandsons on the telephone. What would they be? My second cousins? And I've arranged to visit them all when I go back to Russia in the spring. I had a photograph of you in my wallet, and I left that with Petya. But he wants pictures of all the family.'

Natasha kept turning the photographs over and over, going

back always to the one Hugh had taken of Petya just three days before.

Hugh took a final envelope out of his pocket. 'There is one last thing for you. Petya has written you a letter.'

★ ★ ★

Half a dozen people were slumped around the kitchen table when Hugh came in. Mabel and Katya had their shoes off, and Gregor had propped his feet up on the cooler end of the range. The cats, Picasso and Seurat, now pardoned, were curled up in their basket and Harry was sprawled on the flagstones in front of the range, exhausted by his first appearance on stage.

'Everyone else gone to bed?' Hugh asked, helping himself to a glass of brandy from the kitchen supply (of the same quality as the bottle in the drawing room).

'Peter and Birgit went an hour ago,' said Gregor. 'I think Peter bore up pretty well.'

'Nick and Sally are putting Bob and Chrissie to bed. Sarah woke up and demanded to come back to the "parpy".' Mabel laughed. 'I think she realised that she had missed something! Chrissie is thoroughly over-excited. *She'll* be lying wide awake. Eric has marched Olga off – she was falling asleep on her feet. And Irina is helping William get to bed.' Mabel smiled to herself. Irina had been quite fierce in saying that she could manage by herself.

Anya and Spiro were sitting quietly on the old oak settle, not paying much attention to the others, but Anya did look up and ask: 'Has Natasha gone to bed?'

'No,' said Hugh. 'She said she wanted to sit out under the copper beech a little longer, and think about the day.'

'But it's dark out there!' protested Tony.

'It doesn't seem so dark when you're outside. And she does have a lot to think about. Not just the anniversary party.' He stopped, and they looked at him curiously.

'I have been telling her about my visit to Russia, to St Petersburg. I found her old home and took photographs of it.'

'You found Natasha's old home! Still standing? That's amazing,' said Katya.

'Yes. And I found something else. Natasha's brother didn't die. In fact he's still alive. I met him.'

'Her brother Petya?' Katya gaped at him. 'Then – that means he's Prince Greshlov now.'

'No, Katya, he is a watchmaker called Fyodor Petrovich. That has been his name for nearly eighty years now, and he's happy for it to stay that way. But he has written a letter to Natasha. I think she wants to be alone for a little, while she gets used to the idea.'

'That's all very well,' said Mabel, getting up stiffly and walking across the kitchen to a cupboard beside the range. 'But she is a very old lady and she will be getting chilled. Katya, take this rug to wrap round her knees if you can't persuade her to come in.'

★　★　★

'Is that you, Katya?'

'Yes. I've been sent to fetch you in, or – if you won't come – to wrap you up in this rug.'

Natasha laughed. 'Very well, doushenka, you can wrap me up like a plaid parcel.' She sat patiently while Katya tucked the rug around her.

'Is this the house?' asked Katya curiously, tilting the photograph to catch the light of the lamp. 'It looks as big as Buckingham Palace.'

'Oh, no. Nothing like as big. And even chillier in the winter than St Martins, although we had dozens of servants to stoke the tiled stoves in every room, and make up the fires in the fireplaces.'

'It must have been very different from nowadays.'

'Very different. And yet to my sisters and Petya and me, growing up like that, it seemed quite normal. Looking back, of course, I can see what an unjust society it was, even though my parents were very liberal, politically, and my family had given their serfs their freedom three generations before.'

'But what came afterwards was awful, wasn't it? We learned a bit about it at school – Stalin and the purges, the labour camps, the executions.'

290

'Yes, that also was bad. And who knows what will become of them all now?'

'Which one is Petya?'

'Here he is.' Natasha handed her a photograph. 'It's difficult to recognise the little boy I knew, but his hair always did stick up like that.'

Katya studied the photograph in amazement. She had a whole family in Russia. And they couldn't even speak to each other in the same language. She laid down the photograph and began looking at the others. 'This is the garden, is it? And that's the lake! Look, that's the lake you told us about!'

'Yes, see – there are still people having fun on the lake.'

'I almost can't believe it.'

'I almost can't believe it either, doushenka.'

Katya put down the photographs. 'What are these two big envelopes? Is this something else Uncle Hugh brought from Russia?'

'No,' said Natasha. 'That is something altogether different.' She laid her hands on the envelopes and stared away over the garden to where the dying embers still glowed on the barbecue.

'Child, will you do something for me?'

'Of course!'

Natasha looked carefully first into one, and then into the other stiff white envelope. They had no writing on the outside, and they were unsealed. She handed one to Katya.

'Run down and put this on the last of the fire in the barbecue, will you, Katoushka? Poke it well down and make sure that it burns away.'

Wonderingly, but without a word, Katya took the envelope and did as she was told. The barbecue implements were still lying on the ground. She picked up a long-handled poker and pressed the envelope down hard against the last crumbling embers. At first it only charred sulkily, then the paper caught and an orange flame leapt up suddenly towards her incautious hand. She batted at the blackened frill of paper until the last of it had turned to ash, then she laid the poker, still hot, on the wire shelf under the barbecue and climbed back up the ha-ha to Natasha.

291

'It's burnt away to ashes.'

'Thank you, doushenka. Now off you go to bed. Isn't it good that you and your mother are coming to live here?'

'I can't wait,' said Katya, giving her a hug and planting a warm kiss on the thin cool cheek. 'Good-night, Natasha. Sleep well.'

* * *

'It's a girl,' said Frances, coming in the kitchen door at the same time as Katya. 'They're going to call her Natasha.'

'Wonderful,' said Mabel. 'I am glad. Where's Paul? Did he stay at the hospital?'

'No, he came back with me, but he's gone to telephone his parents – it's their very first grandchild, of course.' She looked around. 'Has Natasha gone to bed? I wanted to tell her.'

'I can't persuade her to come in,' said Katya, turning to Mabel. 'I did try.'

'She isn't still outside?' Frances looked around at them in concern.

'You know how stubborn she can be,' said Mabel. 'Not unlike you, Frances.'

'Well, I'll go and be stubborn with her now. I won't take no for an answer.'

'I'll come and back you up,' said Hugh, pushing back his chair. 'And I'll explain why she wanted to go on sitting alone for a while.'

As they crossed the lawn, in and out of the chessboard of moonlight, Hugh told her the story of Petya. Frances stopped abruptly in the middle of the lawn and stared at him.

'It's beyond belief.'

'It's true.'

'So when Natasha was painting in Paris, when she and Grandpa were helping Peter make his début in London, when we came here as children . . . when we were growing up and you went away all over the world and I was bringing up my children . . . *all that time*, Petya was sitting quietly in St Petersburg or Leningrad or whatever, being a watchmaker?'

'Most of the time. He served during the war against the

Germans. But he was shot in the hip quite early on, and invalided out. That's the hip that still gives him trouble. Then they went through the siege and his young son-in-law was killed. His wife died of pneumonia and starvation. He was left with just his daughter and the two little boys. They're about our age – a little younger.'

In her chair under the copper beech they could see the dim outline of Natasha's figure, her piled-up hair still thick and beautiful in the moonlight.

'She must be feeling . . . ' said Frances. 'I don't know what she must be feeling. She loved him best of all of them, you know. It's like a resurrection.'

They walked slowly on. Natasha sat very still.

'Perhaps she's fallen asleep,' said Hugh. 'I'll carry her back into the house.'

Only one oil lamp was still alight on the table. Beneath it Hugh's photographs were lined up neatly, and below them was Petya's letter. Natasha's hand was resting on a long white envelope, across which a single word, 'Frances', had been scrawled with a shaky hand.

Hugh bent down to lift her, but Frances suddenly stiffened and gripped his arm. The moonlight caught Natasha's eyes, which were blank and open. She was not breathing.

'Oh, God,' said Hugh. 'I've killed her.'

★　★　★

Frances refused to leave Natasha while Hugh went to break the news to the others and start telephoning. 'I can't leave her alone,' she said. 'Soon she'll be alone for the rest of time.'

She knelt down in the grass beside Natasha's chair, where the dew was pearling the grass in the moonlight, and took her grandmother's hand in hers. For a long time she gazed out over the garden, and the rise of the meadow beyond. The night was so still that she could even hear the chatter of the Ludbrook at the far side of the meadow. The day filled her mind, a patchwork of emotions and gestures, of things said and not said.

She had turned frantically to Hugh, when they were sure

that Natasha was indeed dead. 'There were three things. She said there were three things.'

'What are you talking about?' Hugh was shaking.

'She said there were three things she wanted me to do for her, but she only told me two. What was the other thing? What am I to do?'

They opened the white envelope, and found it contained Natasha's will, and a short note addressed to Frances:

If you are reading this, doushenka, it means that I have left you, and I have destroyed my other will. The arrangements in that will are now of no importance. Apart from some small bequests, I am leaving St Martins and all my property to you. I know that you will manage matters as I would wish. I hope you will also live here, and carry on the work I have tried to do for the last half-century. And I hope that you will see it as a new beginning, as an opportunity, and not as a burden.

The letter was dated two weeks previously.

'Could this be the other thing she was going to ask you?'

'I don't know. How can I know?'

'Do you suppose she has destroyed this other will she mentions? What is this all about?'

'Perhaps Nick will know. His senior partner is her solicitor.'

There were voices now, and torches, approaching from the house. Frances laid her head against Natasha's silk skirt. 'You never gave me a chance to say thank you,' she said, 'for giving me another chance.'

★ ★ ★

Two hours later, they were sitting exhausted in the drawing room. The curtains were undrawn and the windows looked black and cold. At some point they had migrated here from the kitchen, perhaps when Tony had carried in Natasha's chair and placed it in its usual position beside the window. They avoided looking at it. The doctor had been and gone. The ambulance had taken Natasha away. Mabel, struggling to stay on her feet had collapsed suddenly and been put to bed by

Frances and Anya. They had decided not to waken Irina and William.

'Time enough in the morning,' said Hugh. 'It might just set Dad back again. There's no need to upset them tonight.'

Tony had fetched Nick over from his house, but persuaded Sally to stay with the children.

'Yes, I know there were two wills,' said Nick, looking at the envelope Frances had handed him. 'Brian was worried about it, and told her she shouldn't do it, but she said she wasn't quite sure how things would work out. He warned her it could cause a lot of trouble. How can we be sure she has destroyed the other will?'

'She didn't,' came an unhappy whisper from the corner behind the door. 'I did.'

They all turned to look at Katya, who was huddled on the floor, clutching a cushion in her arms in front of her like a shield. She stared at them. Her eyes were black with fatigue. 'Natasha gave me another white envelope, just like that one, and told me to burn it on the barbecue, till there was nothing left but ashes.'

'When?' asked Nick.

'When I took the rug out to her. It didn't seem important. I mean, she just told me to burn it, as though it was waste paper.'

'I don't know what I should do,' said Frances. 'What do you suppose the other will said?'

'It doesn't matter now,' said Hugh. 'This is the will Natasha wanted to leave. We all understand that.'

'That's quite right,' said Nick. 'In law, this will is the only one that has any validity.'

There was a sudden gulping sob from the corner. 'It's all my fault. She wouldn't have died if I'd made her come back into the house with me.'

Frances knelt down on the floor and put her arms around Katya. 'Darling, of course it wasn't your fault. Any more than it was Hugh's, for bringing her such joyful news. Natasha had a heart condition. She knew she could go at any time.'

'Then we shouldn't have allowed her to have the anniversary

party,' said Anya, whose face was blotched and tear-stained. 'If anything killed her it was the strain of today.'

Frances smiled sadly and shook her head, looking round at all of them. 'Don't you understand? It was a wonderful day for her. It marked the culmination of all that she has worked for, all her life. We were all here. And Hugh brought the news about Petya. If ever anyone died of happiness, then that is why Natasha died. But I think she just knew that she was finished with the business of living.'

'Frances is right,' said Gregor, who had been sitting silently by the window, half hidden by the long curtain. 'This was the crown of Natasha's days. We may grieve, but she wouldn't have wanted us to. She went fulfilled and joyful.'

★ ★ ★

They drifted off to bed, one by one, till there was no one left but Frances, Gregor and Hugh. They had made tea, and then Hugh had poured brandy, but neither Frances nor Gregor had touched theirs. Hugh looked as though he was sleepwalking. The moon was throwing a great shaft of silver light through the windows, but otherwise they had no light on but a small table-lamp near the fireplace. Hugh leaned his head back in his chair and closed his eyes.

For some time Frances and Gregor sat in silence, preoccupied. Then Gregor held out his hand to Frances, whispering so that he would not wake Hugh. 'Come with me. I want to show you something.'

They let themselves out of the back door and crossed the stableyard to the studio. Inside, Gregor turned on the lights, illuminating the Venus Rampant, straddling her plinth and eyeing them aggressively.

'I suppose I don't like it,' said Frances, 'because I know it's true. And I don't want to be reminded.'

'Reminded?' Gregor looked at her aghast. 'You didn't think that it was supposed to be what I felt about you?'

'Isn't it?'

'Oh, my dear. How have we come into such a state of confusion!' He stepped back and viewed the statue coldly. 'I was trying to say something about sexual appetite, yes. But the kind of destructive addiction that has nothing to do with love. And which isn't even the simple copulation of animals for the continuity of the species. No, I was thinking about the kind of abuse of sex that is an exercise in power. And the figure could just as well have been male as female. Maybe I should have made it hermaphrodite.'

'Would your Texan millionaire have cared for that?'

Gregor laughed. 'Probably not. I've come to hate it myself. If I were younger, I might make the grand gesture and smash the Venus. But to tell you the truth, I need the money, and so does St Martins. And I suppose it would be dishonest to destroy it. After all, it marks a phase in my development, just like everything else I've ever done. But it was a dead end. A road not further taken. Almost a caricature of my real intentions. I'm going another way now.'

'I'm glad.'

'Yes, I think you will be.'

He took her hand again. 'Frances . . . This whole day . . . Natasha meant it to be about celebration. Not just looking back, on the fiftieth anniversary, but looking forward. She was talking to me earlier today about new beginnings.'

'New beginnings. Yes. I've been thinking of new beginnings. But Natasha . . . ' For the first time since she and Hugh had found Natasha in her chair, Frances could not control her voice. Gregor put his arm around her shoulders, and she leaned against his solid bulk.

'Come back here. This is what I really wanted to show you, not the Venus.'

He led her to the far end of the studio, and drew back the curtain which made a partition. His modelling table was here, and a shape covered with damp sacking. On the edge of the table lay a black case that had once held a slide-rule. Its corners were scuffed now, but the leather glowed with years of polishing. Frances touched it with her finger, then picked it up and opened it. The pale wood of the modelling tools had darkened with age and handling to a warm gold. They were spotlessly clean, but showed the marks of heavy use.

'I had no idea you still used these. I wouldn't have thought they would be good enough for a professional.'

'Oh, yes. Quite good enough. And they fit my hand with familiarity and love.'

'All this day,' said Frances, 'I've been feeling as though I have been asleep for years. And now I have woken up. Woken up to so many things that I was stupid about in the past.'

He smiled to himself, and lifted the sacking from the figure he was modelling.

'It is nearly finished. I'm going to cast it in bronze. And then, if you will allow me, I want to give it to you.'

The figure was about three feet high. It was a young girl – kneeling amongst meadow flowers, but in the very act of springing up – her arms joyously raised and her head thrown back so that her hair was caught by the wind.

Frances looked at it silently and smiled. 'Yes,' she said. 'Oh, yes – this is your true vision.'

Then she turned to him. 'Is it Katya?'

He put his arms around her again. 'I call it "The Awakening". It isn't Katya. This girl is a little older. Sixteen or seventeen perhaps? Look again.'

She looked. 'It's me,' she said.

'It's you.'

das